BEST
OF THE SOUTH

Previous Volumes
BEST OF THE SOUTH (1996)

BEST
OF THE SOUTH

From the Second Decade of *New Stories from the South*
edited by Shannon Ravenel

Selected and Introduced by
Anne Tyler

A SHANNON RAVENEL BOOK
Algonquin Books of Chapel Hill / 2005

R
A Shannon Ravenel Book

Published by
ALGONQUIN BOOKS OF CHAPEL HILL
Post Office Box 2225
Chapel Hill, North Carolina 27515-2225

a division of
WORKMAN PUBLISHING
708 Broadway
New York, New York 10003

Library of Congress Cataloging-in-Publication Data
Best of the South, edited by Shannon Ravenel / selected and introduced by Anne Tyler.
    p. cm.
    ISBN-13: 978-1-56512-470-7
    ISBN-10: 1-56512-470-7
    1. Short stories, American—Southern States.   2. Southern States—Social life and
customs—Fiction.   I. Tyler, Anne.   II. New stories from the South.
    PS551.B38   1996
    813'.0108975—dc20   95045857
                                                                               CIP

10 9 8 7 6 5 4 3 2 1
First Edition

CONTENTS

INTRODUCTION

An old woman recollects a trip across a bridge, over and over and over. A child traps his mother on the front-porch roof and refuses to release her. A boy mistakes Death for the landlady's son, come to collect the rent.

What do these people have in common?

They are characters in just three of the 186 stories that Shannon Ravenel has chosen as the best from the South during the past decade.

It's twenty years now since the series first began, which means that for twenty years various people—first Shannon Ravenel herself, later different fiction writers she has deputized volume by volume—have attempted to explain just what it is that makes a story Southern. It's not an easy task. Strictly speaking, it's not even a necessary task, because we could legitimately say that a Southern story is just a story that happens to have a Southern setting, or one that's written by an author who at some point has lived in the South. But the temptation is to argue for more—to suggest that there is still, even in twenty-first-century America, a quality unique to the South that permeates much of its fiction.

Ten years ago, when I introduced the first *Best of the South,* I proposed that at least eight of the twenty stories I chose were dyed-in-the-wool Southern. Relocate those eight to Boston and you wouldn't fool a soul, I said. They would still have a Southern feel to them, deep down in their bones. I was happy to discover this, but also a bit surprised. Even back then our country had begun to seem homogenous—the same fast foods, the same brand names, almost the same language from border to border. I'd expected the stories to be indistinguishable from, oh, New England or Midwestern stories. And privately, I assumed that in another ten years that would most certainly be the case. I thought I must be witnessing the last gasp of regional literature.

Wrong, wrong, wrong, I'm delighted to say.

This new collection—twenty stories from the second ten years of *New Stories from the South*—includes nine that could have taken place in the South and no place else. Or, no, wait: maybe twelve. Or, given other criteria, fourteen. What *are* the criteria, anyhow?

I was pondering this very question on a bitter cold night last January when my doorbell rang unexpectedly and a friend announced that here she was, ready for supper. Actually, I'd invited her for the next night, not that one. But I was glad to see her anyhow, first because Kay is delightful company and second because she chanced to find on my doorstep a UPS delivery of an electric blanket I'd ordered. I thought her arrival was providential. Besides, my pondering had reached the state where it was going in circles. I was starting to wonder if I was kidding myself. Did the South as such even exist anymore? I happily set aside my work and offered her a glass of wine.

So, she said, settling in. That afternoon she'd gone to the most interesting museum exhibit. Oh, and by the way, she'd bumped into a mutual friend of ours there, a man who comes from the small town in Tennessee where Kay herself comes from. Yes, and who should he have with him but *another* Tennessean, a woman Kay used to know as a girl who in fact was somehow related to her and who was also related to so-and-so on both sides of the family and who promptly reminded her of the time such-and-such had happened, the oddest thing—wait till I heard—and who could quote to her word for word all these years later just what everybody in town had had to say about it.

Well, I realize that Southerners don't have a monopoly on sprawling family trees and shared pasts. But what perked up my ears was Kay's narrative style: the run-on stream of associations, the dreamlike interweaving of the past with the present, and the fondness for verbatim he-said-she-said reported with such dead-to-rights mimicry of inflection that the speakers come alive before the listener's eyes.

Tell me, I asked Kay: did she believe that a person even today could be quintessentially Southern?

She said, "I have lived up North for thirty-five years and I still think I'm just visiting."

I decided that the electric blanket was the least of what made her arrival providential.

Many of the stories in this volume might very well have been narrated by one of those three Tennesseans. Listen to the woman in Clyde Edgerton's "Debra's Flap and Snap," for instance, describing the not-quite-right schoolmate who invites her to a dance:

> L. Ray was in shop, and they all met with Mrs. Waltrip down in the shop—where they had electric saws and everything. They didn't do shop—they just met down there. People who went down there for shop would just more or less put up with them. On second thought, some of them did do shop.

The young narrator of Heather Sellers's "Fla. Boys," quoting her sick father, employs a repetitive, almost incantatory tone that you often hear in Southern speech:

> He'd said the cancer of the colon thing was nothing. It was good to get rid of your excess colon. You had two hundred feet of the stuff. What he was getting rid of was just excess. It wasn't anything. He said that about everything—him not going to work, finding me still asleep in the back of the car in the afternoon, stunned in the sun, the Florida room flooding and the television in water sparking, cops at the door at five in the afternoon, a woman trying to stab him on our patio on his birthday, me

drinking beer and floating in the pool so that I could drown. It wasn't anything. None of it was anything.

Nearly as important as the narrative style is the strong sense of place, as in Michael Knight's charming "Birdland," which introduces an entire community gathered around the TV set in Dillard's Country Store. And place altered by time—place destroyed by the passage of time—is the theme of both Paul Prather's "The Faithful," a description of a small church's final religious service, and Stephen Coyne's "Hunting Country," in which an old man mourns the virgin timberland his coon dogs used to roam. In Lucia Nevai's "Faith Healer," a barbecue vendor complains about his customers' impatience with his old-time, slow cooking style—their "Kentucky Fried mentality," as he calls it.

This last story, by the way, reveals an underside of the South's good old days. "Look, miss," the central character tells a faith healer, "I would not have driven all this way if I knew you was black—nothing against blacks." Pam Durban, in "Gravity," gives a perfect-pitch rendition of an old woman's condescending attitude toward a black servant from long ago. And the issue takes an unexpected turn in Gregory Sanders's wonderful "Good Witch, Bad Witch" when the narrator regrets his failure to forgive his aunt's racist language.

But I don't mean to suggest that Southern literature has to relate to the old days, good or bad. The figure of Death in Mark Richard's "Memorial Day" may be haunting a distinctly Southern setting, but his language is almost comically trendy. ("I get along well with others," Death confides. "I'm a people person.") In Scott Ely's memorable "Talk Radio," a North Carolinian finally meets his counterpart from the war in Vietnam. Jill McCorkle's "Intervention" describes the very modern practice of confronting a person about his alcohol abuse, but with an unusual and touching slant of vision. And by pure chronological happenstance, this collection that begins with Marcia Guthridge's "The Host," in which a woman honors her family's ancient practice of respecting the animals they kill, ends with Stephanie Soileau's "The *Boucherie*," an account of how a Louisiana community learns new traditions from a family of Sudanese refugees when they all gather to butcher a cow.

Then there are the other stories—the ones that could be from anywhere but are no less effective for that. Stories of connection: "Second Hand," in which Chris Offutt shows a burnt-out woman pulling herself together for the sake of her boyfriend's little girl; or "Ramone," Judy Troy's description of a hardscrabble family embracing a reluctant new stepdaughter. Stories of character: the magnificently dignified commuter-train proselytizer delivering her public sermons in Jim Grimsley's "Jesus Is Sending You This Message"; the feisty, life-affirming retirement-home resident in Lee Smith's "The Happy Memories Club"; the small boy doing his desperate best to deal with the unpredictable in Max Steele's "The Unripe Heart."

And finally, there are the stories that take us not just beyond the South but beyond our known experience altogether. William Gay's magical "Those Deep Elm Brown's Ferry Blues" places us squarely inside the head of an old man suffering from dementia. Thomas H. McNeely's "Sheep" is a wrenching glimpse into the mind of a serial killer.

Do you notice the range here? Identifiably Southern or not, these stories cover a wide spectrum of styles and subjects and attitudes, and that's not my doing, believe me. Of all the qualities that I admire in Shannon Ravenel (her vision and her integrity and her infectious enthusiasm, to name just three), most remarkable is her lack of bias. She seems open to everything; she approaches her task each year without any preconceptions. Nobody, I am sure, would ever say, "Oh, this is a Shannon Ravenel story." Or if somebody did, it could mean only one thing: This is a very *good* story. This is the best.

Anne Tyler
Baltimore, Maryland
2005

BEST

OF THE SOUTH

1996

Marcia Guthridge

THE HOST

*Marcia Guthridge was born in San Antonio, Texas, and grew up in New Orleans.
She lives in Illinois, where she received her Ph.D. in English language and literature
from the University of Chicago, and now works on behalf of adult literacy. A large
kingfish, the only fish the author ever caught, was the inspiration for this funny story
of a displaced Texan seeking to relive her childhood vacations on the Gulf Coast. Her
husband can't see beyond the reality of her paradise—hot, windy, birdless, oil-
slicked—and is alarmed by her fierce determination to honor the family rule: eat
what you kill. "She would take communion, eat her fish."*

I've never understood about fishing and buffalo stomachs. I
admit it freely. I am no cannibal. But there are connections
between me and the world. I'm not a cog. I'm a bolt. People who
know me find me reasonable—neither gluttonous nor profligate.
It is only my wife who thinks I devour without permission and
eschew what I should eat.

Only yesterday, for example, just back from vacation, I was driving across the city, the water glittering in the lake on one side of
me, skyscraping apartment buildings—clean steel Mies—glittering on the other side, Bach's "Air on the G String" on the radio. I
soared. The road was newly paved and the high places were long,
the dips so smooth and quick the nose of my little car never turned
down, just fell for a second vertically and rose again, me with it.
Two birds pumped upward in the distance and then a perfectly
proportioned curve in the road—a classical Grecian curve—turned
me to see an airplane, barely moving, opposite the birds but on the
same slant, heading down for the airport I had just left. The plane
disappeared behind a building; and when I saw it again, a trick of

I

the sun, I guess, had it sinking straight down now, no slant, falling lazily like a parachute, like me and my little car when the beautiful road dipped. I knew my place.

Even the shells are bleached white here on my seashore. The Gulf of Mexico is so light a gray that the sun above it can blur it nearly to white. Directly across the same Gulf, on the edge of Florida where we went one spring on vacation because he likes color and baseball, the water is altogether different: blue. There are lots of palm trees and sea oats among clumps of long-bladed humid green grass, sea grapes with flat round red leaves, mossy pine trees, and a sky hectic with birds, such birds: blue herons and egrets with necks as slim and wavy as the sea-oat stalks and shockingly yellow beaks, greedy mud-colored pelicans flap-elbowing each other off the crowded fishing piers. The sun is red and sweet, unreal. The shells are striped and glossy. I found one that looked like the hide of a green zebra with one perfect straight orange line up the middle, as if painted on with a fine Japanese brush.

So after we went to Florida that one spring because he wanted to, after I'd spent the whole week comparing where we were to where I'd rather be—the shore of my childhood summers, the resort of my adult dreams—he said he'd see this beach of beaches. "Let's go to Texas. We'll take a few days off at the end of August. I want to see this place." He said it on the plane going home from Florida. Immediately I blanched innerly, like one of my Texas shells, like a brittle white sand dollar with a secret rattling in its closed chambers.

But I said it was a nice idea (indeed it was), and I said to myself that sensing danger would help me to avoid it. I knew he wouldn't like Port Aransas. I knew to him it would seem primitive and bru-tal. I knew to me it would seem primitive and brutal now, except it was inside me in the way places are inside creatures like creatures are inside places, like mountains are inside mountain goats, like mollusks are inside shells. I knew he was not my brother or my father, or even my cousin (he was my husband), and I knew that would be a problem. Blood bonds to places, and everything there is is layered and surrounded.

I thought I was ready. He would be my guest. But I did not foresee the argument about murdering fish. How could anyone foresee such a thing?

We flew into Corpus Christi and drove the short distance to the tip of Padre Island in a rented Buick. Already this was wrong. When I was a child, my family strapped plastic buckets and rubber floats and beer coolers atop the car and drove down from Central Texas, where we lived. We crossed from the mainland on the car ferry, so the water snuck right up under us, car and all, first thing. Every year we took the same vacation, my uncle's family too; all eleven of us stayed in one cabin. One pair of grown-ups slept in the bedroom and the other pair in the sitting room, which was the same as the kitchen. Until my little sister and my youngest cousin grew up a little, they slept in the sitting room too, on a pallet made of beach towels on the sandy floor. The older kids got to sleep on the screened porch, on salt-smelling mattresses that felt as if they were stuffed with ancient oyster shells. We tossed and twitched on our crunchy beds gingerly, because of our sunburns. We giggled softly late into the night, and listened to the roar of trucks on the main island road a hundred yards away, and sometimes, as the trucks glided onto the Corpus Christi highway, we imagined we heard the Gulf waves whispering among the tall wheels.

Every morning we packed the two cars full of food and Coca-Cola and beer, and drove to the beach about a mile away. Sometimes the cars were so full of stuff we older kids were allowed to ride sitting on the doors, our legs inside and the rest of us out. You drive—still do—your car right up to the water, and then you could sit on top of it, stare at the Gulf, and pretend to be a pirate or a renowned fisherperson scouting schools. The car glinted in the sun and heated up like a roasting pan with you on it. We made sand animals. We buried each other: we'd dig a deep hole and put somebody in it, then smooth a mound of sand around his shoulders till it was a perfect dune with a head on it, and finally the buried kid's muscles went crampy, and he'd burst from the white earth like a white-hot rock from a volcano. We floated for hours at a time in the steamy salt water, to boil for a while instead of roast. The grown-ups fished in the surf.

We recognized the end of the day by how red our skin was, not by the color or position of the sun, which stayed high and strong till dusk, when it changed momentarily from white to yellow and popped suddenly into the water while no one was watching. When we were red enough we packed the cars and drove back to our cabin. My mother and aunt cleaned vegetables; my father and uncle cleaned fish. It was the children's job to take the laundry to the laundromat without dragging the towels through the sticker burrs in the pale lawn, and to fetch eggs or fruit or pickle relish from the Island Food Store which smelled of hot wood and bread. One afternoon we resolved to help with supper by trapping crabs. It took us hours to catch a dozen from the pier, none bigger than my youngest cousin's tiny fist, with legs like hairs, fleshless. By the time we got them back to the cabin they were dead in our dry creel. My father and uncle came home from fishing and found the bodies where we dumped them in the grass burrs by the back door. They made us boil them and (though my mother fought them on this—she said they'd already started to smell off) eat them. There was no more than a teaspoonful of meat in each crab. We scraped smidgens from crevices in the enameled labyrinths of inner shell, sucked the juice from spider legs, and then my uncle re-boiled the shards and strained the liquid for broth. My father thought it was necessary to eat what you kill. "It's not magic," I heard him say forcefully to someone later in the house, while I lay with the other children on the screened porch thinking of sleep. "It's common consideration. It's keeping things right between us and the fish."

The condo my husband had booked for us this time had a view of the Gulf and a Weber grill. When I saw the modern kitchen with its butcher-block island, I remembered how my mother and aunt laughed as they moved between the sink and the little table in our kitchen–sitting room, working with shoulders touching. I told him about that, and when he looked at me as if there must be more to the story, I added: "My mother didn't laugh when she cooked supper at home."

Immediately I went hunting the thermostat, turned off the air-conditioning and began tugging at the window over the carport. "Don't you think we'll be hot without air-conditioning?" he asked. "It must be a hundred and ten out there."

"This is urgent. There's got to be a crowbar here somewhere," I said. "I need a window open. I need a window open now." The windows were all painted shut. I pulled barbecue tools out of kitchen drawers until I found a hammer and a sturdy spatula. On my way back to the bedroom I saw his face. It looked all flattened out, pulled tight by the ears, so I smiled affectionately. "We're lucky to have the Gulf so close, you know." I didn't want him to be afraid.

I went to work furiously on the window. From well behind me, he peered toward outside. "There are cars right up on the beach," he called out, plainly astonished. "Would you look at that? People are driving their cars right up to the water!" Wood cracked, the sash zinged, and the window rolled open. I stepped back, sweating. Dead white paint chips littered the sill.

"I know. That's what you do here."

"Don't kids get run over?"

"Every once in a while. Not very often, I don't think."

We spent four days going to the beach. The wind was high the whole week. He sat on a towel decorated with the Coca-Cola logo and weighted on the corners by two Top-Siders, a Pat Conroy novel, and a bottle of SPF 30 sunscreen. He squinted at me through eyelashes studded with sand. He didn't wear sunglasses because he didn't want to tan like a raccoon. "Why are there so few birds here?" he asked. "No pelicans or herons like in Florida."

"There are gulls," I said, pointing to a homely line of them gazing with us at the water and staggering in the hot wind.

"Maybe for the same reason there are so few people," he answered himself. It was a Friday morning, and only a pickup and a sun-silvered Camaro were beached near us, pulled up to the high tide mark in line with the gulls.

I made peanut-butter sandwiches with jalapeño peppers on flour tortillas every noon, and carried mine down from the condo to eat them sitting in the breakers. Bits of tar swirled in the water around me. When one hit me it stuck like a leech. Sand blew into my mouth with every bite. Grit silted among my teeth after I swallowed. He usually stayed in the kitchen to eat his lunch, and then took a nap. He never wanted to go back to the beach after that because he'd already cleaned himself up once. It took quite a while to scrub, with mayonnaise, the tar from our skin. He wondered if it would ever come off his new trunks.

Evenings, we walked on the fishing pier to see what people were catching. We dodged flying hooks cast inexpertly by children off the windy rock jetty a mile or so down from the pier. "Sometimes you can catch crabs around here," I informed him.

Tuesday night we brought some shrimp back from Aransas Pass. I told him we might find a good restaurant over there on the mainland, but what I really wanted to do was ride the ferry. So we did, and we saw one restaurant that looked all right to him—a steak house built with stones on the bottom, logs on top, and a concrete Indian tepee on the roof like a chimney. We got as far as the crowded parking lot (it was the crowd that soothed and attracted him), and he stopped the rental car halfway nosed into a space. He left his hands on the wheel and turned to me. His eyes moved from my feet up to my neck. "You know," he began, still not looking at my face. "I don't want to embarrass you."

I can't say I wasn't surprised. The betrayal was too soon and too overt. "Yes?" was all I said.

"Well, it just occurred to me—I just noticed what you're wearing."

"I never knew you to pay much attention to my clothes." I had on a polyester muumuu I had bought at the Island Food Store and rubber flip-flop thong sandals.

"I never saw you looking like this before. You don't wear this outfit at home, do you?"

"No."

"Anyway, I don't think we ought to go in this place. These people look pretty dressed up." There was a group of women getting out of a car near ours. They had on high heels and carried patent-leather purses.

"Okay, forget it then." I didn't care about eating at a crowded steak house with a tepee on top anyway. I wanted to get back on the ferry. "Let's go back."

A couple of miles before the ferry landing, we stopped at an open-backed van by the side of the road and bought some shrimp in a plastic bag. "We'll take them home and boil them," I said. "You won't believe how fresh they'll taste." The fat woman who sold us the shrimp had three fat children playing in the front seat of the van, no front teeth, and flip-flops the same color as mine.

On the ferry I got out of the car, as usual, to feel the wind and look for porpoises as we chugged across the gassy little strip of water from the mainland. I considered the shrimp. I was fascinated by them, and had taken the plastic bag out with me to the ferry's front rail. They were dead, of course, but still perfect: their feelers and legs unbroken, black eye-beads, pale pink stripes. Their last meals were still visible through their fragile shells in their alimentary veins.

"I'd like to eat them with their skins still on," I said to him after we'd boiled them. "Eyes and all." They were pinker, done being cooked but each one still intact. They drained in a colander. Two of them embraced a limp half-lemon, their legs twined about it on either side. They were like mythological figures balancing a symbolic orb over an antique door. Steam rose from the colander: the absolute last of their pale pink spirits.

I relented and did not eat the eyes and shells; but I refused to let him de-vein my portion. Happily, I ate what the shrimp had eaten. I tried not to chew too many times, as if they were holy things, and so I could imagine them coming to life and swimming in my gut, eating what I ate, pink parasites in a gracious host.

It got hotter and hotter. We lay in bed one night at the end of the week listening to the hungry gulls calling for help. Pools of sweat rose in the hollows between my breasts and ribs when I lay on my back. I felt him sighing beside me, awake.

After a time, he got up. He flopped once, disentangled his long feet from the top sheet and popped out of the bed. He fumbled through a drawer and found his blousy seersucker trousers. He hopped on one leg around the room, fighting for his balance as he put them on. "I'm going for a walk, but I don't have much hope of cooling off. Even the goddamn wind is hot."

Now I sighed, answering his sleepless breathing. "Watch out for the snakes as you're crossing the dunes. They come out onto the paths at night."

He changed his mind, refolded his trousers carefully into the drawer, and returned to the sticky bed. Finally, I felt the springs soften and I could tell he was asleep. As I drifted off myself I remembered, too late, that we could have turned on the air conditioner.

When there was only one more day left, I decided we should go out on one of the party boats to fish. I had thought of it a few other times, earlier, but we hadn't gotten to it. I don't think he much cared what we did, and I had been happy floating in the waves, baking in the sand, and eating peanut-butter and jalapeño sandwiches. Now, I thought, it was time to go fishing.

And what caused the trouble was not the fishing, nor even my putting it off until it was so late. It was my real self, which had been flexing inside of me for the whole trip, and which burst out, wide awake, well grown, and ready to kick ass the minute I stepped onto that boat.

Every married person has a real self, I guess (as well as people who live with their mothers and with roommates), which over the years of being only in common places is slowly bludgeoned unconscious by a gathering of small blows with very blunt instruments: dishrags, bedsheets, dandelion roots, now and then a snow shovel. The real self hides like a small fish in a grotto, coils to save itself like a snake in the dunes, and sleeps. Around it, cell by cell, grows another more pliant personage to live in the common places: it knows how to avoid unpleasantness, Mexican food, excessive sun, ecstasy. Still the real self wakes sometimes at night to moon-bask on the cool dune paths and to star in dreams of rebellion and courage, or to fish in the Gulf for its darkly swimming buried kin.

It was a rough trip out that day. It always was, as I remember from when my father and uncle used to take me and the other kids out on these big boats designed for groups of inexperienced fishermen. One side of the boat is designated for being seasick and the other for fishing. I have never been among the seasick. In fact, the happiest I have ever been, I think, is when standing with my hips fitted snug into the point of the bow riding up a swell and crashing down, shrieking, salt water soaking me, stinging my sunburn. I did it this day too, now adult and undignified, having ignored the warnings of the old sailor who captained the boat. Still I shriek and sing; again I am the happiest I can be.

As soon as we stopped, the men around us made a shiny pop-top reef around the boat and let out their lines. I baited my double hook with a ribbon fish and wiped my hands on my orange terry-cloth shorts, which I had bought years ago for my father. He had died a few days before his birthday. I had kept them in a box and had finally decided to wear them myself.

"These guys are drinking beer?" he said. "Jesus, it's 8:30 in the morning." He looked queasy. He hadn't enjoyed the ride out. "But it is hot."

The steel deck rail was becoming uncomfortable to the touch. He leaned over the side, then came back upright but swaying. "This water looks like it's about to boil. I think I'll buy a soda. You want something?"

"Beer." He headed for the cabin. I fished. "Maybe you should get yourself some crackers to settle your stomach," I called after him.

He was wrong: this water was not about to boil. It was still, bubbleless, foamless, as secret as frozen soil in winter. We had left the clattering gulls behind with the shore. I saw one lone shrimper at the very edge of sight, its nets hoisted up, head past us and home somewhere. I trusted the leathery old sailor who had brought us here. Indeed, he even had an electronic fish-finder up on the bridge, if the sign by the dock was true. There were fish below us. But I firmly felt, staring at my slack line, they were asleep at the faraway mud-misted bottom of the Gulf, as soundly asleep as jonquil bulbs in Yankee January.

It was a half-day trip. We were supposed to be ashore again by noon. By eleven, the captain had moved us twice and all that had been caught was one dark-fleshed jack (my father called them liverfish), two puny kingfish off the stern, and a large pitted gray rock by someone's grandson who had been fishing near me and who, in the process of reeling in his rock, managed to tangle my line hopelessly with his. For a rushing moment, I'd thought we'd awakened the fish and we both had bites; but instead, when the rock was decked I had to squat and cramp my fingers unthreading our lines from it. Many people lost bait. Something down there was nibbling in its dreams.

As I re-baited my hook we moved again. In the new place I lowered my line with a benediction; in answer, ten minutes later, ten minutes before we would have turned for shore, there was a flicker of fish fifteen yards from the bow where I stood. It gamboled near the surface, twisting like a puppy, its energy mixing and shining with the sun. "There's my fish," I whispered.

"That's no kingfish! It's a tarpon," yelled the captain from above me on the bridge.

My line zinged taut. With the calm of the prescient, I raised my pole to set the hook, and in an instant that hook was on its way to Florida. "Let her run awhile," the captain told me. He was right behind me now. "Reel in," he ordered everybody else. "This little lady's got a fish on here, big one. Never expected a tarpon today. Don't see them all that much." He sounded as if he doubted whether I deserved such a fish.

"Now you start inching her in," he advised me. My arms ached already just from holding onto the pole while the fish ran. When the fish rested I braced the end of the pole against my stomach and turned and turned the reel. When it jerked and swam sideways the captain pushed me along with it. Up and down either side of the boat I sashayed and sidestepped to fool the fish into thinking it was pulling me; then, when the captain gave the word, I pulled it. My arms went numb early on. "You want me to take over?" he asked.

I shook my head. "My fish," I gasped. The dearth of breath in my lungs gave this the sound of a question.

It was a fish fight from one of my father and uncle's tales. I had caught a fish or two as a kid, dragged it myself off a boat like this to the scale by the fish-cleaning house, hugging it on the way like a dead child. We used to catch small sharks and kingfish, jack, once a big tuna I didn't like the taste of. They fought, but not like this fish, my fish.

Suddenly the line went slack. I thought my fish was lost. But it was only breathing under the boat, trying to trick me. I waited.

The numbness spread to my legs. By the time the fish started running again I had braced myself against the railing in a V shape, the grip of the pole poking my midsection out into a point, my heels on the deck and my toes smashed up against the side of the boat, my arms stretched to the utmost to keep from losing the tackle. I reeled and waited, holding tight. Finally, I could feel where the fish was: less deep and very close. It lolled, enervated by the warm surface water. I reeled some more, and unbraced my legs enough to lean and peep over at the water. My fish flashed at me a silver greeting from an eighth of a mile underwater.

"I saw it," I sighed.

"Damn straight," the captain whispered in my ear. "You want this fish?" I nodded and shrugged to catch some sweat from my chin. "Then reel." I felt blisters rising on my hands with each heart-beat. I knew how the fish felt. I too had surrendered in warm salt water, unable to swim for the lapping of waves in my mouth. I knew how the hook hurt as it pulled, how it jabbed as I gnawed it; so when my fish began its last run and the pole slipped in my chafed and sweaty hands, I considered going with it over the side, letting my fish catch me.

I re-gripped. And when the fish was done running I reeled with the end of my strength. I bore down like a mother for the last push in a birthing, and up came the fish with a splash like a gunshot. It flipped, looping the line round its tail in the air. It was miraculously silver-blue-and-green, the same colors as the winking hot Gulf. Blood covered its face. The captain and I were both soaked by its explosion out of the water. He climbed to a perch on the deck rail, ready with his gaffing hook, and kept coaching: "*Up.* Keep the tip up!"

The fish out of water was too heavy for me. I let it drop back down. It was gone again. But I sat on the end of my pole as if it were a seesaw and pried it up again. The bones in my crotch ached, but the fish was caught. The captain and one of his teenaged assistants gaffed it through its middle and levered it onto the boat.

"That is a nice fish," the teenager dryly opined. We were all flattened against the side of the boat watching it die. Decked, it flopped and faded from blue-green to gray. Its gills pulsed hugely and irregularly. I could not see its eye for the blood from around the hook. I could hardly breathe. Some of us on deck hopped and slid around to avoid the thrashing fishtail. The grandson who had caught the rock climbed with me onto the railing and stared enviously at me as I watched my fish. The teenaged assistant reversed his gaffer and slammed the fish in the head a few times with the handle. Soon after that it stopped caroming about the deck. It lifted itself twice from the slimy pinkened boards, its middle rising first, then up-ended the curve in the air and thudded down. Finally it died with its gill chamber wide open. Each filament was discrete: you could have counted them, hung like harpstrings. If you were small enough and careful you could have walked among them in the spaces where the breath had been, like a Chinese weaver in an ancient silk factory with the worms next door.

"I can recommend a taxidermist in Fulton," the captain said to me. His teenager had started the boat and was turning us around. Someone had dragged my fish to the cooler astern, where it lay ignominiously among mackerel. For a moment I didn't understand the word.

"Taxidermist. Oh, I don't want a trophy," I said. "I'm going to eat it."

"Oh no ma'am," advised the captain, politely laughing. "Most people around here don't like to eat tarpon." The men around me tittered.

"Why not?"

"It's no eatin' fish. My way of thinking, fish like this, you mount it."

"I'll eat it."

He searched for another way to explain, forcefully: "It ain't good eatin'."

"You expect me to hang it on the wall?"

"Hell yes. That is one good-looking fish. Skull's in pretty good shape." All the men on deck began talking and gesturing about trophies. They didn't know anything about eating tarpon. They were just siding with the old sailor. "Here, we'll see what your old man thinks about it." He had come up behind me, and saluted with his beer can. It was close enough to lunch for him to have one now, and I guess he had gotten used to feeling on the border of sick. He still looked yellow.

"Did you see?" I asked him.

"Of course I saw. I was right here the whole time. Look how wet I am." He jiggled his knees so I could hear his shorts sloshing. "That is a big fish. You should be proud."

"I am proud. I caught it. I'm going to eat it."

"I think we should have it mounted."

"This fish is too important to stuff," I said. The captain wheeled and waved a hand at my face as if I were a fool and words were useless. I hated to lose his approval, but my real self was now in control. He headed for the ladder to the bridge.

My husband reasoned: "It's because the fish is so important that

I think it should be mounted. We'll find someone in Corpus Christi and have them send it to us when it's done. We'll leave early tomorrow for the plane and drop it off."

"No."

"Well, we don't have time to eat it, even if we wanted to. We're going home tomorrow." He was becoming annoyed. I could see the tightness in his throat as the words passed through. "You should have gone fishing earlier in the week, okay?"

"I don't care. I'll find some dry ice and take it on the plane in coolers. I'll have it cleaned and cut up."

"They won't let you on an airplane with dry ice. My daddy's a pilot," offered the boy who had caught a rock.

"How many coolers do you think we'll need for a forty-pound fish? Or more?" he yelled, waving his arms and spilling his beer.

"I'll give some away."

"Nobody wants to eat this kind of fish. You heard him. He says it's not good."

"It is good. I'll figure it all out."

I had to eat what I caught. Or, at least, what I caught had to be eaten. If there were someone to help me eat it, I could share. I didn't have to eat it all myself, but it couldn't be wasted. I had been taught this as a child. It was part of my family's science. My father's people claimed kinship with the Plains Indians, a tenuous connection, which my mother maintained was no more than fancy dress for an ancestor's sexual indiscretion; still my father loved to talk about buffalo hunting—eating the meat, making spoons from horns, clothing from skins, and toys from bladders—wasting nothing. It was important that if you killed something you kept its life going by taking the whole of the dead into yourself. I don't know that he ever said it to me just that way, but I know it to be true.

I've never seen anyone act so crazy and be so convinced she's right. If I pulled the car over by this curb and stopped a hundred people at random and told them the whole story, I bet they'd all side with me. She said her father made her eat dead crabs. She said I had no soul. She said there was nothing real left of me. She said she was descended from Native Americans who used all of the buffalo. She made no sense.

I came home on the flight we had tickets for. Christ, I had to be back at work—and she stayed so she could find enough dry ice and coolers to pack up her stinking fish. Maybe they won't let her on any plane. Maybe she'll have to eat the whole thing there, frying it up in chunks on a hot plate in that lousy beach house. Maybe she'll stay down there forever eating tarpons. She's gone completely nuts. She'll swallow the eyes and crunch up the tail, eat the liver and turn into a fish. Isn't that what the Indians did? I tried to calm her, smooth her down. She was bristly. "Let's not make this into life and death," I said.

"What the hell else do you think it is?" she screamed back at me, spitting. The back seat of the rental car was piled high with slimy, bloody plastic bags containing bits of fish. She'd wrestled the thing by herself down the dock and had it chopped up at a fish house. She was covered with blood and the car smelled awful. (Oh, my own little car calms me, now I'm home. It smells so good, and it fits so well around me.) "My fish is bleeding, bleaching into me. It is exactly just life and death," she raved.

"You're scaring me," I said. Her left forearm was clean of fish blood. I touched the salty skin there. I remember we passed one of those big spiraling plastic slides that dump kids into pools of water and I thought how the kids on that one, shadeless in this wild place, must be getting their butts burnt off, and I remember thinking I was glad we were going home.

At first she wheedled me. Her voice was low and monotonous, humming. She suggested we take the fish back to that hot little condo and stay another week (a week or so is what she said—"or so": how long?). We'd jam the refrigerator full of fish and start eating. "We'll eat the fish together. You'll help me eat it."

I pictured that cheap Formica table in the kitchen dripping with slippery fish, the butcher-block island twinkling with scales. I saw barrels of tartar sauce, mountains of lemons, fried filets, ceviche, tarpon chowder in a washtub, minced-fish-and-onion cakes the size of basketballs. I saw the little Weber grill smoking up the carport full-time for a week "or so," scarring slabs of fish with charcoal stripes, and I saw her sweating and grinning through the smoke. I glimpsed the edge of lunacy myself. I thought of fish fritters for breakfast, and my stomach quivered. "I don't really care that much for fish, you know."

That was all I said, and then she cut loose and sang her anger at me. She chanted like a TV evangelist or a witch doctor in a Tarzan movie. Her face was bright orange and shining—sunburnt I guess, but it occurred to me that she'd caught fire from sitting in this deadly sun all week and was about to combust spontaneously, right there on the bloody car seat. Her features looked blurred, as if they were starting to melt like the plastic on the baking water slide. To touch her now would burn me. Her hair was mashed flat on the top of her head from this ugly fishing cap she'd been wearing, and it jutted out in stiff salty tufts around her ears.

She said I had no connections with things. She went on and on about the sea and the fish and the plains and the buffalo and life and death and her childhood. She said even the Christian culture knows how to redeem violence: through sacrament. She would take communion, eat her fish. If she didn't, nothing made sense. I don't remember half the things she said. She said Indians ate what they loved. She said it was a kind of cannibalism, so I should understand it: I had swallowed her.

1996

Lee Smith

THE HAPPY MEMORIES CLUB

The author of three collections of short stories and eleven much-loved novels, including Fair and Tender Ladies *and* The Last Girls, *Lee Smith has been said to write with "an honesty so severe we are brought to our knees"* (Washington Post Book World). *The narrator of this story is cut from the same cloth. Says Alice Scully of her life in a Virginia retirement center, "Passionate love affairs . . . are not uncommon here. Pacemakers cannot regulate the wild, unbridled yearnings of the heart. You do not wish to know this, I imagine." Now at work on her twelfth novel, Lee Smith lives in Hillsborough, North Carolina.*

I may be old, but I'm not dead.
Perhaps you are surprised to hear this. You may be surprised to learn that people like me are still capable of original ideas, intelligent insights, and intense feelings. Passionate love affairs, for example, are not uncommon here. Pacemakers cannot regulate the wild, unbridled yearnings of the heart. You do not wish to know this, I imagine. This knowledge is probably upsetting to you, as it is upsetting to my sons, who do not want to hear, for instance, about my relationship with Dr. Solomon Marx, the historian. "Please, Mom," my son Alex said, rolling his eyes. "Come on, Mama," my son Johnny said. "Can't you maintain a little dignity here?" *Dignity*, said Johnny, who runs a chain of miniature-golf courses! "I have had enough dignity to last me for the rest of my life, thank you," I told Johnny.

I've always done exactly what I was supposed to do—now I intend to do what I want.

"Besides, Dr. Solomon Marx is the joy of my life," I told them. This remained true even when my second surgery was less than successful, obliging me to take to this chair. It remained true until Solomon's most recent stroke, five weeks ago, which has paralyzed him below the waist and caused his thoughts to become disordered, so that he cannot always remember things, or the words for things. A survivor himself, Solomon is an expert on the Holocaust. He has numbers tattooed on his arm. He used to travel the world, speaking about the Holocaust. Now he can't remember what to call it.

"Well, I think it's a blessing," said one of the nurses—that young Miss Rogers. "The Holocaust was just awful."

"It is not a blessing, you ignorant bitch," I told her. "It is the end; our memories are all we've got." I put myself in reverse and sped off before she could reply. I could feel her staring at me as I motored down the hall. I am sure she wrote something in her ever-present notebook. "Inappropriate" and "unmanageable" are among the words they use, unpleasant and inaccurate adjectives all.

The words Solomon can't recall are always nouns.

"My dear," he said to me one day recently, when they had wheeled him out into the Residence Center lobby, "what did you say your name was?" He knew it, of course, deep in his heart's core, as well as he knew his own.

"Alice Scully," I said.

"Ah. Alice Scully," he said. "And what is it that we used to do together, Alice Scully, which brought me such intense—oh, so big—" His eyes were like bright little beads in his pinched face. "It was of the greatest, ah—"

"Sex," I told him. "You loved it."

He grinned at me. "Oh, yes," he said. "Sex. It was sex, indeed."

"Mrs. Scully!" his nurse snapped.

Now I have devised a little game to help Solomon remember nouns. It works like this. Whenever they bring him out, I go over to him and clasp my hands together as if I were hiding something in them. "If you can guess what I've got here," I say, "I'll give you a kiss."

He squints in concentration, fishing for nouns. If he gets one, I give him a kiss.

Some days are better than others.

This is true for us all, of course. We can't be expected to remember everything we know.

In my life I was a teacher, and a good one. I taught English in the days when it was English, not "language arts." I taught for forty years at the Sandy Point School, in Sandy Point, Virginia, where I lived with my husband, Harold Scully, and raised four sons, three of them Harold's. Harold owned and ran the Trent Riverside Pharmacy until the day he dropped dead in his drugstore counting out antibiotics for a Methodist preacher. His mouth and his eyes were wide open, as if whatever he found on the other side surprised him mightily. I was sorry to see this, since Harold was not a man who liked surprises.

I must say I gave him none. I was a good wife to Harold, though I was at first dismayed to learn that this role entailed taking care of his parents from the day of our marriage until their deaths. They both lived long lives, and his mother went blind at the end. But we lived in their house, the largest house in Sandy Point, right on the old tidal river, and their wealth enabled us to send our own sons off to the finest schools and even, in Robert's case, to medical school.

Harold's parents never got over Harold's failure to get into medical school himself. In fact, he barely made it through pharmacy school. As far as I know, however, he was a good pharmacist, never poisoning anybody or mixing up prescriptions. He loved to look at the orderly rows of bottles on his shelves. He loved labeling. Often he dispensed medical advice to his customers: which cough medicine worked best, what to put on a boil. People trusted him. Harold got a great deal of pleasure from his job and from his standing in the community.

I taught school at first because I was trained to do it and because I wanted to. I was never one to plan a menu or clip a recipe out of a magazine. I left all that to Harold's mother and to the family housekeeper, Lucille.

Anyway, I loved teaching. I loved to diagram sentences on the board, precisely separating the subject from the predicate with a vertical line, the linking verb from the predicate adjective with a slanted line, and so forth. The children used to try to stump me by making up long sentences they thought I couldn't diagram, sentences so complex that my final diagram on the board looked like a blueprint for a cathedral, with flying buttresses everywhere, all the lines connecting.

I loved geography, as well—tracing roads, tracing rivers. I loved to trace the route of the pony express, of the Underground Railroad, of De Soto's search for gold. I told them the story of that bumbling fool Zebulon Pike, who set out in 1805 to find the source of the Mississippi River and ended up a year later at the glorious peak they named for him, Pike's Peak, which my sister, Rose, and I visited in 1926 on our cross-country odyssey with my brother John and his wife. In the photograph taken at Pike's Peak, I am seated astride a donkey, wearing a polka-dot dress and a floppy hat, while the western sky goes on and on endlessly behind me.

I taught my students these things: the first flight in a power-driven airplane was made by Wilbur and Orville Wright at Kitty Hawk, North Carolina, on December 17, 1903; Wisconsin is the "Badger State"; the Dutch bought Manhattan Island from the Indians for twenty-four dollars in 1626; you can't sink in the Great Salt Lake. Now these facts ricochet in my head like pinballs, and I do not intend, thank you very much, to enter the Health Center for "better care."

I never tired of telling my students the story of the Mississippi River—how a scarlet oak leaf falling into Lake Itasca, in Minnesota, travels first north and then east through a wild, lonely landscape of lakes and rapids as if it were heading for Lake Superior, over the Falls of St. Anthony, down through Minneapolis and St. Paul, past bluffs and prairies and islands, to be joined by the Missouri River just above St. Louis, and then by the Ohio, where the water grows more than a mile wide—you can't see across it. My scarlet leaf meanders with eccentric loops and horseshoe curves down, down, down the great continent, through the delta, to New Orleans and beyond, past the great fertile mud plain shaped like a giant goose's foot, and into the Gulf of Mexico.

"And what happens to the leaf *then*, Mrs. Scully?" some student would never fail to ask.

"Ah," I would say, "then our little leaf becomes a part of the universe"—leaving them to ponder *that*!

I was known as a hard teacher but a fair one, and many of my students came back in later years to tell me how much they had learned.

Here at Marshwood, a "total" retirement community, they want us to become children again, forgoing intelligence. This is why I was so pleased when the announcement went up on the bulletin board about a month ago:

WRITING GROUP TO MEET
WEDNESDAY, 3:00 P.M.

Ah, I thought, that promising infinitive "to meet." For, like many former English teachers, I had thought that someday I might like "to write."

At the appointed day and hour I motored over to the library (a euphemism, since the room contains mostly well-worn paperbacks by Jacqueline Susann and Louis L'Amour). I was dismayed to find Martha Louise Clapton already in charge. The idea had been hers, I learned; I should have known. She's the type who tries to run everything. Martha Louise Clapton has never liked me, having had her eye on Solomon, to no avail, for years before my arrival. She inclined her frizzy blue head ever so slightly to acknowledge my entrance.

"As I was just saying, Alice, several of us have discovered in mealtime conversation that in fact we've been writing for years, in our journals and letters and whatnot, and so I said to myself, 'Martha Louise, why not form a writing group?' and *voilà*."

"*Voilà*," I said, edging into the circle.

So it began.

Besides Martha Louise and myself, the writing group included Joy Richter, a minister's widow with a preference for poetry; Miss Elena Grier, who taught Shakespeare for years and years at a girls' preparatory school in Nashville, Tennessee; Frances Mason, whose husband lay in a coma over at the Health Center (another euphemism—you never leave the Health Center); Shirley Lassiter, who had buried three husbands and still thought of herself as a belle; and Sam Hofstetter, a retired lawyer, deaf as a post. We agreed to meet again in the library one week later. Each of us should bring some writing to share with the others.

"What's that?" Sam Hofstetter said. We wrote the time and place down on a little piece of paper and gave it to him. He folded the paper carefully, placing it in his pocket. "Could you make copies of the writing, please?" he asked. He inclined his silver head and tapped his ear significantly. We all agreed. Of course we agreed—we outnumber the men four to one, poor old things. In a place like this they get more attention than you would believe.

Then Joy Richter said that she probably couldn't afford to make copies. She said she was on a limited budget.

I said I felt sure we could use the Xerox machine in the manager's office, especially since we needed it for the writing group.

"Oh, I don't know." Frances Mason started wringing her hands. "They might not let us."

"I'll take care of it," Martha Louise said majestically. "Thank you, Alice, for your suggestion. Thank you, everyone, for joining the group."

I had wondered if I might suffer initially from writer's block, but nothing of that sort occurred. In fact I was flooded by memories—overwhelmed, engulfed, as I sat in my chair by the picture window, writing on my lap board. I was not even aware of the world outside, my head was so full of the people and places of the past, rising up in my mind as they were then, in all the fullness of life, and myself as I was then, that headstrong girl longing to leave her home in east Virginia and walk in the world at large.

I wrote and wrote. I wrote for three days. I wrote until I felt satisfied, and then I stopped. I felt better than I had in years, full of new life and freedom (a paradox, since I am more and more confined to this chair).

During that week Solomon guessed "candy," "ring," and "Anacin." He was getting better. I was not. I ignored certain symptoms in order to attend the Wednesday meeting of the writing group.

Martha Louise led off. Her blue eyes looked huge, like lakes, behind her glasses. "They just don't make families like they used to," she began, and continued with an account of growing up on a farm in Ohio, how her parents struggled to make ends meet, how the children strung popcorn and cut out paper ornaments to trim the tree when they had no money for Christmas, how they pulled taffy and laid it out on a marble slab, and how each older child had a little one to take care of. "We were poor but we were happy," Martha Louise concluded. "It was an ideal childhood."

"Oh, Martha Louise," Frances Mason said tremulously, "that was just beautiful."

Everyone agreed.

Too many adjectives, I thought, but I held my tongue.

Next Joy Richter read a poem about seeing God in everything: "the stuff of day" was a phrase I rather liked. Joy Richter apparently saw God in a shiny red apple, in a dewy rose, in her husband's kind blue eyes, in photographs of her grandchildren. The poem was pretty good, but it would have been better if she hadn't tried so hard to rhyme it.

Miss Elena then presented a sonnet comparing life to a merry-go-round. The final couplet went

> Lost children, though you're old, remember well
> The joy and music of life's carousel.

This was not bad, and I said so. Frances Mason read a reminiscence about her husband's return from the Second World War, which featured the young Frances "hovering upon the future" in a porch swing as she "listened for the tread of his beloved boot." The military theme was continued by Sam Hofstetter, who read (loudly) an account of Army life titled "Somewhere in France." Shirley Lassiter was the only one whose story was not about herself. Instead it was fiction evidently modeled on a romance novel, for it involved a voluptuous debutante who had to choose between two men. Both of them were rich, and both of them loved her, but one had a fatal disease, and for some reason this young woman didn't know which one.

"Why not?" boomed the literal Sam.

"It's a mystery, silly," Shirley Lassiter said. "That's the plot." Shirley Lassiter had a way of resting her jeweled hands on her enormous bosom as if it were a shelf. "I don't want to give the plot away," she said. Clearly, she did not have a brain in her head.

Then came my turn.

I began to read the story of my childhood. I had grown up in the tiny coastal town of Waterville, Maryland. I was the fourth child in a family of five, with three older brothers and a baby sister. My father, who was in the oyster business, killed himself when I was six and Rose was only three. He went out into the Chesapeake Bay in an old rowboat, chopped a hole in the bottom of it with an ax, and then shot himself in the head with a revolver. He meant to finish the job. He did not sink as planned, however, because a fisherman witnessed the act, and hauled his body to shore.

This left Mama with five children to raise and no means of support. She was forced to turn our home into a boardinghouse, keeping mostly teachers from Goucher College and salesmen passing through, although two old widows, Mrs. Flora Lewis and Mrs. Virginia Prince, stayed with us for years. Miss Flora, as we called her, had to have a cup of warm milk every night at bedtime; I will never forget it. It could be neither too hot nor too cold. I was the one who took it up to her, stepping so carefully up the dark back stair.

Nor will I forget young Miss Day from Richmond, a teacher, who played the piano beautifully. She used to play "Clair de Lune" and "Für Elise" on the old upright in the parlor. I would already have been sent to bed, and so I'd lie there trembling in the dark, seized by feelings I couldn't name, as the notes floated up to me and Rose in our little room, in our white iron bed wrought with roses and figures of nymphs. Miss Day was jilted some years later, we heard, her virtue lost and her reputation ruined.

Every Sunday, Mama presided over the big tureen at breakfast, when we'd have boiled fish and crisp little johnnycakes. To this day I have never tasted anything as good as those johnnycakes. Mama's face was flushed, and her hair escaped its bun to curl in damp tendrils as she dished up the breakfast plates. I thought she was beautiful. I'm sure she could have married again had she chosen to do so, but her heart was full of bitterness at the way her life had turned out, and she never forgave our father, or looked at another man.

Daddy had been a charmer, by all accounts. He carried a silver-handled cane and allowed me to play with his gold pocket watch when I was especially good. He took me to harness races, where we cheered for a horse he owned, a big roan named Joe Cord. On these excursions I wore a white dress and stockings and patent-leather shoes. And how Daddy could sing! He had a lovely baritone voice. I remember him on bended knee singing "Daisy, Daisy, give me your answer, do" to Mama, who pretended to be embarrassed but was not. I remember his bouncing Rose up and down on his lap and singing, "This is the way the lady rides."

After his death the boys went off to sea as soon as they could, and I was obliged to work in the kitchen and take care of Rose. Kitchen work in a boardinghouse is never finished. This is why I have never liked to cook since, though I know how to do it, I can assure you.

We had a summer kitchen outside, so that it wouldn't heat up the whole house when we were cooking or canning. It had a kerosene stove. I remember one time when we were putting up blackberry jam, and one of those jars simply blew up. We had blackberry jam all over the place. Glass cut the Negro girl, Ocie, who was helping out, and I was surprised to see that her blood was as red as mine.

As time went on, Mama grew sadder and withdrew from us, sometimes barely speaking for days on end. My great joy was Rose, a lively child with golden curls and skin so fair you could see the blue veins beneath it. I slept with Rose every night and played with her every day. Since Mama was indisposed, we could do whatever we wanted, and we had the run of the town, just like boys. We'd go clamming in the bay with an inner tube floating out behind us, tied to my waist by a rope. We'd feel the clams with our feet and rake them up, flipping them into a net attached to the inner tube. Once, we went on a sailing trip with a cousin of ours, Bud Ned Black, up the Chickahominy River for a load of brick. But the wind failed and we got stuck there. We just *sat* on that river, for what seemed like days and days. Rose fussed and fumed while Cap'n Bud Ned drank whiskey and chewed tobacco and did not appear to mind the situation, so long as his supplies held out. But Rose was impatient—always, always so impatient.

"Alice," she said dramatically, as we sat staring out at the shining water, the green trees at its edge, the wheeling gulls, "I will *die* if we don't move. I will die here," Rose said, though Bud Ned and I laughed at her.

But Rose meant it. As she grew older, she had to go here, go there, do this, do that, have this, have that—she hated being poor and living in the boardinghouse, and could not wait to grow up and go away.

We both developed a serious taste for distance when our brother John and his wife took us motoring across the country. I was sixteen. I loved that trip, from the first stage of planning our route on the map to finally viewing the great mountains, which sprang straight up from the desert like apparitions. Of course, we had never seen such mountains; they took my breath away. I remember how Rose flung her arms out wide to the world as we stood in the cold wind on Pike's Peak. I believe we could have gone on driving and driving forever. But we had to return, and I had to resume my duties, letting go the girl John had hired so that Mama would permit my absence. John was our sweetest brother, but they are all dead now, all my brothers, and Rose, too.

I have outlived everyone.

Only yesterday Rose and I were little girls, playing a game we loved so well, a game that strikes me now as terribly dangerous. This memory is more vivid than any other in my life.

It is late night, summertime. Rose and I have sneaked out of the boardinghouse, down the tiny back stair past the gently sighing widows' rooms; past Mama's room, door open, moonlight ghostly on the mosquito netting draped from the canopy over her bed; past the snoring salesmen's rooms, stepping tiptoe across the wide-plank kitchen floor, wincing at each squeak; and out the kitchen door into moonlight so bright that it leaves shadows. Darting from tree to tree, we cross the yard and attain the sidewalk, moving rapidly past the big sleeping houses with their shutters yawning open to the cool night air, down the sidewalk to the edge of town where the sidewalk ends and the road goes on forever through miles and miles of peanut fields and other towns and other fields, toward Baltimore.

Rose and I lie down flat in the middle of the road, which still retains the heat of the day, and let it warm us head to toe as we dream aloud of what the future holds. At different times Rose planned to be an aviator, a doctor, and a film actress living in California, with an orange tree in her yard. Even her most domestic dreams were grand. "I'll have a big house and lots of servants and a husband who loves me *so much*," Rose would say, "and a yellow convertible touring car, and six children, and we will be rich and they will never have to work, and I will put a silk scarf on my head and we will all go out riding on Sunday."

Even then I said I would be a teacher, because I was always good in school, but I would be a missionary teacher, enlightening natives in some far-off corner of the world. Even as I said it, though, I believe I knew it would not come to pass, for I was bound to stay at home, as Rose was bound to go.

But we'd lie there looking up at the sky, and dream our dreams, and wait for the thrill of an oncoming vehicle, which we could hear coming a long time away, and could feel throughout the length of our bodies as it neared us. We would roll off the pavement and into the peanut field just as the car approached, our hearts pounding. Sometimes we nearly dozed on that warm road—and once we were almost killed by a potato truck.

Gradually, as Mama retreated to her room, I took over the running of the boardinghouse, and Mama's care as well. At eighteen Rose ran away with a fast-talking furniture salesman who had been boarding with us. They settled finally in Ohio, and had three children, and her life was not glamorous in the least, though better than some, and we wrote to each other every week until her death, of ovarian cancer, at thirty-nine.

This was as far as I'd gotten.

I quit reading aloud and looked around the room. Joy Richter was ashen, Miss Elena Grier was mumbling to herself, and Shirley Lassiter was breathing heavily and fluttering her fingers at her throat. Sam Hofstetter stared fixedly at me with the oddest expression on his face, and Frances Mason wept openly, shaking with sobs.

"Alice! Now just look at what you've done!" Martha Louise said to me severely. "Meeting adjourned!"

I had to miss the third meeting of the writing group, because Dr. Culbertson sent me to the Health Center for treatment and further tests (euphemisms both). Dr. Culbertson then went so far as to consult with my son Robert, also a doctor, about what to do with me next. Dr. Culbertson believed that I ought to move to the Health Center, for "better care." Of course I called Robert immediately and gave him a piece of my mind.

That was yesterday.

I know they are discussing me by telephone—Robert, Alex, Johnny, and Carl. Lines are buzzing up and down the East Coast.

I came here when I had to, because I did not want any of their wives to get stuck with me, as I had gotten stuck with Harold's mother and father. Now I expect some common decency and respect. At times like this I wish for daughters, who often, I feel, have more compassion and understanding than sons.

Even Carl, the child of my heart, says I had "better listen to the doctor."

Instead I have been listening to this voice too long silent inside me, the voice of myself, as I write page after page propped up in bed in the Health Center.

Today is Wednesday. I have skipped certain of my afternoon medications. At 2:15 I buzz for Sheila, my favorite, a tall young nurse's aide with the grace of a gazelle. "Sheila," I say, "I need for you to help me dress, dear, and then roll my chair over here, if you will. My own chair, I mean. I have to go to a meeting."

Sheila looks at my chart and then back at me, her eyes wide. "It doesn't say . . ." she begins.

"Dr. Culbertson said it would be perfectly all right," I assure her. I pull a $20.00 bill from my purse, which I keep right beside me in bed, and hand it to her. "I know it's a lot of trouble, but it's very important," I say. "I think I'll just slip on the red sweater and the black wraparound skirt—that's so easy to get on. They're both in the drawer, dear."

"Okay, honey," Sheila says, and she gets me dressed and sets me in my chair. I put on lipstick and have Sheila fluff up my hair in the back where it's gotten so flat from lying in bed. Sheila hands me my purse and my notebook, and then I'm off, waving to the girls at the nurses' station as I purr past them. They wave back. I feel fine now. I take the elevator down to the first floor and then motor through the lobby, speaking to acquaintances. I pass the gift shop, the newspaper stand, and all the waiting rooms.

It's chilly outside. I head up the walkway past the par three golf course, where I spy Parker Howard, ludicrous in those bright-green pants they sell to old men, putting on the third hole. "Hi, Parker!" I cry.

"Hello, Alice," he calls. "Nice to see you out!" He sinks the putt.

I enter the Multipurpose Building and head for the library, where the writers' group is already in progress. Driving over from the Health Center took longer than I'd expected.

Miss Elena is reading, but she stops and looks up when I come in, her mouth a perfect O. Everybody looks at Martha Louise.

"Why, Alice," Martha Louise says. She clears her throat. "We didn't expect that you would be joining us today. We heard that you were in the Health Center."

"I was," I say. "But I'm out now."

"Evidently," Martha Louise says.

I ride up to the circular table, set my brake, get out my note-book, and ask Miss Elena for a copy of whatever she's reading. Wordless, she slides one over. But she still does not resume. They're all looking at me.

"What is it?" I ask.

"Well, Alice, last week, when you were absent, we laid out some ground rules for this writing group." Martha Louise gains composure as she goes along. "We are all in agreement here, Alice, that if this is to be a pleasant and meaningful club for all of us, we need to restrict our subject matter to what everyone enjoys."

"So?" I don't get it.

"We've also adopted an official name for the group." Now Martha Louise is as cheerful as a robin.

"What is it?"

"It's the Happy Memories Club," she announces, and they all nod. I am beginning to get it.

"You mean to tell me—" I start.

"I mean to tell you that if you wish to be a part of this group, Alice Scully, you will have to calm yourself down, and keep your subject matter in check. We don't come here to be upset," Martha Louise says serenely.

They are all watching me closely now, Sam Hofstetter in particular. I think they expect an outburst.

But I won't give them the satisfaction.

"Fine," I say. This is a lie. "That sounds just fine to me. Good idea!" I smile at everybody.

There is a perceptible relaxation then, an audible settling back into chairs, as Miss Elena resumes her reading. It's a travelogue named "Shakespeare and His Haunts," about a tour she made to England several years ago. But I find myself unable to listen. I simply can't hear Elena, or Joy, who reads next, or even Sam.

"Well, is that it for today? Anybody else?" Martha Louise raps her knuckles against the table. "I brought something," I say, "but I don't have copies."

I look at Sam, who shrugs and smiles and says I should go ahead anyway. Everybody else looks at Martha Louise.

"Well, go on, then," she directs tartly, and I begin.

After Rose's disappearance, my mother took to her bed and turned her face to the wall, leaving me in charge of everything. Oh, how I worked! I worked like a dog, long hours, a cruelly unnatural life for a spirited young woman. Yet I persevered. People in the town, including our minister, complimented me; I was discussed and admired. Our boardinghouse stayed full, and somehow I managed, with Ocie's help, to get the meals on the table. I smiled and chattered at mealtime. Yet inside I was starving, starving for love and life.

Thus it was not surprising, I suppose, that I should fall for the first man who showed any interest in me. He was a schoolteacher who had been educated at the university, in Charlottesville, a thin, dreamy young man from one of the finest families in Virginia. His grandfather had been the governor. He used to sit out by the sound every evening after supper, reading, and one day I joined him there. It was a lovely June evening; the sound was full of sailboats, and the sky above us was as round and blue as a bowl.

"I was reading a poem about a girl with beautiful yellow hair," he said, "and then I look up and what do I see? A real girl with beautiful yellow hair."

For some reason I started to cry, not even caring what my other boarders thought as they sat up on the porch looking out over this landscape in which we figured.

"Come here," he said, and he took my hand and led me behind the old rose-covered boathouse, where he pulled me to him and kissed me curiously, as if it were an experiment.

His name was Carl Redding Armistead III. He had the reedy look of a poet, but all the assurance of the privileged class. I was older than he, but he was more experienced. He was well educated, and had been to Europe several times.

"You pretty thing," he said, and kissed me again. The scent of the roses was everywhere.

I went that night to his room, and before the summer was out, we had lain together in nearly every room of the boardinghouse. We were crazy for each other by then, and I didn't care what might happen, or who knew. On Saturday evenings I'd leave a cold supper for the rest, and Carl and I would take the skiff and row out to Sand Island, where the wild ponies were, and take off all our clothes and make love. Sometimes my back would be red and bleeding from the rough black sand and the broken shells on the beach.

"Just a minute! Just a minute here!" Martha Louise is pounding on the table, and Frances Mason is crying, as usual. Sam Hofstetter is staring at me in a manner that indicates that he has heard every word I've said.

"Well, I think that's terrific!" Shirley Lassiter giggles and bats her painted blue eyelids at us all.

Of course this romance did not last. Nothing that intense can be sustained, though the loss of such intensity can scarcely be borne. Quite simply, Carl and I foundered upon the prospect of the future. He had to go on to the world that awaited him; I could not leave Mama. Our final parting was bitter—we were spent, exhausted by the force of what had passed between us. He did not even look back as he sped away in his little red sports car, nor did I cry.

Nor did I ever tell him about the existence of Carl, my son, whom I bore defiantly out of wedlock nine months later, telling no one who the father was. Oh, those were hard, black days! I was ostracized by the very people who had formerly praised me, and ogled by the men in my boardinghouse, who now considered me a fallen woman. l wore myself to a frazzle taking care of Mama and the baby at the same time.

One night, I remember, I was so tired that I felt that I would actually die, yet little Carl would not stop crying. Nothing would quiet him—not rocking, not the breast, not walking the room. He had an oddly unpleasant cry, like a cat mewing. I remember looking out my window at the quiet town where everyone slept— everyone on this earth, I felt, except me. I held Carl out at arm's length and looked hard at him in the streetlight, at his red, twisted little face. I had an awful urge to throw him out the window—

"That's enough!" several of them say at once. Martha Louise is standing.

But it is Miss Elena who speaks. "I cannot believe," she says severely, "that out of your entire life, Alice Scully, this is all you can find to write about. What of your long marriage to Mr. Scully? Your seven grandchildren? Those of us who have not been blessed with grandchildren would give—"

Of course I loved Harold Scully. Of course I love my grandchildren. I love Solomon, too. I love them all. Miss Elena is like my sons, too terrified to admit to herself how many people we can love, how various we are. She does not want to hear it any more than they do, any more than you do. You all want us to *never change, never change.*

I did not throw my baby out the window after all, and my mother finally died, and I sold the boardinghouse then and was able, at last, to go to school.

Out of the corner of my eye I see Dr. Culbertson appear at the library door, accompanied by a man I do not know. Martha Louise says, "I simply cannot believe that a former *English teacher—*"

This strikes me as very funny. My mind is filled with enormous sentences as I back up my chair and then start forward, out the other door and down the hall and outside into the sweet spring day, where the sunshine falls on my face as it did in those days on the beach, my whole body hot and aching and sticky with sweat and salt and blood, the wild ponies paying us no mind as they ate the tall grass that grew at the edge of the dunes. Sometimes the ponies came so close that we could reach out and touch them. Their coats were shaggy and rough and full of burrs, I remember.

Oh, I remember everything as I cruise forward on the sidewalk that neatly separates the rock garden from the golf course. I turn right at the corner, instead of left toward the Health Center. "Fore!" Parker Howard shouts, waving at me. *A former English teacher*, Martha Louise said. These sidewalks are like diagrams, parallel lines and dividers: oh, I could diagram anything. The semicolon, I used to say, is like a little scale; it must have items of equal rank, I'd warn them. Do not use a semicolon between a clause and a phrase, or a main clause and a subordinate clause. Do not write *I loved Carl Redding Armistead; a rich man's son*. Do not write *If I had really loved Carl Armistead; I would have left with him despite all obstacles*. Do not write *I still feel his touch; which has thrilled me throughout my life*.

I turn at the top of the hill and motor along the sidewalk toward the Residence Center, hoping to see Solomon. The sun is in my eyes. Do not carelessly link two sentences with a comma. Do not write *I want to see Solomon again, he has meant so much to me*. To correct this problem, subordinate one of the parts. *I want to see Solomon, because he has meant so much to me*. Because he has meant. So much. To me. Fragments. Fragments all. I push the button to open the door into the Residence Center, and sure enough, they've brought him out. They've dressed him in his Madras plaid shirt and wheeled him in front of the television, which he hates. I cruise right over.

"Solomon," I say, but at first he doesn't respond when he looks at me. I come even closer. "Solomon!" I say sharply, bumping his wheelchair. He notices me then, and a little light comes into his eyes.

I cup my hands. "Solomon," I say, "I'll give you a kiss if you can guess what I've got in my hands."

He looks at me for a while longer.

"Now, Mrs. Scully," his nurse starts.

"Come on," I say. "What have I got in here?"

"An elephant," Solomon finally says.

"Close enough!" I cry, and lean right over to kiss his sweet old cheek, being unable to reach his mouth.

"Mrs. Scully," his nurse starts again, but I'm gone, I'm history, I'm out the front door and around the parking circle and up the long entrance drive to the highway. It all connects. Everything connects. The sun is bright, the dogwoods are blooming, the state flower of Virginia is the dogwood, I can still see the sun on the Chickahominy River and my own little sons as they sail their own little boats in a tidal pool by the Chesapeake Bay, they were all blond boys once, though their hair would darken later, Annapolis is the capital of Maryland, the first historic words ever transmitted by telegraph came to Maryland: "What hath God wrought?" The sun is still shining. It glares off the snow on Pike's Peak, it gleams through the milky blue glass of the old apothecary jar in the window of Harold Scully's shop, it warms the asphalt on that road where Rose and I lie waiting, waiting, waiting.

1997

Judy Troy

RAMONE

The late Stanley Elkin described Judy Troy's fictional characters as "busted families, ditched husbands and abandoned wives, stepparents and stepkids [who], despite their bleakness, somehow manage to leave a light shining in the heart." This story, set in the tiny crossroads of Ramone, Texas, exemplifies that shining as well as Troy's brilliant use of dialogue. A midwesterner by birth and raising, Judy Troy has lived in Auburn, Alabama, long enough to recognize the particular poignancy of Alabama cotton farmers dying in Texas. She is alumni writer-in-residence at Auburn University.

At the beginning of August, a week after my fourteenth birthday, my stepfather, McKinley, my mother, and I left Houston for Ramone, Texas. McKinley's dying father was our reason for going. He was eighty-three years old and sick with lung cancer and had only a few months left to live, and McKinley wanted us to care for him. He said that he and my mother could get jobs in Lubbock.

We left on a humid Friday morning before the sun came up. In the pale sky we could see Venus and a half moon. McKinley turned on the inside light to show me how Texas took up five pages in the road atlas. "We're driving six hundred miles without crossing a state line, Roberta," he said.

I was in the back seat, and my mother was driving. She was afraid that McKinley, talking about his father, or his sister, who also lived in Ramone, would start to cry. He hadn't been home in nine years—he'd been in the Army, and had married the wrong person before he married my mother—and he was an emotional person, just as my real father had been. My father, who my mother never talked about except sometimes after church, had died of a heart attack five years before.

The sun came up, and as we left refineries and oil wells behind we came upon empty flat fields, nowhere towns, and more historical markers than probably exist in any normal-sized state.

"Let's stop," McKinley said, each time we passed one. My mother stopped twice; each time, the marker was for a man who'd come from Alabama and tried to grow cotton.

"Isn't this interesting?" McKinley said to us.

"To be truthful, no," my mother said.

"I'd rather just get there," I said. "The sooner you start a new life the sooner it becomes an old life."

"What's your hurry to make it old?" McKinley asked.

"I don't know," I said. But I felt my heart speed up, which told me that the answer had to do with being afraid. My father had told me once that I was hooked up inside to a kind of lie detector.

"I like the travelling part," my mother said. "I'd just as soon never get anywhere."

"That's weird," I said.

"It's not," my mother said.

"You two argue because you're so much alike," McKinley told us.

It took us all day to get there, even though we'd left so early—loading the car and U-Haul the night before, in darkness, because my mother was worried that we'd be robbed by somebody watching. The only person I saw was Roy Lee Hollis, standing under a stairway at our apartment complex, trying to apologize. He was my best friend—the only person I'd bothered to tell I would miss—and he had refused to kiss me. He proved for me something that my mother had always said—that it was foolish to like a boy more than he liked you. But it made moving away easier. I'd be in a tiny town in West Texas with a dying person I'd never met, but at least I would never again have to see Roy Lee Hollis.

I didn't expect him to show up at the last minute. I hardly let him speak. I walked away—in the stiff-legged way I'd seen high-heeled women in soap operas do—just as McKinley came down the stairs with a suitcase. "Why wouldn't you say goodbye to that boy?" he asked me later.

That question and Roy Lee's sad expression were on my mind as we drove into Ramone. The sky was darkening over a one-block street of one-story buildings. At the end of the block the pavement ended and the street became dirt. That's where our neighborhood began.

McKinley drove past three shabby houses, raising behind us a storm of dust, then stopped in front of a two-story, caved-in, paint-peeling dump.

"Jesus Christ," he said. He didn't move to get out. My mother put her hand over her mouth.

The door opened, and an ancient, smaller, yellow version of McKinley stepped onto the broken porch. He slowly lifted one hand in a wave.

"I guess that's Grandpa," I said.

My mother laughed.

"That's not funny," McKinley said to us.

McKinley's father had emphysema and liver disease in addition to cancer; he'd been sent home from the hospital to die.

"At least they came straight out and told him," my mother said later that night. "At least they didn't sugarcoat it."

'You wouldn't want any sympathy creeping in," McKinley said.

It was after ten. McKinley's father, Emerson, had gone to bed, and we'd investigated the house and the neighborhood and walked the short distance into town. We'd had dinner at Luigi's Lone Star Pizza, which was a convenience store and gas station as well as a restaurant. Now we were settled outside, in back, on the weedy lawn. We couldn't see each other in the hot darkness. Behind us in an empty field cicadas were buzzing. My mother and I were too depressed to talk, but for some reason, sick as Emerson was, McKinley had gotten happier being around his father. McKinley said he hoped his daddy would live long enough to see the house repaired.

"Repaired by who?" my mother said meanly. It was doubly

mean, because both my mother and McKinley had been construction workers before they married. It was how they'd met.

"I know you're disappointed," he said, "but sniping at me won't make it better."

"What will, then?" she asked.

"Cheering up. Seeing the good things. Finding a little brightness in the dark corners."

My mother scratched her leg. "I'll tell you what's in this corner," she said. "Chiggers." She stood up and walked off toward the house. Overhead you couldn't see a single star.

"I think we'll end up liking it here," McKinley said.

I slept in a tiny room upstairs. McKinley and my mother were next door, in the double bed McKinley's father had been born in. Sometime in the night I heard McKinley cry out in his sleep.

"It's no wonder you're having a nightmare," I heard my mother say.

I fell back to sleep and dreamed that my father wasn't dead but only in a room that I couldn't find the door to. Then I dreamed that Roy Lee chose me as his partner in biology class but couldn't remember my name.

McKinley woke me at seven.

"Your Aunt Mavis Jean used to sleep in that bed," he told me. "Wait till you meet her."

"She's not my aunt," I said.

"I forget that," McKinley said. "It seems to me you've always been mine."

"I've never been yours," I told him.

"Don't you get tired of being so tough?" he asked me.

Then he disappeared. A moment later I heard him downstairs, saying to Emerson, "Just hold on to me, Pop. I won't let you go."

Across the narrow hall, in the bathroom, I could hear my mother trying to get clean water out of the bathtub faucet. I'd tried the night before.

"I think it's sewage," I shouted through the wall.

"Goddam shit," my mother said. It was such a shock to hear her say those words that I went in and looked at her sitting on the floor in McKinley's boxer shorts and undershirt.

"Why are you wearing that?" I asked.

"Why shouldn't I wear it?"

"Well, it's not exactly attractive."

"Pardon me," my mother said. "Let me get on a negligee."

"Don't do it for my sake. I'm not married to you."

"So those are the words you choose to start the day with," she said. "Fine."

We stared at each other stubbornly. As usual, I looked away first.

When my mother and I came downstairs, McKinley said, "Daddy was just asking about you two."

It was hard to tell if that was true. Emerson was partly deaf and looked confused. McKinley had fed him and got him into a lop-sided chair on the broken porch. McKinley sat down next to him. I thought that the two of them, side by side, were like a before-and-after "Don't Smoke" advertisement.

"Hello," Emerson said.

"Hi," I said.

"Step out here into the yard," McKinley said.

My mother and I went to stand in the dandelion grass. Last night's clouds had blown off; the sky was bluer and wider than it had ever seemed in Houston. Wind was moving through the branches of the cottonwood trees and rippling the wheat field across the road.

"I told you it was pretty, didn't I?" McKinley said.

"Where did you get that thing on your head?" my mother asked. He was wearing a cowboy hat.

"Hello!" Emerson said again. He needed to shout.

"Hello!" I shouted back.

"I knew you two would have a lot to talk about!" McKinley said.

I was afraid he'd gone crazy. But he hadn't. He was just happy and sad at the same time.

A few minutes later, McKinley's sister, Mavis Jean, drove up with her husband in a boat-size Chevy. They were both large people. Mavis Jean was as tall as McKinley but not as skinny, and had reddish hair like his. She walked right over and hugged me; my mother moved herself out of range. Mavis Jean's husband was big and bald, and a tobacco chewer. I thought he might not know how to talk until I heard him say "Thank you" very quietly, in the dilapidated kitchen, when Mavis handed him a doughnut. She'd brought two boxes of them, plus a thermos of coffee. She'd brought orange juice for me.

"I have pictures of the both of you in my living room," she said, beaming down at my mother and me, where we stood side by side in front of the rusty refrigerator. "You're already family."

"Neither one of us takes a good picture," my mother said.

At the cluttered table, Mavis's husband and McKinley were writing up a list of tools and supplies they'd need to fix the house. After they left to get them, Mavis sat down with us and showed us Emerson's pills—which ones he needed to take when.

"He gets the pain pills whenever he wants them," she said. "Sometimes I give him one just when he looks real bad." Her eyes got wet, and she let tears run down her face. "I've seen Daddy almost every day for the past thirty years," she said. "It's like seeing the sun. You don't expect it to disappear."

My mother looked out the window. She tapped her nails on the table. "Is there a Presbyterian church around here?" she asked.

"The minister's already got your name," Mavis Jean said. "McKinley said you were religious."

"I don't like that word," my mother said. "I prefer 'churchgoing.'"

"I don't go myself," Mavis told her. "Maybe I should. But I feel I have God in my heart."

When my mother didn't respond, Mavis said gently, "Not everybody makes it personal like I do."

In the afternoon, my mother and I shopped for supper groceries at the convenience store. The temperature was up to a hundred and six degrees, we heard on the radio, and on top of that there was a drought. We were both having trouble with our hair, which turned limp with no humidity.

"We look like dogs," my mother said as we got out of the car. "If we're lucky they'll put us in the pound."

Inside, she got a cold, quart-size beer and drank most of it as we walked around the store. On the way home, she pulled the car over and stepped out into an overgrown field and threw up.

"Don't mention that when we get home," she warned me.

"Why would I?"

We didn't talk after that, not even when we pulled up to the house and saw Mavis Jean in the yard, swinging a rug beater at the moldy gray living-room carpet she'd hung from a tree.

McKinley, on the porch, was carefully holding up a stained pea-colored plate. "Mama's china," he said reverently to my mother.

Inside, Emerson, positioned next to the window air-conditioner, was wheezing out some sort of song.

Just then my mother snapped. "Get the groceries in, Roberta!" she yelled at me.

She tore at the loose, rotten upholstery on the couch and the chair; ripped up a corner of the kitchen linoleum, which had half risen and curled; yanked down the bathroom wallpaper, which had a kind of yellow dampness seeping through.

We all got out of her way, including Emerson: Mavis Jean's husband came in and lifted up him and his chair and deposited them both in the back bedroom.

McKinley stood in the doorway and watched. He'd never seen my mother exercised like that, although I'd told him once how right after my father's funeral she went into their bedroom and boxed up all his things. "Helen, let that go for now," my grandmother had said. She and I had stood in the doorway—just as McKinley was now—watching my mother sort through mismatched socks. She'd wanted to pair them up, even though she was putting his clothes in boxes to give to the charity-drive ladies at our church.

It was almost dark by the time my mother stopped. We had all—except for Emerson—tried to stay on the outskirts but still help.

"Just think of us as worker bees," Mavis Jean had said light-heartedly to my mother, when Mavis got in her way for a second. My mother had been holding a putty knife, though, and for a moment none of us were sure what she might do next.

Finally, she collapsed on the front porch, where she'd been prying up boards. Her sweaty hair was sticking to the back of her neck. Her sleeveless shirt was so wet you could tell where her bra was held together with pins.

"Honey, you need some new underwear," Mavis Jean said quietly.

We had supper in the cramped kitchen and then sat in the cool dimness of the living room. I fell asleep and dreamed again about Roy Lee—he was kissing and touching me—and I woke afraid that I'd been making noises. But the noises I'd heard must have been Emerson's breathing. He'd seemed all right earlier, although he hadn't eaten any dinner. "Sometimes the only food you want is sweets," I'd told him—that was how my father used to tempt me to eat when I was sick. But Emerson hadn't wanted so much as a cookie.

"Daddy?" Mavis Jean said. "What's wrong? What do you need?" She was sitting close to him, holding a pair of his trousers in her lap; she was sewing up a ripped hem.

He opened his mouth to speak but all he did was take in air. McKinley got up and went to his side; my mother went into the kitchen and came back with a glass of water. We all, except my mother, crowded around him, watching his chest rise and fall, and the look in his eye, and the way his hands were clutching the arms of his chair.

"Give him some room!" my mother shouted in a high-pitched voice.

Mavis Jean was taking his pulse, her head bent down, her eyes on her watch. Her husband put his hand on her shoulder. McKinley was all but holding his daddy in his arms. I stood right next to McKinley, leaning against him even, although I hadn't meant to. I heard him tell his father he loved him.

Then it was over. Emerson's breathing grew regular; he looked less scared; and he didn't die—not for another six months, and it was in his bed, during the night, while he was asleep.

It was an hour before we trusted that he was O.K. During that time only my mother left the house; she went out to the porch and sat on the steps.

"Come help me get coffee and cake," Mavis Jean said to me.

I followed her into the kitchen, and when she picked up the coffeepot I saw that her hands were shaking.

"I can do that," I said.

She went over to the sloping counter under the window, looking off into the dark back yard. Then she turned around and looked at me.

"What was it like," she asked softly, "having your daddy die?"

"I only know what it was like afterward," I told her. "I wasn't there when it happened."

"Oh, no," she said. "You didn't get to say goodbye."

She came close and pushed back my straggly hair, and I saw that her own hair was more gray than red. I'd forgotten that she was older than McKinley.

"'Cross at the light, Roberta,'" I said. "That was the last thing he said to me."

"That has some sweetness in it," she said. "Sweetness and good advice."

In the living room, Mavis Jean set the coffeepot down and put a blanket over Emerson's shoulders.

"You don't need a chill on top of everything else," she told him.

"It's ninety-seven degrees outside," my mother said, her voice still strange. She stood in the doorway, ignoring that she was letting in hot air and letting out cool.

"He seems most comfortable at a hundred and two," Mavis Jean said.

"Close the door, honey," McKinley said to my mother. "Come sit here by me.

My mother went outside instead. She left the door open, and her work boots were noisy on the broken boards and the cracked sidewalk. After a few minutes McKinley went out after her. Through the window I could see them standing in the road, my mother facing the empty field on the other side, and suddenly I knew how afraid she was—not of Emerson's dying but of how it made her feel, to feel too much. It was like loving a boy more than he loved you, I thought; you couldn't help it, and you couldn't stop it, and you made him love you in your dreams.

They stayed outside a long time. I sat down finally and ate a piece of cake, watching the way Mavis Jean double-rolled the hem of the pants leg before she sewed it.

Behind her, Emerson was eying me. He leaned forward to speak.

"Does that little girl belong to me?" he asked Mavis Jean.

She told him yes.

1997

Pam Durban

GRAVITY

Pam Durban says that writing this story was, in part, her attempt to "question the stories on which I was raised, stories about history and culture and especially race handed down through generations of white Southerners in my home state of South Carolina." She set the story in Charleston because it is "the place where South Carolina's history and idea of itself are still alive and flourishing." The author of two novels and a collection of stories, Pam Durban is the Doris Betts Professor of Creative Writing at the University of North Carolina.

Whenever she visited her mother in the last weeks of the elder woman's long, long life, Louisa knew that if the nurse's aide had turned Mother's wheelchair to face the bridges over the Cooper River, she would have to listen to the Mamie story again. On Mother's bad days, which seemed to fall at the beginning and end of the week, bracketing the lucid days, Mamie looked back at her out of every black woman's face. The nurse, the woman who brought her meals or helped her to the bathroom—if she was black, her name was Mamie.

Also, any footsteps might be hers. "Mamie?" Mother's voice would wobble out to meet Louisa as she walked down the hall toward her Mother's room. "Mamie?" When Louisa came into the room, Mother would be watching the door, her swollen hands folded in her lap, a look of pained brightness on her face, until she saw her daughter and the brightness dimmed. On the good days, Louisa's mother laid down her search for the actual Mamie (dead, now, for fourteen years), was content to tell Mamie's story again. In her last weeks, the Mamie story became, Louisa thought, like a

46

lighthouse beam: whenever Mother sailed too far out of sight of land, she swung toward its light and traveled home.

Why Mamie? Louisa asked herself often that spring. In the small, walled garden behind their house, in the brief cool of early morning as she watered the ferns and impatiens, the question would trickle through her mind like the thin stream of water that splashed in the garden fountain. Surely it was not Mamie herself, the person, the individual human being, that Mother was trying to keep alive by telling that story. Mamie's family had been part of their family for so long that any questions about them—if there had been any to begin with—had long since been answered. Mamie's family had served the Hilliard family since time was, her mother always said, in slavery and in freedom down through the generations until the last: Mamie's granddaughter Evelyn, who at sixteen left the kitchen house apartment in their yard where her grandmother had raised her and went to live with relatives out on Yonges Island. Who came in to work at ten, then at noon, and finally, not at all.

Besides, Mother's descriptions had all been of Mamie's labor and usefulness, her place in their world. *A good pair of black hands,* Mother had called Mamie with such affection, sometimes with tears in her eyes, you'd have thought she was praising Mamie's character or remembering the light the woman's soul gave off. In Mother's more formal moods, she called Mamie *the laundress and housekeeper and cook.* Finally, when the useful part of her life was done, she became *the family retainer* who lived out her days in their old kitchen house. ("Who else would take care of her, tell me that?" Mother asked.) How old was Mamie? No one knew. No white person anyway. "They destroyed my dates" was all Mamie would say if you asked her age, then set her jaw as if she'd clamped a plug of words between her back teeth.

"Who, Mamie?" Louisa would ask.

"I be just born, time of the shake," she would say. At least that date was fixed by something other than an old colored woman's memory: the earthquake of 1886. Then would follow a long, tangled account of dates written in a family Bible, a fire.

That morning, the Friday before Palm Sunday, Louisa wondered again— why Mamie?— as she stood out of sight behind the tea olive tree and waited for the tour guide, who had stopped his carriage in front of her house, to finish his speech to the tourists he carried and move on. Just that morning she'd hung the sign on the brick gatepost beside their wrought-iron gate. "Kindly Admire the Garden from the Street," it read, green words painted on gray slate with flowering jasmine twined around them to sweeten the message: go away, no one here wants to talk to you about this house, its people, or its history.

The guide, blond and friendly, a college boy, wore a gray Confederate army cap on his head and a red, fringed sash tied around his waist. His horse, a muscular chestnut Percheron, dozed with one back hoof cocked on the pavement. The boy stood up in the front of the carriage and turned to face his passengers, the reins draped loosely over one hand. This much she could see. And what she could hear was the story she knew so well she heard mostly tone when he spoke. The Hilliard house was one of the finest examples of the typical Charleston house still standing. Set gable end to the street, with piazzas up and down and a garden tucked behind a brick wall, its architecture was West Indian. Specifically, its influences came from Barbados, from which windward isle many of the planters had made their way to the Holy City of Charleston. She flinched at the oversized and pompous strokes with which the boy painted his picture of ease and wealth, the soft movie-mush of a Southern accent that made his speech sound like a parody and himself like the Southern aristocrat in a bad melodrama.

"Please note the exceptionally ornate ironwork of the gate," he said, "and the chemin de fer, a bristle of iron spikes set along the top of the brick wall as protection against the pirates who once freely roamed and pillaged through these streets. Notice the bricks of which the house and its attendant wall were constructed," he said. "They were fired in the brickyard at Fairview, the Hilliard family's plantation, out on the Edisto River.

"Now, the Hilliard family," he said, bowing slightly, "as was the custom with wealthy rice planters of their day, owned this house in town and the plantation house at Fairview—between which residences they divided their time. In late winter, they came into the city for the balls and races of the social season, then left for the plantation in time to oversee the planting of the rice crop in the spring. During the summer, the sickly season, they lived in town, then journeyed back to the plantation for the fall harvest and stayed there through the Christmas season."

Finally, it was over. The guide clucked to the horse and the carriage moved on, leaving a drift of horse smell in the warm air. Closing the iron gate behind her, Louisa stepped carefully over the slate flagstone sidewalk in front of the house that Hilliards had built, where Hilliards had lived forever. Even though she'd been born a Marion—her father's name and fine in its own way, with Francis Marion, the Swamp Fox, back in the line—she and her mother always thought of themselves as Hilliards first. That spring Louisa was seventy-five; her body felt rickety, full of drafts and cracks. Crossing the uneven flagstone sidewalk in front of her house, she felt her frail ankle bones, her brittle spine, and rigid hips. Sometimes at night she imagined the calcium sifting out of her skeleton as though her body were dissolving, bone by bone. Soon, she would be a rounded soft lump of a woman, like a tabby foundation after a few centuries in the weather. Soon, she would be an old woman who scuttled along, humped over and studying the ground.

Still, thanks to a daily dose of estrogen and to willpower, she walked erect as she moved steadily north, a woman with a wide, quiet face, a Prince Valiant helmet of white hair, a raw-silk shirt-waist dress, teal, set off with a dramatic scarf. She carried a flowered portmanteau and walked with her head held high and quiet on a long neck, enjoying the subtle prickle of salt air on her face, the smells from the gardens she passed, the sound of trickling water, the cries of gulls. Passing the market and the wharves, she walked through the smells of fish, coffee, and incense. The door to the ship's chandler's shop stood open, and she inhaled the oily, hayfield smell of rope that drifted from the narrow door. Out in the harbor the sheer green side of a freighter rose, the red and white Danish flag flying from its bridge.

At the place where Mother lived now, a private nursing home in an old house on Society Street, Louisa walked on tiptoe up the stairs and down the hall until she came to her mother's room, poked her head in the door.

"Mamie?" her mother asked from her wheelchair which, this being Friday, faced the window and the bridges.

"It's Louisa, Mother—here we are," she said as she always said, as though they'd arrived together at some destination. Then pulled a chair close to the wheelchair and sat with her needlepoint (Pax and the paschal lamb that she was stitching on the linen Easter banner for St. Phillip's Church) through her mother's first grieving silence. While her mother huffed, whimpered, muttered, Louisa crossed her ankles, straightened her back, smoothed her face, submerged her mind in a quiet pool of patience and cultivated charity, practiced forbearance.

Soon the bundle of pink quilted satin with a failing heart and lungs inside that was her mother began to stir. She had room in her and breath enough, but just enough, to tell her story. "The Cooper River Bridge was the bridge we had to cross, you see . . ." she said, catching the story's current and eddying into it. Louisa pushed her needle in and out of the linen, knotted the paschal lamb's woolly fur. Maybe, Louisa thought, the old soul (the words made her see something tarnished and heavy, smooth and almost round, like an old iron egg) told the story of Mamie and the bridge because it was the only story she remembered that could still carry her out and over the water, away from her present life. What amazed Louisa (and on her own bad days, literally caused her skin to itch, made her want to jump up and scream, "Get to the point, for God's sake, Mother!") was how the story never varied from telling to telling by one detail, pause, or inflection; how it seemed to be asking a question, by which construction a person might assume that the story had a point, a destination. How, though it traveled in that direction, it never seemed to arrive.

Once, browsing through old newspapers in the reading room of the Charleston Library Society in search of a mention of some nineteenth-century Hilliard, Louisa had come across this advertisement in a copy of the *Charleston City Gazette* published in the summer of 1820: "$10 Reward. Drifted from Haddrill's Point, a CANOE, painted red or a bright Spanish brown, branded with my name in several places, has row locks for 6 oars." That is how she thought of her mother's mind: a one-hundred-and-two-year-old bright Spanish-brown canoe of a mind, drifting here, drifting there, stranded on an oyster bank at low tide, lifted again and set adrift when the tide came in, drawn by tides and currents always back toward Mamie and the Cooper River Bridge.

"The Cooper River Bridge was the bridge we had to cross, you see, to get from the Charleston peninsula over to our beach house on Sullivan's Island. We spent our summers there away from the city's heat," she confided to Louisa as if she were giving one of her famous talks on local geography and history to a stranger. As if her own daughter were a tourist.

Her mother did not say this, but the Cooper River Bridge was not always the wide concrete six-lane road of a bridge it is today, a chunk of Interstate 26 lofted over the river, with reversible lanes and concrete walls to keep you from looking down or sailing off the edges. Crossing the new bridge you might as well be flying over the river in an armchair. The old bridge, however, which still stands beside the new one and carries traffic one way into the city from the north, was once the only bridge coming or going: a narrow two-lane steel girder suspension bridge with rusty open railings (like some rickety roller coaster at a county fair) through which you could look down onto the wings of gulls and onto rusty barges, sailboats, tankers and, now and then, the periscope of a submarine heading downriver from the navy base toward the harbor and the open ocean beyond.

That was the bridge Mamie was required to cross with their family every summer on the way to the beach house where she was the one who picked the crab meat from the bushels of crabs the family hauled in. Where she peeled shrimp, cooked, walked the children to the beach, swept the sand out of the house. Where she lived in a room underneath the house and slept on a rusty iron bed and pomaded her hair in front of a mirror with most of the silver peeled off. Where she read her Bible out loud to herself every night or sang and ironed in front of the oscillating fan until long past midnight.

"Well, Old Mamie had an absolute and utter terror of that bridge," Mother said. She was launched now, Louisa saw, and there would be no turning back. Louisa pushed her needle harder through the stiff linen. "Something about being high up in the air like that, crossing water, scared her so much that when I told her it was time to get ready to go to the beach, those little bitty pig-tails she used to wear would practically stand straight out from her head, and she'd drop to her knees in the kitchen or wherever I'd spoken to her and start wringing her hands. 'Lord, Missis,' she'd wail. 'Lord God. Leave I back behind on solid earth. I too old. Be crossing that water soon enough.' I'd tell her I'd carry her petition to my husband, but I knew it wouldn't do any good. He never would put up with nonsense from the colored. 'She'll ride with us, as usual,' he always said. 'I'm not going to inconvenience my fam-ily to accommodate Mamie's superstitions.'"

Listening that day, Louisa asked herself: was this perhaps a story of injustice, historic and ongoing? Not likely. When the concept of injustice finally pushed its way into their world, her mother had been outraged. "Injustice?" Mother would say, revolted by the taste of the word. "What injustice? When we carried them all those years. Who turned on whom? Who deserted whom?" She came from that generation whose childhoods had touched the outer rim of the time in which the conclusions about race still felt like cer-tainties. Such as: The Hilliards had been good masters, kind mas-ters who seldom had to raise the whip to their people. So after freedom the Fairview slaves had stayed on the place: Teneh and Cuff, Binah, Scipio, Daniel and Abby and Maum Harriette, Mamie's mother. Her own mother had been born there and cared for by Mamie's mother. Such as: The Hilliards take care of their own. When King Hopkins, Mamie's husband, got drunk and cut a man at a juke joint up on Calhoun Street, who bailed him out of jail? (Hugh Marion Sr., himself.) Who went to court with him and got him off? (Mr. Marion, again.) Such as: Evelyn grew up in their yard, too, didn't she? After Mamie's daughter died, who allowed Evelyn to come live with her grandmother? They didn't have to do that, Mother insisted, or let Mamie stay in the kitchen house in their yard either, for that matter. When Evelyn graduated from South Carolina State, who drove Mamie up to her granddaughter's graduation? It was Louisa herself, that's who." Round and round the stories went, round and round, miraculous wheels that rolled through time and never warped or splintered as they rolled.

When the civil rights movement came along and the hospital workers went on strike, demonstrators had lined King Street singing and chanting, holding their signs: FREEDOM NOW. WE SHALL NOT BE MOVED. Evelyn had marched into Pierce Bros. department store, which did not serve Negroes, and asked to try on a pair of shoes. Mother had been personally hurt and affronted that blacks should have seen themselves damaged by the cordial and correct distances the races had agreed to keep from one another, the obvious and necessary ranking that kept them apart, in the separate worlds they lived in so comfortably, side by side. Once, in a bitter mood about the city's handling of the protests, after his fifth trip to the cut-glass decanter of port on the dining room sideboard, Louisa's brother Hugh had said, "Keep Mother away from the windows. She's liable to ask Martin Luther King if he's looking for yardwork." She might have, too. Mother was as invulnerable to the idea of injustice as a turtle latched in its shell.

"Well, for about two weeks before we left for the beach there were some odd comings and goings around our kitchen house. Her pastor must have visited her half a dozen times. Then there were the other characters. That old scarecrow of a man who used to run errands for us. The vegetable cart man. A one-eyed woman who sold baskets down at the market. You'd hear them knocking on the screen door of the kitchen house all hours of the day or night. 'Aunt Mamie,' they'd call. 'Aunt Mamie.' But we knew what they were doing. They were root doctors and so forth, bringing charms to her. We pretended we didn't know," she leaned forward and confided in her daughter, "but we did. On the morning of our departure, Mamie would appear with her Bible clutched in one hand, her suitcase in the other. She'd have her lucky dime on a string around her ankle, nutmeg around her neck along with a big silver cross on a red ribbon and a cloth pouch she'd sewed herself. She never would tell us what was in it. Graveyard dirt, I suppose. They were big on that. Crab claws, maybe. I'd just have to turn my back to keep from laughing at the poor old thing and hurting her feelings.

"Mamie sat in the back between you and Hugh. As soon as we started up the bridge, she'd grab the door handle with one hand and the rope across the back of the front seat with the other. Remember that big, black, sixteen-cylinder Buick we owned, your father's pride and joy? Those little ropes across the backs of the seats? Up we'd go onto the bridge, Mamie hanging onto that rope for dear life, with her eyes squeezed shut, praying. 'Sweet Jesus! Lord have mercy! Great God! Do, Jesus! Great King!' I think she used up every name they have for their God before we'd gotten over the first span. She'd start off low, grumbling and muttering to herself—she knew your father didn't want to listen to her carrying on—but before we'd reached the top of the first span, she'd practically be shouting. Of course I'd see what was coming by the way your father scowled into the rearview mirror with increasing severity, and then all of a sudden, '*Mamie*,' he would say, so quietly *I* almost couldn't hear him, and I was sitting beside him in the front seat, but Mamie would jerk straight up as if he'd yanked her by a chain. 'Do I need to remind you that you are riding in my family car, you are not at some camp meeting out in the Congaree Swamp?'

" 'No suh,' she'd say, 'sure don't,' and all the while she'd be studying the floor with her old bottom lip poking out about a mile.
Mamie was light skinned—*high yellow* we called those kind—much
lighter than your blue-black Negro, with more refined features and
a few freckles across her nose and cheeks. She had light hazel eyes.
But she sure prayed like an African. Well, after your father spoke
to her, she'd simmer down and mumble her prayers to herself until
we were safely across the bridge and down onto Mt. Pleasant. Old
Mamie. Didn't she make the best biscuits?"

And right there, her mother stopped, as she always stopped, as
though the thread had all run off that spool. She nodded an
emphatic period, smoothed down the skirt of her bathrobe over
her knees, and stared out at the bridges until her eyes began to
droop. This drowsiness was Louisa's signal that the story and the
visit were over. Mother would not talk again that day. She had
come to the end of the story; there was nothing more to tell. It was
time for Louisa to fold up the linen banner and pack it away in her
portmanteau along with her embroidery floss and the small silver
scissors—the ones with handles shaped like the curved necks and
out-stretched heads of flying cranes—that had once belonged to her
ancestor Eliza Hilliard, another spinster seamstress. Time to help
her mother out of the wheelchair and onto the bed. Time to draw
the covers up around her mother's neck, kiss the pink scalp that
showed through the white hair that stood out like mist around her
mother's head, and tiptoe out of the room, closing the door behind
her. Time to walk out into the nursing-home parking lot, into the
smells of fish and oil and sun on water, and to remember how the
water had looked from the top of the highest span of the old
Cooper River Bridge: like a floor, hard and glittering, swept with
light.

It was not her mother's drifting Spanish-brown canoe of a mind
that had landed her in the nursing home; it was her body. One
night earlier that spring Louisa had waked to her mother's call.
Though her voice had thinned, it was sharp as a needle, and like a

needle it had pierced Louisa's sleep. "Louisa, Louisa, I need to tee-tee."

Sleep-clogged, stiff, Louisa had dragged herself out of her canopied bed in the upstairs corner room. Snapping on the light in the bedroom next to hers she'd found Mother propped on pillows on the chintz-covered chaise lounge where she slept upright in order to ease her breathing. Oxygen tubes ran up her nose, a canister of oxygen on wheels sat at her side.

Louisa meant no disrespect when she thought of her mother as grotesque. One hundred and two and elephantine with a face like a pudding, she was bloated from medications and edema and from an appetite which (until her most recent and steepest decline soured her stomach) she had not even attempted to curb since her husband died. No sooner had Hugh Wyman Marion gone to St. Phillips churchyard than she began to pour half-and-half on her breakfast cereal, to stir four thick pats of butter into every plate of rice, to set her shrimp bubbling in two inches of melted butter and bacon grease. Now she was hung with slabs, folds, and pouches of fat, as if she were outfitting herself in flesh for a long trip into a land of famine.

As Mother had ballooned, so had her stubbornness, her imperial selfishness (this much resentment Louisa would allow herself—more would be unhealthy), which kept her from listening to the doctor ("*My God, Elizabeth, you've gained another fifteen pounds. What are we going to do with you?*") or from agreeing to a wheelchair or allowing Louisa to hire someone to help them. Absolutely not. No. If Mother's silver cane tip marred the floors, the floors would be refinished. If in the middle of the night Mother required a four-letter synonym for *decaying plant matter* or a reminder of the precise location of the cruet stand, Louisa tried to answer. Hiring help was out of the question—her mother's demands rested on historical precedent. Juliana Hilliard (Elizabeth's mother) had cared for *her* mother; now Louisa would care for hers. In that way the generations would hold and a shining vein of loyalty and devotion would run through dark and crumbling time. Sometime that spring, watching her mother munch toast, jaws rolling, watching her lips reach for the rim of the coffee cup and delicately suck the hot liquid in, Louisa decided that to call her grotesque (in private, of course, and only to herself) was simply to state a fact, something with which Louisa had made the firmest and longest-lasting relationship of her life.

The night of the bathroom call, Louisa had knelt and forced her mother's feet into the bedroom slippers that she needed then, mustard-colored corduroy loafers from the Woolworth's on King Street, the kind that Mother had never allowed Mamie to wear around the house because they slapped against her heels with such a slovenly sound. Size twelve and still the heel had to be cut away to keep them from squeezing Mother's swollen feet. Hoisting her mother, Louisa said "Upsy-daisy," just to hear the optimistic lilt of those words in the dark. Louisa rolled the oxygen tank with one hand, kept the other arm around her mother's waist. Together they struggled and staggered toward the bathroom at the far end of the hall. Louisa felt her mother's weight bear down on her, her damp armpits and clammy neck; she heard her mother's breath whistle past her ear. It was too hot for this work, but Mother always ordered the air conditioning shut off at 8 P.M. sharp and the windows opened—even when it was still stifling outside and the air so muggy it seeped through the screens like fog through a sieve.

"She's leaning her whole weight on me," Louisa thought as they inched toward the bathroom. "We're going to fall. We're going to collapse right here in the middle of the hall." Louisa felt the beginning of a panicky tightening in her lungs.

But they didn't collapse in the hall. They had made it all the way to the bathroom and then—as she tried to ease her mother down onto the toilet seat, holding her around the waist with one arm while Mother grappled with her underpants and yanked at the oxygen tank—Louisa's feet slipped on the tile floor. To keep herself from falling she let go of her mother, who sat down hard on the floor with the high furious cry of a baby. When Louisa couldn't get her mother up, and the old woman could no longer hold back

her water, Mrs. Elizabeth St. Julian Hilliard Marion had peed on
the bathroom floor in the house where Hilliards had made their
high or low, prolonged or shortened transits from birth to death
for more than two centuries. When her mother was done, Louisa
picked up the wet towels and dropped them down the laundry
chute in the bathroom closet. Then she called 911 from the phone
in the upstairs hall. "My mother has fallen in the bathroom," she
said, "and I can't get her up."

After she'd returned from making the call, Louisa had sat on the
cool tile floor and leaned against the toilet, holding her mother,
who dozed with her head resting against Louisa's thin breasts and
one hand splayed out on her cheek as if she were thinking something over. The thin hiss of oxygen up the tubes into her mother's
nose was the only sound in the room besides the whine of a mosquito, that had discovered them helpless on the floor and attacked
Louisa's ankles. As they sat and Mother dozed, her chin pillowed
in the fat of her neck, and as the sound of the siren came toward
them through the night, Louisa looked down and saw the slack,
puckered elastic of her mother's yellowed nylon underpants. At
least she, Louisa, had thought to put on her robe.

That was the night Louisa knew that she'd come to the end of
something. She knew that she would date some ominous acceler-
ating of time from the moment she'd laid three thick mono-
grammed towels on the floor next to her mother, then stepped out
of the room and stood in the hall with her hand on the heavy glass
doorknob of the bathroom door while her mother wet the towels.
Before that night, age had worked on Louisa one piece at a time.
In cold, rainy weather, her knuckles swelled and ached. Her hips
felt stiff every morning. Some days the smell of her pillow—like
gray iron—startled her. Or the smell that rose from her mouth
when she flossed her teeth, that carried her back to her grandmother and what had been on her breath. How foreign and startling it had seemed then, how familiar now. There were migrating
patches of numbness and constriction, fine lines that radiated out

from her mouth, into which her lipstick spread. Signs of aging, true, but never overwhelming, never all at once.

On the floor of the bathroom that night, propped up against the toilet with her mother's slack weight resting against her, she'd felt old all over, as though age were something she was swamped in, as if she were curing in it, like the nineteenth-century Hilliard Madeira and peach brandy still curing in barrels down in the cellar. Both of them, herself and the liquor, steeped in time, which caused the collapse of one and deepened the flavor and value of the other. And she wept for the two old women they'd become, two old women with their stains and flows. Two old women not able to keep up with the laundry anymore, and the younger, who was herself, unable to help the older, who was her own mother, up from the bathroom floor or even to pull her nightgown out from under her body and cover the underpants and slack thighs and ugly slippers that the ambulance attendants would notice.

Later, sitting over coffee in some Waffle House up on Ashley Phosphate Road, those men would shake their heads and laugh together about the old ladies they'd hauled up off the bathroom floor of their house in the historic district. "They pee just like the rest of us," one of them would say from behind his cigarette smoke—she imagined he would have a knuckly, mournful face and a big Adam's apple, his hair so thickly oiled the drag marks of the comb stayed in place all day—and the waitress would laugh too. That night, after the vision of the Waffle House left her, Louisa had laid her cheek down on her mother's head and whispered, "Mother, don't you think it's time to move on?"

Later, she wondered if Mother had heard her that night. The week after the bathroom crisis, at their doctor's insistence, Mother had gone to the nursing home without complaint. She'd even sent Louisa a note—shaky handwriting that skated down her heavy cream notepaper—thanking her daughter for finding her such a nice place, a private care home in an old house like their own.

Quiet and clean, it did not smell, and the help were the courteous, almost invisible, old-style colored you seldom found working any-where anymore. The woman who ran the home was a woman like herself, Louisa thought, a *discreet matron* as they used to describe themselves in the *Mercury* when they advertised their music or sewing or watercolor lessons for young ladies.

Mother had been in the home for three months when the owner called in the middle of the night. "Miss Marion," she said, "I'm sorry, but I must inform you that your mother has passed away." Even while the woman went on talking (just died, she said, not half an hour ago) Louisa felt restless. Hugh needed to know that their mother had died, and she was the oldest; she must make the call. Besides, the news of her mother's death had gone into her and started growing, pushing everything else out until it was just a big, spinning hollow place inside, like the swirling cloud of wind on a hurricane tracking map, and she was in danger of dropping into this fact of death without another soul to know it with her. "I'll be right there," she said, "but first I must call my brother."

She switched on the gooseneck lamp on the telephone table in the hall and took her address book out of the drawer. She ripped through it, looking for Hugh's page, while fear rose inside her, hissing softly like Mother's oxygen. She had to find his number before the fear filled her and she was lost in it. This terrified Louisa over every other terror—to be lost in time. Not to know where you were, who you were, to look and not to recognize what you saw, to lose your bearings.

By the light of the small gooseneck lamp, she found her brother's page in the address book. HUGH, she'd printed in block letters across the top. His addresses, entered and crossed out, filled the entire page. The apartment on King Street that he'd moved into after he gave up on law school at the University of South Carolina. The house on the marsh on Isle of Palms where he'd lived one summer while he rented floats on the beach out of a little shack made of raw pine boards covered with palmetto fronds. The apartment near the Navy base in North Charleston where it was never quite clear what he did.

And the house on Station Creek in McClellanville. Hugh liked to laugh about how termites had been swarming there when the real estate agent had showed it to him, a twitching carpet of them laid over the downstairs floors, but Hugh had waded through them and rented the house anyway. So close to the creek that the full-moon spring and autumn tides had washed up under the porch. Hugh had pulled his batteau up onto the mud bank there and tied it to one of the brick pillars that held up the front porch. He spent his days fishing, crabbing, drinking, traveling in his batteau down the tidal creeks to the ocean. Sometimes he threw parties that lasted for days, cooked up kettles of shrimp that he'd pulled from a creek with his cast net. He'd call her at two in the morning, a chaos of merriment going on behind his voice, to invite her to the party, and when she'd refuse, he'd turn maudlin and insist: she was his sister, she belonged there, partying with him and his friends.

This had been in the late sixties, early seventies, and what Hugh had really been doing was unloading marijuana off the boats that slipped up the creeks near McClellanville, then running the dope down to Charleston to sell. Hugh was getting rich at it, too, for once in his life, having spent all of the money their father had left him between the year he started law school at Carolina and the time two years later when he left school for good.

When state drug agents set out to break up the smuggling along that part of the coast, they went to the real estate agencies in Charleston that sold houses in the historic district and collected the names of people who'd made large cash down payments on houses. They did the same at marinas and luxury car dealerships. Hugh's name came to them from the Mercedes-Benz dealership in North Charleston, but they never did catch up with him. He moved too fast.

Then she was fully awake and Hugh was dead, as he'd been for twenty years. She closed the address book and put it back in the drawer, turned off the lamp, and with one hand on the wall, found her way back to her room, where she sat on the edge of her bed and rocked a little, preparing herself. The dark from the hall seemed to flow into the room. It smelled of old wood and wet air, something green trailing through it. The smell of ghosts, Mamie had said. She wouldn't go into the hall at night, where the ghosts were so thick, jostling each other. "Black and white, all jam up together" was how Mamie described what happened up in the hall at night. Once, Mamie said, a witch jumped her and rode on her back all the way down the stairs and out into the yard, where she shook it off and stuffed it down the well. Louisa remembered being up there with Mamie, the feel of Mamie's fingers plucking at her sleeve. "Walk over this side the hall, Miss," she'd say, and Louisa would know that they were detouring around one of her ancestors, or Mamie's. She'd find Mamie standing on the flag-stones in front of the house, broom in hand, staring up at the chimney. "They pouring out now, Miss," Mamie would say, mean-ing, Louisa knew, the ghosts. Pouring out like smoke.

It happened quickly, the owner said, as she opened the front door and let Louisa into the entrance hall of the big house. It hap-pened in her sleep, she said, steering Louisa by the elbow toward the stairs. Louisa was grateful that the woman was dressed for work, that her hair was combed. She wore glasses, low-heeled pumps, and she carried papers in her hand as though she'd been awake for hours. Louisa appreciated the woman's efficiency. No bathrobe, no straggling hair or slack, bewildered face to show that death had surprised her.

"I'm going to let you talk to Yvonne, the nurse's aide who was on duty when your mother passed away," the woman said as she and Louisa climbed the stairs. Walking down the hall toward her mother's room, Louisa caught herself listening. *Mamie?* It was quiet except for the sound of their feet on the carpet, and the moon sent the shape of the window at the end of the hall ahead of them as they walked.

In her mother's room, the bedside lamp was turned down low. A woman sat in a rocking chair beside the bed, one hand on the spread, rocking and patting the spread and humming to herself. Then she stood up when Louisa came in, smoothing down her uniform and smiling. Louisa saw a gold front tooth, a quick, kind smile.

"This is Mrs. Marion's daughter, Yvonne," the owner said, and went out of the room closing the door with a soft click as she went.

"She was a sweet, fine lady," Yvonne said. "She didn't struggle against it. Look here, sheets smooth, face sweet." She touched the dead woman's cheek. "You blessed. Some struggle and fight. One lady try to climb out the window—had to call in two mans for to hold her back." She had checked on Mother at midnight, then gone down the hall to look in on someone else, and when she'd come back at 12:45, Mother had ceased to breathe.

"So she didn't say anything?"

"Not as I am aware of."

"Thank you for all you've done," Louisa said, anxious for the woman to leave, and when Yvonne had gone, she sat down beside her mother on the bed. Her mother lay on her side with her eyes closed, her hands tucked between her knees. They'd disconnected the oxygen tubes from her nose and rolled the canister away. On her mother's upper lip, Louisa saw the outline of the tape that had held the tubes in place. She licked her thumb and moved to scrub, then stopped. The undertaker would clean those away, she thought. He would clean all the marks of life away. Now there was only silence in the room, and the sound of her own breathing.

The expression on her mother's face was peaceful. In fact, Louisa thought, it was the same expression that she'd seen a hundred times when her mother had caught up with Mamie and her biscuits and put them back where they belonged and finished her story. It occurred to Louisa that at the moment of death her mother might have been dreaming of Mamie's biscuits. She remembered that they felt dense and heavy in your hand, then dissolved like buttery clouds when you bit into them. And she saw that it was comfort her mother had been looking for, telling that story—comfort and consolation and certainty in the memory of those biscuits and of Mamie's silly old colored-woman terrors, so much more primitive and obscure than their own.

Sitting beside her mother's body, Louisa felt she'd entered another world of silence and stillness that lapped out from the body on the bed and surrounded her. It was the stillness, the vacancy, that she could not bend her mind around. She almost said, "Mother?" the way she used to do, to wake her. But she brushed back wisps of hair from her mother's forehead and kept still. Whatever life is, she saw, it visits the body, then goes, taking nothing you could catch, store in a bottle, or press and keep under glass. Taking nothing visible and taking everything. And she remembered a darkened room stuffed with summer heat, the wooden shutters latched over the windows and herself sick with diphtheria on the canopied bed, the cool feel of her mother's fingers rubbing hand cream on her lips. The last person who knew her before she knew herself, the last one who could say, "When you were a baby . . ." and hand her a piece of her life that had existed before she even knew herself to be in it.

Looking up, Louisa saw the lights of the bridges over Cooper River and thought of how Hugh might have driven north across the new bridge to Sullivan's Island. He had let himself into the beach house, rummaged in drawers, drank half a bottle of port, sat in every chair and lay on every bed. (For weeks the imprint of his backside was left in the chair cushions and the restless twist of his body stayed in the white chenille bedspreads until someone smoothed them.) Then he had driven his dark blue Mercedes up onto the dunes in front of the house until the tires sank in the sand, cut the engine, and shot himself in the head.

Looking at the bridges, remembering Hugh, she felt afraid again. To this day, when crossing that bridge, her throat tightened, her heart beat slow and hard, and her face felt as if a bright light shone on it. She wanted only to make it safely to the other side. She remembered the scene from her mother's story: all of them in the car together, crossing the bridge high over the water, listening to Mamie's prayers and her father's outburst. Now she was the only survivor of those who had lived that story. It was her story now, and there was no comfort in it, for she also remembered how her father had grown philosophical after he'd silenced Mamie. Looking down at the water, he'd offered them the same detail every time. Water would feel like concrete if you fell into it from this height, he'd say. And just like that, how high they were became how far they could fall, how close they were to falling. Silent as one of Mamie's ghosts, the knowledge of their actual and precarious place on earth had traveled with them to the other side.

1998

Mark Richard

MEMORIAL DAY

Death stars in this story of a family struggling to ward it off. Death, who "stood lean-
ing against a tree scraping fresh manure off his shoe with a stick," wears white pants
and a white dinner jacket. He says, "It looks to me like your brother's got a neural
infection that may be at the stem of his brain. . . . Of course, that's just a layman's
guess." Mark Richard grew up in Texas and Virginia. He is the author of two col-
lections of short stories, The Ice at the Bottom of the World *and* Charity, *and* Fish-
boy, *a novel. He lives in Los Angeles with his wife and three sons.*

The boy mistook death for one of the landlady's sons come
to collect the rent. Death stood leaning against a tree scraping fresh manure off his shoe with a stick. The boy told death he
would have to see his mother about the rent, and death said he was
not there to collect the rent.

My brother is real sick, you should come back later, the boy said.
Death said he would wait.

They had sent the boy's brother home from the war in a box.
When the boy and his mother opened the box, the brother was not
inside. Inside the box was a lifesize statue of a woman holding a
seashell to her ear. A messenger's pouch hung around the statue's
neck. Hide this for me, the note in the pouch read. Love, Brother.

Then came the brother a week later. He was thin and yellow and
sorry-looking, too weak to fend off his mother when she struck
him, too weak to be held. The mother and the child carried him
into the house and put him to bed.

The next morning, a black healer woman walked down the white
shell driveway and straight into the house to squeeze the older

brother's guts and smell his breath. She looked over her shoulder at the high weeds and the statue box and the bitter, brown gulf beyond and she said This place flood flood flood. Stink, too.

The mother bathed the brother with an alcohol sponge and the black healer woman twisted his spine to break his fever. The brother saw monkeys in the corners of the ceiling that wanted to get him, their mouths full of bloody chattering teeth. The black healer woman and the mother fought with the brother and told the child to Get out! when he came in to tell them that someone was waiting in the yard.

It was not unusual that the child could see death when the mother and the healing woman could not. Once at a church picnic the child had seen Bad Bob Cohen walk through the softball game and past the barbeque tables with a .22 rifle slung barrel down over his shoulder on a piece of twine. The child had watched Bad Bob walk right past where mothers and small children were splashing on the riverbank, had watched Bad Bob reach up and select two sturdy vines to climb up, and Bad Bob had turned and looked at the child, feeling him seeing him, and Bad Bob had nodded because they both knew that Bad Bob was invisible, and then later when the deputy and the road agents came to the picnic looking for Bob no one had seen him and no one would have believed the child if he had said he had, so he said nothing. Also, one Easter, the child had seen an angel.

Tell them they have to wait, the mother said. The rent's not due until tomorrow.

You have to wait, the child told death sitting in a tree. Death ate a fortune cookie from his pocket. His lips moved while he read the fortune to himself.

I'll come back tomorrow, death said finally, jumping down from the tree.

The black healer woman stood on the porch and said she would keep death from the doorstep as long as they had faith in Christ

Jesus Our Savior and a little put-away money to cover her expenses coming down the long white broken shell driveway to their house. Death, that day, was wearing white pants and a white dinner jacket, a small, furled yellow cocktail umbrella buttonholed in his lapel. There were three good scratches across death's cheek from the beautiful woman who had not wanted to dance the last dance with death aboard a ship somewhere the previous evening. I don't get much time off from this job, death confided in the child under the tree. Work work work. I am much misunderstood. I actually have a wonderful sense of humor and I get along well with others. I'm a people person, death told the child. Death climbed the front porch steps to make faces behind the black healing woman. Death folded his eyelids back, stuck out his tongue, then pinched his cheeks, forgetting about the scratches. Ow! death said. The black healer woman did not hear death nor see death but to her credit, she shivered when death blew on the back of her neck.

The child followed the black healer woman and his mother into the back bedroom where his brother stank. The black healer woman burned some sage cones and rubbed charcoal on the brother's temples and on the soles of his feet to draw out the fever.

How come you don't work? the black woman said to the child.

He's just a child, the mother said. The mother was stripping the brother's bed around them to boil the sheets on the stove.

When I young, I work, said the black healing woman.

I can make baskets from reeds, the child said.

What do people need reed baskets for when they give wooden ones away for free at the tomato fields, said the woman.

When the brother sat up and shouted Get the monkeys! the black healing woman said to him Your little brother here going to get them monkeys, your little brother going to get them monkeys and put them under baskets, under *wooden* baskets, she said to the child. Won't no *reed* basket hold no monkey, she said, and the brother lay back down.

Here's the rent money, the mother said. I don't want anybody to come in the house while we get your brother's fever down.

The child said Yes ma'am. He took out the messenger pouch his brother had sent home in the box with the statue. It was not a purse. It had two long pockets and a waterproof pouch in case you had to swim a river. The child put the rent money in the waterproof pouch because it had two good snaps on it.

When the landlady's son came to collect the rent, death told the child to ask for a receipt.

I want a receipt, the child told the landlady's son.

You want to be evicted? the landlady's son said. You want us to throw your sorry asses out on the highway?

Don't worry, death said, he's afraid he might catch what your brother has. He won't go in the house. Tell him you want a proper receipt, tell him to bring a proper receipt for the rent.

Before the child could say all that, the landlady's son said Give me the money I bet you got in that purse!

It's not a purse! the child said and yanked back on the strap.

All right, I'll be back tomorrow, said the landlady's son.

Death sat on the edge of the porch and lip-read a new fortune cookie. It looked like a word near the end hung him up.

That's a good one, death finally said, and he crunched the cookie in his big white teeth.

The brother's tongue grew fuzzy and his ravings were barking up the bad neighbor's dogs down the road all night.

The black healer woman came out on the porch.

You get me a shoebox of scorpions, what I need, she told the child. Try get me white ones. They stronger than the piddly brown ones. Go on and get me them.

They had scorpions in the woodpile, scorpions in the sandbox, scorpions in the clothespin pouch, scorpions in the cinderblocks where they burned trash, scorpions under the bathroom sink, scorpions in the icebox water tray, and scorpions in the baby crib. They didn't have a baby anymore, so it was all right.

I wouldn't fool with scorpions, death said. Some people are highly allergic. It's a neurotoxin thing in the stinger, death said.

Death followed the child around trying to find a shoebox. The child could not find a shoebox. He had an old wooden-style cigar box. The lid was broken.

I wouldn't use that cigar box, it's got no lid, death said. The child said he could see that.

The child took the rent money out of his waterproof pouch and put it in his pocket. He cut a good stick and found three brown scorpions and one white scorpion by lunchtime. He put the scorpions in the messenger pouch and snapped it shut carefully so as not to crush them, and shook the bag down every time before he opened it so he would not get stung. He had never been stung before and had heard it was ten times worse than a wasp, maybe fifty times.

It looks to me like your brother's got a neural infection that may be at the stem of his brain, death said. Of course, that's just a layman's guess.

The child was beginning to tire of death hanging around so much and talking talking talking. Death never seemed to shut up. Down where the bitter brown gulf water foamed dirty, death talked about time zones and the speed of light. Under the big yard tree, he talked about pine cones that broke open their seeds only when they burned. Under the brother's window looking in on the mother and the black healer woman, death said the brown statue of the girl holding the seashell to her ear was pedestrian terra-cotta.

I bet it's valuable, the child said, and death said Yeah, maybe as a boat anchor.

The mother took back the rent money to fetch a real doctor. The landlady's son came by with a friend who smelled like vomit and the friend who smelled like vomit threw a dirt clod that hit the child in the mouth. The landlady's son kicked open the front gate. The child had forgotten he had taken the rent money out of the messenger pouch so he held on to its strap until the landlady's son broke it and said Here's your receipt, and he rabbit-punched the child twice in the ear. The landlady's son and the friend who smelled like vomit roared off in their car with the messenger pouch, taking with them, inside the pouch, the little yellow furled fruit cocktail umbrella, twelve white scorpions, and thirty, maybe even fifty, brown scorpions in the waterproof pocket. Death laughed in the treetops.

Death flocked down beside the child. He said maybe the scorpion cure would have worked and maybe it would have killed the brother outright. It would have depended on if the black healer woman could figure a good way to extract the neurotoxin and put the brother into moderate shock to break the fever. I guess it could work, maybe in a laboratory, death said, and the child, holding his ringing ear, said You just want an easy way to take my brother from me, and death said the child had completely misunderstood him. That was all right, because he was much misunderstood, death began again, and maligned, and the child left death in the front yard making speeches, and to the child's one good ear, it all sounded like wind in the stovepipe.

The doctor hardly thought it worth breaking a car axle to drive down and look at the brother, so he took the rent money for his trouble walking and said to bathe the brother in alcohol and put these sulphate powders in honey tea. The doctor gave the brother a shot and on his way out said the child needed some fish oil but did not give him any.

You find them scorpions for me? the black healer woman whispered after the doctor had gone.

I had a bunch that got away from me, the child told her. She said to get her a new bunch unless he wanted his brother to die. Tonight, she said. The black healing woman had no faith in the shot or the sulphate or the doctor. She said she had seen him swing little newborns by their heels against tree trunks back where the real white trash lived. Go get them scorpions and get them quick, she said.

Death sat on the levee pipe and watched the child weave a reed basket. Death said baskets done well like that could fetch maybe two, three dollars from tourists. Of course, the child would have to learn to weave the popular check-cross design, and not just the standard lanyard double-tuck.

This is for scorpions, the child said. The child said he noticed death had not come around the house when the doctor came, and death laughed and said he liked doctors, that you could make a career following doctors. No, death said he had just had an appointment that had taken a little longer than he had planned for, and he offered the child a fortune cookie.

No thanks, said the child, weaving his basket.

Death read his fortune. Sometimes these things are incomprehensible, he said, and he let the little white paper float away.

That night the brother broke the mother's jaw. Punched her right in her damn monkey teeth, red and chattering at him.

No one knows their time. The brother recuperated and returned to the war, and afterwards, operated a small, profitable import business until his death at age fifty-eight from smoke inhalation. He had been trying to retrieve an old three-legged dog from a warehouse fire.

The man who smelled like vomit died of emphysema at age seventy-two living on the benevolence of the state. The state ridded itself of Bad Bob Cohen at age forty-one with a lethal injection.

It is believed among the black healing woman's family, and among those to whom she administered, that she was commended by God, that God spared her from death entirely, that He lifted her directly into heaven, for one day she simply disappeared.

The mother died seven years after the older brother recuperated. Her jaw did not heal well and her weight dropped to slightly below normal for her height, diet, and hereditary dispensation. The mother's passing away at age forty-eight was generally ascribed to grief, from finding her youngest remaining son at the edge of the hot brown gulf. According to the deputy and to the coroner who drove the station wagon to fetch the body, it appeared that the bottom of the reed basket the child had been carrying had flung itself open somehow, as if whoever had made the basket had folded the reeds backwards, upside down into the spiraling center instead of outward to the edges, and the action and weight of several hundred scorpions inside the basket had broken through the bottom. The child had been stung too many times to count. The neurotoxin, to which the child was highly allergic, had caused his windpipe to close, and when they found him at the edge of the gulf, he had already turned blue, his protruding tongue black and flyspecked. It was as if the child had run down to the gulf while being stung to drink the bitter water and could not drink, could not force down what he thought he felt he could not swallow, and only death had seen him try, death saying to him Run to the water and drink, come on, run with me to the gulf and drink, and the child had taken death's outstretched hand because he was beginning to stumble, and death encouraged him Run with me! and the child ran with death and finally he was no more, for death had taken him.

As for the landlady's son, he is one of many who have long since been forgotten.

1998

Scott Ely

TALK RADIO

This story—about a Vietnam veteran who in the decades since the war has become a very successful Southern radio host—draws some unexpected parallels having to do with danger and with luck. Scott Ely says he has always wondered about the life of his counterpart in the North Vietnamese Army and wrote the story to evoke him. Ely teaches at Winthrop University in South Carolina. He is the author of two novels and three collections of stories. His stories have appeared in many magazines, from Shenandoah *to* Playboy. Eating Mississippi, *a new novel, will appear in fall of 2005.*

I'm having a great night. Folks from all over the Carolinas are dialing me up, filling the air with their howls, like a bunch of ancient warriors gathered about a campfire, working themselves up into a killing mood. Bob, the station manager, as if he knows what I'm thinking, dances a war dance outside the booth, what he always does when I'm really rolling. Peggie, who sells advertising, shakes her head, but she knows that tomorrow will be a good day for her, that she won't have to wiggle her ass or shake her tits to make those sales.

We're talking about gun control. They're calling in from mobile phones as they drive into our signal on the interstate; they're calling from bars and bedrooms and phone booths. I imagine all that hate pulsating through the night like colored gas in a tube.

"Guns could disappear," I say to a caller. "The Japanese did it in the seventeenth century. Tokugawa Ieyasu halted the production of guns, and the country returned to the sword for 250 years. He lopped off a few heads, and folks came around to his way of thinking."

"I got a made-in-America .357 right here in my truck," he says.

"I got it loaded with Teflon-coated rounds. Go right through a flak jacket. I just hope somebody tries to carjack me. I just hope they do."

In North Carolina it's legal to carry a handgun in a car, and you can carry it on your person if you have a permit. All you have to do to get a permit is prove you don't have a criminal record or haven't spent a few months in a mental institution. And take a course in gun safety, and pay a small fee. It's easy.

I wonder what some of the callers would say if they knew I don't own a gun of any kind. Once Bob had us do a show from a pistol range that caters to women. The sign advertising the place shows a woman in a two-fisted firing stance, filling a male torso full of holes. They had me shoot a few rounds at one of those torsos, but I didn't do well at all, even though I'd qualified with a .45 when I was in the army. Bob told me he was shocked at my ineptitude.

Then the caller becomes inarticulate. He snorts like a wild hog, makes sounds that are half words and half snarls. I let the listeners enjoy a little of that before I cut him off.

We go to a commercial break.

"Ease up a little on the intellectual stuff," Bob tells me. "Ease up. This isn't public radio."

I had enjoyed my job with public radio, where I hosted a talk show devoted to the standard liberal causes. Sometimes I long for the slower pace of that life, but I don't hold it against them for firing me. I came to work drunk one too many times. They did me a favor. Now I'm making plenty of money. I still drink, but I haven't come to work drunk a single time. I do that at home. I've got it under control.

"But I'm hot," I say.

"Back off a little."

"Everybody loves me. All those truck drivers and mill hands and hog farmers. You've seen the mail."

"That's right, Luther. Remember that."

I live in the two-story white house I grew up in on one of those oak-lined Charlotte streets. My father is dead. My mother is in a nursing home. I go to see her every Sunday, and she has no idea who I am.

With all the money they're paying me to be a local radio personality, it was no problem to put in a tennis court, the kind surfaced with brick dust like at Monte Carlo and Roland Garros. It's the only red clay tennis court in the city, and probably in the whole of North Carolina.

I pick up the phone for the next call.

"Every man, woman, and child in the United States should be given an AK-47," a voice says.

I know who it is, although I can hardly bring myself to even think his name. It's a voice I remember well, coming out of the night, wrapping itself around me just as it's doing now. If I speak, I imagine some spell will be broken and that voice will be gone, spinning off into the night, lost out there amid the clamor of the mob.

"Is that you, Thac?" I ask.

I know that voice from when I was in a radio research company in Vietnam. We monitored radio traffic from a base camp near Pleiku. With the help of interpreters, we tried to identify individual units down to the platoon level. That way we could keep track of the movements of regiments and divisions. Everyone in Saigon was worried about losing a provincial capital like Pleiku to the enemy; they all remembered Dienbienphu. It was in the back of command's mind, some bad dream that might come true.

"Where are you, buddy?" I ask.

"Roland Garros," he says.

We often talked about playing a match at Roland Garros after the war was over. Thac had spent time in Paris as a student at the Sorbonne.

I transfer the call to another line, so I can talk off the air, and go to an unscheduled commercial break. Bob is outside the booth, looking at me strangely, probably wondering if I've started coming to work drunk.

Thac says he's staying at a hotel. I agree to meet him in the morning. I tell him that I have to get off the line and back to the show. We hang up.

Thac was my counterpart on the other side, a brother officer. He appeared on our tactical frequency one night, asking to speak to anyone who knew how to play tennis.

We became friends in the same way that soldiers in the trenches at Vicksburg became friends, or Germans and British soldiers in World War I. Later they would kill each other. Thac and I would have done that if we had met in the jungle, but we only met over the radio.

The talk about AK-47s stirs the audience into a frenzy, makes listeners reach for their telephones. Soon I'm having a conversation with someone who argues that no child under six should be issued a rifle. Bob has returned to the booth with the engineers. He sits there with a satisfied look on his face.

Bob started the show with Jack Perkins, but Jack quit one night, announced on the air that he was going to live in Alaska, that he didn't think much of anyone stupid enough to listen to his show. Told his listeners that he didn't much care for Charlotte, that city of trees and churches. Said he wanted to live somewhere where he was not necessarily at the top of the food chain. Bob told me that Jack is up in Anchorage, doing the midnight-to-six shift, broadcasting the music of the '60s to army guys and trappers and Indian villages. I was drafted as a temporary substitute. To everyone's surprise, I was wildly successful.

"Who was that?" Bob asks. The show is over, and I'm preparing to go home.

"Some guy I knew in Vietnam," I say.

"A tennis player?"

"Yeah."

Bob worries about me making references to tennis on the air — or classical music or jazz or books. He says elitist talk is bad for advertising.

During those long nights in Vietnam, Thac and I talked about exceptionally good Wimbledons or Paris Opens. He had learned to play tennis in France and claimed to have served once as a ball boy at the French Open. His interest in the game was frowned upon by his superiors, who regarded it as a bourgeois sport.

In the morning I drive to the hotel. I call from the lobby, and Thac tells me to come up to his room.

When he opens the door he's about what I expect to see, a small man whose hair is turning gray around the temples.

"Come in, Luther," he says as he shakes my hand. "I heard your voice and knew it was you. Let me make you a drink. Whiskey and water?"

"Sounds good," I say. I notice right away that he walks with a limp.

"Bullet through the ankle," he says. "I can run, but I can't jump."

He explains that he is here on business. He wants to import pharmaceuticals into Vietnam, so he's been up around Durham talking with those big companies. That's where he first heard my voice on the radio. I'm surprised, because our signal doesn't usually reach that far north.

We had been talking to each other for a couple of months when abruptly he disappeared. I had promised to play him a new Jimi Hendrix tape. He was playing me *The Magic Flute*.

Major Wallace, who ran the operation, thought I was a little strange, but he didn't take my eccentricities seriously. After all, I was just a reserve officer, and he was a West Point man.

Under his direction we looked for deviations from standard radio procedure, individual idiosyncrasies that would help us identify the operators. But it had been difficult, because their discipline was excellent. I told Thac how our South Vietnamese interpreters had made fun of their northern accents, the same way that Major Wallace, who was from New York, had made fun of my Savannah accent: "It's *room*, Luther," he used to say. "Not *rum*. Jesus, but you talk strange."

"What happened to you?" I ask.

"My superiors discovered that I was having those conversations," Thac says. "They did not approve. I was put in command of an infantry platoon."

"No more Mozart," I say.

"No, we had difficult times."

I think of Thac wandering around in the jungle with his platoon, all because of his conversations with me. It makes me sad thinking that happened to him, and I tell him so.

"I was fortunate," he says. "A B-52 strike got our bunker. Everyone was killed. I would have died if I had been there."

"Saved by Jimi Hendrix," I say.

"Do you listen to him now?"

"No."

"I still love Mozart."

"We'll go to my house and listen to Mozart. Why don't you have dinner? Spend the night."

Thac says he will, so I call Verna at work to let her know I'm bringing someone home. She moved in with me about six months ago. She works at a health club, where she teaches aerobics. I suppose you could say that she's Miss Hardbody. One of these days I'm going to think more deeply about why she's with me, a man who prefers his women soft. Maybe it's her big breasts that attracted me. Verna dislikes them. She'd rather be much smaller, more athletic.

No woman like her, beautiful and twenty-five, would ever have taken up with Luther Watkins, the public radio disc jockey. On the air I'm called "The Professor." Bob came up with that name. What the audience likes, Bob says, is to listen to a liberal like me espousing conservative causes. It's like they are watching me being born again every afternoon on the radio. They take a sort of joy in my denigration, I once observed. And Bob said I was exactly right—that was what he had in mind, he just didn't have the words to express it.

Verna says she's dying to meet Thac. She does tend toward hyperbole. I know that simply means it's OK with her. We'll eat shrimp. I volunteer to pick some up on my way home.

We go to the grocery store and buy two pounds of king-sized shrimp, fresh from the waters off Charleston, the kid behind the counter tells us. Thac puts a couple of six-packs of German beer in the buggy. I buy a chocolate amaretto cake at the bakery. Verna won't touch that, but I can eat whatever I want.

Thac is impressed with the house. He doesn't say anything, but I can tell he is. He looks everything over carefully.

"They pay you well for insulting people on the radio?" he says.

I haven't told him about the court, which I've saved as a surprise. He sees it through the kitchen window when we bring in the groceries.

"Terre battue?" he says.

"That's right," I say. "If there's another one in North Carolina, I don't know about it. We'll play that match before you leave. You still play, don't you?"

"Yes," he says. "Whenever I can."

I put *The Magic Flute* on the player and make us drinks. Thac begins to explain to me what is going on in the music. He knows about it; he knows about the libretto. He never did that in Vietnam, probably thought it wasn't worth the trouble, but now I can see that he really wants me to understand it, to appreciate it in the same way he does. The rest of the morning we listen to it, playing sections of the disc over and over until I can feel that music in my bones.

I order us pizza for lunch, and we drink the German beer with it. We eat half of the cake. After lunch we give Mozart a rest. Thac puts *Carmen* on the player. After *Carmen* we play *Tristan und Isolde.* Every now and then I ask a question, and he always has the answer. Thac knows those operas backwards and forwards. For some reason I haven't listened to opera in a long time. Verna likes New Age stuff, which I can't stand.

When Verna comes home from work, we are in the middle of *La Bohème.*

"I could hear that out in the driveway," Verna says.

I turn down the sound and introduce her to Thac. She's dressed in a spandex exercise suit. Thac looks at her with fascination, as if he has never seen a beautiful woman before.

"So you knew each other in Vietnam," she says.

I explain how we talked on the radio, how we never saw one another, and how Thac had suddenly disappeared. Verna was asleep when I came home after my telephone conversation with Thac and was gone before I woke. I had considered waking her to tell her about Thac but decided against it.

"We lived like animals in the jungle," Thac says. "We ate such food as pigs eat."

"Tell me about it," Verna says.

Neither Thac nor I has said a word about Vietnam all afternoon.

"I ate steaks," I say.

It was true. We had it easy in base camp. Occasionally the enemy would lob a few mortar shells into the camp or drop a rocket in on us, but mostly it was pretty quiet.

Neither of them laughs at my comment about the steaks. They ignore me.

"They hunted us from the air," Thac says. "My men died from bombs and malaria and dysentery. We had little medicine."

Thac goes on talking about the six months he spent in the jungle. He tells the story in great detail. I'm not that interested, but Verna is riveted. That surprises me. He describes how he was shot in the foot, how he was evacuated back to Hanoi for treatment. He spent the rest of the war directing the repair of a bridge that American planes blew up at least once a week. Thac brags that his men had trucks running across it within two hours of each attack. His wife died in a B-52 raid on Hanoi.

All this flows out of Thac, who speaks it to Verna and not to me. It's like I'm not in the room, or that he assumes it's a story I already know. But we never talked about the war on the radio. I get fresh drinks for Thac and me; Verna doesn't drink. Thac takes one sip and puts it down. He talks while I watch the ice cubes in his drink melt. He talks on and on. I expect that Verna will get impatient with him and make some excuse to break off the conversation, for Verna is not a good listener. The war was over when she was still a baby, and I can't imagine her having any interest in it. But she sits on the floor with her legs crossed and listens intently, every now and then asking a question. An hour goes by, and he's still talking.

I want a cigarette. At Verna's urging I stopped smoking those, but she likes the smell of cigars. I get one for myself and offer one to Thac, who accepts. He's stopped talking. He sips his drink. I offer to get him some ice, but he says he doesn't need any.

We light up. There's nothing I want to ask Thac about his life in
the jungle. He's told it all to Verna. He sits on the couch beside me
and leans his head back and blows a smoke ring toward the ceiling.
I don't know why I find that amazing, but I do. I tell him I do.

"I was a great smoker of cigars in Paris," he says.

Verna says that she's going to do something with the shrimp,
that we should sit and talk.

"Y'all reminisce," she says.

Thac surely cannot have anything more to say about the war,
nothing to add to that litany of disease, starvation, and violent death.

"We'll play tennis in the morning," I say. "Maybe you can wear
a pair of Verna's shoes."

"I have shoes and a racket," he says. "I have played every day for
a week."

"Do you play in Hanoi?" I ask.

"There are courts in Saigon," he says. "We play on them during
the monsoon. Everyone calls us amphibians." He tells me that balls
and strings are difficult to obtain and expensive. He is the number
one player in Saigon. "The level is not high if an old man who cannot jump can be number one," he says.

At dinner we switch to wine. Verna has put chopsticks at our
places instead of knives and forks.

"I'll get a fork," I say. "I'm not very good with these things."

I know that Verna is even worse than me. Thac shows her what's
wrong with her technique, and soon she's handling those chopsticks like an expert. I stick with my fork.

I begin to tell Verna about my year with the radio research
company. I know that my experience is bland compared to Thac's,
but once I get started I can't help myself. And Verna seems interested. Thac concentrates on his food and the wine. Soon we're into
a second bottle.

I tell Verna about listening to the war at night, of all that radio
traffic from companies and platoons, of men calling desperately for
evacuation helicopters and the calm, professional voices telling

them they had none to send. We were eavesdropping on the war, those transmissions sailing across mountains and rivers and savannahs. The tropical night was alive with them.

We have ice cream for dessert, and then coffee. Afterward I serve brandy. Thac and I smoke another cigar. Verna excuses herself and goes off to bed.

I turn on the player, and we listen to *La Traviata*. When Thac goes to sleep toward the end, I turn off the player and wake him. After he heads off to bed, I drink a beer and listen to the rest of the opera. Then I go to bed.

Verna doesn't stir. She sleeps through thunderstorms. Last year when the hurricane came, she slept through that.

As I drift off, I think of Thac wandering about in the jungle, watching his men die. The army could have sent me anywhere. I never asked for radio research. I have nothing to feel ashamed about.

When I wake to the sound of Jimi Hendrix, it isn't light yet. Verna is gone. I get out of bed and walk into the hallway. The hall is in darkness and so is the room below, but in the glow from the streetlights outside I can see Verna kneeling before Thac with her head between his legs. He is seated on the sofa. I know his head is thrown back, because the red tip of his cigar is pointed at the ceiling.

I go back to bed and lie there, listening to my heart pounding. It's not that I am completely surprised, but if it happened I expected it would be with one of those young studs at the health club.

I decide to say nothing to Verna or Thac. Thac will be gone tomorrow, and I'll never see him again. In a few weeks I'll start some quarrel with Verna. It will be easy to get rid of her, and I'll be left alone and at peace. Charlotte is filled with women who like the sound of my voice in the night.

Though I try to go to sleep before Verna comes back to bed, I can't. When she does return, she smells of cigar smoke. I pretend to be asleep. Soon she dozes off, and I lie there listening to the regular sound of her breathing. I try to imagine that I can smell Thac on her, underneath the cigar smoke, but all I can detect is the sweet scent of the soap she uses.

Then I sleep too.

In the morning Verna wakes me. I avoid looking directly into her eyes.

"I made you breakfast," she says. "Thac is already up."

When I go downstairs, Thac, dressed in tennis clothes, is seated at the kitchen table eating eggs and bacon. Verna has gone to work.

"Eat," he says. "We can play. I must be on a plane to Atlanta at two o'clock."

It's eight o'clock. We have plenty of time. I sit down and eat. I wonder what I will be thinking the next time Verna has her head between my legs.

Instead of talking to Thac, I concentrate on my breakfast. He smokes a cigarette while I finish.

After I dress we cross the dew-wet grass to the court. It is already a very hot day, but I imagine that Thac is as acclimated to the heat as I am.

When we start to warm up, I see why he is the number one player in Saigon. If it weren't for that shattered ankle, I wouldn't stand a chance. But his lack of mobility is going to be the difference, I tell myself. That and the fact that most of his play has been on fast surfaces. On concrete, in Saigon.

We both play sluggishly at first. Thac doesn't have much of a volley and can't jump for overheads, so on important points I bring him in and lob him. Most of his smashes go into the net. I win the first set easily.

I think play has gotten rid of my anger, but toward the end of the second set it returns as blind rage. I net a couple of easy shots. I have a chance to hit Thac with an overhead, but I miss. Now I wish we were boys on a football field. I would take much pleasure in hitting Thac with a hard tackle.

Thac looks like he's tiring. Perhaps, I think, he is still jet-lagged, and staying up half the night with Verna couldn't have helped. I give him a point here and there until the score is even. We agreed not to use tiebreakers, so by the time he wins the second set, the score is 14–16.

And the third goes better than I could have expected. Though I don't give him any points, he jumps out to a three-game lead, which I manage to close. Then it is six all, and we begin to trade games. I'm hoping he'll cramp up. I want to see him writhing on the clay.

At ten all I can tell he's close to cramping. He lifts his left leg and pulls it up behind him to stretch the muscle.

"I am obliged to retire," he says.

"We'll call it a tie," I say.

We drink some water together at the net.

"Sit down and rest," I say.

"No, if I sit I will cramp," he says.

I wonder why I've done this to Thac. I never pretended I was in love with Verna, and the only thing she loves is her own body. I think about saying these things to Thac but decide not to.

"You have time to sit in the Jacuzzi," I say. "We'll get some fluids into you."

We walk back to the house. Thac has taken off his shirt. A shrapnel scar wanders under his right nipple.

He showers and then gets into the Jacuzzi. I fix myself a drink and give Thac a quart of Gatorade. I sit in a rocking chair and smoke a cigar. Verna likes to make love in the Jacuzzi, to cavort as if we are a pair of porpoises.

Thac and I have leftover pizza for lunch, and the rest of the German beer. Then I call him a cab.

When the cab arrives and Thac starts out the door, I offer him the Jimi Hendrix disc.

"No," he says. "I have no way to play it."

There's not the slightest hint, no tremor in his voice, that would let me know that he knows I know.

I walk out to the cab with him, and we shake hands.

"Call me the next time you're in town," I say.

He smiles. "Come to Ho Chi Minh City and play on my courts," he says.

Then he's gone. I go back inside. I call Verna, but she's at lunch. I sit on the couch and have another drink and think about tonight's show. We're going to talk about busing.

I kick off my shoes and put my feet up. I set my drink on the table.

Then I close my eyes and think of those nights when Thac's voice would appear, how I'd listen and wonder what the man was like who was sitting in a bunker outside Hanoi, both of us plugged into the war, listening to the heartbeat of battle. I hear the confused babble of those voices from the past, a great chorus of pain and despair, rising out of those forest-covered mountains, sweeping over the coastal plain, and sailing out above the South China Sea. I sit very still and attentive before my memory, searching for individual voices, as if I am trying to identify the singer of an aria on a faulty disc.

I imagine playing tennis with Thac in Saigon during one of those days of the monsoon, the warm wind steady off the sea, the clouds low and thick over the city, the air filled with a fine mist. The concrete courts are slick. The balls are heavy with water. We move carefully, as if we are playing on ice, but I know that neither of us is going to fall. We are safe.

I wonder if Verna considers herself safe, protected by her perfect body. Maybe she was born safe, could have wandered through that jungle with Thac and never received a scratch. I imagine touching her, running my hands over those beautiful breasts and thighs. To my surprise, instead of being moved to anger or disgust by thoughts of her and Thac, I imagine something entirely different, something I cannot quite name. All I know is that it will be a good feeling. Then I realize that she will be a connection with Thac, like his voice on the radio.

I am not going to drive her away. I am going to hang on to her for as long as I can.

1999

Michael Knight

BIRDLAND

Alabama native Michael Knight tells a love story fraught with football fervor, par-
rots, politics, and hope. It's set in the tiny town of Elbow, Alabama, whose eleventh-
term mayor is eighty-one years old and where a flock of African parrots spends the
winters. Knight, who says he has been a Crimson Tide fan since childhood, is the
author of a novel, Divining Rod, *and two collections of stories and has published his*
fiction in many magazines, including Esquire, The New Yorker, The Paris
Review, The Virginia Quarterly Review, *and* GQ. *He lives in Knoxville, where*
he teaches creative writing at the University of Tennessee.

Between the months of April and September, Pawtucket,
Rhode Island, is inhabited by several generations of a particular African parrot. A millionaire philanthropist named Elgin
Archibald brought a dozen or so over from Kenya around the turn
of the century and kept them in an aviary built against the side of
his house. A few days before his death, in 1907, in a moment more
notable for generosity than for good sense, he swung open the
cage and released the birds into a wide summer sky. According to
eyewitness reports, the parrots, surprised by their sudden freedom,
made a dazed circle beneath the clouds and, not seeing anything
more to their liking, lighted amid the branches of an apple orchard
on the back acreage of Archibald's property. There, following the
habit of nature, they flourished, and have continued to thrive for
more than ninety years. But in September, when winter creeps in
from the ocean and cold air evokes hazy instincts, the parrots flee
south for warmer climes and settle here in Elbow, Alabama, along
a slow bend in the Black Warrior River, where perhaps they are

reminded of waters, slower still, in an almost forgotten continent across the sea.

I know all this because the Blonde told me it was true. The Blonde has platinum hair and round hips, and a pair of ornithology degrees from a university up in New Hampshire. She has a given name, as well, Ludmilla Haggarsdottir, but no one in town is comfortable with its pronunciation. The Blonde came to Elbow a year ago, researching a book about Archibald's parrots, and was knocked senseless by the late-August heat. Even after the weight had gone out of summer and the parrots had arrived and football was upon us, she staggered around in a safari hat and sunglasses, drunk with the fading season, scribbling notes on the progress of the birds. She took pictures and sat sweating in the live-oak shade. They don't have this sort of heat in New England —bone-warming inertial heat, humidity thick enough to slow your blood. She rented a room in my house, the only room for rent in town. At night, we would sit on the back porch, fireflies blundering against the screen, and make love on my grandmother's old daybed. "Tell me a story, Raymond," the Blonde would say. "Tell me something I've never heard before." The fireflies glowed like cigarette embers. The Blonde was slick with perspiration.

"This," I said, throwing her leg over my shoulder, "is how Hector showed his love to Andromache the night before Achilles killed him dead."

Elbow, Alabama, is easy enough to find. Take Highway 14 north from Sherwood until you come to Easy Money Road. Bear east and keep driving until you're sure you've gone too far: past a red barn with the words HIS DESIRE SHALL BE SATISFIED UPON THE HILLS OF GILEAD painted on the planks in gold letters, past a field where no crops grow, past a cypress split by lightning. This is modest country, and nature has had her steady way for years. My house is just a little farther, over a hill, left on the gravel drive.

The only TV around here sits on the counter at Dillard's Country Store. Dillard's has a gas pump out front and all the essentials inside: white bread and yellow mustard and cold beer. Dillard him-self brews hard cider, and doubles as mayor of Elbow. He is eighty-one years old and has been elected to eleven consecutive terms. On fall Saturdays, all Elbow gathers in his store to watch the Alabama team take the field: me and the Blonde, Mayor Dillard, Lookout Mountain Coley, the Foot brothers, and Mae and Wilson Camp, who have a soybean farm north of town. Lookout Mountain Coley is the nearest thing we have to a local celebrity. He grew up in Mentone, Alabama, near the mountain with that name. These days, Lookout stocks shelves and does the bookkeeping in the grocery and mans the counter when the Mayor is in the head, but thirty-five years ago he was only the second black man to play football for the great Bear Bryant. Once, he returned a punt ninety-nine yards for a touchdown against Tennessee. The Crim-son Tide is not what it used to be, of course, and we all curse God for taking away our better days. Leonard and Chevy Foot, identi-cal twins, have the foulest mouths in Elbow, and their dialogue on game day is a long string of invective against blind referees and unfair recruiting practices and dumb-ass coaches who aren't fit to wipe Bear Bryant's behind. The parrots perch in pecan trees beyond the open windows and listen to us rant. At night, with the river curving silently, they mimic us in the dark. *"Catch the ball,"* they caw in Mayor Dillard's desperate tones. *"Catch the ball, you stupid nigger."* Mayor Dillard is an unrepentant racist, and I often wonder what the citizens of Pawtucket, Rhode Island, must think when the birds leave us in the spring.

When I was fourteen, Hurricane Frederick whipped in from the Gulf of Mexico, spinning tornadoes upriver as far as Elbow. Dillard's Country Store was pancaked, and a sixty-foot pine fell across the roof of my grandmother's house. My father had been gone almost a year, and we huddled in the pantry, the old woman and I, and listened to the wind moving room to room like a search party. The next day she sent me to town on foot to borrow supplies and see if everyone was all right. Telephone poles were stacked along the road like pick-up-sticks. But the most terrifying thing was the quiet. The parrots were gone, the trees without pigment and voice. We thought they had all been killed, and to this day no one is certain where they spent the winter, though the Blonde has unearthed testimony for her book regarding strange birds sighted in the panhandle of Florida during the last months of 1979. We rebuilt the grocery, and my grandmother turned her roof repairs into a party, serving up cheese and crackers and a few bottles of champagne she'd saved from her wedding. Despite our efforts at good cheer, and exempting New Year's Day, when Bear Bryant licked Joe Paterno in the Sugar Bowl, a pall hung over town until Lookout spotted the birds coming back, dozens of them coloring the sky like a ticker-tape parade.

Our river is named for the Indian chief Tuscaloosa, which means "Black Warrior" in Choctaw, and in the fall, while we sit mesmerized and enraged by the failings of our team, its dark water litters Dillard Point with driftwood and detritus—baby carriages and coat hangers, Goodyear radials and headless Barbie dolls. When the game has ended and I need an hour to collect myself, I wander the riverbank, picking up branches that I later carve into parrot shapes and display in the window of Dillard's Country Store. We have bird-watchers by the busload in season and, outside of the twenty dollars a month I charge the Blonde for her room and board, these whittlings account for my income. But I don't need much in the way of money anymore.

The Blonde doesn't understand our commitment to college football. Ever the scientist, she has theorized that a winning team gives us a reason to take pride in being from Alabama, after our long history of bigotry and oppression, and our more recent dismal record in public education and environmental conservation. I don't know whether she is correct, but I suspect that she is beginning to recognize the appeal of the Crimson Tide. Just last week, while we watched Alabama in a death struggle with the Florida Gators, our halfback fumbled on their twenty-yard line and she jerked out of her chair, her fists closed tight, her thighs quivering beneath her hiking shorts. She had to clench her jaw to keep from calling out. Her face was glazed with sweat, the fine hairs on her upper lip visible in the dusty light. The sight of her like that, all balled-up enthusiasm, her shirt knotted beneath her ribs, sweat pooling in the folds of her belly, moved me to dizziness. I held her hand and led her out onto the porch. Dillard's is situated at a junction of rural highways, and we watched a tour bus rumble past, eager old women hanging from the windows with binoculars at their eyes. The pecan trees were dotted with parrots, blurs of brighter red and smears of gray in among the leaves. *"Catch the ball!"* one of the parrots called out, and another answered, *"Stick him like a man, you fat country bastard."* She sat on the plank steps, and I knelt at her bare feet. "Will you marry me?" I said. "You are a prize greater than Helen to Paris." The Blonde is not the only one around here with a college education.

She looked at me sadly for a minute, her hand going clammy in mine. The game was back on inside, an announcer's voice floating through the open door. After a while, she said, "I can't live here the rest of my life." She stood and went inside to watch the end of the game, which we lost on a last-second Hail Mary pass that broke all our hearts at once.

The Blonde is still working on her book. She follows the birds from tree to tree, keeping an eye on reproductive habits and the condition of winter plumage. "Parrot," she tells me, is really just a catchall name for several types of bird, such as the macaw, the cockatoo, the lory, and the budgerigar. Common to all genera, including our African grays, are a hooked bill, a prehensile tongue, and yoke-toed claws, whatever that means. The African parrot can live up to eighty years, she says, and often mates for life, though our local birds have apparently adapted a more swinging sexual culture, perhaps from an instinctive understanding of the necessity of perpetuation in a nonindigenous environment. Her book will be about the insistence of nature. It will be about surviving against the odds.

By the time April came along and the birds began to filter north, the Blonde and I were too tangled up for her to leave. One day, the Blonde says, she will return to Pawtucket and resume her studies there. She mentions this when she is angry with me for one reason or another, and leads me to her room to show me her suitcase, still standing unpacked beside my grandmother's antique bureau. And the thought of her leaving does frighten me into good behavior. I can hardly remember what my life was like without her here, though I managed fine for a long time before she arrived.

The Blonde won't sleep a whole night with me. She climbs up the drop ladder to the attic, which is where I make my bed, and we wind together in the dark, her body pale above me, moonlight catching in her movie-star hair. When she is finished, she smokes cigarettes at the gable window, and I tell her stories from the Iliad. I explain how the Greeks almost lost everything when Achilles and Agamemnon argued over a woman. I tell her that male pride is a volatile energy, and that some feathers are better left unruffled, but I know she only listens to these old stories for the sound of my voice. She is more interested in the parrots, a few of whom have taken roost in an oak tree beside my house. If there is a full moon, the birds are awake for hours, calling, *"Who are you? Why are you in my house?"* back and forth in the luminous night. According to the Blonde's research, old Archibald was deep in Alzheimer's by the time of his death and was unable to recognize his own children when they visited. She goes dreamy-eyed imagining the parrots passing these words from generation to generation. Before she returns to her bed, she wonders aloud how it is that the birds could have learned such existential phrases in Rhode Island and such ugly, bitter words down here.

Sometimes Lookout Coley gets fed up with Mayor Dillard shouting "nigger" at the TV screen. Having played for Alabama in the halcyon sixties, Lookout knows what football means to people around here, and he restrains himself admirably. But when they were younger men and Mayor Dillard crossed whatever invisible boundary exists between them Lookout would circle his fists in the old style and challenge him to a fight. A couple of times they ended up rolling around in the dirt parking lot, sweat running muddy on their skin. Nowadays Lookout presses his lips together and his face goes blank and hard as if he were turning himself to stone. He walks outside without a word and stares off at the trees across the highway. After a few minutes, Mayor Dillard gets up and follows him. The rest of us focus our attention on the game, so they can have some time alone to sort things out. No one knows for sure what goes on between them, but when they return they are patting each other on the back and making promises that neither of them will keep. Each time, Mayor Dillard offers a public apology, saying he hopes the people of Elbow won't hold this incident against him come election. He buys a round of bottled beers and Lookout accepts the apology with grace, waving his beer at the TV screen so we'll quit looking at him and keep our minds on simpler things.

Her first season in town, the Blonde was appalled by these displays. She is descended from liberal-minded Icelandic stock and she couldn't understand why Lookout or any of us would allow Mayor Dillard to go on the way he does. Once she sprang to her feet and clicked off the television and delivered an angry lecture welcoming us to the "twentieth fucking century." Her fury was gorgeous. She tried to convince Lookout to report Dillard to the N.A.A.C.P. or, short of that, to run for mayor himself, arguing that only a sports celebrity would have the clout to unseat an old incumbent. But Lookout told her he wasn't interested. Though she would never admit it, the words don't offend her so much anymore. You can get used to anything, given time. Some nights, however, when she is moving violently over me, she grits her teeth and says, "Who's the nigger, Raymond? Who's the nigger now?" I don't think her indignation is aimed directly at me. When she has gone, I tangle myself sleeplessly in the sheets and promise never to think another closed-minded thought.

Raymond French was my father's name, now mine. I am the only child of a land surveyor. My mother died giving birth to me, and my dad began to wander farther and farther afield, finding work, until one day he never returned. I was thirteen when he went, left here with my grandmother and the house. She paid for my education, but she was always disappointed with my chosen field of study. "Classics, Raymond?" she would say. "You ought to be studying the future." She loved this town and hoped that I would bring my learning home and give something back. But all I have given unto Elbow is driftwood parrots and the Blonde. Everyone knows she lingers here because of me, and no one is quite sure how they feel about that.

A few days ago, I panicked when I returned from Dillard Point and found an empty house. I waited on the porch and watched the road for cars, but she didn't show. I don't have a phone, so I drove from house to house, stopped by to see Lookout, swung past the Foots' mobile home, whipped the town into a posse. Prowling country lanes, I began to suspect that she was gone for good. Then I spotted her jeep parked beside one of the Camps' fields. This deserted road and vacant field are like horror-movie sets, with a defunct grain silo rising from the ground like a wizard's tower. I called her name, but only the parrots answered. *"Who are you?"* they said, their voices flat and distant. *"Catch the ball."* Then, faintly, I heard her voice, a stage whisper coming from inside the silo, and when I crawled up beside her she shone a flashlight on a nest, so I could see the baby parrots, their feathers still slick and insufficient, heads wobbly on their necks. She threw her arms around me and wept and pressed her lips against my collarbone. The roof of the silo had fallen in years before and stars blossomed in the open space.

One Saturday in the fall and one in spring, the town celebrates Parrot Day. In October, Mayor Dillard stands outside the store, where Lookout has rigged a hand-painted banner, delivers a short speech, and has his picture snapped for the record. He always arranges it so that Parrot Day comes during an off week for the Crimson Tide. This year, we gather in the parking lot and listen to the Mayor give his speech. The parrots jeer him from the trees.

"Run, darkie, run," they call, and he pretends not to notice. The Blonde is disappointed with the day. She wants more from these proceedings, wants something meaningful and real, but this year most of us are grateful for a break from football. Six games into the season and already we've lost four. Another stinker and 'Bama is out of contention for a bowl. We'd settle for anything at this point—the Jeep Aloha, the Outback Steakhouse, even the Poulan Weedeater Bowl, over in Louisiana.

All our mail is addressed to Dillard's Country Store, and in the evenings, when the sun is like molten glass over the river, Mayor Dillard hands out our letters and such. Once a month, the Foots hang their heads in a stew of shame because their subscription to *Titty* has arrived. The Camps get postcards now and then from Wilson's brother Max and his other brother, Andre, whose marriage broke up years ago. Lookout gets religious pamphlets and sports-recruiting news, but letters never come for me. I no longer have connections beyond the boundaries of our town. The Blonde dawdles nearby when Mayor Dillard passes out the mail, her hair sweat-damp against her neck. She cracks her knuckles and goes for nonchalance. She has, it seems, applied for a government grant. She wrote the proposal without telling me and will head north in the spring if her funding comes through. We are sitting at a picnic table behind my house eating peanut-butter sandwiches when she announces her intentions. I force down a mouthful and ask her for a second time to marry me, but her answer is the same. She covers my hand with hers, and sends a look of apology across the table. The Blonde holds all history against me. When it is clear that I have nothing else to say, she stands and walks around to the front of the house. I find her staring up into the trees at a pair of fornicating parrots. "Don't mistake this for love," I hear her murmur to the birds. "Don't be talked into something you'll regret." She watches, unblinking, her arms crossed at her chest. I ask her why she stayed last spring, why she didn't follow the parrots when they left Elbow for the season. She tells me she was broke, that's all. She would have vanished if she'd had the cash. I remind her that she paid her rent, that she was never short of cigarettes and oils for her hair. "Shut up," the Blonde says. "I know what you want to hear."

At night, she types her notes and files them away on the chance the government will write. It's warm enough still, even in October, that we can leave the windows open, air grazing her skin and carrying her scent to my chair in the next room. There is something familiar about the way she smells, though I can never place it. I whittle and listen to sports radio and wish I had a phone so I could call all the broadcasters in New Jersey who have forgotten how great we used to be, how we won a dozen National Championships, and how Alabama lost only six games in the first ten years of my life. To listen to them talk, you'd think they never heard that Bear Bryant was on a U.S. thirty-two-cent stamp. I pace the floor when I get agitated and shuffle wood shavings with my feet. I talk back to my grandmother's Motorola portable. When I make the fierce turn toward my chair, I see the Blonde standing in the doorway, her hands on the frame above her. She smiles and shakes her head. "You people," she says. "When are you gonna put all that Bear Bryant stuff behind you? That's all dead and gone." I cross myself Catholic style and look at her a long moment, my heart tiny in my chest. She is wearing a man's sleeveless undershirt and boxer shorts, her hair pinned behind her head with a pencil. I would forgive her almost any sacrilege for the length of her neck or the way she rests one foot on top of the other and curls her painted toes. I remember Calypso casting a spell on the Greeks to keep Odysseus on her island, and I want to teach the birds a phrase so full of magic that the Blonde will never leave.

I want to tell her that the past is not only for forgetting. There are some things, good and bad, that you can't leave behind. According to the record books, Bear Bryant didn't sign a black player until 1970 because the State of Alabama was not ready even for gridiron integration. A decade earlier, however, he had recruited a group of Negro running backs who were light-skinned enough to pass for white. They hid their faces beneath helmets and bunked in a special dorm miles away from campus. They were listed in the program under names Bear himself selected. Lookout's playing name was Patrick O'Reilly.

Every now and then, Mayor Dillard will set up his ancient reel-to-reel projector on a card table outdoors and, against the rear wall of his store, show black-and-white movies of Lookout's punt return. We sit in the grass in the early dark, pressing beer bottles against our necks to ward off the heat, and watch his image shimmering and breaking around chips in the paint. There is Lookout, sleek and muscled and young, with the punt dropping into his arms. He shifts his hips side to side and gives a Tennessee defender a stiff-arm that takes your breath away. The image flickers as he shimmies toward the sideline, and then he breaks upfield, his back arched with speed, the rest of the world falling away behind him. The movie is without sound, and whenever Mayor Dillard rewinds the film, so we can watch the touchdown over and over, Lookout goes streaking backward in front of the Alabama bench, past his exultant teammates and granite-faced Bear Bryant, then forward again toward the end zone, all swift and silent grace. None of us have ever done anything so wonderful in all our lives. Chevy Foot, as if witnessing a cosmic event, whispers, "Old Number Forty-one, man, you sure could fly."

I ask the Blonde why the parrots keep returning to Elbow, and she says it's instinct. We are sitting on the riverbank, with our feet in the water. It's morning on another football Saturday. Downstream, a hot-air balloon hovers on invisible currents in the sky. The Blonde slips into her academic's voice as she tells me that, because the birds are native to equatorial Africa, because their food supply of seeds, nuts, and fruit dries up in the Rhode Island cold, they are obliged to embark on a southerly migration in order to survive. "It's a miracle *Psittacus erithacus* endures in this country at all," she says, and lies back on the ground, crossing her hands behind her head. There is a parrot perched on a cypress branch across the river watching us with the side of his head. I find a stone on the bank and skip it across the water in his direction, and he screeches and flutters his wings at me.

"But why here?" I say. "They could live anywhere in the world." The Blonde lifts up on her forearm, her hair falling over her eyes, and opens her mouth to speak before she realizes that for once she doesn't have an answer to my question.

In the second quarter of the Ole Miss game, a freshman quarterback named Algernon Marquez comes off the bench for Alabama and throws a pair of touchdowns before the half. For nine minutes, as our team works to tie the score, we are beside ourselves, leaping about Dillard's Country Store, pitching our bodies into one another's arms, but at halftime we fall silent, fearing a jinx, and cross our fingers and apologize to God for all the nasty things we have said about Him in the recent past. Even the Blonde wants to bear the suspense in quiet. She carries her cigarettes outside and sits smoking in her jeep. I stand behind my parrot sculptures, and watch her through the window, as she pretends she is above all this.

The second half, God bless, belongs to Alabama. Our defense is inspired, our offense fleet and strong. Algernon Marquez isn't Joe Namath or even Snake Stabler, but he is more a dream than we could have hoped. "A no-name wonder from Boulahatchie," the announcer says, "whose only goal in life was to play for the Crimson Tide." I wonder how it would feel to have achieved all your aspirations by your eighteenth year. I wonder what Lookout would say about that. A busful of Delaware parrot lovers rolls up while the score is 35–17, and Mayor Dillard gives them whatever they want for free.

That night, I tell the Blonde Andromache's story—how she was made a slave to Pyrrhus, the son of Achilles, after Hector's death, but grew to love him a little bit, over time. "She was happy there, even though she never guessed it could be true," I say, sitting on the bed, with my back propped up. We are in her bed now, my grandmother's sleigh bed, which has been in our family since the Revolutionary War; it made the journey down here by wagon from Virginia. The Blonde is on her back, with her feet against the wall beside my head. She is naked, still flushed from our coupling. "I'm pregnant," she says. "I can feel it in my bones." She traces concentric circles on her stomach with a finger, the parrots frantic beyond the windows. Then she sits upright and looks at me, as if she wanted to see something behind my eyes. I'm just about to haul her into my arms and waltz her joyously around her room when she slaps my face, leaving an echo in my head. I watch, too stunned to stop her, while she jumps up and down on the wood floor, landing hard and flat-footed each time, shaking windowpanes, sending ripples along the backs of her legs. She is crying and pounding her knees, and I wrap my arms around her and pin her down. "This is not my baby," she says. "This is not my life." She keeps shouting until her voice is gone, and she cries herself to sleep beneath me.

Morning finds me alone, still sleeping on the floor. I check the house to be sure, but she is nowhere to be found. Her suitcase is gone from beside the bureau, her hair-care products have vanished from the shelf beside the bathroom sink. I sit drinking coffee on the sleeping porch while the parrots call softly, *"Who are you? Why are you in my house?"* It is not quite a new day yet, and I watch the world come to life, winter buds opening in the light, the river far below hauling water toward the sea. I tell myself that I will give up hope at lunch. And though I hold off eating until two o'clock, I keep my promise and carry a melancholy peanut-butter sandwich out into the yard. The grass is cool on the bottoms of my feet. I wonder about the Blonde, see her streaming down the highway in her jeep, sunglasses on her head to keep the hair out of her eyes. I wonder if she will put an end to our baby in a clinic or if she only wants to get some distance between history and the child. I want to tell her that even bland Ohio is haunted by its crimes. I want to tell her, with the air full of birds like this and the shadow of my house still lingering on the yard, that she is exactly what I need. Behind me, as if on cue, the Blonde says, "I drove all night, but I didn't know where else to go." I turn to face her, blood jumping in my veins. There are tired blue crescents under her eyes, and her hair is knotted from the wind. She smiles and smooths the front of her shorts. I am so grateful I do not have the strength to speak. "I took a pee test in Gadsden," she says. "It's official." Then she walks over, grabs my wrist, and guides the sandwich to her lips.

Election day is nearing again, November 17th. Though Mayor Dillard will run unopposed, as usual, he is superstitious about complacency. He pays Lookout overtime to haul boxes of campaign buttons out of the storage shed behind his store and stake DILLARD DOES IT BETTER signs along the road. He visits each of his constituents in person, bribing us with hard cider and the promise of a brighter future here in Elbow. Things are looking brighter for the Alabama team as well. We've won two games in a row and the Yankee radio personalities are beginning to see the light. They say our team has an outside shot at the Peach Bowl, over in Georgia, where we will likely face Virginia's Cavaliers. But we do not speak a word of this in town. We hold our breath and say our prayers because hated Auburn is looming in the distance and one false step could bring all this new hope down around us like a house of cards. At night, the Blonde and I drink non-alcoholic beverages beneath the Milky Way. We have reached an acceptable compromise: spring in Rhode Island, fall back here, until she has finished her book, but she will give birth in Alabama. Elbow will have a new voter in eighteen years, and the Blonde has convinced Lookout to contend for mayor himself. He will not run against his friend, Lookout says. Too much has passed between them. But it won't be long before Mayor Dillard gives in to time, and Lookout Coley can sweep injustice from our town like an Old West sheriff.

My life purls drowsily out behind me like water. Parrots preen invisibly in the dark. I shuttle inside for more ice and listen to the Blonde spin stories about our unborn child. Her daughter, she says, will discover a lost tribe of parrots in the wilds of Borneo, and invent a vaccine for broken hearts. She will write a novel so fine that no other books need writing anymore, and she will marry, if she chooses, an imperfect man and make him good inside. And maybe, if the stars are all in line, our daughter will grow up to be the hardest-hitting free safety who ever lived.

1999

Heather Sellers

FLA. BOYS

Heather Sellers says, "I set the story in the landscape I'm most acquainted with: a backside, no-place strip of Florida, between Bithlo, Christmas, and Narcoosee. That setting—flat and scrubby, unseen by outsiders—seemed a perfect metaphor for the adolescent girl body." Born and raised in Orlando, Sellers earned her doctorate in English literature at Florida State University and lived in Florida for nearly thirty years. She teaches creative writing at Hope College in Holland, Michigan, and is the author of a collection of stories, Georgia Under Water, *and a collection of poems,* Drinking Girls and Their Dresses, *as well as a book about writing and a children's book.*

I started driving early. I was twelve. I am a girl. It was not what I lived for.

At first my main fears driving were 1) a dog would run out in front of me and I would crush it and never be able to drive again I would be so upset and 2) my door would fly open and I would fall out and get run over by my own back wheels, my neck tangled hopelessly in the rear axle.

By the time I was thirteen, I was fairly confident on the road. My dad in the front seat, sort of conducting. My uncles once in a while packed into the back seat, their drinks in ice tea glasses. They loaded me with compliments. We didn't see them that often.

Most often it was me driving my dad at four in the afternoon out the two-track to Amber's, where there were chickens and beer and what my father called moonshine but was just regular Gordon's in regular fifths.

Other times I drove to school, and put the car in the teacher lot, and walked in through the front doors. Sometimes I drove the

Trail to the ABC, in the morning. Sometimes even the highway when Dad wanted to go downtown for a drink.

Nothing bad happened, except when we got pulled over, and then I did everything my father told me to do, and miraculously, it worked. I cried, and my father had explained we were on the way to the hospital. He just kept talking, and somehow he had made his drink disappear—I still didn't know how he did that. Once the cop ended up giving me money, two damp twenty-dollar bills. Figure that out.

When I was fourteen my father got me a thirty-day restricted driver's emergency license. I would get to drive him to the hospital. Then, I would take care of myself for two weeks. This time, the hospital part was true. I wasn't worried about my father.

"They just take out six inches of colon, Sweetie, it's nothing." His belly was pregnant with fluid—he was huge, and his skin was yellow. We sat in the kitchen drinking—I was having a beer. His little suitcase was on the dining room table. On top of his aqua pajamas, little white cloudy plastic flasks, full.

The license was bigger than a normal license. It was laminated. There was no photo of me. My restrictions were printed on the back in red. A) Operator may only drive 7 A.M.–7 P.M. B) Forty-five miles per hour maximum speed.

The restrictions seemed dangerous. With these instructions I was a slow-moving target.

To get the license, I had driven down to the Orlando City Hall with my father. I drove, illegally, as I did most of the time. He liked to have his gin and tonic going, in his smoky tall glass, a cigarette dangling dangerously above the drink. This was how I learned to drive. You learn to not spill any fluid.

I'd dressed up in my favorite outfit; I was still sure there'd be a photo and I was thrilled—I mean I actually thought this might lead to a modeling portfolio. I clasped purple puka shells around my neck. I had a bitchin suntan, because my father and I had a pool—in the front yard—of our Southside stucco ranch. I wore my white sundress and I loosened the ties at the shoulders so my breasts would look bigger—you couldn't tell really, I thought, if it was the dress flipping around or my boobs. I was thinking, I will invite a guy over to the house, and we will have a little champagne by the pool. I was thrilled to be on my own for two weeks. My father had stocked the freezer in the garage with meat.

"Don't dawdle," my father said, and he held out his palm for the keys. I got out of the car and went to put money in the city hall meter. The palms were scratching together, their fronds like legs. Itch itch.

"Don't fuck with that, I'm right here," he growled out the passenger window.

I turned on my heels and walked up the forty stairs, into the city hall. I pretended I was a lawyer. I was in stiletto Candies, red.

I gave the clerk my fat folder of papers, documenting my father's surgery, the hardship, the loss of work, and giving them a fake address, my uncles' Kissimmee ranch. Farm kids could get the Temporary even without an Emergency.

Here you go, she said.

I wanted it to be harder. I wanted my photo taken. These would be my dominant reactions to many situations for the rest of my life.

When I was a little girl, I would climb into the back seat of my father's car, late late at night, but so bright in Florida, in summer, and I would lie back there on his newspapers and bottles and the fertilizer sacks and papers and carbons and I would pretend a man was making love to me. I don't know where I got that stuff. I guess you just know what goes where.

The next night, when he passed out on the couch, his pale, almost green gaseous belly stiff on top of him, I took his keys and sat in the giant brown Olds out in the green cement driveway, on my side, the passenger side. I had the license in my hand. My sweat was buckling the lamination. I sat out there for hours, and thought of men, and how they drive women around. I didn't need to drive secretly at night, like most kids. I did all that driving during the day.

The next day my father didn't get out of bed. I swam in the lake. I was pretending I was a seal, shooting up from the white mucky bottom of Lake Conway every time a plane came over the blue lake, and barking *orr orr orr.* Right then the Carrington boys came by in their Mercury boat and asked me if I wanted to ride around. I said no.

They sped off and I went down to the bottom. I don't know why. Their white bathing suits, little flags flapping in the wind, scared me, like dinner napkins and mothers and rapes and won races.

That night, I cried out in the Olds. I was so sad I hadn't gone with those Carrington boys. I started the engine, backed out of the driveway, hitting the neighbor's curb, and I drove slow and smooth as Johnny Hartman singing "My Favorite Things" on 88.4, my father's favorite station. I sang loud, and I put on his pilot sunglasses. I prowled around the Southside in the big car, pretending I was a pimp, or a Colonel or a cat or a woman with small children or a woman with no children at all.

The last night before he went in to Orange Memorial I was completely happy just to sit in the driveway with my hands on my father's sticky steering wheel. It was like I was hiding and everyone I knew had quit looking for me.

I was fourteen. I didn't even own a wallet yet. The Emergency license sat in my red plastic purse alone, among my lip gloss and eyeshadow and concealer and tiny plastic Hallmark calendar and calculator and Troll doll, all the things I would get to keep forever.

I drove him to the grocery store. It was his last day.

"Monday dinner," I said, just to get him thinking on it. I threaded us between the cars, trolling and idling and parked in places that weren't even really places in the Winn Dixie parking lot. I worked around broken bottles, and grocery carts and a large St. Bernard who looked to be suffering a heat stroke out by the cart corral.

"Why do you want to park in bum-fuck Egypt?" he said.

"Is there something wrong with your legs?" I said.

"As a matter of fact," he said.

And he bought me everything I wanted that day, and finally I wanted some things. More makeup. A giant pink iced angel food cake. A tiny bottle of champagne. I don't even know if it was real or play.

And the ABC, we stopped there, and he sat inside at the revolving bar for one hour and twelve minutes while I waited in the car, reading *Seventeen* and staring at the men who went in and out. Everything was fine except I was melting inside, I was so worried he would die of cancer. And he was. He was to have his ear cut off and six inches of colon taken out.

"I'll tell you what to worry about," he said. He was frying fish that night. Dad always made us wonderful dinners, chop suey and chicken Buck. Buck is my father's name, Buck Jackson, and chili. He could do Mexican, he could do Indian, he could do steak and potatoes. Everything he cooked tasted so good.

"Thanks for making this wonderful dinner," I said, most unworried voice.

"Jesus, who the fuck can't cook," he said. "If you can follow directions, you can cook."

I didn't point out that he didn't follow any directions at all, he just seemed to stumble around throwing things on the counter and making an enormous mess. My job was to clean up that mess. I didn't point out that one of his refrains was "people in this world can't follow goddamn directions."

We ate out on the patio in the purple starlight. He threw his bones into the pool. Bones float sideways.

Then it was the morning of Tuesday, June 7th. I drove him to the hospital. He told me again where I was born, pointing five floors up to a dirty greenish window.

"You looked like Rocky Marciano." He always said this. And he laughed in a sad way, like it was the end of something, my birth, his seeing me like Rocky.

"How much did it hurt my mother?" I wanted to say. I was having trouble keeping my eyes on the road, much less doing the circle of rotations between the road, the rearview, and the siderear, duh, duh, dunh. *That my face was so flattened then. Did she scream? Was sex worth this? Why was a baby so big? Couldn't it start off much smaller, much much smaller, something to fit in your palm, something the size of a penis, something appropriate for the woman? Couldn't we find a way to grow them out here, in the open, an easier way?*

I looked at my father, transmitting my questions to him subliminally, as always. He didn't like to be asked things, unless he asked you to ask.

"Ask me if I fucking care." "Ask me how to wire a goddamn house, I will fucking tell you. Hell I will fucking show you." "Ask me what you should do with your life, Georgia. Ask me."

I didn't ask him, never about her. He'd left her and taken me with him, and he had what he called mixed feelings. This always made me think of cement. Mixed feelings. Our lives, the products of mixed feelings.

"Turn around back. Not here. This whole part is for ambulances. Damn it."

She was in Wisconsin, so who knew what was what. This was not the day to ask my father particulars. We were into the Emergency period. He was getting cancer out of his colon. He was getting the colon out of his system. When you live with an alcoholic, if you are fourteen, you learn quickly and sweetly. You learn that many things can be put off. You learn how to stay in a place of not-knowing. You never would consider asking prognosis, odds, or how much money there is. Not-knowing. You learn to find this somewhat relaxing.

Earlier in the morning he had showed me how to fix the toilet, that creepy rusty water, the green corroded chain, and how to load his gun, those slimy shells—he didn't think there was anything else

I ought to need to know. A gun and a commode is what I had to hold me through the next two weeks. Hormel tamales and fourteen frozen cube steaks. Onions in our yard. Enough muriatic acid for the pool for a year. And the Emergency License.

I was driving perfectly, around the back of the hospital, up into the parking garage, wrapping around, not gunning the engine at this very low speed—I was going two miles an hour, not spilling a drop, even though inside I thought my father would die during this operation, I would never see him again, I would drive to his funeral with an expired Emergency license.

We didn't have the radio on. He was nervous, but he was always nervous. He always had a lot going on. He was drinking the whole way down to the hospital, long drinks out of his smoky gray glass.

He looked hard into his fist, which had just swallowed his cigarette, his eyebrows untamed wires, his complexion yellow from the colon blockage, his eyes sweating, his blue jumpsuit unzipped too far. He had gotten all skinny in the face and shoulders and legs and arms. His middle was more enormous, as if he were pregnant way past the time, like sixteen months or something.

On level three, I braked and gas-pedaled at the same time I think. My legs were all mixed up, the car chortling, my father coughing, and I wanted to just take a breather at this four-way stop, I just really wanted to stop and not think, just pause the world for the moment, a big moment. It spilled. It spilled, my father's fist, around his drink, the drink was on the floor, and ice slid around, and I lurched through the intersection and somehow the Olds was spinning, a wide circle, like how guys drive on purpose, at night, doing their donuts, sometimes. Spinning, and then Buck socked me in the throat. He socked me hard. The parked cars slipped past my windows. We lurched on through. I could make no noise. Up to level five.

I concentrated on the burning on my neck and the red golf cart in front of me, with its pails of paint stacked like white heads.

"Sorry about that," he said. He had ochre eyes, always wet. "Get going. Now, get going. You're going to get rear-ended. And in a

couple of hours I'm getting out six inches of my colon. Get vehicle out of goddamn intersection. Go up to the top."

My hands tingled on the steering wheel. My stomach whooshing. This was pretty much my constant state.

"We oughta get em to put it in formaldehyde so we can display
my contribution on the mantel. What do you think about that as
a conversation piece, baby?" My dad smiled and you could tell he
was seeing a crowd of people around our mantel and all of us talking and laughing.

I pulled up to the Admitting doors at the top of the parking
garage.

There was no plan.

"Just let me out," he said. He didn't have the suitcase. Standing
in the sun, he drained the rest of the bottle, a jug of gin he had in
the back seat. There wasn't a lot left.

"Dad," I was going to say, "are they going to cut you open? Is it
going to hurt? Will you know when they are inside you? Will you
not be able to feel them?" But my throat hurt from where he hit
me and I just turned on the radio, I didn't know the tune, and he
walked into the building.

I waited, idling for a few minutes, like moms do when they drop
you off at school or dance lessons.

How do you know what gets inside of you? Why was I born?
How could you ever figure out something like that? How could
you not? I wanted to drive into the lake behind the hospital. By
way of a cure.

I didn't know much about cancer. What it was. It seemed like
stones. I knew about guns and toilets and making drinks, mim-
osas, molotov cocktails, his favorites. I knew about butt-fucking.
My father's pornography collection was vast and specific.

I didn't know any people who had died. I didn't know that
many people.

My mother and brother had moved to Wisconsin seven years
ago. I had a memory block from age twelve to age seven. And what

can you remember before age seven? Wanting stuff made out of sugar or plastic and crying and some ducks at a park. I remembered my kid brother's hair. It was cute and white, like the Christmas angels my mother hung around our kitchen. It was so white you wanted to taste it, it was so shiny.

My dad didn't come back out. He hadn't forgotten anything, not anything that he had, anyway.

He'd said the cancer of the colon thing was nothing. It was good to get rid of your excess colon. You had two hundred feet of the stuff. What he was getting rid of was just excess. It wasn't anything. He said that about everything—him not going to work, finding me still asleep in the back of the car in the afternoon, stunned in the sun, the Florida room flooding and the television in water sparking, cops at the door at five in the afternoon, a woman trying to stab him on our patio on his birthday, me drinking beer and floating in the pool so that I could drown. It wasn't anything. None of it was anything.

I believed that I was going to be okay while I had the E. L.

I circled down out of the parking garage, pretending I was twenty-seven years old. I put on some more lip gloss, and my father's sunglasses. I changed the radio station to WDIZ, Rock 100, and it was Van Halen and I knew the song. "Pretty Woman." Ah, I said. "Oh Baby." That was a shame, because those words hung around in the car with me.

I drove down the Orange Blossom Trail, with the radio on really loud. I was looking for a drive-thru liquor window. I was going to try out the credit card I had been given by my pops.

The Olds was chugging funny. I wondered if spinning out, if losing it back there in the parking garage, had that hurt the car? He'd told me to take the car to Earl if I had any trouble. Earl at the Shell station was always trying to feel me. Earl had a cot behind the Coke cooler and a mattress in his Rescue Van. The misnomer of the century.

"Hey baby you sure look wonderful," a guy on a motorcycle yelled into my open window at the red light on Bumby.

"Oh, thank you," I said. It was so funny to me how no one knew what you had just done.

I wanted to use up this part of my life driving on the highway. I decided to take the Beeline to the beach, to Daytona Beach. I would just sit there in the sun. I was wearing diaper shorts. Those shorts that are printed with parrots and palm trees, of thin cotton, that you wrap up between your legs, and then the ties wrap around your waist. And my pink tube top. I looked pretty cute and skinny and tan and significantly older than fourteen. I could just sit on the beach on my diaper shorts, and if they got wet, I had on great underwear, that could just be my bathing suit and I could drive home in that easily.

The shins always lost their color first. I would get my shins back even with my arms and thighs. The tan was important.

I hurtled up the I-4 access ramp and took the Beeline Exit, a cloverleaf that I handled like an expert, and I loaded myself onto the highway. It felt like roller skating, going this fast after having been limited to low speeds for all these weeks. The rumble in the engine disappeared and I started breathing better. I sped up. I went a little faster than the speed limit, like everybody else. Something my father would never let me do.

Highway 50 draws a neat straight line across Florida, like a belt from the sea to the gulf. It was Tuesday in the middle of the after-noon. It was hot and salty, and the palms and the crotons and the oleanders planted along the sides of the highway looked scratchy and tired and somewhat poisonous, which they were. The sky was a washed-out blue, and I had tears in my eyes. I liked my high-way—no other cars. I liked my lane. It made a rhythm like my heart.

I headed to the sea.

I started steering with one hand. I powered down all the win-dows to one-half.

But then I changed my mind. I would go back and make myself a mimosa and sit in the pool, keep an eye on the Olds, and watch the stars come out and reheat some of the chicken Buck left for me in the microwave and then watch the Clint Eastwood channel. I didn't want to get stuck at the beach hungry and then have to drive back home in the dark. I didn't want to get stuck anywhere at all.

I pulled over, to a Fat Joe's. Gas. I needed gas. You always need gas if you have an Olds. They are true gas hogs. But I didn't want to buy gas at that juncture. I wanted to go right home and reset my head, break through the walls.

Highway 50 had quickly become peculiar to me. I couldn't tell which way was back to my dad's house, couldn't tell which way went on out to the ocean or the gulf. I went a ways and then, no, wrong way. To get back I had to go east. I looped around on the median, ten miles back the other way and then I would do it scared all over again. I kept passing the Fat Joe's. There were no signs that were useful to me. I must have turned around ten times. I was lost on a straight line.

I was lost on a straight line. The town back over in the marsh was Christmas. In Christmas, Florida, a town of 1,322, I was lost. I was lost, crying, then screaming. My throat hurt on both sides, like I had a scalpel there in my neck. The same kind of Florida scrub—palmettos and sword bushes passed in my windows. I couldn't read the sky. I couldn't figure it out.

One thing I remembered from my mother, the death scream. It's just a scream you can do when you are really upset and you want people to back off, to give you some room to work in. I screamed her scream, pleasant little legacy. Then I was shaking the car by the steering wheel, by the neck it seemed—everything was coming loose, the sky was one big blue eye and I could hardly see, soaked, red, a puff—let go and screamed thinking I'd fall. My dad's Olds rolled into a ditch.

My head didn't hit the windshield when the car banked and rocked over, so I slammed it against the windshield myself. It didn't crack. The jug of empty gin rollicked up to my feet, lay there like an accusation, a destiny. I pitched it out the window.

I was so wet between my legs I thought I had had an accident, or a female emergency, but it was just sweat. I thought, well, the back seat. A little sleep. But I was too sideways and I couldn't get back there. I had to sit on my own door. I had no idea which way to go. I wanted to walk down the highway with the steering wheel. That would be funny. Straight to the hospital, please. I did want to just share a room with my father. We could be together now.

I waited. No blood. I was just soaked with sweat. I kept looking at my face and head in the rearview mirror. No one came. I turned the rearview mirror to me so I could stare at myself without having to crane my neck. No contusions arose to the surface like lovely rose tattoos.

It was so hot. No cars passed me. Would I be a person walking into Christmas? I was sticking to the vinyl bad. It was hard not to think about Earl and his creepy van and my dad and his colon like a sausage in brine on our mantel. You can't get stuff like that out of your head unless you are willing to sacrifice years of memory around it, and at my age, that would pretty much wipe me out.

The pine trees were only about a foot outside the ditch. Their needles were so green, so dark, they seemed like ink up there, through my dad's window.

"Shut up, trees," I said. I spoke out loud. "Good-bye," I said, and turned the rearview mirror around so to face them, those scaly trees, and not me anymore. "Bad bye," I shouted. "How don't you do!"

Nothing seemed wrong, except the crowd was missing, and I knew my dad had been asked to lie down and breathe in a blue gas, and he was not thinking about me. There were dirty magazines at home on the dining room table. There was porn in the suitcase and both bathrooms. So I needed a boyfriend somewhat older than the Carrington boys and their innocent red boat with its sharp white flags.

Keep it on the road. I knew what he meant by that now.

In my next little dream he lived. And I died because I went off the road and that was the last thing. No one would know! This was my constant fix. I wanted to live in order to tell people, but in order to be interesting my good stories required my death.

I started screaming again, out loud or not, I don't know. Three big green Publix trucks passed fast and I felt my car wiggle and shudder, even though it was locked into mud. You know how some people start laughing to keep from crying, or so they say, I've never really seen anybody do that. I do the opposite.

In a ditch, in an Olds Delta 88, in Christmas, Florida, so sweaty I am smelling like formaldehyde, I started howling harder maybe than I have ever howled, and I have howled, because everything takes so long when you are a kid. I started screaming so hard my whole body hurt. I tried to rip my short blue shorts, but there wasn't a way to get a good grip on the denim. I was wet and huge mucous was everywhere. I was screaming red screams and scratching my face. No one came. There weren't that many people in Christmas. A cougar escaped from Circus Land two weeks ago, and they hadn't caught it yet. It was kind of a flat jungle. There aren't that many people in Florida. I know it must seem like it if you just see Florida on television, but the crowds here are clustered in pockets. It is mostly trees, cows, bushes, and bugs and more field scrub, a cougar or three. Not that many people. Fat Joe's. I didn't see the cougar.

I got out by opening up the passenger door, my dad's door now, and climbed out like from a box. Like the lady out of the cake. I said "Hello" when I got out. The car was so hot, like an eye on your stove. Man. My thighs sizzled. My diaper shorts were scooched up into my butt. Adjusting, I slid off of the car. It was hurt pretty bad. It made me think of an abandoned jungle gym, the brown knot of it.

I hopped down into the reeds.

I wiped my face off on the soft weeds, cattails, in the ditch. I threw my Emergency License and then my whole purse into the hyacinths because I would never ever be driving again. No one could make me.

I was lost, ankle deep in humus. It was noon, and the sky just kept going higher and higher, like each breath I took puffed my clean blue blanket off of me a little bit more.

I felt naked in my tube top and my parrots shorts. They were so short when you sat down it was like a bathing suit up around your thighs, tight and into the skin.

On my way up to the highway, I saw a baby alligator in the water in the ditch with my car, sunning on a stick in the muck— they always look like they are smiling, and I felt just like him. I wanted to slip into his mud with him, stay small and soft and have little bright teeth like that.

He couldn't remember a thing. He couldn't know why my car was lodged like a spaceship on his nest. He couldn't care less. He wasn't even really grinning.

It's like I was in a fog, but without the fog. Not that I was slow. I went to a special school called PEP. You had to be smart and you had to have some kind of problem. The same kids had always known me. One had a rod in her back, Sara. She'd been my best friend since I was seven, she said all the time to everyone. She made me wear her jewelry and her flower blouses over my halters. The others that went to PEP were all boys, brilliant nerds with epilepsy or hemophilia or something else like attention deficit disorder, something that didn't really show up to us or seem at all important. Me and Sara tied their shoes together while they did enormous and tormented math problems. We were supposed to teach each other. Sara and I taught the boys how to love us, how to be our lovers. I did all of this without speaking or remembering. The boys taught us how to balance checkbooks and exactly what the gonads were capable of. We had to translate Dolly Parton's measurements into metric. They were interested in learning that kind of thing. They liked the idea of taking pi out to the millionth digit, working it out on rolls of toilet paper. They got into fist fights over infinity and the Big Bang and the size of the largest mammalian penis.

"It's not the elephant. It's the guy from Austria in the *Guinness Book of World Records.*"

"It's a shark."

"Well, how are we defining largest? Length, bulk, circumference, or total cubic volume when erect?"

"You have to factor in flaccid weight, or you are an asshole, butt face."

Blue whale, I didn't say.

You will write us a love letter every morning, first thing when you get to school, okay boys? Sara had them all churning the stuff out. Now, we move to roses, she said. She actually said that. Next, promise rings! We'll make em, and you just give them to us when I say.

It was a great school.

We were allowed to write on the walls and to play the stock market in theory. The teacher talked on the phone all day, selling real estate.

I played along but I wasn't happy to receive presents from Sara's hostages. It didn't feel like love, it felt like school. I just wanted to cheat.

I wasn't really interested in anything except the film room down the hall because it was dark. There was only one movie in all those tin circles—*Michelangelo: Tragic Genius.* I was allowed to go there on Fridays and only if Sara came with me. We watched it and watched it and watched it on the wall. None of the boys were allowed in there with us. It was too much focus on the breast, Mr. Rose said, with Michelangelo, the tragic genius. I loved the stealing corpses part. I just loved it that you had to have an arm in order to draw an arm.

All those boys liked me and they made me the Queen of Dogs before school let out. They would follow me around the PEP classroom on their all fours, and bark and I spoke my secret language—"Zimba Marton. Cray Cray." They went crazy rolling at my feet. Sara got mad when I was made Queen, especially at her fiancé John Trombley rolling around and barking and salivating at my feet, the one she loved best, but you know she'd never marry him. She was just playing eighth grade. She would be different next year.

Now Sara Simko was the type who would go over to Fat Joe's and call the police, I think. She wasn't allowed to ride motorcycles or wear bikinis because of the rod in her back. She was a police caller. But I was scared to call. I was always a criminal-feeling girl. Like when the coffee money was stolen from the teachers' lounge at PEP I wondered: could it have been me? It wasn't, but I always worried.

I creeped over to that Fat Joe's, making it seem like I was just walking on in from any old direction.

I cried by the pumps. Maybe I would just get in someone's car. I walked up to the little booth with the money woman in it and pulled my shorts down better. They were hiked and wrinkled and all wet. I couldn't see the car and that was good. It was just below the horizon. Like the little yellow alligator, I couldn't see what happened.

The woman in the booth at the pumps gave me some questions, and tried to be helpful.

"Where you trying to go, Sweetie?"

I explained that I lived in South Orlando, and I had a car, not far away, and I was just lost.

"Oh sugar, it's okay, you want a Coke?" I didn't. She gave me directions to my subdivision. It was just a line she drew, a line that was also an arrow, and she put an "x" where my house was, at the end of the line. It angered me, this map. It was not what I needed. How was I supposed to figure out which way to hold that arrow? You could turn it an infinite number of directions.

"No, thanks," I said. My throat hurt like it had had something jammed into it.

I just wandered off across the parking lot, over to the line of pumps where truckers filled up their tanks. I mouthed the words "Taxi Cab" into the sky, and then I started humming Van Halen. Little bit of a dance, a sexy dance.

I stepped in front of a large red truck with a man filling two gas tanks, one on each side. His engine was running. This was illegal. I stood in front, aligning myself with where he stood in the back, looking into his grille, which had a piece of a bird, a pigeon, caught in it. The wing was fine, but the rest was a smeary mess. I looked at the road, and could tell I wouldn't ever know which way to go.

I said I was lost.

"Are you lost, girl?"

"My horse ran away," I said. "Our best paint." I fell onto him, and tried to cry. I wondered if maybe I should ask him to take me to a hospital, an orderly well-run mental hospital, but then how could I pick my dad up in two weeks, how could I keep the toilet on track?

His name was Michael it said on his shirt in red writing. He had hair like the fake icicles that hung on the gas pumps, dried-out white hair, salt and sun hair, but he was young. He had all kinds of deer horns and fish bait cartoons and turtle shells laid out across his dashboard. I thought of my egg. All this stuff. All this life that he had, all this that never spilled. I sat on the edge of the sofa-like seat in his truck while he paid and got me a Coke and him a carton of Marlboros.

"I can't find my way home." I had let the map blow off, even though there was no wind. I had no pockets. No change of clothes. I had no purse, no bra, not a dime, even the Emergency License was not on me. My long blonde hair was all around my hot pink tube top, like waves.

"Well, what's your name?"

"Georgia," I told him. "Like the state."

He smiled. "Where are you trying to get?" His lips were thin and white and his eyes were like horse's eyes, big and brown.

I liked it that he didn't ask where I was coming from.

"I don't know," I said. I knew this was the most radical thing I had done, even more radical than putting my dad's Olds in that deep wet ditch. It was a lie. A public lie. I thought it was a little sad that my lying debut had to take place at Fat Joe's in Christmas. But I was driving off the road, fast and hard. I had already spilled.

That afternoon, late, red, orange, and blue, in Room 2-7, in a hotel by the beach, a Daytona 500 truckers' hotel with no name, two stories, and long black railings wrapping around the second floor like a little prison or a Spanish condo, an odd long hour away from Orange Memorial Hospital, Michael showed me how much money he had on him. We went through his boots, $500 in each. His wallet on a chain, pictures of kids, $100 bills behind each of them, and $1000 in a secret pocket. We went through his shirt together, and there were secret inside places with $100 bills.

I wanted to lay it all out on the little round table and get all of the heads facing the same way. I pushed some of the bills towards each other, a little family of Franklins.

"Don't even fuck with me, not once, or I will kill you."

"Thank you," I said. "I won't." I felt I was doing well.

I got under the covers. I pulled the white sheet up to my neck and lay there with my arms at my sides. This made me think of my father. I smiled. This was my life! The brown scratchy bedspread smelled like cigarette smoke and when Michael sat down on the end of the bed, the smoke smell puffed and made me cough. He leaned forward, lit a cigarette with his silver lighter, and changed the channels on the television.

"You sure are quiet, girl," he said. He didn't look back at me. He had cartoons on really loud. "Let's get ourselves hungry," he said.

He put the cigarette in his mouth backwards, and pulled his shirt, a button shirt, over his head. His slim wrists slipped through the cuffs, and he threw the inside-out shirt on the television and kicked the cigarette back out. The arm of the shirt draped over the cartoons. He slid his belt out, and said, "What are you lookin' at?" in a mean voice but he was smiling. "Your hair looks so beautiful, gold on white," he said. "Against the sheets. My God," he said. "This is not what I was expecting when I woke up this morning. Angel hair."

"Where do you live?" I said. He turned up the air conditioner.

"To block out noise," he said, and I didn't follow up or imagine or do anything except take my diaper shorts off under the covers, and push them with my feet down to the end of the bed, under the spread, where things were heavy and tight.

"You never fucked a nigger, I hope," he said.

"No one," I whispered to him when he lay down next to me, on top of the spread. I could hardly move. I could feel my legs sweating and between my legs spreading. The light in the room was blue and although it was stuffy and close and strange, I liked it. I liked being away from the car, far from the freezer of chuck steak, the hospital. I liked not having my purse.

"I wish I had a photograph of you," I said.

"Why don't you get out from under there and let me look at you," he said. "Let me see a little bit more of ya." His voice was soft and sweet. He was watching television, the part you could see around the sleeve, while he talked to me, but it wasn't like my dad. He wanted to see me.

"No," I said. And Michael looked at me then, his white icicle hair didn't move, but he did. He took me in his arms and laughed. "You get down in here with me," I said. And I started kicking and kicking the heavy brown spread, making smoke smells puff into the room, and I got the stuff over him at last, and I said, "Let me take off your pants."

"What. Are you my angel?" he said and I was glad I was under the covers, in the brown tent, because I would have started laughing or maybe I would have burst into tears had I seen his face when he said *that*.

I unzipped his pants slowly, and then I started scooting them down his slim hips, over his funny bent hipbones. This is much harder to do than you would think. You have to really yank. It's nothing like a doll, which is smooth and plastic and purely dry. His skin looked older and his hair was blonde, all the way up his legs, curlier and curlier as you got to his gray underwear. The smell was of acid and lemons and sulfur. It was like playing tent with my brother when we were little, except for that complex smell.

I could not tell if he had a hard-on or not. I started kissing his knees, pulling the hairs with my teeth, and licking and kissing the skin, which was salty and fearless. And I worked my way up to the above-the-knee.

His hands came down under the covers like two cheerful squids. I was happy to feel them. He kneaded my butt and stroked me like I was a car, then a bird, then a saddle.

I was so wet it was like I had my period, and it was gross and strange and wonderful under those covers. I could hardly breathe, so I sounded like I was panting with pleasure, which I thought was a good thing.

"Are you my angel? Am I going to fall in love with you?" Woody Woodpecker made his famous noise, and it was like Woody talking to me. I had my eyes open and could only see the wall. I was licking the white scratchy sheet. I was numb from the waist down. I couldn't feel anything. My feet were sweating buckets, though. I could tell that.

"I hope not," I said as softly as I could talk which was very very soft.

We had shrimp dinner down at the pier late that night and he bought me a rose from the girl with them in her little white plastic basket.

"She's gorgeous," the girl said. "And you're going to get ten years. They have laws, Tackett," she said, laughing. I had this feeling they knew each other, but I had that feeling about every single set of people I encountered ever since I got my memory back. I liked the rose. It had black edges, and it was a tight bud.

It would never open. I knew that. Just looking at it.

"That will open up really nice in the next few days," he said. He was building River Country, part of Disney. He got paid in cash at the end of every day. He had cement poisoning, and I felt sure

I was going to get it on my legs too. He had a woman on his crew. He wouldn't be able to hire me on. There were too many problems with this one woman. She couldn't carry two buckets. She was willing to make two trips, but it wasn't fair. The men all hated her ways.

"I know what an Allen key is," I said. "I can fix a toilet. I know I could be very useful at River Country."

"Oh, you could be useful," Tackett said, and he put three shrimp tails into his mouth and crunched them in. "Ah," he said. I thought, the joke is on me. But, I didn't care. I wanted anything. Just to have more to think about than my dad, that life. People always are saying teenagers are difficult and crazy. We just want something other than the trouble we have.

We sat on the mess of bedcovers like we were in a nest. He was skinny without his clothes, a true stick. Like my dad without the pregnant belly, but this man was hard, whip thin, yellow-eyed, but a hard yellow, not that watery yellow. We watched cartoons on television for a long time, not talking. I put on his blue work shirt and snapped it up to the top of my neck. He made me take it off and go shower and dry off really good before he let me put it back on. He didn't say anything about the way I handled things. Maybe it had gone okay. It was easy to forget. It was so easy to know that things had always been this way.

He fell asleep with the television on at 10:33 P.M. I smelled him while he slept. The ceiling had a stain on it in the exact shape of the sausage-curled head of Marie Antoinette.

Sometime late in the night, the cartoons had turned to a black-and-white movie that didn't have any cars in it, just women who yelled out all these beautiful sentences at the men in a tiny office, big women in suits with big buttons, yelling but in the most sexy way you could imagine, like trumpets, many notes all spilling out at once—it was wonderful but it was too many words. I kept fearing a car would come on screen, or a car commercial, or even a horse-drawn carriage. I couldn't understand who was who or what the point was.

Michael Tackett was sleeping like a stick would sleep. Stiff and straight with his arms at his sides. Not a leaf stirred. I got up quick like a snake and put on his jeans. They had so much stuff on them. Dirt and writing and clots of cement. I felt like a building in progress. White streaks of caulk and sand in the pockets. I emptied his pockets. I didn't want to get killed.

I didn't want anything to happen. I didn't want one single moment anywhere in the world to go forward. Not because I was so happy, but because it seemed this was a good place to stop. Everything as yet undiscovered but completely changed—that was how I wanted to stay, but that isn't a way that can stay.

The door made a sucking sound as it locked behind me. I had the feeling I was leaving something behind, but I realized I was always going to have that feeling. That was the car, that was my dad, that was my dinner, and that was my stomach. That was my memory block, that was my brother in Wisconsin with our mother, that was the Emergency License. I walked outside, tip-toeing on the Astroturf into the parking lot.

It could have been anywhere in the whole world of Florida, I thought. The light was my same old lonely no-lover back seat of the car light at way past midnight in my dad's driveway light. The ROOMS $20 SEA PEARL L UNGE OPEN sign blinked in gold and peach letters and I looked back at the motel, all those dark windows like a hospital. Down the strip I could see more neon problems. BUG BOY. IMPER   GARDEN.

As I walked away from the hotel, his truck, down to the highway, I thought—everyone is going to be able to see me now. I am no longer invisible.

Right after he drifted off, he had started rolling his lips, saying "Shelley, Shelley, Shelley," over and over. It was hard to tell if he was mad at her, having sex with her, or she was driving, or what. I knew she would be the mother of the kids in his wallet, the hundred-dollar-bill kids. Then later he was humming emotionlessly.

He'd told me things about women and I kept thinking of those things, those shapes, those quantities, those colors, those holes, those words he said, all he knew.

I worked towards the highway where trucks were passing with the same noise that I always felt in my stomach, the whooshing. In a while, those trucks, they would pass by the yellow shiny baby alligator and my dad's yellow car in the ditch, as they closed in on Orlando. I started walking that way. The pavement was still hot from yesterday and my sandals were already wet and salty from my sweaty feet. The pines were all inky and sharp and salty alongside me. I touched my face—it had lines deep into it, from the coarse sheets, scratching. I smelled like cigarettes. His pants, now my pants, shifted around my body as I walked, like in a denim barrel, chafing. His shirt felt like a pelt on me.

I felt like my self was a vital organ beating, somehow staying alive inside an ancient husk that was not my own. My hair stuck to itself. A truck's horn blasted me off the highway, like it was the first sound I ever heard, the siren I had been waiting for all this time. It was a good kind of frightened to death.

The road, that straight line, was a geometry lesson. The air, its salt making me a kind of chemical reaction I cannot even describe. That new space inside of me.

It scared me, all of it. As much as the thought of the next thing.

1999

William Gay

THOSE DEEP ELM BROWN'S FERRY BLUES

William Gay is the author of two novels, The Long Home *and* Provinces of
Night, *and a collection of stories,* I Hate to See That Evening Sun Go Down.
*This story, like most of his fiction, is set in rural Tennessee, where he was born and
where he lives now. He says the inspiration for it was an old man with Alzheimer's
who could remember the tiniest details of a place he once lived, though he couldn't say
where that place was. "The memory seemed cut off and isolated. Nothing led up to it,
nothing led away. He became frustrated, and finally angry at his own impotence. I
felt an enormous empathy for him."*

I heard a whippoorwill last night, the old man said.
  Say you did? Rabon asked without interest. Rabon was
just in from his schoolteaching job. He seated himself in the armchair across from the bed and hitched up his trouser legs and
glanced covertly at his watch. The old man figured Rabon would
put in his obligatory five minutes then go in his room and turn the
stereo on.
  It sounded just like them I used to hear in Alabama when I was
a boy, Scribner said. Sometimes he would talk about whippoorwills or the phases of the moon simply because he got some perverse pleasure out of annoying Rabon. Rabon wanted his father's
mind sharp and the old man on top of things, and it irritated him
when the old man's mind grew preoccupied with whippoorwills
or drifted back across the Tennessee state line into Alabama. Scribner
was developing a sense of just how far he could push Rabon into
annoyance, and he fell silent, remembering how irritated Rabon

had been that time in Nashville when Scribner had recognized the doctor.

The doctor was telling Rabon what kind of shape Scribner was in, talking over the old man's head as if he wasn't even there. All this time Scribner was studying the doctor with a speculative look on his face, trying to remember where he had seen him. He could almost but not quite get a handle on it.

Physically he's among the most impressive men of his age I've examined, the doctor was saying. There's nothing at all to be concerned about there, and his heart is as strong as a man half his age. But Alzheimer's is irreversible, and we have to do what we can to control it.

Scribner had remembered. He was grinning at the doctor. I've seen you before, ain't I?

Excuse me?

I remember you now, the old man said. I seen you in Alabama.

I'm afraid not, the doctor said. I'm from Maine and this is the farthest south I've ever been.

Scribner couldn't figure why the doctor would lie about it. Sure you was. We was at a funeral. You was wearing a green checked suit and a little derby hat and carryin a black shiny walkin stick. There was a little spotted dog there lookin down in the grave and whinin and you rapped it right smart with that cane. I hate a dog at a funeral, you said.

The doctor was looking sympathetic, and Scribner knew he was going to try to lie out of it. Rabon was just looking annoyed. Who were you burying? he asked.

This confused Scribner. He tried to think. Hell, I don't know, he said. Some dead man.

I'm afraid you've got me mixed up with someone else, the doctor said.

Scribner was becoming more confused yet, the sand he was standing on was shifting, water rising about his shoes, his ankles.

I reckon I have, he finally said. That would have been sixty-odd years ago and you'd have to be a hell of a lot older than what you appear to be.

In the car Rabon said, If all you can do is humiliate me with these Alabama funeral stories I wish you would just let me do the talking when we have to come to Nashville.

You could handle that, all right, the old man said.

Now Scribner was back to thinking about whippoorwills. How Rabon was a science teacher who only cared about dead things and books. If you placed a whippoorwill between the pages of an enormous book and pressed it like a flower until it was a paper-thin collage of blood and feathers and fluted bone then Rabon might take an interest in that.

You remember that time a dog like to took your leg off and I laid it out with a hickory club?

No I don't, and I don't know where you dredge all this stuff up.

Dredge up hell, the old man said. I was four days layin up in jail because of it.

If it happened at all it happened to Alton. I can't recall you ever beating a dog or going to jail for me. Or acknowledging my existence in any other way, for that matter.

The old man was grinning slyly at Rabon. Pull up your britches leg, he said.

What?

Pull up your britches leg and let's have a look at it.

Rabon's slacks were brown-and-tan houndstooth checked. He gingerly pulled the cuff of one leg up to the calf.

I'm almost sure it was the other one, Scribner said.

Rabon pulled the other leg up. He was wearing wine-colored calf-length socks. Above the sock was a vicious-looking scar where the flesh had been shredded, the puckered scar red and poreless and shiny as celluloid against the soft white flesh.

Ahh, the old man breathed.

Rabon dropped his cuff. I got this going through a barbed-wire fence when I was nine years old, he said.

Sure you did, the old man said. I bet a German shepherd had you by the leg when you went through it, too.

Later he slept fitfully with the light on. When he awoke, he didn't know what time it was. Where he was. Beyond the window it was dark, and the lighted window turned the room back at him. He didn't know for a moment what room he was in, what world the window opened onto. The room in the window seemed cut loose and disassociate, adrift in the space of night.

He got up. The house was quiet. He wandered into the bathroom and urinated. He could hear soft jazzy piano music coming from somewhere. He went out of the bathroom and down a hall adjusting his trousers and into a room where a pudgy man wearing wire-rimmed glasses was seated at a desk with a pencil in his hand, a sheaf of papers spread before him. The man looked up, and the room rocked and righted itself, and it was Rabon.

The old man went over and seated himself on the side of the bed.

You remember how come I named you Rabon and your brother Alton?

Yes, the man said, making a mark on a paper with a red-leaded pencil.

Scribner might not have heard. It was in Limestone County, Alabama, he said. I growed up with Alton and Rabon Delmore, and they played music. Wrote songs. I drove them to Huntsville to make their first record. Did I ever tell you about that?

No more than fifty or sixty times, Rabon said. But I could always listen to it again.

They was damn good. Had some good songs, "Deep Elm Blues," "Brown's Ferry Blues." "When you go down to Deep Elm keep your money in your shoes," the first line went. They wound up on the Grand Ole Opry. Wound up famous. They never forgot where they come from, though. They was just old country boys. I'd like to hear them songs again.

I bought you a cassette player and all those old-time country and bluegrass tapes.

I know it. I appreciate it. Just seems like I can't ever get it to work right. It ain't the same anyway.

I'll take Brubeck myself.

If that's who that is then you can have my part of him.

It's late, Papa. Don't you think you ought to be asleep?

I was asleep. Seems like I just catnap. Sleep when I'm sleepy. Wake up when I'm not. Not no night and day anymore. Reckon why that is?

I've got all this work to do.

Go ahead and work then. I won't bother you.

The old man sat silent a time watching Rabon grade papers. Old man heavy in the chest and shoulders, looking up at the schoolteacher out of faded eyes. Sheaf of iron-gray hair. His pale eyes flickered as if he'd thought of something, but he remained silent. He waited until Rabon finished grading the paper he was working on and in the space between his laying it aside and taking up another one the old man said, Say, whatever happened to Alton, anyway?

Rabon laid the paper aside ungraded. He studied the old man. Alton is dead, he said.

Dead? Say he is? What'd he die of?

He was killed in a car wreck.

The old man sat in silence digesting this as if he didn't quite know what to make of it. Finally he said, Where's he buried at?

Papa, Rabon said, for a moment the dense flesh of his face transparent so that Scribner could see a flicker of real pain, then the flesh coalesced into its customary opaque mask and Rabon said again, I've got to do all this work.

I don't see how you can work with your own brother dead in a car wreck, Scribner said.

Sometime that night, or another night, he went out the screen door onto the back porch, dressed only in his pajama bottoms, the night air cool on his skin. Whippoorwills were tolling out of the dark and a milky blind cat's eye of a moon hung above the jagged treeline. Out there in the dark patches of velvet, patches of silver where moonlight was scattered through the leaves like coins. The world looked strange yet in some way familiar. Not a world he was seeing, but one he was remembering. He looked down expecting to see a child's bare feet on the floorboards and saw that he had heard the screen door slap to as a child but had inexplicably become an old man, gnarled feet on thin blue shanks of legs, and the jury-rigged architecture of time itself came undone, warped and ran like melting glass.

Naked to the waist Scribner sat on the bed while the nurse wrapped his biceps to take his blood pressure. His body still gleamed from the sponge bath and the room smelled of rubbing alcohol. Curious-looking old man. Heavy chest and shoulders and arms like a weight lifter. The body of a man twenty-five years his junior. The image of the upper torso held until it met the wattled red flesh of his throat, the old man's head with its caved cheeks and wild gray hair, the head with its young man's body like a doctored photograph.

Mr. Scribner, this thing will barely go around your arm, she said. I bet you were a pistol when you were a younger man.

I'm a pistol still yet, and cocked to go off anytime, the old man said. You ought to go a round with me.

My boyfriend wouldn't care for that kind of talk, the nurse said, pumping up the thingamajig until it tightened almost painfully around his arm.

I wasn't talkin to your boyfriend, Scribner said. He takin care of you?

I guess he does the best he can, she said. But I still bet you were something twenty-five years ago.

What was you like twenty-five years ago?

Two years old, she said.

You ought to give up on these younger men, he said, studying the heavy muscles of his forearms, his still-taut belly. Brighten up a old man's declinin years.

Hush that kind of talk, she said. Taking forty kinds of pills and randy as a billygoat.

Hellfire, you give me a bath. You couldn't help but notice how I was hung.

She turned quickly away but not so quickly the old man couldn't see the grin.

Nasty talk like that is going to get a soapy washrag crammed in your mouth, she said.

With his walking cane for a snakestick the old man went through a thin stand of half-grown pines down into the hollow and past a herd of plywood cattle to where the hollow flattened out then climbed gently toward the roadbed. The cattle were life-size silhouettes jigsawed from sheets of plywood and affixed to two-by-fours driven in the earth. They were painted gaudily with bovine smiles and curving horns. The old man passed through the herd without even glancing at them, as if in his world all cattle were a half-inch thick and garbed up with bright lacquer. Rabon had once been married to a woman whose hobby this was, but now she was gone, and there was only this hollow full of wooden cattle.

He could have simply taken the driveway to the roadbed but he liked the hot, astringent smell of the pines and the deep shade of the hollow. All his life the woods had calmed him, soothed the violence that smoldered just beneath the surface.

When he came onto the cherted roadbed he stopped for a moment, leaning on his stick to catch his breath. He was wearing bedroom slippers and no socks and his ankles were crisscrossed with bleeding scratches from the dewberry briars he'd walked through. He went on up the road as purposefully as a man with a conscious destination though in truth he had no idea where the road led.

It led to a house set back amid ancient oak trees, latticed by shade and light and somehow imbued with mystery to the old man's eyes, like a cottage forsaken children might come upon in a fairy-tale wood. He stood by the roadside staring at it. It had a vague familiarity, like an image he had dreamed then come upon unexpectedly in the waking world. The house was a one-story brick with fading cornices painted a peeling white. It was obviously unoccupied. The yard was grown with knee-high grass gone to seed and its uncurtained windows were opaque with refracted light. Untrimmed tree branches encroached onto the roof and everything was steeped in a deep silence.

A hand raised to shade the sun-drenched glass, the old man peered in the window. No one about, oddments of furniture, a wood stove set against a wall. He climbed onto the porch and sat in a cedar swing for a time, rocking idly, listening to the creak of the chains, the hot, sleepy drone of dirt daubers on the August air. There were boxes of junk stacked against the wall, and after a time he began to sort through one of them. There were china cats and dogs, a cookie jar with the shapes of cookies molded and painted onto the ceramic. A picture in a gilt frame that he studied until the edges of things shimmered eerily then came into focus, and he thought: This is my house.

He knew he used to live here with a wife named Ellen and two sons named Alton and Rabon and a daughter named Karen. Alton is dead in a car wreck, he remembered, and he studied Karen's face intently as if it were a gift that had been handed to him unexpectedly, and images of her and words she had said assailed him in a surrealistic collage so that he could feel her hand in his, a little girl's hand, see white patent-leather shoes climbing concrete steps into a church, one foot, the other, the sun caught like something alive in her auburn hair.

Then another image surfaced in his mind: his own arm, silver in the moonlight, water pocked with light like hammered metal, something gleaming he threw sinking beneath the surface, then just the empty hand drawing back and the muscular freckled forearm with a chambray work shirt rolled to the biceps. Somewhere upriver a barge, lights arcing over the river like searchlights trying to find him. That was all. Try as he might he could call nothing else to mind. It troubled him because the memory carried some dark undercurrent of menace.

With a worn Case pocketknife he sliced himself a thin sliver of Apple chewing tobacco Rabon didn't know he'd hoarded, held it in his jaw savoring the taste. He walked about the yard thinking movement might further jar his memory into working. He paused at a silver maple that summer lightning had struck, the raw wound winding in a downward spiral to the earth where the bolt had gone to ground. He stood studying the splintered tree with an old man's bemusement, as if pondering whether this was something he might fix.

Say, whatever happened to that Karen, anyway? he asked Rabon that night. Rabon had dragged an end table next to the old man's bed and set a plate and a glass of milk on it. Try not to get this all over everything, he said.

Scribner was wearing a ludicrous-looking red-and-white-checked bib Rabon had tied around his neck, and with a knife in one hand and a fork in the other he was eyeing the plate as if it were something he was going to attack.

Your sister, Karen, the old man persisted.

I don't hear from Karen anymore, Rabon said. I expect she's still up there around Nashville working for the government.

Workin for the government? What's she doin?

They hired her to have one baby after another, Rabon said. She draws that government money they pay for them. That AFDC, money for unwed mothers, whatever.

Say she don't ever call or come around?

I don't have time for any of that in my life, Rabon said. She liked the bright lights and the big city. Wild times. Drinking all night and laying up with some loafer on food stamps. I doubt it'd do her much good to come around here.

I was thinkin about her today when she was a little girl.

She hasn't been a little girl for a long time, Rabon said, shutting it off, closing another door to something he didn't want to talk about.

• • •

Past midnight Scribner was lying on top of the covers, misshapen squares of moonlight thrown across him by the windowpanes. He had been thinking about Karen when he remembered shouting, crying, blood. When he pulled her hands away from her face they came away bloody and her mouth was smashed with an incisor cocked at a crazy angle and blood dripping off her chin. One side of her jaw was already swelling.

Where is he?

I don't know, she said. He's left me. He drove away. No telling where he's gone.

Wherever it is I doubt it's far enough, he said, already leaving, his mind already suggesting and discarding places Pulley might be.

Don't hurt him.

He gave her a long, level glance but he didn't say if he would or he wouldn't. Crossing the yard toward his truck he stepped on an aluminum baseball bat that belonged to Alton. He stooped and picked it up and went on to the truck, swinging it along in his hands, and threw it onto the floorboard.

He wasn't in any of his usual haunts. Not the Snowwhite Café, the pool hall. In Skully's City Café the old man drank a beer and bought one for a crippled drunk in a wheelchair.

Where's your runnin mate, Hudgins?

Bonedaddy? He was in here a while ago. He bought a case of beer and I reckon he's gone down to that cabin he's got on the Tennessee River.

Why ain't you with him? The old man did not even seem angry. A terrible calm had settled over him. You couldn't rattle him with a jackhammer.

He's pissed about somethin, said he didn't have time to fool with me. I know he's gone to the river though, he had that little snake pistol he takes.

The night was far progressed before he found the right cabin. It set back against a bluff and there was a wavering campfire on the riverbank and Bonedaddy sat before it drinking beer. When Scribner approached the fire, Bonedaddy glanced at the bat and took the nickel-plated pistol out of his pocket and laid it between his feet.

Snake huntin? the old man asked.

These cottonmouth hides ain't worth nothin, Bonedaddy said. Nobody wants a belt made out of em. Too muddy lookin and no pattern to speak of. I mostly shoot copperheads and rattlesnakes. Once in a while just whatever varmint wanders up to the fire.

Scribner was watching Bonedaddy's right hand. The left clasped a beer bottle but the right never strayed far from the pistol. The hand was big and heavy-knuckled and he couldn't avoid thinking of it slamming into Karen's mouth.

You knocked her around pretty good, he said. You probably ain't more than twice her size.

She ought not called me a son of a bitch. Anybody calls me that needs to have size and all such as that into consideration before they open their mouth.

The old man didn't reply. He hunkered, watching the hammered-looking water, the farther shore that was just a land in darkness, anybody's guess, a world up for grabs. He listened to the river sucking at the banks like an animal trying to find its way in. He saw that people lived their own lives, went their own way. They grew up and lived lives that did not take him into consideration.

I don't want to argue, Bonedaddy said, patient as a teacher explaining something to a pupil who was a little slow. Matter of fact I come down here to avoid it. But there's catfish in this river six or eight feet long, what they tell me. And if you don't think I'll shoot you and feed you to them then you need to say so right now.

The hand had taken up the pistol. When it started around its arc was interrupted by Scribner swinging the ball bat. He swung from the ground up as hard as he could, like a batter trying desperately for the outfield wall. The pistol fired once and went skittering away. Bonedaddy made some sort of muffled grunt and crumpled in the leaves. The old man looked at the bat in his hands, at Bonedaddy lying on his back. His hands were flexing. Loosening, clasping. They loosened nor would they clasp again.

His head looked like something a truck had run over. Scribner glanced at the bat in mild surprise, then turned and threw it in the river. Somewhere off in the milk-white fog the throaty horn of a barge sounded, lights arced through the murk vague as lights seen in the muddy depths of the river.

He dragged Bonedaddy to the cabin then up the steps and inside. There was a five-gallon can of kerosene and he soaked the floors with it, hurled it at the walls. He lit it with a torch from the campfire. With another he searched for blood in the leaves. Bonedaddy's half-drunk beer was propped against a weathered husk of stump, and for a reason he couldn't name Scribner picked it up and drank it and slung the bottle into the river.

He stayed to see that everything burned. When the roof caught, an enormous cedar lowering onto it burst into flame and burned white-hot as a magnesium flare, sparks rushing skyward in the roaring updraft, like a pillar of fire God had inexplicably set against the wet, black bluff.

Hey, he said, trying to shake Rabon awake.

Rabon came awake reluctantly, his hands trying to fend the old man away. Scribner kept shaking him roughly. Get up, he said. Rabon sat up in bed rubbing his eyes. What is it? What's the matter?

I killed a feller, Scribner said.

Rabon was instantly alert. What the hell are you talking about? He was looking all about the room as if he might see some outstretched burglar run afoul of the old man.

A feller named Willard Pulley. Folks called him Bonedaddy. I killed him with Alton's baseball bat and set him afire. Must be twenty years ago. He had a shiny little pistol he kept wavin in my face.

Are you crazy? You had a bad dream, you never killed anybody. Go back to sleep.

I ain't been asleep, Scribner said.

Rabon was looking at his watch. It's two o'clock in the morning, he said, as if it were the deadline for something. The old man was watching Rabon's eyes. Something had flickered there when

he had mentioned Willard Pulley but he couldn't put a name to
what he had seen: anger, apprehension, fear. Then it all smoothed
into irritation, an expression Scribner was so accustomed to seeing that he had no difficulty interpreting it.

You know who I'm talkin about?

Of course I know who you're talking about. You must have had
a nightmare about him because we were talking about Karen. He
did once live with Karen, but nobody killed him, nobody set him
afire, as you put it. He was just a young drunk and now he's an old
drunk. It hasn't been a week since I saw him lounging against the
front of the City Café, the way he's done for twenty-five years. You
were dreaming.

I ain't been asleep, Scribner said, but he had grown uncertain
even about this. His mind had gone over to the other side where
the enemy camped, truth that had once been hard-edged as
stone had turned ephemeral and evasive. Subject to gravity, it ran
through the cracks and pooled on the floorboards like quicksilver.
He was reduced to studying people's eyes for the reaction to something he had said, trying to mirror truth in other people's faces.

In the days following, a dull rage possessed him. Nor would
it abate. He felt ravaged, violated. Somewhere along the line his
life had been stolen. Some hand furtive as a pickpocket's had
taken everything worth taking and he hadn't even missed it.
Ellen and his children and a house that was his own had fallen by
the wayside. He was left bereft and impotent, dependent upon
the whims and machinations of others. Faceless women prodded
him with needles, spooned tasteless food into him, continually
downloaded an endless supply of pills even horses couldn't swallow. The pills kept coming, as if these women were connected
directly to their source, so that no matter how many he ingested
there was always a full tray waiting atop the bureau. He pon-
dered upon all this and eventually the pickpocket had a face as
well as a hand. The puppeteer controlling all these strings was
Rabon.

At noon a nameless woman in a dusty Bronco brought him a Styrofoam tray of food. He sat down in Rabon's recliner in the living room and prepared to eat. A mouthful of tasteless mashed potatoes clove to his palate, grew rubbery and enormous so that he could not swallow it. He spat it onto the carpet. This is the last goddamned straw, he said. All his life he'd doubled up on the salt and pepper and now the food everyone brought him was cooked without benefit of grease or seasoning. There was a compartment of poisonous-looking green peas and he began to pick them up one by one and flick them at the television screen. Try not to get this all over everything, he said.

When the peas were gone he carried the tray to the kitchen. He raked the carrots and mashed potatoes into the sink and found a can of peas in a cabinet and opened them with an electric can opener. Standing in the living room doorway he began to fling handfuls of them onto the carpet, scattering them about the room as if he were sowing them.

When the peas were gone he got the tray of pills and went out into the back yard. The tray was compartmentalized, Monday, Tuesday, all the days of the week. He dumped them all together as if time had no further significance, as if all days were one.

Rabon had a motley brood of scraggly-looking chickens that were foraging for insects near a split-rail fence, and Scribner began to throw handfuls of pills at them. They ran excitedly about pecking up the pills and searching for more. Get em while they're hot, the old man called. These high-powered vitamins'll have you sailin like hawks and singin like mockinbirds.

He went in and set the tray in its accustomed place. From the bottom of the closet he took up the plastic box he used for storing his tapes. Wearing the look of a man burning the last of his bridges, he began to unspool them, tugging out the thin tape until a shell was empty, discarding it and taking up another. At length they were all empty. He sat on the bed with his hands on his knees. He did not move for a long time, his eyes black and depthless and empty-looking, ankle-deep in dead bluegrass musicians and shredded mandolins and harps and flattop guitars, in old lost songs nobody wanted anymore.

Rabon was standing in the doorway wiping crushed peas off the soles of his socks. The old man lay on the bed with his fingers laced behind his skull watching Rabon through slitted eyes.

What the hell happened in the living room? Where did all those peas come from?

A bunch of boys done it, Scribner said. Broke in here. Four or five of the biggest ones held me down and the little ones throwed peas all over the front room.

Do you think this is funny? Rabon asked.

Hell no. You try bein held down by a bunch of boys and peas throwed all over the place. See if you think it's funny. I tried to run em off but I'm old and weak and they overpowered me.

We'll see how funny it is from the door of the old folks' home, Rabon said. Or the crazyhouse. Rabon was looking at the medicine tray. What happened to all those pills?

The chickens got em, Scribner said.

The going was slower than he had expected and by the time the chert road topped out at the crossroads where the blacktop ran it was ten o'clock and the heat was malefic. The treeline shimmered like something seen through bad glass and the blacktop radiated heat upward as if somewhere beneath it a banked fire smoldered.

He stood for a time in the shade of a pin oak debating his choices. He was uncertain about going on, but then again it was a long way back. When he looked down the road the way he had come, the perspiration burning his eyes made the landscape blur in and out of focus like something with a provisional reality, like something he'd conjured but could not maintain. After a while he heard a car, then saw its towed slipstream of dust, and when it stopped for the sign at the crossroads he was standing on the edge of the road leaning on his stick.

The face of the woman peering out the car window at him was

familiar but he could call no name to mind. He was wearing an old brown fedora and he tipped the brim of it in a gesture that was almost courtly.

Mr. Scribner, what are you doing out in all this heat?

Sweatin a lot, Scribner said. I need me a ride into town if you're goin that far.

Why of course, the woman said. Then a note of uncertainty crept into her voice. But aren't you . . . where is Rabon? We heard you were sick. Are you supposed to be going to town?

I need to get me a haircut and a few things. There ain't nothin the matter with me, either. That boy's carried me to doctors all over Tennessee and can't none of em kill me.

If you're sure it's all right, she said, moving her purse off the passenger seat to make room. Get in here where it's air-conditioned before you have a stroke.

He got out on the town square of Ackerman's Field and stood for a moment sizing things up, getting his bearings. He crossed at the traffic light and went on down the street to the City Café by some ingrained habit older than the sense of strangeness the town had acquired.

In midmorning the place was almost deserted, three stools occupied by drunks he vaguely recognized, bleary-eyed sots with nowhere else to be. He sat down at the bar, just breathing in the atmosphere: the ancient residue of beer encoded into the very woodwork, sweat, the intangible smell of old violence. There was something evocative about it, almost nostalgic. The old man had come home.

He laid his hat on the counter and studied the barman across from him. Let me have two tall Budweisers, he said, already fumbling at his wallet. He had it in a shirt pocket and the pocket itself secured with a large safety pin. It surprised him that the beer actually appeared, Skully sliding back the lid of the cooler and turning with two frosty cans of Budweiser and setting them on the Formica bar. The old man regarded them with mild astonishment. Well now, he said. He fought an impulse to look over his shoulder and see was Rabon's rubbery face pressed to the glass watching him.

You got a mouse in your pocket, Mr. Scribner? a grinning Skully asked him.

No, it's just me myself, Scribner said, still struggling clumsily with the safety pin. He had huge hands grown stiff and clumsy and he couldn't get it unlatched. I always used one to chase the other one with.

I ain't seen you in here in a long time.

That boy keeps me on a pretty tight leash. I just caught me a ride this mornin and came to town. I need me a haircut and a few things.

You forget that money, Skully said. I ain't taking it. These are on the house for old time's sake.

Scribner had the wallet out. He extracted a bill and smoothed it carefully on the bar. He picked up one of the cans and drank from it, his Adam's apple convulsively pumping the beer down, the can rattling emptily when he set it atop the bar. He turned and regarded the other three drinkers with a benign magnanimity, his eyes slightly unfocused. Hidy boys, he said.

How you, Mr. Scribner?

He slid the bill across to Skully. I thank you for the beer, he said. Let me buy them high-binders down the bar a couple.

There was a flurry of goodwill from the drunks downbar toward this big spender from the outlands and the old man accepted their thanks with grace and drank down the second can of beer.

We heard you was sick and confined to your son's house, Skully said. You look pretty healthy to me. What's supposed to be the matter with you?

I reckon my mind's goin out on me, Scribner said. It fades in and out like a weak TV station. I expect to wake up some mornin with no mind atall. There ain't nothin wrong with me, though. He hit himself in the chest with a meaty fist. I could still sweep this place out on a Saturday night. You remember when I used to do that.

Yes I do.

I just can't remember names. What went with folks. All last week I was thinkin about this old boy I used to see around. Name of Willard Pulley. I couldn't remember what become of him. Folks called him Bonedaddy.

Let me see, now, Skully said.

He's dead, one of the men down the bar said.

Scribner turned so abruptly the stool spun with him and he almost fell. What? he asked.

He's dead. He got drunk and burnt hisself up down on the Tennessee River. Must be over twenty years ago.

Wasn't much gone, another said. He ain't no kin to you is he?

No, no, I just wondered what become of him. And say he's dead sure enough?

All they found was ashes and bones. That's as dead as I ever want to be.

I got to get on, the old man said. He rose and put on his hat and shoveled his change into a pocket and took up his stick.

When the door closed behind him with its soft chime, one of the drunks said, There goes what's left of a hell of a man. I've worked settin trusses with him where the foreman would have three men on one end and just him on the other. He never faded nothin.

He wasn't lying about cleaning this place out, either, Skully said. He'd sweep it out on a Saturday night like a longhandled broom but he never started nothin. He'd set and mind his own business. Play them old songs on the jukebox. It didn't pay to fuck with him though.

The old man sat in the barber chair, a towel wound about his shoulders and he couldn't remember what he wanted. I need a, he said, and the word just wasn't there. He thought of words, inserting them into the phrase and trying them silently in his mind to see if they worked. I need a picket fence, a bicycle, a heating stove. The hot blood of anger and humiliation suffused his throat and face.

What kind of haircut you want, Mr. Scribner?

A haircut, the old man said in relief. Why hell yes. That's what I want, a haircut. Take it all off. Let me have my money's worth.

All of it?

Just shear it off.

When Scribner left, his buzzcut bullet head was hairless as a cue ball and the fedora cocked at a jaunty angle. He drank two more beers at Skully's, then thought he'd amble down to the courthouse lawn and see who was sitting on the benches there. When he stood on the sidewalk, the street suddenly yawned before him as if he were looking down the sides of a chasm onto a stream of dark water pebbled with moonlight. He'd already commenced his step and when he tried to retract it he overbalanced and pitched into the street. He tried to catch himself with his palms, but his head still rapped the asphalt solidly, and lights flickered on and off behind his eyes. He dragged himself up and was sitting groggily on the sidewalk when Skully came out the door.

Skully helped him up and seated him against the wall. I done called the ambulance, he said. He retrieved Scribner's hat and set it carefully in the old man's lap. Scribner sat and watched the blood running off his hands. Somewhere on the outskirts of town a siren began, the approaching *whoop whoop whoop* like some alarm the old man had inadvertently triggered that was homing in on him.

All this silence was something the old man was apprehensive about. Rabon hadn't even had much to say when, still in his schoolteaching suit, he had picked Scribner up at the emergency room. Once he had ascertained that the old man wasn't seriously hurt he had studied his new haircut and his bandaged hands and said, I believe this is about it for me.

He hadn't even gone in to teach the next day. He had stayed in his bedroom with the door locked, talking on the telephone. Scribner could hear the rise and fall of the mumbling voice but even with an ear to the door he could distinguish no word. It was his opinion that Rabon was calling one old folks' home after another trying to find one desperate enough to take him, and he had no doubt that sooner or later he would succeed.

The day drew on strange and surreal. His life was a series of instants, each one of which bore no relation to the one preceding, the one following. He was reborn moment to moment. He had long taken refuge in the past, but time had proven laden with deadfalls he himself had laid long ago, with land mines that were better not stepped on. So he went further back, to the land of his childhood, where everything lay under a troubled truce. Old voices long silenced by the grave spoke again, their ancient timbres and cadences unchanged by time, by death itself. He was bothered by the image of the little man in the green checked suit and the derby hat, rapping the spotted dog with a malacca cane and saying: I just hate a dog at a funeral, don't you? Who the hell was that? Scribner wondered, the dust of old lost roads coating his bare feet, the sun of another constellation warming his back.

He looked out the window and dark had come without his knowing it. A heavy-set man in wire-rimmed glasses brought a tray of food. Scribner did not even wonder who this might be. The man was balding and when he stooped to arrange the tray, Scribner could see the clean pink expanse of scalp through the combed-over hair. The man went out of the room. Scribner, looking up from his food, saw him cross through the hall with a bundle of letters and magazines. He went into Rabon's room and closed the door.

Scribner finished the plate of food without tasting it.

He might have slept. He came to himself lying on the bed, the need to urinate so intense it was almost painful. He got up. He could hear a television in the living room, see the spill of yellow light from Rabon's bedroom, the bathroom.

His bandaged hands made undoing his clothing even more complicated and finally he just pulled down his pajama bottoms, the stream of urine already starting, suddenly angry at Rabon, why the hell has he got all his plunder in the bathroom, these shoes, suits, these damned golf clubs?

Goddamn, a voice cried. The old man whirled. Rabon was

standing in the hall with the *TV Guide* in his hand. His eyes were wide with an almost comical look of disbelief. My golf shoes, he said, flinging the *TV Guide* at Scribner's bullet head and rushing toward him. Turning his head, the old man realized that he was standing before Rabon's closet, urinating on a rack of shoes.

When Rabon's weight struck him he went sidewise and fell heavily against the wall, his penis streaking the carpet with urine. He slid down the wall and struggled to a kneeling position, trying to get his pajama bottoms up, a fierce tide of anger rising behind his eyes.

Rabon was mad too, in fact angrier than the old man had ever seen him. He had jerked up the telephone and punched in a series of numbers, stood with the phone clasped to his ear and a furious impatient look on his face, an expression that did not change until the old man struck him in the side of the head with an enormous fist. The phone flew away and when Rabon hit the floor with the old man atop him, Scribner could hear it gibbering mechanically at him from the carpet.

The hot, clammy flesh was distasteful to his naked body but Scribner had never been one to shirk what had to be done. With Rabon's face clasped to his breast and his powerful arms locked in a vise that tightened, they looked like perverse lovers spending themselves on the flowered carpet.

When Rabon was still, the old man got up, pushing himself erect against Rabon's slack shoulder. He went out the bedroom door and through a room where a television set flickered, his passage applauded by canned laughter from the soundtrack, and so out into the night.

Night air cool on his sweaty skin. A crescent moon like a sliver of bone cocked above the treeline, whippoorwills calling out of the musky keep of the trees. He stood for a moment sensing directions and then he struck out toward the whippoorwills. He went down into the hollow through the herd of plywood cattle pale as the ghosts of cattle and on toward the voices that called out of the dark. He came onto the spectral roadbed and crossed into deeper woods. The whippoorwills were drawing away from him, urging him deeper into the shadowed timber, and he realized abruptly that the voices were coming from the direction of Brown's Ferry or Deep Elm. Leaning against the bole of a white oak to catch his breath he became aware of a presence in the woods before him, and he saw with no alarm that it was a diminutive man in a green plaid suit, derby hat shoved back rakishly over a broad pale forehead, gesturing him on with a malacca cane.

They're up here, the little man called.

Scribner went on, barefoot, his thin pajama bottoms shredding in the undergrowth of winter huckleberry bushes. Past a stand of stunted cedars the night opened up into an enormous tunnel, as wide and high as he could see, a tunnel of mauve-black gloom where whippoorwills darted and checked like bats feeding on the wing, a thousand, ten thousand, each calling to him out of the dark, and he and the man with the malacca cane paused and sat for a time against a tree trunk to rest themselves before going on.

2000

Thomas H. McNeely

SHEEP

The narrator of "Sheep," Thomas McNeely's first published work of fiction, is accused of a terrible crime of which he has no knowledge. And he gravely misinterprets the intentions of the sheriff who arrested him and those of his court appointed lawyer. The author, who once worked for a nonprofit law firm in Texas that defended death row cases, says, "All of my models for Lloyd, unfortunately, are dead. The story is a tribute to their courage, and the courage of the people who defended them." A Wallace Stegner Fellow in creative writing at Stanford University where he is currently a Jones Lecturer in fiction, he is at work on a novel.

Before the sheriff came to get him, Lloyd found the sheep out by the pond. He'd counted head that morning and come up one short. He did the count over, because he was still hazy from the night before. And he'd waked with a foul smell in his nose. So he had gone into Mr. Mac's house—it was early morning; the old man would be dead to the world—and filled his canteen with white lightning. He felt shaky and bad, and the spring morning was cold. He shouldn't have gone to town the night before.

The sheep lay on its side in some rushes. A flow of yellowish mucus was coming from its nose, and its eyes were sickly thin slits that made it look afraid. Lloyd thought the sheep honorable—it had gone off to die so that it wouldn't infect the rest of the flock. Lloyd knew that the sheep's sickness was his fault and that he couldn't do anything about it, but he squatted down next to the animal and rubbed its underside. In this hour before sunrise, when the night dew was still wet, the warmth and animal smell felt good. Lloyd moved his hand in circles over the sheep's lightly furred pink skin and lines of blue veins, its hard cage of ribs, its slack, soft belly.

Across the pond the sun peeked through the Panhandle dust over a low line of slate-gray clouds. With his free hand Lloyd took his canteen from a pocket in his jacket, clamped it between his knees, opened it, and drank. For a moment the liquor stung the sides of his tongue; then it dissolved in him like warm water. The sheep's lungs lifted up and down; its heart churned blood like a slowly pounding fist. Soon the sun broke free and the pond, rippled by a slight breeze, ignited in countless tiny candle flames. When Lloyd was a child, Mr. Mac used to tell him that at the Last Judgment the pond would become the Lake of Fire, into which all sinners would be cast. Lloyd could still picture them falling in a dark stream, God pouring them out like a bag of nails. The sheep closed its eyes against the light.

When Sheriff Lynch walked up behind him, Lloyd started. He still caressed the sheep, but it was dead and beginning to stiffen. His canteen felt almost empty; it fell from his fingers. By the sun Lloyd saw it was almost noon. Big black vultures wheeled so high above that they looked the size of mockingbirds. Uneasiness creeping on him, Lloyd waited for the sheriff to speak.

Finally the sheriff said, "Son, looks like that sheep's dead."

"Yessir," Lloyd said, and tried to stand, but his legs were stiff and the liquor had taken his balance.

"You look about half dead yourself." The sheriff picked up Lloyd's canteen from the dry grass, sniffed it, and shook his head. "You want to turn out like Mr. Mac? A pervert?"

Lloyd wagged his head no. He thought how he must look: his long blond hair clumped in uncombed cowlicks, the dark reddish-gray circles around his eyes, his father's dirty herding jack hanging off his broad, slumped shoulders. Sheriff Lynch stood there, his figure tall and straight. He wore a star-shaped golden badge hitched to a belt finely tooled with wildflowers. His face was burnt the rust color of Dumas County soil, the lines on it deep, like the sudden ravines into which cattle there sometimes fell. His eyes were an odd steely blue, which seemed not to be that color itself but to reflect it. He studied Lloyd.

"That probably doesn't make much of a difference now," he said, lowering his eyes as if embarrassed.

"What?" Lloyd said, though he'd heard him.

"Nothing. We just need to ask you some questions."

Lloyd wondered if Mr. Mac had found out about the sheep somehow. "But I ain't stole nothin'," he said.

"I'm fairly sure of that," the sheriff said. A grin flickered at one corner of his mouth, but it was sad and not meant to mock Lloyd. "Come on. You know the drill. Hand over your knife and shears and anything else you got."

After Lloyd put his tools in a paper bag, the sheriff squatted next to the sheep and ran his hand over its belly. His hand was large and strong and clean, though etched with red-brown creases.

When they got up to the house, Lloyd saw three or four police cars parked at odd angles, as if they'd stopped in a hurry. Their lights whirled around, and dispatch radios crackled voices that no one answered. Some policemen busied themselves throwing clothes, bottles, and other junk out of Lloyd's shack, which was separated from the house by a tool shed. Others were carrying out cardboard boxes. Lloyd recognized one of the men, name of Gonzales, who'd picked him up for stealing a ten-speed when he was a kid. Lloyd waved at him and called out, but Gonzales just set his dark eyes on him for a moment and then went back to his business. Mr. Mac stood on the dirt patch in front of the house, his big sloppy body looking like it was about to fall over, talking to a man in a suit.

"If you're gonna drag that pond," he said, his eyes slits in the harsh, clear sunlight, "you're gonna have to pay me for the lost fish. I'm a poor old man. I ain't got nothin' to do with thisayre mess."

The man started to say something to him, but Mr. Mac caught sight of Lloyd. His face spread wide with a fear that Lloyd had never seen in him; then his eyes narrowed in disgust. He looked like he did when he saw ewes lamb, or when he punished Lloyd as a child.

"Mr. Mac," Lloyd said, and took a step toward him, but the old man held up his hands as if to shield his face.

"Mr. Mac." Lloyd came closer. "I 'pologize 'bout that 'er sheep. I'll work off the cost to you someway."

Mr. Mac stumbled backward and pointed at Lloyd; his face was wild and frightened again. He shouted to the man in the suit, "Look at 'im! Look at 'im! A seed of pure evil!"

Lloyd could feel his chest move ahead of his body toward Mr. Mac. He wanted to explain about the sheep, but the old man kept carrying on. The sheriff's hand, firm but kind, gripped his arm and guided him toward a police car.

The sheriff sat bolt upright on the passenger side and looked straight ahead as the rust-colored hills passed by outside. A fingerprint-smudged Plexiglas barrier ran across the top of the front seat and separated him from Lloyd. As always, the hair on the nape of the sheriff's neck looked freshly cut. Lloyd had expected them to take his shears and bowie knife, but why were they tearing up his shack? And what was Mr. Mac going on about? Still drunk, probably. He would ask the sheriff when they got to the jail. His thoughts turned to the sheep. He should've put it out of its misery—slit its throat and then cut its belly for the vultures. Not like at slaughter, when he would've had to root around with his knife and bare hands and clean out its innards. What a Godawful stink sheep's insides had! But this would've been easy. It wouldn't have taken a minute.

In the jail two guards Lloyd didn't know sat him down inside a small white room he'd never seen before. The man in a suit who had been talking to Mr. Mac came in, with Sheriff Lynch following. Lloyd hadn't gotten to ask the sheriff what was going on. The man put what looked like a little transistor radio on the table and pressed a button and began to talk.

"Is it okay if we tape-record this interview?" he asked Lloyd.

Lloyd shrugged and smiled a who's-this-guy? smile at the sheriff. The sheriff gave him a stern, behave-yourself look.

"Sure," Lloyd said. "I ain't never been recorded before."

"Okay," the man said. He said all their names, where they were, what date and time it was. Then he opened a file folder. Lloyd didn't like his looks: he had a smile that hid itself, that laughed at you in secret. Mr. Mac could get one of those. And the man talked in one of those citified accents, maybe from Dallas.

"Okay," the man said. "My name is Thomas Blanchard. I am a special agent with the Federal Bureau of Investigation. I work in the serial-homicide division." He shot his eyes up at Lloyd, as if to catch him at something. "Do you understand what that means?"

"Which part?" Lloyd said.

"Serial homicide — serial murder."

"Nope."

"It means to kill more than once — sometimes many people in a row."

"Okay," Lloyd said.

The man gave him another once-over and said, "You are being held as a material witness in seventeen murders that have occurred in and around this area. You have not been charged in any of them. Should you be charged, you will have the right to counsel, but at this time you have no such right per se. However, as a witness, should you wish to retain counsel, that is also your right. Do you wish to do so?"

Lloyd tried to put the man's words together. Blanchard bunched up his shoulders, like a squirrel ready to pounce. The sheriff leaned back his chair and studied the ceiling.

After he had drawn out the silence, Lloyd said, "I don't know. I'm still pretty drunk to think about suchlike. Would I have to pay for him?"

Blanchard's hand snaked out to the tape recorder, but the sheriff looked at Lloyd and said, "Lloyd, you think you're too drunk to know what you're sayin'? I mean, to the point of makin' things up or disrememberin'?"

"Oh, no," Lloyd said. The sheriff asked him if he was sure, and he said yes. Then the sheriff told him that to retain a lawyer he would have to pay for one. In that case, Lloyd said, he didn't want one.

"Sheriff," he said. "What's thisayre all about?"

The sheriff told him he would find out.

But he didn't, not really. Blanchard asked Lloyd about the night before. He'd gone to Genie's Too, where the old Genie's used to be. He'd brought a canteen of Mr. Mac's stuff with him for setups, because they'd lost their license. He saw all the usual people there: Candy, Huff, Wishbone, Firefly. Dwight, Genie's old man, did the colored-baby dance, flopping around this brown rag doll and flashing up its skirt. Everybody seemed to be having a real good time. Big plastic bottles were on nearly every table; people were talking—men arguing, women listening. People leaned on each other like scarecrows, some dancing slow and close, others just close, doing a little bump-and-grind.

Blanchard asked him if he had met anyone, danced with anyone. Lloyd grinned and blushed and sought out the sheriff, who smiled this time. Lloyd said, "I always been shy. I guess it's my rearing, out on that old ranch. And they got their own group there at Genie's, everybody always foolin' with everyone else's."

By the end of his answer the sheriff's smile had gone.

Blanchard asked Lloyd the same thing about ten different ways —had he seen anyone new there? The questions got on his nerves. He said, "Sheriff, now what's this about?"

The sheriff told him to have some patience.

Blanchard asked about places in Amarillo, Lubbock, Muleshoe, Longview, Lamesa, Reno, Abilene—bars Lloyd had sneaked away to when he wanted to be alone. The ones he could remember were all about the same as Genie's, each with its own little crowd. Blanchard mentioned places from so long ago that Lloyd began to feel as if he were asking about a different person. He drifted off into thinking about Mr. Mac.

Mr. Mac, when Lloyd would ask him where they were, used to say that all he needed to know was that they were in the United

States of America. He used to tell Lloyd that where they were was just like Scotland, and then he'd start laughing to himself until his laughs trailed off into coughs. The sheriff had never, ever laughed at him like that. He didn't have those kinds of jokes inside him.

Blanchard began asking personal questions: Did he have a girl-friend? Had he ever? No. How long had he been out at the ranch? All his life—about thirty years, according to Mr. Mac. Was he a virgin?

"Now, Sheriff, have I got to answer that?" In truth he didn't know what he was, because, as he often reflected, he didn't know whether what Mr. Mac had done made him not a virgin.

Perhaps sensing this, the sheriff told him no, he didn't have to answer any more questions. In fact, it might be better to quit for the day. "I'm afraid, though, son, we're gonna have to hold you as a suspect."

"Suspect of what?" Lloyd said, a sweat creeping on him like the cold rain when he herded in winter.

Lloyd woke to the stink of his own sweat, and he seemed wholly that sweat and that stench—the stench was him, his soul. The overhead light had been switched on. It was a bare bulb caged by heavy wire. He glanced at the steel place he was in: steel walls, floor, ceiling, toilet, stool, table. Everything was bolted down. The steel door had a small square high window made of meshed security glass, and a slot near its bottom, with a sliding cover, for passing food. Lloyd hid his face in the crook of his arm and shook and wished he could go to Mr. Mac's for some white lightning.

The door clanked open. Lloyd could tell it was the sheriff even though he kept his face hidden and his eyes shut tight. The sheriff put a plastic plate on the table and said, "I was afraid of this." Then he left.

Maybe the food would help. Lloyd stood up, but his legs felt wobbly and his eyes couldn't focus right. He lurched to the stool, planted himself on it, and held the edge of the table. When he picked up the plastic fork, it vibrated in his fingers. His touch sent a jangling electrical charge through his arm and down his back. The harder he gripped, the more he felt as though he were trying to etch stone with a pencil, yet only this concentration made any steadiness possible. Keeping his face close to the plate, he scooped the watery scrambled eggs into his mouth. He fell to his knees and threw up in the toilet. Curled facedown on the floor, Lloyd felt a prickly, nauseous chill seep into his muscles and begin to paralyze him.

Someone not Sheriff Lynch, who seemed by his step to be burly and ill-tempered, grabbed Lloyd's shoulder and twisted his body so that he faced the ceiling. The floor felt cold and hard against the back of his head. The man spread Lloyd's eyelids, opened his shirt, and put a cold metal disc on his chest. Lloyd had not noticed until now, but his heart was racing—much faster than the sheep's. That seemed so long ago. Mr. Mac was angry with him. The man started to yank down Lloyd's pants. Lloyd moved his lips to say no! No! But his limbs and muscles had turned to cement. His mouth gaped open, but he couldn't catch any air. The chill sweat returned. He was a boy again. Mr. Mac's heaviness pressed the air from his lungs, pinned him from behind, faceless, pushing the dull, tearing pain into him; he choked Lloyd's thin gasps with old-man smells of sweat and smoke and liquor and his ragged, grunting breath. The man rubbed something on Lloyd's right buttock and then pricked it with a needle. He left without pulling up Lloyd's pants.

Lloyd's body softened, and the cement dissolved; a cushiony feeling spread through him, as though his limbs were swaddled in plush, warm blankets. He could breathe. He could not smell himself anymore. "Son," he heard the sheriff say. "Put your pants on."

The two of them sat in the little white room, this time without Blanchard.

"Sheriff?" Lloyd's words seemed to float out of his mouth. "Sheriff, what's all thisayre 'bout?"

Sheriff Lynch sat across the table. His face changed faintly as animals and unknown faces, and then the spirits of Mr. Mac and Blanchard, passed through it. He popped a peppermint Life Saver, sucked on it hard, and pulled back into focus.

"Let me ask you a question, first, son, and then I'll answer yours." He reached down next to his chair and put two Ziploc bags with Lloyd's shears and bowie knife in them on the table. Both the shears and the knife were tagged, as if they were in hock. The sheriff pressed them a few times with the tips of his long rust-colored fingers, lightly, as though to make sure they were there, or to remind them to stay still. "Now," he said, "I think I already know the answer to this question, but I need to know from you." He pressed them again. "Are these your knife and shears?"

How should he answer? The sheriff leaned back, waiting, with a look on his face that said he didn't want to hear the answer.

"Maybe," Lloyd said.

"Maybe." The sheriff joined his hands behind his head and pointed his eyes up and away, as though he were considering this as a possible truth.

"Maybe," Lloyd said.

"Lloyd Wayne Dogget," the sheriff said, turning his not-blue eyes on him. "How long have I known you? I knew your daddy and your grandpappy when they were alive. I know more about you than you know about you. And you ain't never been able to lie to me and get clear with it. So I'll ask you again — are these your knife and shears?"

Mr. Mac had given Lloyd the shears when he was sixteen. They were long and silvery. At the end of each day of shearing, after cutting the sheep's coarse, billowy hair, Lloyd would sharpen them on a strop and oil them with a can of S'OK to keep off the rust. The merry old man on the green can, a pipe in his mouth, always reminded him of Mr. Mac.

"What if I say yes?" Lloyd said.

Sheriff Lynch sucked on the Life Saver and blew out a breath. He leaned close to Lloyd and put his elbows on the table. "To tell you the truth," he said, "it doesn't make a whit's difference." He pressed the plastic bags again. "There's blood on these tools matches the type of a young lady people saw you leave Genie's with, a young lady who turned up murdered. And I confiscated these two things from you. So it doesn't make a whit's difference what you say, whether you lie or not. I'm just trying to give you a chance to get right with yourself, to be a man." He sank back and ran his hands through his stubbly iron-gray hair as he bowed his head and looked at the bags. He massaged his clean-cut neck. "Maybe to get right with the Lord, too. I don't know. I don't believe in that kind of thing, but sometimes it helps people."

To Lloyd, the sheriff seemed embarrassed about something. Lloyd wanted to help him. But he was also afraid; he could not remember any young lady, only smiling dark-red lips, the curve of a bare upper arm, honky-tonk music, Dwight flinging the colored baby doll around.

"Okay, Sheriff," he said. "Since it don't make any difference, you know they're mine."

The sheriff escorted him to the showers, where he took Lloyd's clothes and gave him an inmate's orange jumpsuit and a pair of regulation flip-flops. After Lloyd had showered and changed, the sheriff told him he was under arrest for capital murder, read him his rights, and handcuffed him. They got in his car, Lloyd riding in the front seat, and drove the two blocks to the courthouse. The judge asked him if he had any money or expected any help, and he said no, which was the truth.

Every morning Sheriff Lynch came to Lloyd's cell and walked with him down to the little white room, where Lloyd talked with his lawyer. When the sheriff opened the door to the room, Lloyd watched his lawyer and the sheriff volley looks under their pleas-antries. He remembered a cartoon he'd seen: Bluto and Popeye had each grabbed one of Olive Oyl's rubbery arms. They were stretching her like taffy. He couldn't remember how it ended.

Raoul Schwartz, the lawyer Lloyd had been assigned, said the judge had granted Lloyd a competency hearing, but not much money to do it with. He, Schwartz, would have to conduct the tests himself and then send them to a psychiatrist for evaluation. In two months the psychiatrist would testify and the judge would decide whether Lloyd was competent to stand trial. Schwartz said they had a lot of work to do. Schwartz said he was there to help.

Schwartz was everything the sheriff was not. He had short, pale, womanish fingers that fluttered through papers, fiddled with pencils, took off his wire-rimmed granny glasses and rubbed the bridge of his nose. When he got impatient, which was often, his fingers scratched at a bald spot on the top of his forehead. Lloyd thought he might have rubbed his hair off this way.

Schwartz wouldn't let him wriggle out of questions, sometimes asking the same ones many times, like Blanchard. He asked about Lloyd's whole life. Sometimes the glare of the white room and Schwartz's drone were like being in school again, and Lloyd would lay his head down on the slick-topped table between them and put his cheek to its cool surface. "Come on, Lloyd," Schwartz would say. "We've got work to do."

Also unlike the sheriff, Schwartz cussed, which was something Lloyd could never abide, and the little man's Yankee accent raked the words across Lloyd's nerves even worse than usual. When Lloyd told him that Sheriff Lynch had been out to talk to Mr. Mac after a teacher had spotted cigarette burns on his arms, Schwartz murmured, "Excellent, excellent. Fucking bastard."

"Who's the effing bastard?"

"Mr. Mac." Schwartz's head popped up just as Blanchard's had when he'd wanted to catch Lloyd at something, only this time it was Lloyd who had caught Schwartz in a lie.

Schwartz began giving Lloyd tests. Lloyd was worried that he might fail them, but he didn't say anything; he had already gotten the impression that this man thought he was stupid. But it was the tests that were stupid. First Schwartz asked him about a million yes-or-no questions. Everything from "Do you think your life isn't worth living?" (no) to "Do you ever see things that aren't there?" (sometimes, in the woods). Then came the pictures. One showed a man and a boy standing in opposite corners of a room. At first Lloyd just said what he saw. But this wasn't good enough; Schwartz said he had to interpret it. "Tell me what you think is going to happen next," he said. When Lloyd looked at it closely, he figured the boy had done something wrong and was about to get a good belt-whipping. Schwartz seemed pleased by this. Finally, and strangest of all, Schwartz showed him some blobs of ink and asked him to make something out of them. If Schwartz hadn't been so serious, Lloyd would have thought it was a joke. But when he studied them (Schwartz had used that word—"interpret"—again), Lloyd could see all different kinds of faces and animals, as he had when he'd talked to Sheriff Lynch about his knife and shears.

It took only one little thing to tell him what the sheriff thought about this testing.

One morning the sheriff walked Lloyd down the hallway without a word, and when he unlocked the door to the white room, he stepped back, held it open, and swooped his hand in front of Lloyd like a colored doorman.

"Mr. Dogget," he said, for the first time making fun of Lloyd in some secret way.

The sheriff turned and let the door close without so much as a glance at Schwartz. Lloyd wanted to apologize to the sheriff. He was beginning to understand that it came down to this: the worse the sheriff looked, the better he, Lloyd, looked. He felt he was betraying the sheriff, with the help of this strange, foul-mouthed little man. Schwartz seemed to see everything upside down. When Lloyd had told him about Mr. Mac, even though Schwartz said it must have been awful, Lloyd could tell that in some way he was pleased. When he told Schwartz about times when a lot of hours passed without his knowing it, like when he'd sat with that sheep, or about drinking at least a canteen of Mr. Mac's white lightning every day for the past few years, Schwartz began scribbling and shooting questions at him. Same thing with the pills and reefer and acid and speed he'd done in his twenties. Even the gas huffing when he was just a kid. Lloyd felt dirty remembering all of it. Schwartz wanted details. Lloyd could almost see Schwartz making designs out of what he told him, rearranging things to make him look pitiful.

"I don't want to do no testin' today," Lloyd said as soon as the door had shut. He sat and leaned back in his chair, arms dangling, chest out.

"Okay," Schwartz said. "What do you want to do?"

"I been thinkin'," Lloyd said. "It don't make no difference if I was drunk or not. That don't excuse what I did."

"But you don't know what you did."

"That don't make no difference. They got the proof."

"They have evidence, Lloyd, not proof."

Another bunch of upside-down words. "But if I can't remember it, then ain't what they got better than what I can say?"

"Lloyd," Schwartz said, his head in his hands, massaging his bald spot. "We've been over this about every time we've talked. I know that it doesn't make common sense at first. But our criminal-justice system—that misnomer—is predicated upon the idea of volition. It means you have to commit a crime with at least an inkling of intention. You can't be punished in the same way when you don't have any idea what you're doing."

This kind of talk made Lloyd's head ache. "All I know," he said, "is I don't want to go foolin' around with truth. It's like the sheriff says—I got to get right with myself and be a man."

"The sheriff says this?" Schwartz's head popped up.

Lloyd nodded.

"Do you talk to the sheriff often?"

"I been knowing Sheriff Lynch since forever. He's like my daddy."

"But do you talk to him? How often do you talk to him?"

"Every chance I get." Lloyd felt queasy. He knew he'd said something he shouldn't have. But his pride in his friendship with the sheriff, perhaps because it was imperiled, drove him to exaggerate. "When we come from my cell, mostly. But any time I want, really. I can call on him any time."

"I don't think it's a good idea for you to be talking to him about your case," Schwartz said.

"And why not?"

"Because anything—*anything*—you say to him becomes evidence. As a matter of fact, I don't think it's a good idea for you to talk to him at all."

"So who'm I gonna talk to? Myself? You?"

For the next couple of days the sheriff didn't speak to Lloyd unless Lloyd spoke to him first. Schwartz must have done something. But the sheriff never looked at him hard or seemed angry. He mainly kept his words short and his eyes on the floor, as if he was sad and used to his sadness. Lloyd wanted to tell him how he was trying to get right but it was hard. Eventually Lloyd realized that even if he said this, the sheriff probably wouldn't believe him. If he were trying to get right, then he wouldn't be letting this Schwartz character make him look pitiful. Each morning Lloyd rose early, dressed, and rubbed his palms to dry them as he sat on the edge of his bunk, waiting. When he walked in front of the sheriff down the hallway to the white room, Lloyd could feel the sheriff's eyes taking him in. He tried to stand up straight and walk with manly strides, but the harder he tried, the smaller and more bent over he felt. He was careful not to wrinkle his prison outfit, pressing it at night between his mattress and a piece of plywood the sheriff had given him for his back. He combed his hair as best he could without a mirror.

At night Lloyd lay on his bunk and thought about Schwartz. Of course, Schwartz had tricked him into more tests. Next they were going to take pictures of his brain. Lloyd studied Schwartz's words: "volition," "interpret," "diminished responsibility." They all meant you couldn't be punished for your mistakes. This didn't square with Lloyd; he had been punished for plenty of mistakes. That was what Mr. Mac had punished him for; that was what the sheep died of. When you missed one on a head count and it got lost and fell into a ravine; when you forgot to give one a vaccination and it got sick, like the one that had died before Lloyd was taken away, you were punished. But how could he expect Schwartz, a womanish city boy, to understand this?

On one side were Schwartz and the law, and on the other were the sheep and God and the earth and Sheriff Lynch and Mr. Mac and everything else Lloyd had ever known. Who was he to go against all that—to hide from that terrible, swift sword the Almighty would wield on the Final Day? His fear was weak and mortal; it drove him out of his cell to plot with this fellow sinner to deceive God. Some nights Lloyd moaned in agony at the deceit of his life. For in his pride he had latched onto the notion that since he could not remember his gravest sins (and he believed they were all true, they must be true), he should not have to pay for them in this life. Oh, he would pay for them in eternity, but he flinched at paying here. What upside-down thinking! What cowardice in the face of sins that were probably darker, cloaked as they were in his drunken forgetting, than any he could have committed when he had "volition," as Schwartz called it. Because Lloyd did not know his sins, he could not accept his punishment; but for the same reason they seemed to him unspeakably heinous.

Lloyd lay on his bunk in the darkness and thought about the pictures he had seen of his brain. Two officers he didn't know had driven him to a hospital in Lubbock to get them taken. The hearing was in a week. Schwartz had pointed out patches in the pictures' rainbow colors, scratching his bald spot and pacing. He'd said that although parts of Lloyd's brain were damaged so that alcohol could cause longer and more severe blackouts in him than in normal people, such damage might not be enough for the court to recognize him as incompetent. And the rest of the tests had proved that he had a dissociative condition but not multiple-personality disorder. Lloyd had wanted to ask if Schwartz thought he was incompetent, but he figured he wouldn't get a straight answer.

In the darkness of the steel room Lloyd touched his head, trying to feel the colored patches of heat and coolness that the pictures showed in his brain. He imagined he could sense some here and there. He had come a long way—not many people knew what their brains looked like. But the thought that he might be incompetent frightened him. What if some day one of those big machines they put over his head was put over his chest and a picture was taken of his soul? What would it look like? He saw a dark-winged creature with tearing claws, cloaked in a gray mist.

The knock came to Lloyd in a half dream, and at first he thought he had imagined the sheriff's voice. The whole jail was quiet; all the inmates were covered in the same darkness.

"Lloyd? Lloyd? You awake, son?" The voice didn't sound exactly like the sheriff's, but Lloyd knew that's who it was. He rose and went to the door, too sleepy to be nervous. He peered out the square window. The glare of the hallway made him squint. The sheriff stood in silhouette, but his steely eyes glinted. Looking at him through the crosshatches of wire in the security glass, Lloyd thought that he, too, looked caged.

"I'm awake, Sheriff."

The door opened, and the sheriff said, "Come on." Lloyd could smell whiskey. He followed the sheriff out past the booking area. Everything was still and deserted in the bare fluorescent light. Gonzales dozed in a chair at the front desk with a porno magazine in his lap. The sheriff opened the door to his office, making the same mocking gesture as before, though this time he seemed to be trying to share his joke with Lloyd. He snapped the door's lock and sat down behind his desk. A single shaded lamp glowed in a corner, casting shadows from the piles of paper on the desk and reflecting golden patches from plaques on the walls.

The sheriff pointed at a low-backed leather chair and told Lloyd to have a seat. "Excuse me gettin' you out of bed, son. I figured this was the only time we could talk."

"It's no trouble."

"You can prob'ly tell I been drinkin'," the sheriff said. "I don't do it as a habit, but I apologize for that, too. I been doin' it more lately. I do it when I'm sick at heart. At least that's my excuse to myself, which is a Goddamned poor one, unbefitting a man, if you ask me. But I am. Sick at heart."

He took a long pull from a coffee mug. Lloyd followed it with his eyes, and the sheriff caught him.

"And no," he said, "you can't have any. One of us got to stay sober, and I want you to remember what I'm gonna tell you." He leaned across the desk. "You know what a vacuum is, son? I mean in a pure sense, not the one you clean with."

Lloyd shook his head.

"Well. A vacuum is a place where there ain't anything, not even air. Every light bulb"—the sheriff nodded at the lamp behind him—"is a vacuum. Space is mostly a vacuum. Vacuum tubes used to be in radios. And so on. A place where there ain't nothin'. Is that signifyin' for you?"

Lloyd nodded.

"Good. So we, because we're on this earth with air to breathe, we are in a place that's not a vacuum that's in the middle of a vacuum, which is space. Think of a bubble floating out in the air." The sheriff made a big circle above the desk with his fingertips. "That's what the earth is like, floating in space. Are you followin' me?"

"I think so."

"Well, are you or aren't you?" the sheriff said with sudden violence. Not waiting for an answer, he yanked open his desk drawer and took out a large folding map of the world. He tumbled it down the front of his desk, weighted its top corners with a tape dispenser and a stapler, and came around the desk to stand next to Lloyd. He told Lloyd what it was and said, "I study this all the time. Do you know where we are right now?"

To Lloyd, the shapes on the map looked like those inkblots. By reading, he found the United States and then Texas, and then he gave up. He shrugged his shoulders. "I don't know, Sheriff."

"That's okay," the sheriff said gently. He pointed to a dot in the Panhandle which someone had drawn with a ballpoint pen. Cursive letters next to it said "Dumas." "This is where we are. Two specks within that dot, on the dark side of the earth, floating in space. Over here"—he pointed to Hong Kong—"it's lunchtime. Japs eatin' their noodles or whatever. Here"—he pointed to London—"people just risin', eatin' their sausages and egg sandwiches."

He stepped back, behind Lloyd, and put his hands on the chair. The heat of his body and the smell of his breath washed over Lloyd.

"But look, son," the sheriff said, "how many places there are. It's some time everywhere, and everybody is doin' something."

The sheriff stood there for a few moments. Lloyd felt as he had when he was a child watching TV—he couldn't imagine how all those people got inside that little box. Now he couldn't fathom people inside the little dots. The world was vast and stranger than he had ever imagined.

"We are all here doin' things," the sheriff said, "inside this bubble that is not a vacuum. We all breathe the same air, and everything we do nudges everything else." He stepped over and propped himself on the edge of his desk, next to the map, and crossed his legs. The lamp's soft light cast him in half shadow.

"And this is why I'm sick at heart. Because I thought I knew you. Separation is the most terrible thing there is, especially for a man like me." The sheriff gestured to take in the whole room. "This is what I got. It ain't much. You and I aren't that far apart, son. Both of us solitary. But what you done, son, and I do believe you did all that, that separates a man from the whole world. And that's why I said you need to get right with yourself."

Lloyd bowed his head.

"You don't need to tell me you ain't done that." The sheriff's voice rose and quickened, began to quiver. "You and I both know you ain't. But that itself—a negativity, a vacuum—ain't nothin' to breathe in. Things die without air. So what I'm askin' you is, I want to do my own competency exam, for my own self. This is between Lloyd Wayne Dogget and Archibald Alexander Lynch. I need to know what's inside you to know what's inside myself. So you tell that lawyer of yours I'll stipulate to whatever he wants. Remember that word—'stipulate.' Now get out a' here." He turned from Lloyd and began folding the map with shaking hands. The corner weighted by the tape dispenser tore. Lloyd could not move.

"Shit," the sheriff muttered. He wheeled unsteadily on Lloyd, his eyes wide with panic and surprise at what he'd said. Lloyd could tell he was afraid, but not of him, as Mr. Mac had been. The sheriff was afraid that he might show his own soul to Lloyd and so break out of the bubble in which he lived. "Git!" he yelled. "Go tell Gonzales to take you back! Get outta here before I say somethin' foolish!"

"He wants you to do *what*?" Schwartz paced in the little white room, looking at the floor.

Lloyd was sitting at the table, turning his head to follow Schwartz. Was Schwartz right with himself? He repeated what the sheriff had told him.

"What does that son of a bitch want?" Schwartz said to himself.

"I wish you'd stop cussing around me."

Schwartz made a distracted noise.

"I mean it," Lloyd said. "It's offensive."

Schwartz made another noise. He had gathered his lips together into a pucker with his fingers, and he looked at the floor as he paced.

"Especially cussing on the sheriff." When Schwartz didn't answer, Lloyd said, "Are you hearing me? Don't cuss on the sheriff."

"I don't know what kind of game he's trying to play." Schwartz did not stop or raise his eyes from the floor. "But I would guess he's trying to trick some kind of confession out of you."

"Sheriff don't play no games with me," Lloyd said. "He don't have no tricks. You're the one with all the tricks."

"I'll take that as a compliment."

"Sheriff's the one tryin' to help me get right."

"Sheriff's the one tryin' to help you get dead," Schwartz said, mimicking Lloyd.

"Okay, man." Lloyd stood up and pushed his chair away. It

squealed on the floor, and Schwartz stopped. Lloyd saw that his own fists were clenched. He hesitated.

"What are you gonna do, Lloyd? Beat me up? Go ahead. I've been expecting this."

"You think I'm stupid," Lloyd said. "And all them tests is to make me look pitiful and incompetent. What do you think that's done to my trying to get right?"

"What do you think that means, Lloyd—'getting right'?" Schwartz moved close to him. He stared straight at Lloyd as he spoke. "It means giving up."

That night, and for the days and nights to come, Lloyd turned over in his mind all he had seen and heard. What he had known before was like some foreign language that now he couldn't understand. The worlds of Schwartz and the sheriff, of man and God, of what was in the law and what was in the fields, began to blur, and yet between them grew a chasm in which he hung suspended. He tried to remember what had happened in the places Blanchard had said he'd been, but he couldn't. He could not make them connect the way the sheriff had said all the people in all those dots on the map did. An indifference grew around him, a thin glass glazing that separated him from the rest of humankind.

The sheriff led him down the hallway to the white room without a word or a look, and left him with Schwartz. The hearing was the next day. Lloyd felt as though he were about to take another test. He had fought with Schwartz tooth and nail over the sheriff's proposal, and in the end had gotten his way by threatening to fire him. After Lloyd sat down across the table from him, Schwartz explained that he and the sheriff had struck a deal: the sheriff had agreed that he would not testify about his "competency exam," as he called it, on the condition that he not have to reveal to Schwartz beforehand what it was going to be about.

"I don't like this," Schwartz said, pacing, clicking the top of a ballpoint pen so that it made a *tick-tick* sound, like a clock. He sat down again, his elbows on the table and his hands joined as though in prayer, and brought his face close to Lloyd's.

"I want to tell you the truest thing I've ever seen, Lloyd. I've seen a man executed. When you are executed in Texas, you are taken to a powder-blue room. This is the death chamber, where the warden, a physician, and a minister will stand around the gurney. Since executions can take place in Texas only between midnight and dawn, it will have that eerie feeling of a room brightly lit in the middle of the night. Before this, in an anteroom, a guard will tell you to drop your pants. Then he will insert one rubber stopper in your penis and another in your anus, to prevent you from urinating and defecating when your muscles relax after you have died. When you are lying on the gurney, the guard will secure your arms, legs, and chest to it with leather straps. The guard will insert a needle, which is attached to an IV bag, into your left arm. Above you will be fluorescent lighting, and a microphone will hang suspended from the ceiling. The warden—I think it's still Warden Pearson—will ask whether you have any last words. When you're finished, three chemicals will be released into your blood: sodium thiopental, a sedative that is supposed to render you unconscious; pancuronium bromide, a muscle relaxant, to collapse your diaphragm and lungs; potassium chloride, a poison that will stop your heart.

"I could tell that my client could feel the poison entering his veins. I had known him for the last three of his fifteen years on death row; he was old enough to be my father. At his execution I was separated from him by a piece of meshed security glass. There was nothing I could do when he began writhing and gasping for breath. The poison—later I found out it was the potassium chloride, to stop his heart—had been injected before the thiopental. Imagine a dream in which your body has turned to lead, in which you can't move and are sinking in water. You have the sensations given you by your nerves and understood in your brain, but you can't do anything about them. You struggle against your own body. But really, it is unimaginable—what it is like to try to rouse your own heart.

"What if everything goes as planned? A nice, sleepy feeling—the sedative tricking your nerves—will dissolve your fear. The question is, will you want it taken away, fear being the only thing that binds you to life? Will you want to hold on to that, like the survivor of a shipwreck clinging to a barnacled plank? Will you struggle, in the end, to be afraid?"

Schwartz slumped back in his chair and began again to *tick-tick* the top of his pen so that it made a sound like a clock. The whiteness and silence of the room seemed to annihilate time, as though the two men could sit there waiting forever. They fell on Lloyd like a thin silting of powdered glass.

"You spend a lot of time thinkin' about that, don't you?" Lloyd said.

"Yes."

"You told me that to scare me, didn't you?"

"Yes."

Lloyd thought that Schwartz might have gotten right with himself, in his own way, by seeing what he had seen and thinking on it. But something still didn't add up.

"How do you know I'd be afraid?" Lloyd said. "How do you know that would be the last thing I'd feel?"

"I don't know that." Schwartz *tick-tick*ed the pen. "You can never know. That's what's terrible about death."

"Lots of things you don't know when you're alive. So what's the difference?"

Schwartz's fingers stopped, and he stared at Lloyd as though he had seen him purely and for the first time. A knock at the door broke the brief, still moment, and Sheriff Lynch entered. He carried under his arm a stack of manila folders, which he put down on the table. Schwartz rose, studying Lloyd. He shook the sheriff's hand when it was offered. His eyes, though, were fixed on Lloyd. The sheriff caught this, but smiled pleasantly and told Schwartz it was good to see him again.

"Lloyd," he said, and nodded at him. He lifted a chair from the corner, put it at the head of the table, and sat.

"I think I need a little more time to consult with my client," Schwartz said.

The sheriff pressed his fingers a few times on top of the folders. "Okay. How much time do you think you'll need?"

"We don't need no more time," Lloyd said, rocking back and forth in his chair. "I'm ready."

"I'd like to look at what you've got there first."

"But that wasn't the agreement, Mr. Schwartz."

"Come on," Lloyd said. "I'm ready."

"Why don't you listen to your client?"

Looking from Lloyd to the sheriff, Schwartz paled. He seemed pinned in place for a moment; then he took off his glasses and rubbed them on his shirt. He put them on again. Sheriff Lynch stared at the stack of folders, his fingertips resting on them like a pianist's, his expression one of patient indulgence toward a child who was finishing a noisy tantrum. Lloyd clenched his hands between his thighs, wondering what would be revealed to him.

"Do you mind if I stand?" Schwartz said.

"Go right ahead." Sheriff Lynch pressed his fingers again to the top folder, as if for luck or in valediction, took it from the stack, and opened it in front of Lloyd. Lloyd did not see at first what was there, because Schwartz had made a sudden movement toward the table, but Sheriff Lynch, with the slightest warning lift of his hand, checked him. He faced Schwartz a moment and then turned to Lloyd.

"Go ahead, son," he said. "Tell me what you see."

When Lloyd looked down, he was disappointed. It was another one of those crazy tests. He saw shapes of red and pink and green and black. It was the inkblot test, only in color. He studied more closely to try and make sense of it. He realized it was a picture of something. He realized what it was.

"I think I got it," he said to the sheriff. The sheriff nodded to help him along. "It's a sheep," Lloyd said.

"Look at it a little more closely, son." Lloyd saw Schwartz again move and the sheriff again check him while keeping his neutral blue eyes on Lloyd. Lloyd went back to the picture. He had missed some details.

"It's a sheep gutted after slaughter," he said.

"Turn the picture over, son," the sheriff said. This time Schwartz did not move and the sheriff did not hold up his hand. Paper-clipped to the back of the picture Lloyd found a smaller photo of a young woman. She had straight brown hair, wore blue jeans and a red-and-white checkered blouse, and sat in a lawn chair, smiling to please the person who held the camera.

"Now turn the picture over again," the sheriff said, in his calm, steady voice. "What do you see?"

Lloyd tried to puzzle it out, but he couldn't. There must be something he wasn't seeing. He studied the picture. As he followed the shapes and colors of the sheep's emptied body, a trickle of pity formed in him for all three of them—the woman, the sheep, and himself—and dropped somewhere inside him. The glaze over him tightened. He could only tell the sheriff that he saw a sheep.

After the sheriff left, gathering the folders under his arm, the room went back to its silence.

"If I'd known," Schwartz said, "I would've had him testify."

"What?" Lloyd said. "If you'd known what?"

"Never mind." Shielding his face with his pale fingers, Schwartz laid his other hand on Lloyd's shoulder. "Never mind, Lloyd. You're perfect the way you are."

They had sat there a long time, the sheriff opening a folder in front of him, asking him the same questions, and then putting it aside. And in each folder Lloyd had seen the same things: a gutted sheep and a pretty young woman. He knew that the sheriff was trying to do something to help him get right, but as the glaze thickened, that chance seemed ever more remote. Before he left, the sheriff had nodded to Lloyd, to acknowledge that he had found his answer, but his gesture was as distant as that of a receding figure waving a ship out to sea. With each drop of pity Lloyd felt himself borne away yet drowning, so that he knew the heart of the man in the execution chamber, suffocating and unable to move, and he wondered how he would survive in this new and airless world.

2000

Clyde Edgerton

DEBRA'S FLAP AND SNAP

Clyde Edgerton is the author of eight novels and a just-published memoir, Solo: My Adventures in the Air. *About "Debra's Flap and Snap," he says, "Being a former (in some ways, forever) Southern Baptist, I find it troubling to write about sex, and so I'm working my way up toward intercourse. . . . I may not live long enough to get there." He also offers a quote from François Mauriac: "We had to live united with a wild beast whom it was important not to know." Born and raised in the North Carolina Piedmont, Clyde Edgerton teaches writing at the University of North Carolina at Wilmington.*

Lying here now, I can look back.

I was always overweight, though not a whole lot, and was never popular with the boys in high school because of my weight. But L. Ray Flowers liked me enough to, you know, do something ugly in front of me in his car one night, the night of the eighth grade dance—after the dance—and I want to go ahead and tell about that night.

It was the only time I went to a school dance. I never was invited to the prom. There were lots of dances after the high school football games and I went a few times with other girls but didn't dance.

L. Ray was in special education, but he went on to be an evangelist, and had a radio show and for a while, a television show out in the Midwest somewhere. He got to be pretty famous—got a big hair hairdo, the works.

He killed a woman trying to heal her one time. It was a freak accident. You can look it up. It happened out there in the Midwest and the local papers here carried the story. What happened is that they were up on a pretty high stage and she walked backwards in ecstasy off the edge of the stage, hit her head on the base of a flag stand and died on the spot. Honest. Her husband sued L. Ray and lost. Think about the places they put American flags. At restaurants they fly them in the rain and at night. My daddy was always concerned about the flag. He fought in World War II.

L. Ray was seventeen when I was in the eighth grade and he was in shop. They didn't have special ed back then. They just called it shop. I was fourteen. And I don't think the fact that I was overweight made one bit of difference to him. It was not something that mattered to him it seemed like. He didn't feel like he had to be like everybody else in this respect and shun the overweight, or ugly in the face, or anything else. In fact one of the ugliest girls in our school, in the face, had a body I would have killed for and nobody would date her except L. Ray and L. Ray ended up marrying her. That's the truth. But it didn't last. Another story.

See, I have always hated L. Ray for doing that—masturbating is the word—in front of me the way he did. But the more I've thought about it, and the way he's ended up—his radio show failing and him losing everything to the IRS—there is a way in which I feel sorry for him, too. Although that is not exactly what I mean. I can't quite say it right. He didn't have to take me out is one of the things. He chose me over everybody else. I also can tell about it now because it was long before what all you see on television and especially the movies nowadays.

This happened in 1956 and that's all it was—what he did. Think about what people do in cars and everywhere else nowadays. But even back then my dancing and his dancing was on the same wavelength. Even though I'm feeling a little contradictory I can also say that the experience at the time left me feeling filthy, and thus mad at L. Ray. And I'm sure he forgot me. See how complicated it gets. And he never asked me out again after that night, which I regretted only after I got married. You can see something about my husband from that. My first husband.

As to L. Ray these days, I've seen him up here twice visiting his aunt. She's just been here a few days. I asked Traci, because I thought it was L. Ray. He stood outside my door talking to somebody—looked in here but didn't recognize me. I guess he's over sixty now. Let's see . . . he should be sixty-one. He looks a lot the same, except for his white hair. He's about six feet two, narrow shoulders, little pot belly, fairly long white hair he combs forward and then sweeps around. He's got a kind of redhead complexion, and those black snake eyes, set back in his head and sometimes looking almost crossed. And real narrow lips. His eyes are quick, quick, quick. I saw him one time maybe a year ago, when I was in the checkout line at Food Lion before I got sick. He was two people in front of me, had done bought his food and had come back to the checkout girl with his long receipt. Wanted to see a coupon he'd just used—or something about a coupon. The coupon was for fifty cents and he hadn't got credit he said. He showed the receipt to her and she told him the coupon was for something different, slightly different, than what he'd got—like a wrong kind of cereal or something. Would he like to change them, she said, and he said yes and looking kind of intent, headed back into the store up the checkout line, right by me. Just then he caught the eye of the man standing behind me, somebody who might have been a little perturbed about him holding things up, and he gave him that big, gentle, little boy smile and said, "How do you do?"

It was the eighth grade end of the year dance. And in assemblies and parties and trips and all that, shop was considered eighth grade. Whenever all of us in eighth grade went roller-skating, shop went along.

I was a very friendly overweight person, not the depressed, withdrawn type. I was like Miss Piggy in a way, if you can get a picture of Miss Piggy in your head—her sort of like a cheerleader jumping in the air, tossing flowers out behind her. I was this kind of person, always very happy, with lots of girlfriends, always talking, always giggling about the boys and things and always full of curiosity about who liked who and who was going steady with who. And for the entire eighth grade, L. Ray kind of liked me. I could tell it but at the same time I wouldn't admit it to anybody because L. Ray was in shop, and they all met with Mrs. Waltrip down in the shop—where they had electric saws and everything. They didn't do shop—they just met down there. People who went down there for shop would just more or less put up with them. On second thought, some of them did do shop.

So, anyway, I had bunches of girlfriends and then too I was a go-between between girlfriends and boyfriends. You know what I mean. I was somebody overweight who would take messages from a girl to a guy and back, giggling when I needed to and looking forward to gossip in general. I made all As, too, and teachers liked me. I was not bad looking at all. I never had the first pimple if you can believe that. And I was class secretary my sophomore and junior year in high school. Not much other than that, though. Not much to write home about.

L. Ray was really dressed up that night. My mama and daddy were okay with him picking me up. Most anything was okay with them. I had five brothers and sisters and a lot going on, and I lied to Mama and told her that L. Ray was in the tenth grade, which of course he would have been if he hadn't been in shop. No, he would have been a junior or senior.

He was intense looking like he is now, but of course he had red hair then, a kind of dark red, and his eyes had that quickness and he had that thin-lipped mouth that would always break into a big smile at nothing, right when he was looking so hard through those eyes. That gives you a picture.

He brought along a present when he came to pick me up, and I knew enough to know that that wasn't required. It was a brown leather billfold—with the flap and snap and a change purse and zip-up paper money holder. It was in a box, wrapped nicely, with a big white bow. It was green paper. When the doorbell rang and I opened the door, there he stood with that green present.

As you might can tell, L. Ray was not unpopular, nor was he like other people in shop. It was like he, and therefore everybody else, knew in some kind of way that he didn't belong there. He actually seemed pretty smart, and back then in times when boys combed their hair, he combed his very nicely. Dark red hair.

L. Ray was always talking to people, patting them on the back, laughing out loud at his own jokes, making fun of people in nice, very acceptable ways, and all this. He actually had a kind of adult presence about him. I do admit that I'd always felt something a little bit strange about him, but because he liked me, I overlooked this feeling, and now looking back on everything, I'm convinced that the strangeness which caused him to do that in front of me is the strangeness that I felt.

He was standing there in a light grey suit, white shirt, bow tie, and black shoes—holding that green present with the white ribbon and he gave a little bow with his hands under his chin like a Japanese. Which is something I forgot—that Japanese bow. He stuck the present under his arm just before he made the bow. Just about anytime L. Ray came up to you and spoke, he'd do that—give a little head bow with his hands in prayer-fashion below his chin. But this was before he really got religion and went on the road as an evangelist. That happened mainly when he left the Baptist Church and joined the Pentecostals.

It was to be a big night for me. It was my first date. (And, it turns out, the last to any kind of dance. I only had six real dates as a teenager.) I didn't imagine at the time anything could go wrong. I of course was wondering if he'd try to kiss me goodnight, but in the main I was seeing this as the beginning of a high school career of dates and fun times. I hadn't for some reason connected being slightly overweight to being unpopular with the boys. All that didn't dawn on me until later. After all, L. Ray was a boy and had been interested in me for a whole school year.

Daddy was a housepainter and Mama worked at the Laundromat and they both worked unpredictable hours which is why they weren't home. This was not long before they broke up, which was when I was in the tenth grade.

I was wearing my sister Teresa's blue crepe-like dress with the silk top and frilly bottom and fake pearls and earbobs and lots of lipstick and eye makeup. Teresa was seven years older than me and married. She had always been normal sized until after her first child and then during the next year or so she got to be about the size I was at fourteen.

I remember me and L. Ray walking down the walk to his car. We had a rock walkway, flat slate rocks lined up, but they were too close to each other so that if you took regular steps you'd hit in between every other one or two unless you took short steps. I took short steps to hit every one and so did L. Ray—I guess, coming behind me. He let me go first. It had rained and the wet grass hadn't been cut. L. Ray's black shoes were patent leather. He was always saying something funny, always making a joke. When we got to the end of the walkway he showed me the beaded water drops on his shoes and got real serious and said something like, "Looks like little water worlds resting on the hard dark universe, don't it." See. He'd surprise you. He was not a bad evangelist— even that early.

He opened the passenger car door for me. It was his daddy's Oldsmobile or Pontiac, one of those big ones with a lot of chrome, but it was very old and worn-out looking also. L. Ray's daddy sold eggs.

"I think I'll stop and get us a pack of cigarettes," said L. Ray. He pulled the car into the Blue Light, which was a main nightspot back then. "And then how about we stop back in here after the dance for a couple of tall Busches."

Me and Belinda McGregor had drunk beer twice. I was ready to bop. There were lights in my eyes. Blue lights from the Blue Light. Red lights from the cigarette I was about to smoke. White lights from the dance. Green lights from the dashboard of the car when we drove off somewhere later, maybe out to lake Blanca. I knew a lot about life. I had gone to the movies with Diane Coble more than once—us sitting in the back row when Duane Teal would come in and I would sit quietly and watch them out of the corner of my eye. They would kiss for an hour while his hands wandered ever so gently all over her, all approved, accepted, wanted and needed by her. And by me. Not to speak of what I'd seen my sister and her boyfriends do when they stayed over sometimes and all that when Mama and Daddy were gone.

So we arrived, after smoking a cigarette on the way.

The dance was in the library. We parked by the tennis courts and walked around to the front of the school and up the high outside brick steps and in through the doors, and then down that long, long wooden hall. If floors were still made of wood in America then there would be less horror. Wooden halls meant safety, and God knows plastic and cable TV helped bring a horror to America that in my day and my teenage years was peaked out only by this retarded boy doing something in front of me in his daddy's old Oldsmobile or Pontiac. I know what's going on these days. People are killing each other in schools, but so what—people have always killed each other. But not in schools. The problem is that we used to each have a separate nervous system and now people who are alive all have the same nervous system and everybody feels everything on the surface and there's so much to deal with on the surface nothing ever seeps down to your heart.

I regret I never sat on the ground and stared at a tree for a long time just thinking about all the stuff that was going on inside it— I mean a big tree. You sit there, look at it and think about the water going up inside it, just inside the bark and on out a limb to visit the leaves and then getting in the leaves and doing what all it does. Photosynthesis and all that. It is something I never had time for of course. But then you have something like a helicopter sitting on the ground not cranked up, and absolutely nothing is going on inside a helicopter unless somebody cranks it up, and then you've got all that expense of fuel, and little fires going off in the engine. It is so different from a tree. We couldn't be satisfied with a tree, we had to go manufacture a helicopter.

Mr. Albright, my teacher, was standing at the library door greeting students. We got in line behind a few couples. We had to show our tickets that had been handed out in school that day. "Debra, L. Ray," he said. "And how are you all tonight?"

"Just fine, Mr. Albright," said L. Ray, in his very adult way. Did his little Japanese bow.

"Have a good time," said Mr. Albright. "No smoking or profanity."

"I'm here to boogie," said L. Ray.

We made our way in through the door, L. Ray stepping back to let me go first, because one of the double doors was closed.

The library had a book smell that held on above the punch and cookie and balloon and crepe paper smell. There was a record player operated the whole time by Paul Douglass who was also in shop, but Paul was certified retarded. He was a favorite of Mrs. Latta, another chaperone, who got him to participate in all sorts of things, for some reason nobody every knew. He was just her pet, and not even in her class. She taught sixth grade.

Anyway, I could dance like a fool—Teresa, my older sister, had taught me and Melanie, my younger sister—and so could L. Ray, so that's exactly what we did. We danced just about every dance. We were be-bopping. People would stop dancing to watch me and L. Ray dance and I will tell you this: it turned me on. It really turned me on like nothing else. When I did it real hard, I could pick up a leg and twist and turn and bend in a way that it felt like little lightning bolts of gold. It was delightful, and the way L. Ray moved when he was dancing made me hungry for love even at my age or maybe especially at my age. If L. Ray had just had sense enough he could have worked wonders. If any boy over a period of four years of high school had had sense they could have worked wonders.

You get the idea of how it was—people dancing, and us dancing like fools, sweating our heads off, and me having one of the best times of my life. We danced and drank punch and danced and drank punch and ate cookies and potato chips, and more than once people stood and watched me and L. Ray dance all over the place, and all that gold lightning through me, and I was thinking to myself, this is what my life in high school is going to be like. Boys will watch me dance and are going to be asking me to football games and dances all the way through high school, and I'll be a cheerleader and popular and very happy. And three or four times I went to the bathroom with my girlfriends and we freshened our lipstick and makeup and giggled and talked about each other's date and what we were wearing. There seemed to be no jealousy, no bickering. It was a dream night.

Mostly parents came to pick up their children, sticking their heads in the library for their son or daughter, or stepping inside for a minute or two.

L. Ray and I were among the last to leave. We walked down that long wooden hall, and out the door. I remember that door, the clanky handles, and how heavy it was, though on this night L. Ray held it open for me. Then down the steps and around to his car.

"Boy, that was fun, fun, fun," said L. Ray. "Want to go out to the Club Oasis for a little while?"

"Sure." I was game for just about anything.

The Club Oasis advertised on the radio and had live bands and all that. We stopped at the Blue Light and L. Ray went in and got two tall Busches in a paper bag.

"Reach in that glove compartment and get me that church key," he said. He got out the beers and opened them, making the swush sound, and then punched a little hole at the other side of the beer can top.

"Drink up, Debra," he said. "Here's to a long and happy life," and we clunked our beer cans together and I took a swallow. It was cold and it helped me move right on toward the top of the world where I knew I was headed. Then he pushed in the lighter, and, since he was driving, I lit us both a cigarette. I was in the boat of my life heading down the River of Heightened-and-Met-Desires.

Inside the Club Oasis I didn't know too many of the girls, because for one thing they were all older than me. But we danced and danced and danced and sweated and sweated and sweated and went outside and smoked a cigarette and I thought L. Ray might try to kiss me, but he didn't, and then we showed the stamps on our hands and went back inside.

The eighth grade dance had been from seven to nine, and I had to be home I figured no later than about midnight. We left the Club Oasis at about eleven. When I got in the front seat with L. Ray this time, I moved a little ways away from the passenger door toward him. He didn't say anything at all as we left, which seemed a little odd, and he hadn't driven more than I'd say a mile when he simply turned onto a side road, drove maybe a half mile and then pulled over on the shoulder and cut off the ignition. I thought to myself, this is where we neck. I was nervous and I wondered about cars that might drive by.

No sooner was his hand off the car keys, he said of all things, "Debra, have you ever seen a man's pecker?"

I was surprised to death. I thought about my brothers and daddy when they went swimming in the pond. I wasn't afraid or anything—this was just L. Ray Flowers up to something strange. "Yes," I said.

"Well, let me tell you what I'm going to have to do," he said. "I'm going to have to take mine out and give it a beating. It's been a naughty boy, and what you can do for me is sit right there and I think you'll like what you see."

What could I do? I felt like I was locked in a casket.

He sat right there under the steering wheel, unzipped his pants and pulled out his thing. I slipped over against the passenger door and looked out the window but it was like looking in a mirror— the window reflected everything that was in the green light from the dashboard. "Oh, blessed Jesus," he said, and he started masturbating and I just looked out the window at the night and my mind was blank, everything suspended-like, and suddenly there were headlights coming from behind us, and a car whizzed by, and he kept at it, "Oh, blessed Jesus, would you look at me, Debra? Would you look at me?" I couldn't help but see his reflection. He threw his head back and started his hand going faster and . . . well,

I don't need to go into all that here. I just want to somehow explain two things.

The first is the collapse of my insides, of my heart and my hopes. Everything about this was sad and filthy. But at the same time it was clear to me that I wasn't going to get hurt. I did not feel threatened in a physical way, but what had happened might as well have been physical for the hurt and dirty and completely useless and invisible way it made me feel. I tried to look out the window and he said, "Look, look, look," and I said, "I can see you in the reflection, L. Ray. I don't want to look if you don't mind." And he said, "Arrrrrrrrr. Hallelujah! Praise the Lord. Praise the Lord!" Then he opened his door and the inside light came on and he slung his hand toward the ground. I don't mean to gross you out or anything. I'm trying to describe what happened. Then he says, "This is what God gave me, Debra. I can get it going again right away, if only you'll do it with me, if only you do it while I do it and we watch each other. It can make really fun things happen."

I didn't ask him what he meant or anything. I said. "L. Ray, you have to take me home now, or I'm going to tell Mr. Albright."

"Okay," he said. "Let me clean up a little here." He got out his handkerchief. And in no time we were driving home. Total silence. I could feel my face and neck red as a beet.

He walked me to the door, said goodnight, did his little Japanese bow and was gone. I would not look at him in the face.

On the table beside the couch was the box and green paper and white bow. I had the billfold he'd given me in my pocketbook. I sat down on the couch and realized my legs were shaky. And then I started crying.

Mama and Daddy weren't home yet, nor my older brothers and sisters, but my little sister, Melanie, came in and said, "Where have you been?" She was in her pajamas. She was seven then. They were soft pajamas, flannel, white with yellow ducks—they had been mine when I was little. She was wearing her thick glasses and her eyes were looking in different directions.

"Where's Mama and Daddy?" I asked her.

"They went to the drive-in."

"Why didn't they take you?"

"They said it was a dirty movie and I couldn't go. Where have you been?" She was standing there. She was the sister I ended up being closest to.

"To a dance."

"Who did you go with?"

"A boy I know."

"Who?"

"Just a boy."

"Was it fun?"

"Yes. I even went to two dances."

"Then why are you crying?" She jumped up on the couch beside me, crossed her legs, and grabbed her toes.

"I'm crying because I'm happy," I said.

"You can't do that."

"Yes, you can. Sometimes you laugh so hard and so long and you have such a good time that there's nothing left inside except crying. You can be so happy you cry and you can be so sad you laugh. The good thing is that I'm not laughing after all I've been through tonight."

"What have you been through?"

"I told you. A dance. Two dances."

"What did you get for a present?"

"I'll show you." I got my pocketbook from the floor at my feet and pulled out the leather billfold.

"Can I have that bow?"

"Yes."

I still have the billfold. I kept it in my pocketbook all the way through the ninth grade, saying to myself that the next time I had a dance date, I would throw it away and buy myself a new one, and somewhere in there I put the billfold, worn-out, in my top dresser drawer, and then along came this disease with me holding on to that billfold, still. In my life it was L. Ray, my husbands, my children, my grandchildren, then my life with illness.

So is it possible for you to understand that that night was supposed to be the first big dance night of my life? Can you understand if you lived this long without ever having much of a nightlife, when dancing was what you were born for, a gift?

Jim Grimsley

JESUS IS SENDING YOU THIS MESSAGE

The author's message in this story is one of several weaving through the disgruntled narrator's account of his Atlanta commuter-train encounters with Jesus' messenger. At once completely honest and completely unreliable, the narrator's voice is one of bias, prejudice, righteousness, confusion, and recognition. Jim Grimsley was born, raised, and educated in North Carolina and is the author of seven novels, including Winter Birds *and* Boulevard, *and a collection of one-act plays. The recipient of a Lila Wallace–Reader's Digest Writers' Award and an American Academy of Arts award for literature, he teaches writing at Emory University.*

No telling how many times I had ridden home beside her on the train before she gave the message and I noticed. Sitting sleek and composed with her hands clamped firmly on her purse, she was, that day, dressed primly in a pleated skirt and sensible shoes of navy blue, with a bright, fluffy tie at her throat. An older woman, of the generation in which proper ladies wore gloves, like those she carried, folded in her hands, she was blessed with smooth, supple skin the color of dark roast coffee beans; it would have been a flawless skin except for the tiny moles growing out of some of her pores. Her nose was broad and rounded at the end. Her silver-blue hair, streaked, straightened, and shaped into sweeping curves, encased her skull like a helmet, and when she moved the whole stiff mass moved with her, protecting the delicate workings inside, the receiver into which Jesus beamed the message.

She wore a hat that first day I heard her speak, of navy blue felt, with a round brim nicely upturned, and a satin ribbon around the crown, resting gently on the waves and spikes of her hairdo. She rocked forward in her seat, hands clasped around her purse, and glanced at everyone around her. Her eyes brushed mine with the slightest hesitation and moved on. Moments later, she said, in a loud, firm voice, "Good evening, everybody. How is everybody doing?"

She waited, with a fresh, open look, perfectly unafraid. I felt a moment of discomfort, standing so close to her, thinking she was just another crazy person talking on the train while the rest of us made our way home from a day's work in downtown Atlanta. Quiet grew around her and she allowed it to reach its maximum radius, then continued. "Jesus told me to give this message to the people. The Lord is coming back soon, the wait is nearly over. You need to be getting right with God, you don't have much time. Woeful days are coming, when he will bring a destruction on all wickedness of all peoples. Fire will burn in the cities and hellfire and damnation will come to them that have earned it. Then Jesus will come like the light of all things, amen. So you need to hear the message this time, because the Bible says it will come a destruction on the cities, even on this city, too, and it will be too late for you once Jesus gets here. That's what Jesus told me to tell the people. Thanks for listening."

Sitting back with a sense of gliding, at the end she gave a nervous look in various directions, including a glance into my face, the only glimmer of fear she showed, or so I fancied; and she showed that same moment of fear and hesitation every time I saw her, or else I imagined it each time.

The moment passed and I was left with a vague irritation, that first day, but nothing more. But the next morning I boarded the train and found her waiting again, in the exact same seat but this time wearing one of those cotton dresses made of hunter-green fabric covered with white polka dots, a white collar, big white buttons down the front, a white belt and a full skirt. Her bosom swelled ample and high over the cinched belt. A white hat rode the whorls of her hair. She had the same look on her face, as if an invisible page hung before her eyes, words only she could see. Moments after the train left King Memorial Station, she shifted forward, rolling on those ample hips, and glanced at me and opened her mouth and spoke.

I felt, then and later, that she aimed her message at me, though this must have been my imagination, since outwardly she gave no sign of noticing me in any particular way, other than to glance at me with all the rest. But even as early as that second hearing she made me angry with this message, spoken that time so early in the morning. The train arrived at the Georgia State Station and I burst out the door, hurtling toward the escalator. On the short, humid walk to my job at a nearby hospital, I seethed with thoughts of the message-giver which only subsided when I reached my office and found the classical music station playing Bach's Goldberg Variations, soothing piano by Konstantin Lifschitz, enabling me to breathe again.

She became a fixture in my life, after that. She gave the message mornings and afternoons, though most often in the afternoons, always from a seated position, always on the tracks between the Georgia State Station and the Martin Luther King, Jr., Memorial Station. I heard her give the speech going in both directions, and the message never varied, even by one word. She had clearly rehearsed these sentences, and the thought of this added to my resentment of her. She spoke calmly, not with the fervor of a prophet but rather with the grace of a Sunday School teacher. Completing the message as the train pulled into one station or the other, she composed herself and settled back against her seat. By the time the doors opened and new passengers boarded, no one would ever have known that she had, only moments before, shared with us her certainties about the end of time.

Each day, each instance of the message, filled me with contempt for this need she had to put herself forward, to flaunt her Christianity in that manner. Each moment when she shifted forward in her seat to commence her little sermon, I glared at her with narrow eyes as if I could silence her with the completeness of my disapproval.

I am an educated man, a cultivated man. I am not the type of person who would ever speak aloud on a train, unless there were some purpose to it, as saying to the person next to me, "Excuse me, you are standing on my foot" or "Please take your elbow out of my lungs." I am the type of person who believes other people should obey the same rules I do, among them, namely, that no one should presume to deliver Golgothan messages on a commuter train when people are tired and simply want to get home as peaceably as possible. It seemed clear to me that this message could not come from Jesus because He would be too polite to send it. So I listened to her words every day, during a period of peak ridership, in transit from Georgia State to King Memorial or vice versa; and I disliked her every day as well, increasingly.

I see that I have claimed this happened every day. But when I examine my memories, I understand that, while frequently we did ride in the same car on the same train, just as frequently we did not. In the afternoon, I most often caught the 4:36 P.M. eastbound on my way home. Being a creature who takes comfort in habits, I always entered the Georgia State Station from the same direction, crossed the vaulted lobby at the same angle, climbed the same four flights of granite steps to the platform, and waited there next to the same wooden bench. Never sitting on the bench, for fear of dirtying my trousers. But I waited precisely in that spot for the train, because I had calculated from experience that most of the time the lead car pulled up to that point and I had only to step forward to be aboard.

In the mornings I followed a similarly exact routine riding from Inman Park to King Memorial and then on to Georgia State.

On some afternoons I reached the platform only to find the train waiting, and in that case I stepped into the nearest door; or I reached the platform as the door chimes rang and the doors slid closed in my face and then I had to wait for the 4:43 P.M. train; or someone was standing in my waiting place and I had to wait somewhere else and board the wrong car; or someone from work offered me a ride; or I was sick or on vacation or holiday; on many days I never saw her, never heard her give the message. But most afternoons my precise timing and luck brought me to the same place, to the space in the alcove, studying the faded roses on the message woman's cloth bag.

She was a creature of habit like me and liked to sit in one of those seats next to my support pole, or the ones across from me and my pole, so that she was always riding sideways on the train. When I had heard the message often enough to expect her, even to presume she would be sitting there, I began to dread her as well, as soon as I climbed to my waiting place on the platform; though I refused to vary my own routine. I listened for the sounds of the approaching train, watched for the splash of light along the tunnel wall. By the time the train pulled to a stop in front of me and I stepped forward to be the first in line, to board the train first, I had already begun to hate her, as though I knew she were there, as though I could see her sitting with that air of purpose in her usual seat. When I stepped onto the train, when I saw her sitting with that purse raised up like the defensive wall of a highly rounded city, my contempt boiled to loathing and I stood in my usual place fuming that she was certain to speak again, that she would say those words from Jesus that were so intrusive, words that should not be spoken in a public place where people are trapped and have no choice but to listen.

She did, without fail, speak that message each time I saw her. Moving forward in her seat and glancing at her audience, in spite of my longing for her silence, she spoke.

I began to feel, during her soliloquy, the impulse to answer her back, to say, Jesus did not send any message through you for me. The idea of talking back to her, once formed, became part of the whole routine. In my head I framed messages that I would like to give her, brief scenes in which I triumphed over her there on the train; in which I, in fact, transformed her, causing her to understand that there are people in this world who do not need revealed truth on commuter trains or, indeed, in any other setting, excepting perhaps that of the church. There are decent, Christian folk who do not care to live with visions of burning destruction, who are content whether Jesus should come back or not; who are, in fact, happy to wait for him as long as He chooses to tarry. In my fantasy she was overcome with shame at her own effrontery and slid, chagrined, flat against her seat back, never again uttering even a sigh.

My fantasies entirely convinced me of my own way of thinking, so that, when she slipped slightly forward in her seat and gave that sweeping glance to those standing closest, for a long time I thought my silent fury rose up because of the rudeness of her remarks, because her words were not wanted by anybody. I was a Christian myself, a churchgoer, and I did not wish to hear them.

But then one day, at the close of the message, when the woman was easing back into her seat, another black woman seated near her said, "Amen, sister," in a loud clear voice, and an elderly white man nodded his head serenely, as if Jesus had told him the same thing; and I became more angry than ever.

The next day, trembling in my waiting place, the certainty that she would be present delivered me a shivering rage. I heard the familiar drawn-out hoot of the train in the tunnel and witnessed its glide into the station, and I stepped across the platform in the usual way and suddenly realized the train had pulled up too far, that my special door was not where it was supposed to be, and I was actually forced to push and shove my way onto the train with the rest. The train filled to overflowing, I suppose because the train before it had been delayed, and when the doors closed I could not see whether the message woman was there or not. I remained ignorant, my heart fluttering, until, a few dozen yards down the track, her familiar voice rang out, "Good evening everybody. How is everybody doing?"

I ground my back teeth together and pursed my lips and frowned to get the hard line between my eyebrows. I am a tooth grinder, as my dentist will tell you, and I flex my jaw almost constantly, and waken some mornings with tension headaches and the fear that I will soon have facial cancer. But at especial times I grind my teeth in anger, and I did so that afternoon on the train.

I began to study the other people. At first I detected only those who agreed with her, the other older black woman, dressed as she was dressed, with what one might describe as a churchwoman's flare for the benign; and, sometimes, older, white women dressed in a similar vein who signaled their approval demurely with their eyes; or else women of a lower class who nodded, their faces elastic with expanding wrinkles, and said, "You're speaking for the Lord now," and raised their hands for a little of that invisible holy ghost that is always present in the air.

My only allies were, in fact, silent men and groups of teenagers, who were always guaranteed to burst into gales of laughter when she finished speaking the message. Once a loud and sassy girl with huge round thighs and buttocks waited till the end of the message and said, in a crisp, loud voice, "Old grammaw," and her friends hooted and ducked their heads slapping each other this way and that. The message woman simply blinked and watched the space on the wall directly across from her head, as if nothing penetrated the world in which she sat.

A moment later, with breathtaking grace, she leaned forward without looking down and pulled, from the cloth bag, a Bible so worn and thumbed it could only be called formidable, covered in black leather, with patches of bright gold on the edges. She opened the book and started to read silently from the New Testament, one of the gospels where all Jesus's speeches flared up from the page in red ink. The teenagers watched her and fell mostly silent, though one of them would snicker now and then.

One night I dreamed of her lips as she shaped the word "woeful," the fact that the shape of her lips scarcely resembled the sound; her need to replenish her lipstick became very clear to me. She favored a strong red, though not too much of it. Her lips were dark brown at the edges, tapering to pink on the inside. In the dream I saw all this very clearly. Then I awoke with the sheets damp at my neck and a drop of sweat on my meager chest hairs and I became terrified.

I attended St. Luke's Episcopal Church on Peachtree Street, a fine old liberal church with a respectful pastor who occasionally challenged his congregation to greater sacrifice but certainly never threatened us with fiery destruction. While our congregation offered less prestige than a Buckhead church, I felt it was the next best thing. During services, I found myself watching my neighbors on the pews, the young professionals side by side with the old professionals, the gays, the blacks, the well-dressed and the gauchely dressed, the matrons, the widowers, the boys, the girls, the children, the teenagers, the wild bunch, the quiet ones: I studied them, the mostly white faces, and wondered what touch of God would be required to get any of them to speak on a train? Or to hear a message from God at all?

I have heard of white people attending church services in black congregations, like the African Methodist Episcopal Church, or, more often, the Ebenezer Baptist Church in Sweet Auburn, the historic district of downtown Atlanta where Martin Luther King was a preacher and Martin Luther King, Jr., came into the world. But now, when I rode through the shadows of those black churches, I wondered what sort of religion could be practiced there, to arouse in such an ordinary woman the need to predict the end of time to perfect strangers. To speak on a train, actually to do so, to move forward in her seat and open her mouth, how long did she feel the need to take this action before the first time she delivered the message? And the words that she spoke, where did they come from? Did Jesus speak to her in a way He never employed with me?

Seated in the wooden pew of the St. Luke's Episcopal sanctuary, listening to the swell of the organ playing one more verse of "Just As I Am Without One Plea," I listened for the voice of God, even for the echo of the voice of God as He spoke to someone else, and I heard only our thin, reedy voices risen somewhat in song. Then it occurred to me, the question that finally drove me to take action: Was the Christ in her church, who filled her mouth with speech, more real than the Christ in mine?

One day she wore a gold brooch with a silver enamel center and I stood so close to her I could see myself reflected in its surface, a helpless, ridiculous expression on my tiny, pinched face. She had yet to give the message that day, the train having only begun to slide out of Georgia State Station along the curve of track beyond, and I had been forced to stand far closer to her than ever before; added to that, the brooch offended me deeply, being so large and rounded, jutting out from her white rayon blouse with its fussy ruffled collar. But even more offensive was the presence of my own reflection in the milky surface of the brooch, nested near the center of her cleavage. Impossible that I should be so reflected, that my image should seem so tiny and insignificant. The volcano of anger at last boiled over as she rolled those large hips forward and smiled and said those words of preamble, "Good evening, everybody. How is everybody doing?"

"Everybody is doing fine without your message," I said. "Why don't you, for once, sit there and shut your mouth."

As if she had foreseen just such a moment, she hesitated in her forward motion and raised her eyes to mine. In the eyes I saw neither mildness nor serenity but a sharp pinpoint of fury. People around us were tittering and whispering and pointing as the ripple of my words spread out across our pond. "Who does he think he is, what's wrong with him?" I heard, but she kept her eyes glued to mine through that instant, and spoke without hesitation back to me. "I believe I am welcome to speak Jesus's words on this train," she said, "and God bless you in your heart." Then, smiling again, she leaned forward and began, as always, as if I had said nothing, as if I were not present at all. "Good evening, everybody. How is everybody doing? Jesus told me to give this message to the people."

Those around us listened raptly, and I stood there, unable to recede. She spoke with the calm that had been absent from her eyes when she turned her face up to mine, and she delivered the message with the same precision, even the same pauses, as on every other occasion. Her hands she folded over her purse, her white gloves folded in her hands, the small bit of veil from her hat arranged attractively over her forehead. She spoke, "Woeful times are coming," with that movement of lips of which I had dreamed, in need of a touch of lipstick, I noted, even in my distraction and mortification. I had dreamed this actual moment, I too had fore-seen everything.

She completed the message and returned to her resting position. She never so much as glanced at me. Those around her approved of every word, a few "Amens" were whispered, and many faces, black and white, glared at me disapprovingly for my rudeness.

Why had I spoken? Was it simply my reflection in the awful brooch? Had my workday at the hospital piqued my temper to that point? Or was it worse than that? Had I felt so free to speak to this woman for reasons I hardly cared to imagine?

At Inman Park Station I stumbled from the open door and felt the relief of all those who remained behind me. I wondered what they said to one another after I fled. In my mind, like an endless reel of film, the whole sequence of moments replayed itself again and again: my anger, my reflection in the brooch, my sudden, unthinking need to spit words at her, and all that followed, the whole moment of her triumph and my humiliation.

Afterward, I could no longer follow the course of my old habits. I changed everything to avoid her, taking an earlier train from Inman Park and heading home on, as a rule, the 4:50 P.M. train from Georgia State Station. I abandoned my old standing-and-waiting place for a location far down the platform, on the bridge that crosses over Piedmont Avenue below the State Capitol Build-ing where I could see the gleaming dome of real gold leaf. But, as happens, one afternoon when hurrying to the train, I found it had already arrived at the station and I darted heedlessly into the first open door. She was sitting in her usual place and saw me at once, she lifted her face and knew me, I am certain of it, but she said nothing at all. My heart pounded and I nearly fled to the other end of the car; but then I got my breath and held my ground and waited. This time I will listen, I thought. This time I will hear her message as if it really comes to me from Jesus, and I will receive these words into my heart, and I will change, I will never be angry again.

But she merely sat there and never moved forward, never spoke. Her worn Bible showed itself in the faded flowered bag but she never lifted it out, never opened it or read it. The train reached King Memorial Station and still she had not spoken, nor would she meet my eye again. She simply gazed, placid and withdrawn, at the advertisement for Bronner Brothers hair care products behind my head, and at the passing landscape through the windows, the cemetery where Margaret Mitchell was buried, the old cotton sack factory and the chic renovated cottages of Cabbagetown. We rode to Inman Park and I left the train, feeling hollow and even bereft.

At home I bagged the garbage and walked and fed Herman, my aging schnauzer. The life of a bachelor has always suited me, I have never wanted much company, but that evening I called a friend from church and asked her out to dinner. She made some excuse, clearly embarrassed by the invitation, and I hung up the phone feeling even more lonely than before. I felt as if I had been drifting out to sea for a very long time without noticing, and that today I had lost sight of land forever, my continent disappearing over the horizon, while I drifted on and on. I felt the urge to cry and wish, now, I could report that I actually had.

I have seen the message woman since, on occasion. She rides the train as I do, every day, though where she boards and where she departs I have never learned. I picture her as a schoolteacher or teacher's aide, or as a librarian, perhaps employed in Midtown or in West End near the Joel Chandler Harris house. I picture her surrounded by children to whom she tells stories, and sometimes I try to imagine the stories she might tell, rolling words pouring out of her in that voice that had become, at one time, so very familiar to me. Most often I picture her in the front pew of a church, enraptured by the power of some thunderous sermon descending over her from the mouth of a faceless preacher, surrounding her with the voice of God.

When I am present with her, I know she recognizes me and always will, as the white man who told her to shut up, who tried to stifle Jesus's message. She sits neatly and silently folded in the seat, and I stand in my narrow space with my arms glued to my side, my breath coming a bit labored. She waits, and I wait, but no message comes. I slide out of the train at my appointed place and picture her then, moving forward in the seat as the train accelerates toward the next station up the line; she glances around at everybody and begins again, wetting her lips and speaking those words that I hear, these days, all the more clearly in her silence.

2001

Stephen Coyne

HUNTING COUNTRY

Here an old couple faces the winding down of a life of hard work and hard-won plea-
sure. The wife contemplates her aging husband: "He was familiar to her in every
wrinkle and pain. He was hers to have and to hold, but it was as if her hand had
closed on sand, and the harder she squeezed, the quicker it ran between her fingers."
Stephen Coyne sets the story in the rural South, where he once met an old man and
his disapproving wife in search of lost coon dogs. A professor of English literature at
Morningside College in Sioux City, Iowa, he has published his short stories in many
literary journals.

She heard the old fool pull into the driveway. How could she
miss him? A hundred times she had told him to get his truck
fixed, but he never would do it. He couldn't hear was the problem,
and he wouldn't admit that he couldn't hear, so what did he care
if he drove something that sounded like a castrated pig?

His dogs were gone again. Edna could tell that just by the
sound of things. Three thousand dollars' worth of bluetick mixes
running loose in the woods somewhere. It wasn't such a big number anymore—three thousand dollars—unless you were a pulp-
wooder and didn't make but eight or nine thousand a year. Oh, a
young man might make more than that, but then again, young
men these days had better sense than to be pulpwooders.

But forty years ago, when she first met him, pulping was the
thing to do. All you needed was a chain saw and enough courage
to use it. Lots of men were afraid of such saws back then, and good
reason, too. Many a one sawed through a boot top or cut a branch
that sprung back and snapped him into the next world. But not
Coy. He was strong. A chain saw was nothing more to him than a

tamed scream at the end of his big arms. In five minutes he could bring down a tree it'd take two men with a crosscut an hour to fell. That was back before the big woods were cut over. Back when you could get three loads of pulpwood from the laps of a single tree. It seemed to her that in those days everywhere Coy turned another tree was coming down, and there was Coy, standing over the carcass, cutting off the money and loading it onto his truck. Now, all these years later, his forearms were still bigger than most men's calves, but they were laced with varicose veins, and sometimes they hurt so bad that Coy couldn't cut. Even though it was only planted pine not much bigger around than her leg, he still couldn't cut. He never said anything. But he'd come home with half a load or less, and she'd know.

When they were young, though, their wood lot was always stacked high, and as far as they knew, they were rich. First thing Coy always wanted was good dogs. Bluetick and redbone— howlers and criers. On nights when the moon shone down on mist that filled the hollows, the two of them would load the dogs into the truck and drive into the country. They'd turn the dogs loose and sit in the truck, listening to the howls echo through the woods. It put the hair up on Edna's arms, it was so beautiful and eerie. Seemed like it was the sound of their two spirits spinning through those trees, chasing after what they knew they needed while their bodies stayed in the truck doing what bodies could think to do.

Then came kids, and he went without her after that, he and his buddies. They weren't content to sit in the truck and listen but had to get liquored up, put pistols in their pockets, and light out through the woods, chasing the sounds and sometimes finding the dogs around a tree. She never understood why they had to carry it that far, why they wanted to see the coon's eyes shine in their flashlight beams, why they'd shoot until it fell, or until it died in the arms of the tree. Sometimes Coy told her about coons that seemed to disappear, right out of the tree, somehow, so that the dogs had to be tied up and dragged back to the truck.

And sometimes, of course, they'd lose the dogs. There'd be a howling out there, but liquor and the hollows confused the sounds. The men would wander into briars or cripples until finally they'd quit. Coy'd come home alone, then, and she'd be able to tell whether he was mad from the way he closed the truck door and by the sound of his steps on the back porch. If the dogs had struck hard and tracked fast, they might have just left the men behind. He'd be excited then, and his steps would be quick and loud—what a coon, strong and smart. You could lose dogs over an animal like that and feel proud. But if the dogs had wandered and fretted and never struck hard but wouldn't come when they blew the horn, he'd be mad. His steps would be slower and quiet like he was trying to sneak up on something. He'd tell her he didn't care if he never found them dogs again. She'd remind him what they cost, but he'd swear and say it was a small amount to lose to be rid of something that couldn't do what it was put on Earth to do.

But anymore, it was hard to tell how he felt by the sound of his steps because he didn't step so much as shuffle. She heard him head toward the shed to put away his pistol and take off his boots. He ought not hunt was what she thought. For one thing there was nobody to go with him. His last friend, Mr. Logan, was in the White Oak Nursing Home now because it got to the point where he had forgotten how to get home from the store. And there was no way Edna would go with Coy into the woods. Not now, not at her age. No, she had long ago given up foolishness like that. So he went by himself, and it wasn't safe. Time was you had to worry about bears and even panthers. Thank goodness those times were gone, but it wasn't any safer now because the things that stalked old people were a whole lot fiercer than wild animals.

She knew all she needed to know about that. She was old when she had kids—thirty by the time the last was born. And each one brought more trouble—more falling down and foolishness, more sickness and fussing. Wasn't until the kids were grown and gone that she felt safe again. But by then her joints ached when the weather got bad, and one day she tripped over a rug and hit a chair before she wound up on the floor with a broken wrist. It never healed right, and so she was never again the woman she once had been.

No, it was plain as chestnuts—by a certain age a person ought to admit that he can't catch what runs in the woods anymore. He ought to stay home and be glad he's got a clean, warm place where he can sit in comfort and remember a time when he could catch most anything he wanted to. Stay home. Watch TV. Read the paper. Lock the door.

Coy stepped into the kitchen and stood there in his dirty socks, looking at her across the room.

"Well?" she said. He turned away and got a drink of water. "Where are they this time?"

"Ain't no woods no more," he said. "You can drive all the way to Polk County and not pass nothing but saplings no bigger 'round than a dog's waist, and the ground underneath choked with weeds and green briars. Take a weasel to find a coon in such a mess as that. I don't even know why I keep dogs no more."

"Well," she said, "sounds like you don't."

"Ain't even hardly a tree big enough to hold a good-sized coon."

"You ought to sell them dogs."

"Down to Polk County, right there by the Green River, there's still some woods, but they've cut over parts of it, so you walk a while and then you come to a thicket can't a gnat get through. And if they do strike in there, why you can't halfway hear because the sound don't carry through a mess like that."

No, she thought, the old fool's ears were twice as big as when he was young, but the bigger they got the worse they seemed to work.

"Better get some sleep," she said. "So you can hunt them tomorrow."

"I'm going to bed," he said, and she nodded.

But he didn't get up early the next morning and drive the dirt roads looking for the dogs. And he didn't go out in the evening either. All he did was mess around in his shed all day, filling boxes and trash bags. When he came in to wash his hands for supper, she stood right next to him and looked him in the eye. "It's good money," she said, "just starving to death out there."

He turned from the sink and said, "Huh?"

It was bad being deaf, but she had to admit it had its uses.

They sat in the living room all evening watching her shows. He stared at the TV, but she didn't think he was paying attention. He never once asked her to run the volume up, and he only seemed to come to himself when girls in bathing suits flashed across the screen.

"Get up," she wanted to tell him. "What sort of a man sits there and watches shows like this, like he's in a trance?"

In the middle of *Murder, She Wrote*, he pushed himself out of his chair. "I'm going to bed," he said, like he had lost some sort of battle he had been fighting. She watched him slouch up the stairs, then turned back to her show. It was no use trusting an old man. Once they couldn't work, they weren't good for a single thing. She was half-tempted to go find those dogs herself—find them and sell them.

He didn't go out looking the next morning either. And at supper he wouldn't say anything to her but "Huh?" After dinner, he sat in the living room all evening while the room got dark. He didn't even hear the phone when it rang.

The young man on the other end said he had found some dogs at his place and the tags had this number on it.

"Yes," Edna said. "Let me let you talk to my husband."

She held the phone toward Coy, and he groaned coming out of the chair. "Where?" he said into the phone. "Wait a minute."

He gave the phone back to her. "I can't tell what he's saying."

She got the location and hung up. "Let's go," she said.

He filled two bowls with food and put them in the back of the truck next to the dog cages. "You drive," he told her.

She headed them down the Coxe Road, the truck screaming all the way. They turned onto the Watson Road, which was dirt, and then onto a farm road, which was just two ruts through the woods. The road climbed a hill and wound between white oaks into the driveway of an old log house.

"I know this place," Coy said. "There was a bear tore the convertible top off a man's car lived here. Must've been forty years ago. Fool left food in the backseat, and the bear went right through the top. Fellow run him off by throwing stones. Saved some of the food, but the roof of that car was ruint."

The first thing that came to greet them was a Labrador retriever. It looked like a shadow in their headlights. The dog lifted its leg and marked their tires.

"That dog ain't no kind of use around here," Coy said.

Next came three dogs, their tails between their legs. Edna recognized the bluetick markings, but the dogs seemed smaller, somehow, than their dogs. They bred them down, these days. Coy had explained it to her. They mixed in bird dog so they could hunt better in brush. He didn't like it. Little dogs for chasing little coons through little woods. Not a thing to be proud of, but it was all you could do anymore since the world had gotten so small and so filled up with children and pups and saplings that there was hardly anyplace for something full-grown. The Lab jumped back and forth, bowing to play. One of the mixes wrestled with it.

"Useless," Coy mumbled.

Next came a young man in short pants. He had a little goatee and a big smile.

Edna smiled back at the boy and glanced over at Coy. He didn't seem to notice the boy, though. He was looking straight ahead, and she followed his eyes. A girl, also in short pants and wearing the top to a bathing suit, was headed their way. She stopped to pet the dogs, which gathered around and followed her to the truck.

The boy was talking a streak about how they had seen the dogs yesterday at twilight but that they wouldn't come out of the woods. Then this evening they must have gotten the courage to come up and make friends with Jessie (Edna didn't know whether this was the black dog or the girl). The boy had managed to read the number on one of their collars, and so he had called, and goodness they really loved the sound coon dogs made in the woods at night, but Laura didn't like the idea of killing coons. (So Edna knew, then, that Laura most likely was the girl.) The boy had told Laura that lots of times hunters didn't even bother to follow the dogs but just let them run to hear their music and then called them back and went home. Sometimes, though, the dogs wouldn't come, and so they left them, knowing they would go someplace or other when they got hungry enough. Just a good thing they found somebody honest this time, the boy said. Yes, Jessie and Laura both liked them just fine. Real nice coon dogs.

Edna had never heard the like. This boy was some sort of Yankee, or maybe he was just from Charlotte, but either way he was one of those people that comes at you talking and leaves you talking and never shuts up enough to let the world catch its breath. Nice coon dogs. What foolishness. The young could have it worse than the old. A good coon dog didn't care a thing about people except for food. No, all a coon dog cared about was the woods and what his nose could take him to.

"Well, they sure are friendly," the boy was saying, "and pretty— they sing fine at night. Why, with the moon full and . . ."

She turned to Coy. "You going to feed them?"

"Ain't mine," he said.

"What?" she said.

He looked her straight in the eye and said, "Huh?"

How long? she wondered. How long before Coy wouldn't be able to find his way home from the store either? She had fallen in love with this man. She had wanted to spend her life with him, and she had. She had lived with him until, now, it seemed like there was hardly anything left.

She got out of the truck and put the food bowls on the ground. The dogs didn't even bother to smell what was there.

"Oh," said the boy. "Laura made bacon and eggs for them a little while ago."

"They sure were hungry," said Laura, and she smiled sweetly at the dogs.

"Let's go," Coy said. "Get in the truck."

"I'll help you load them up," the boy said, and he bent down and picked up one of the dogs. It wasn't like Coy did it. Coy picked dogs up by the scruff of the neck and the skin of their rumps, and he pitched them like bales of hay. This boy put his arms underneath and held the dog the way Jesus holds the lamb in that picture. Edna didn't open the cage door. She just looked at the boy with his arms under the dog, and the dog looking surprised and yet somehow content, like it didn't care if it never ran in the woods again.

Coy leaned out the window. "That ain't mine," he said.

"But it's got your number right here on the collar," the boy said.

Coy squinted at the boy. "What do you reckon you'd do, short pants, if a bear come through the roof of *your* car?"

The boy cocked his head and smiled. "Huh?" he said.

Edna was about to argue with the old fool, right there in front of strangers. This was good money here, their money, but it'd do no good to argue with him now—she knew that—not with his foolish mind made up. She put the bowls back in the truck and got behind the wheel. They could come back another day, or she could. The truck screamed when she started it. Then she turned around and drove down the ruts, leaving the boy and girl standing there in a swirl of dogs and exhaust.

When they turned onto the Watson Road, Edna said, "Have you gone completely crazy, or are you only halfway there? That's three thousand dollars' worth of dogs."

"Ain't mine," he said.

They were a mile down the road, just crossing White Oak Creek, when he told her to pull over and shut the truck off. The trees were still big along the creek because the law wouldn't let loggers cut there. The darkness was deep, and it smelled cool and rich.

"Now," he said, and his head cocked like he heard something. "Them's my dogs."

She listened to the breeze high in the leaves and to the water hissing across rocks in the creek. If there had been some hounds sounding it would have been like the old days—back when she and Coy thought that the woods would go on forever and that they would go on forever, too, back when a whole forest of tall trees held the stars higher in the sky.

"Forty years," he said. "It ain't a long time to kill every bear and cut every tree."

She nodded. "It's enough," she said.

They stared through the windshield at the darkness. "I done my share of it," Coy said. "Must've cut a million trees, but I can't work no more, Edna. I can't hear the dogs no more. And there ain't no woods no more. Only little patches, like this, to make a man miserable."

Well, it was true. He couldn't work, and he knew he couldn't work. She started the truck and pulled onto the road. The woods glided past, and she could smell the soft, rich smells.

"Can you hear 'em?" Coy said.

She did not look at him. She didn't need to. He was familiar to her in every wrinkle and pain. He was hers to have and to hold, but it was as if her hand had closed on sand, and the harder she squeezed, the quicker it ran between her fingers.

The leaves were turning yellow already. Another winter would be on them soon. Well, so what if he didn't want his own dogs? That was fine with her, but to leave them at some stranger's house, well, it was foolish—a waste of money they didn't have. Just when she thought she knew the exact shape of the old fool's foolishness, here it had gone and taken on a new shape, and now she was going to have to figure him out all over again.

Tomorrow. She would come back tomorrow and gather them up and sell them.

"Do you hear?"

She stopped at the intersection with Coxe Road. The truck screamed, and the cicadas were working themselves up into crazy rhythms. No, she did not hear old hounds running through the woods of a deaf man's memory. She did not hear their mournful cries when they struck trail, did not hear how their music got sadder and more desperate the closer they got to what they wanted. What was it, she had always wondered, what was it that drove them to chase after things that made them seem so unhappy?

Coy was leaning his head out the window, listening. He was out there somewhere, spinning on ahead of her. She wanted to cry his name, wanted to say, "Coy, what's happening to you? Where is the man I used to know?" She wanted to bring him back to her, wanted to have him and to hold him, but getting what you wanted—holding it in your hand or in your heart—getting what you wanted only meant that it was going to be gone from your life forever.

She pulled onto the highway. Countless times she had driven this road, but all of a sudden she wasn't sure if it wound left or right. Left, she thought left, but she slowed down anyway, just in case there might be a surprise for her up ahead.

Max Steele

THE UNRIPE HEART

Max Steele says that when he was asked by The Washington Post Magazine *for a story about summer, the image of a watermelon came to him immediately. "From fifty years of writing I knew to follow any image, or character, or line of dialogue that presents itself at such a moment. So when I pressed the ripe piece of the imaginary watermelon to the roof of my mouth, the story was there, intact. I am often thankful to the grand Nancy Hale for saying to me: 'After all, memory is the best fiction writer.'" Max Steele was head of the creative writing program at the University of North Carolina from 1966 to 1987. He is the author of three collections of stories and a novel,* Debby.

for Rick Moody

Those old enough remember the summer of 1932 as the summer of the Lindbergh case. I remember it as the hottest time of my childhood, when I was not allowed to go out of the yard, not for fear that I would be kidnapped in that small Southern town but because I had done a thing to my mother too dreadful ever to be mentioned in my family, or by the neighbors, or by those people who slowed their cars that afternoon to look up at the porch roof, where my crime was committed.

Hot! The regular paperboy had had heatstroke and been sent off to camp by some rich subscribers. The new paperboy was too young to be carrying the huge canvas bag, packed tight with news of the kidnapping-murder of the Lindberghs' young son and the determination of New Jersey officials and the FBI to find the killer. The ugliest rumor was that the boy was in some way defective or retarded and the Lindberghs had killed him or had him killed.

Neighbors, sitting on their porches or seeking a breeze in their side yards, waited for the afternoon paperboy. Eager for the news but also alert to see where the paper might land. The twelve-year-old boy had no aim at all. He threw papers into bushes, fishponds (the new craze) and even, as was the case with us that day, onto the roofs of porches.

First of all, you need to know that I was barely eight and my mother fifty that hot summer. She had been in a bewitched change of life since I was three and was to stay in it until I was thirteen. Nothing could be done to stop or ease the symptoms of panic and what she considered sheer defensive rage. Her feet never seemed to touch the ground. She blazed through the house giving orders, starting jobs, starting others; the world was falling to pieces before her very eyes. And there was no money for anything. My older brothers and sisters stayed away from home as much as possible. But since I was not allowed to cross streets, she always knew where to find me.

My father simply took me aside from time to time when he would find me hiding and say: "I know. Just stay out of her way as much as possible. But don't hide. It breaks her heart when she finds you hiding from her. Someday you'll see how much she loves you." And he was right, because by the time I was grown she was known as a charming woman, much admired for her calm demeanor and nurturing consideration.

But that afternoon she called me from the gazebo in the back-yard where I was rolling the watermelon in a shallow tub of cold water, getting ready for the slicing after dark.

At the back door she seized my wrist and said: "The paperboy's thrown the paper on the roof." She was really reminding me that my father expected the paper to be unopened and still neatly folded on his chair where he would read it, drinking iced tea and waiting for supper to be set on the dining room table. Nothing in the world seemed more important than that my father be given during these Depression days whatever little things would make him happy. She marched me through the house and up the stairs and into a bedroom with a window that opened onto the porch roof. There she picked up a cushion from an old leather chair and put the cushion on the roof. "Sit on that," she said and pointed me out onto the roof, toward the paper, down near the gutter. "Be careful," she said, and at those words I forgave her all her morning voice, shrill as an untuned violin.

Out on the hot slate roof I edged on my bottom and heels down the steep slope toward the paper. When I looked back for her approval, she waved encouragement, I know now, but in one crazed moment it looked as if she were thumbing her nose at me. "She's got me out here to kill me," I thought. The dead Lindbergh boy was on the minds of everyone, especially children. Most of us had never thought of death before.

She apparently thought I was slipping, falling. Out through the window she came. I screamed, knowing she was going to push me off. She was sure I was falling and came crawling top speed.

I swung over the peak of the hip roof, ran back of her to the baked brick house and back through the window opening. I latched the screen, pulled down the window and locked it. I ran through the bedroom and down the stairs. I flipped the night lock on the front door and slammed it behind me. I sat for a moment in my father's chair listening to her on the roof. What to do? Then my father's voice came back to me: "Don't hide from her."

When my heart quit racing and my breathing slowed, I sauntered, I thought, down the curved brick steps and down the flagstones to the street, where an iron hitching post stood next to a granite block. I had been told ladies once descended in their long dresses from their carriages to the block. (My mother, brought up Victorian, still wore her dresses long, and her collar pinned with a cameo. More Gibson girl than modern.) Without looking at her on the roof, I swung with one hand round the hitching post, stepping up on the granite block and down on each turn.

Sweat was running down my legs, and my good white shirt was clinging to me. She had made me two, this short-sleeved one and a long-sleeved one for school, from two of my father's old ones that had split down the back. Before I could even try them on she had said: "Now, go tear them up like you do everything else." Someone had told me she didn't even hear herself but I heard her.

Gradually I would steal glances at the house and the porch roof where my mother was sitting on the leather cushion, her back to the bricks, the newspaper held stretched out in front of her. The black-and-white skirt of her voile afternoon dress tucked neatly around her ankles. It would never have occurred to her to call or shout over such a distance. Dying, she would have had more dignity than that.

When I started to wheeze from the jumping and from the heat, I moved cautiously to the shade of the pecan tree in the side yard. Few in those days had fences that Southerners would have considered hostile, and so the yards were tactfully separated by bushes and hedges. (The azalea craze had not yet hit the Carolinas and so between our house and the Athertons' next door was a rosebush on a three-foot retaining wall the length of the yard.) Mr. and Mrs. Atherton were sitting in their side yard, almost hidden by the wall and roses. I sat playing with pecan shells on the grass almost above their heads. They could not see me and I could not see my mother.

After a long while and much rustling of the paper, Mrs. Atherton said, "Is that what I think it is?" She was looking at our roof.

"It is," Mr. Atherton said, glancing discreetly over the top of his paper. He was from Charleston, not really even from Charleston, just the outskirts, some even said Summerville, and had married a woman from Pennsylvania and always acted as if he had married beneath himself.

"What is she doing up there?" Mrs. Atherton asked.

Mr. Atherton coughed, meaning lower your voice, and said, "Reading the paper, obviously."

For a long while Mrs. Atherton thought about what she had been told, then dared a reprimand by asking: "But why is she reading it up there?"

Mr. Atherton turned a page and said, "I'm sure she has her reasons."

Mrs. Atherton had to ponder that but finally said: "I wonder what they are."

"They think it may be the work of a foreigner. From the ransom notes."

"Oh," Mrs. Atherton said, befuddled by the mixture of national and local news. She began fanning herself with a palm-leaf church fan with a mortuary ad stenciled on it. "I hope she's found a little breeze up there." She sounded confident that that was why my mother was out on the roof. By then people walking home from work began slowing and looking up at our roof, then people in cars were beginning to slow, puzzled over the loitering pedestrians, and then they, too, were staring up at my mother.

"When are you going to quit trying to mind other people's business?" Mr. Atherton asked.

"I . . ." she began. "It just seems a little odd to me, her sitting out there on the roof . . ."

"It's her roof," Mr. Atherton insisted.

"And her paper," Mrs. Atherton agreed quickly, "I suppose."

At the moment, it didn't seem an especially safe place for me to be. A few people had stopped dead on the sidewalk and were looking up, whispering, then moseying along.

I dropped the pecan shell canoes and ran to the backyard and the watermelon. Some mornings I was given a nickel and it was my job to buy the biggest watermelon I could get for the money. I had made friends with an old black man who had a mule and a wagon full of straw and watermelons. He enjoyed my bargaining and would even tote the watermelon, too heavy for me, to the gazebo. Now, slapping the cool watermelon, I could feel it tremble and knew the heart held but was almost ready to fall out when sliced. I stood absolutely still and slapped my own chest to make it tremble and wondered when my heart would be ripe. The watermelon was the best bargain I'd got since the Fourth of July, huge and exactly ripe. It almost seemed that the day had not gone all wrong and crazy.

Ordinarily my father drove into the driveway and parked under the oak trees, but today I did not hear him. He had parked on the street and I saw him only as he came up the gravel drive. Trying not to run but swinging his arms in a fast pace. He didn't even stop to talk about the perfect watermelon. "Why is the front door locked?" We never locked it except when the circus was in town. He didn't wait for an answer but was up the back steps and through the screen door.

It didn't seem like an especially safe place here in the gazebo, either. So I played a bit until I was behind the four fig trees, which were covered with linen napkins drying in the sun. I was almost hidden from the house.

I lay in the itchy grass and listened as my brothers came home on bicycles and I could hear my sisters playing a duet on the piano, and the rattling of china and clinking of water goblets and ice through the dining room windows. I wanted to cry, wondering if I'd be allowed to have supper, or watermelon at least. Or if I would be allowed back in the house. Again I wished I had a collie dog to cuddle up to even if I would have an asthma attack. (Why did my brothers tease me and tell me asthma was "smother's love"?)

It was funny: Here I was dripping with sweat in the same spot where in the winter I had been lying on the ground "like a dunce" freezing. That February day Dr. Rutledge had made a house call and had brought a New York doctor with him because my mother had fainted twice. Once in the kitchen and once in the back hall, where I had found her. They could not stop her "flooding."

Dr. Rutledge had explained that "flooding" meant bleeding and that was why she was so white and needed to stay off her feet. Both said they had never heard of a case of menopause so obdurate or so corrosive. I did not understand what they were talking about but I did understand when they said someone needed to be with her every moment. She was no longer nervous and angry and I wanted to be the one to be with her.

I sat in the darkened room and held my breath so I could see if she was breathing or not. She was lying, her back to me, fully clothed, with my delivery blanket over her shoulders. I tried not to make a sound. But suddenly she was nervous again and said, "I can't stand all that hovering. I'm not going to die. Go on out and play. Anywhere." When I didn't move, she said: "Just please go. Get out!"

Now, sweating in the tall grass, I wondered if she were up on the roof bleeding. I wanted to sneak along the house to see if blood was gushing or even dripping out of the downspout from the porch. Would the blood turn the daisies red? Did people push up red daisies? I lay so still even a snail couldn't have seen me move.

Finally, feeling I had dozed off, I could hear my sisters on the back steps calling my name, and then my father's voice. I could see him ducking under the fig trees, coming to get me. I curled up on my side and shut my eyes, pretending to be asleep.

"It's all right," he said. He was stooping down beside me and his firm hand was large on my shoulder. "We won't ever mention it," he promised. "None of us." And no one ever did.

2002

Lucia Nevai

FAITH HEALER

This is a love story, told by a man at the end of a harrowing second chance romance.
Lucia Nevai says it "began as the voice of an unloveable, unredeemable bastard in
my ear, trying to make his point to me. . . . I wasn't sure how he'd make out down
South, but I wasn't going to help him." Nevai's short stories have been published in
The New Yorker, Zoetrope: All-Story, The Iowa Review, *and other publications.*
The author of two collections of stories, Normal *and* Star Game, *and a novel,* Seri-
ously, *she lives in upstate New York.*

There are things you will automatically do for an ex no matter how many years you've been divorced. Eppie had me
figured to the penny. She had the amount down. She had the frequency. I enjoyed that aspect of giving her money. She knew me
when no one else knew me. It gave me pleasure to listen to her ask
in her familiar little voice for the right amount for the right thing.
One year it was $600 to have our German shepherd put down and
properly buried in a pet cemetery because her hips went (the
dog's). Another year, it was $2,000 for root canals. Things like that.

When I was still married to Jacquelyn, boy did that burn Jacquelyn up. *What does she want now? Are you going to give it to her? You*
treat your ex better than your spouse. Maybe you want two exes. She
stayed mad for two weeks when I gave Eppie money. It wasn't
about money—money wasn't a problem for Jacquelyn and me.
Not like it was when Eppie and I were married and sometimes
didn't have the sixty bucks to pay the fuel bill or the thirty bucks
for a new carburetor. It was the knowledge Eppie had about how
to handle me, how much to ask for and when to ask. And the way
I always said, *No problem.* After we divorced, Jacquelyn and I, she

tried it, same trick, asking for money above and beyond what I'd agreed to, and I said no. Boy, was she surprised.

It was March—back to Eppie—when I took care of a legal fee, $1,200 for a suit to stay in her apartment because they were trying to illegally evict her. So imagine my surprise when she called me in April from a pay phone at a rest stop on I-79, asking me to do her a favor. She usually paced her requests.

"A favor," I said. "What kind of favor?"

She asked me to drive her to a faith healer in Pikeville.

"Pikeville. Where's Pikeville?" I said because I was afraid something was wrong with her and I didn't want to know what.

"In Tennessee," she said. We both live in Pittsburgh. I live outside Pittsburgh on a lake and she lives downtown.

"Tennessee," I said, cool as a cucumber. "When?"

"Now."

"Where are you?" I asked.

And she told me the name of the rest stop. I listened to the truck traffic for a moment, gathering my courage. "What's wrong?" I asked.

"I had a ride set up, but he turned out to be a psycho." Her voice was brave and matter-of-fact, so mine was too.

"That's what's wrong with the world," I said. "I want to know what's wrong with you."

She paused. I knew what she was going to say because that kind of cancer ran in her family. I said it for her. "It's the liver, isn't it."

We got our first taste of spring in Virginia. The dogwoods were out and the redbud trees were in bloom. There was a Civil War battlefield behind the gas station and a souvenir store next door where Eppie bought a good-sized painting of John Wayne, oil on velvet. I watched her bargain with the fellow. He started out wanting twelve dollars for John Wayne. She got him down to two. Standing there in that Virginia souvenir store, she looked like any woman, not necessarily a sick one. She was wearing a little blue cotton dress and a bulky white cardigan sweater with big machine-embroidered flowers on the two front pockets. On her feet, she wore her little yellow flip-flops. Her face was as round and blank and sweet as a sugar cookie with her two little no-color eyes not quite looking at you. Her hair was still that wispy pale brown color, falling about her shoulders every which way. She burped a lot. That was the only change I could see in her. And every time she burped, she said, "Excuse me all to pieces," as if it was the first and only time that day—that year even—that she'd burped.

There was a 7-11 next to the souvenir store where I wanted to have a quick cup of coffee before getting the 4×4 back on the interstate. "What *now?*" I called to Eppie because although I was hightailing it in the direction of the 7-11, she was standing stock still with John Wayne under her arm.

So much of our marriage had taken place at that distance—roughly 26 feet—me always half turned away as I charged off in a direction I assumed to be our mutual goal, though I hadn't put it into words, Eppie always standing stock still at home plate, the point where my assumptions and hers parted ways. And nine times out of ten, you-know-who went sulking back to home plate with his tail between his legs. For a sweet little blank-faced woman, Eppie always got her way.

"Let's have coffee where we can meet real Virginians," she said. God, I missed her. Jacquelyn was not one-tenth the fun. I followed Eppie past the hardware store, past the church to a little luncheonette still serving breakfast. A ginger-colored cat was sleeping in the bay window next to a big African violet. It's funny. You hear the words *African violet* all your life without ever picturing the continent of Africa full of violets. We went inside and sat in a booth. A few regulars were lounging at the counter, drinking coffee. NO FOUL LANGUAGE read a stained sign over the coffee pot.

"Give us two breakfast specials," I said to the waitress without asking Eppie. I knew what she wanted.

"Yes sir," the waitress said with a sweet little obedient twang. She looked to be about ten years old. She went into the kitchen and waved a wand over two plates, piling them up with sausage, cheese grits, hash browns,and freshly fried eggs. Here I'd been going to Friendly's every morning, thinking THAT was breakfast, that frozen, reheated, overly manufactured stuff they cook the same from New York to California.

"Faster next time," I said. She laughed.

"Y'all looked so hungry!" she said. "I said to myself, *They are hungry—I bet they've been on the road traveling.* I wouldn't have known how hungry you can get traveling except I just got back from driving my three kids to Florida and it was real hard."

"Three kids," I said. "How old are you?"

"Nineteen," she said. "See, I met my husband at fifteen and got pregnant right away. But I told him I didn't want to get married if he was already thinking about getting a divorce. I wouldn't put my kids through what I went through."

"What's that," I said.

"Well, my stepdad, he used to beat me like a dog," she said. She said it descriptively, no blame attached, like the way you'd say *my stepdad used to teach me arithmetic.* "But first I was raised by my father," she said, "because my mother was *unfit.*" She said unfit as if it were a State word, part of some proclamation. "See, the strange thing is my dad and my stepdad used to be best friends and drink together. And my mom and my stepmom, they used to be friends. Because my stepmom used to be married to my stepdad!" Her voice was joyful as if she felt important to be part of such a coincidence.

"See, one night my stepdad said to my dad when they were out in a boat, fishing, *I'm tired of the fat lady*—'cause my stepmom, she's real fat. So he says, *I'm tired of the fat lady. Do you want to switch?* And my dad thinks and he says, *Yeah, let's switch.* Now my stepdad beats my mother like a dog. She doesn't admit it, but he does. Like a dog. He beat all of us, me, my little brother and my little sister. My little brother, he got the worst of it. And now he's in the orphanage. But my stepmom—I love her to death. Bless her soul! She taught me everything I know. Ain't I lucky?"

• • •

We crossed the border into Tennessee. "Did you tell the god-damn kids?" I said. We had been driving in silence since Virginia after arguing briefly about where John Wayne was born. She said California. I knew damn well John Wayne was born in Winterset, Iowa, because my mother was born in Winterset, Iowa, and that's all they ever talked about there. It's not the kind of thing you get wrong.

I was mad at Eppie for not eating her breakfast. All she ate was one hashbrown and part of one egg. I had to eat the rest for her while that gal told us her life story. It made me feel terrible that Eppie was too damn sick to eat the things she used to enjoy so much.

Eppie went into her mute phase. She pressed her lips tightly together like a nun hearing a dirty joke and stared straight ahead as if I wasn't there.

Nothing I ever said about those kids was good enough for Eppie. For God's sake, they're children, she used to say to me ten times a day. I couldn't spank them. I couldn't even talk to them. It was because of them we got the divorce. And it hadn't helped them any. If anything, it hurt them. Charles, our son, still lived with Eppie. He was a sneaky, whiny little mama's boy. Deeana, our daughter, lived in Egypt. Deeana, she was a kid you could be proud of. But she liked blacks. Eppie and I were damn lucky she married an A-rab instead of a black. In high school, that's all she went out with, blacks, because we lived in a neighborhood where the blacks were taking over and the only good-looking, strong, healthy smart boys with a future in front of them were all black.

I kept looking at Eppie's profile out of the corner of my eye, applying the one thing I had learned in our marriage: if you ask a nasty question, ask it only once and then wait for a reply, don't repeat it over and over, saying each time, *I said blank, now answer me.* I waited and watched. Her little eyes drifted down to her lap. Her lips relaxed. She was about to speak. "No," she said.

I was floored. It was the closest she'd ever come to saying

straight out, Clark, I was wrong all those years, keeping those selfish little brats away from the strong hand of their father.

As soon as I got the lump out of my throat, I said, "I never loved nobody but you all my life."

"Me too," she said.

We drove for a while. "How'd you find this place we're going?" I said.

Eppie reached into her purse and pulled out a crumpled piece of newspaper. She laid it on her thigh and set about flattening it, smoothing it with her palm over and over. I had not thought about her thighs for a long time. After blocking it out of my mind for many years, I could now remember exactly how we used to go about making love. She was the kind of gal who started out all stiff and unsure, but once you got her going, she didn't want to stop. I wondered if the good Lord was going to let me fuck her again.

"Faith Healer," she read from the classified section of *The Pittsburgh Telegraph*. "Willie Mae Dupray. One mile south of Jo-Jo's BBQ near Pikeville. I am waiting for your call. 315. 555 1772." She felt guilty. She wouldn't look at me.

"Jesus Christ, one mile south of a barbecue place?" I said. I put my foot on the brake and pulled the 4 × 4 onto the shoulder. I saw something on *60 Minutes* about bogus healers who prey on innocent victims and take their life savings. In this case, *my* life savings. "How much does this Willie person charge?" I noticed my voice was condescending. I learned that from Jacquelyn, that I'm condescending. Once Jacquelyn pointed it out to me, instead of me giving it up and speaking to her respectfully, I began to do it more often and enjoy it even more. It's kind of fun. It's as if you have rights and powers and can see the obvious when others can't. It's not true, of course, and that's what makes it fun.

"There's no charge," Eppie said.

"How does she pay for that advertisement?" I touched the ad on her thigh.

"She said people make donations. She said one lady from Dallas gave her a million dollars when she cured her son of leukemia."

"Well, all right then," I said. I took the truck back up to the limit. "What," I said because she was looking at her lap in that way she had when she couldn't accept the hard part of life. "What, hon," I said, a little bit softer and more gentle.

"I wanted her to cure me over the phone."

"Jesus Christ," I said. "These people can't cure over the phone. Christ himself couldn't cure over the phone. Did she say she could?"

"She said to come in person. She said to call you."

I straightened up. I looked at myself in the rearview mirror. "Did she call me by name?"

"She said a man who lived on the water still loved me and would do anything for me."

I almost drove off the road. I had only lived on the lake for three months. Score one for Willie Mae Dupray. "How'd you end up with the psycho, then?" I asked.

"I didn't believe her."

At the Knoxville rest stop, Eppie put a quarter into a vending machine where you fish for toys with a mechanical set of claws designed to drop anything of value before you win it. Somehow she held on tight and beat the machine, winning a little stuffed yellow duck worth at least fifty cents. "What the hell are we going to do with a duck," I said.

"Put him next to the Duke," she said. God, I loved her.

"Is there anything but Baptists here?" she said at 10 P.M. when we finally found a motel. In our search for something fairly clean with the AAA seal of approval sign on display, we had passed maybe 800 churches and all were Baptist.

"Guess not," I said. "You first." I indicated the bathroom. We each had a double bed to ourself. I sat on mine and listened to the rhythm of the water running in the sink as she gave herself her nightly sponge bath the same way she had for years. Left side of her face, right side. Neck, left and right. Shoulders, arms, breasts.

Why, I wondered. *Why did we divorce? Why did we marry? Why were we born?*

What in the hell she did all night long I do not know, but it was not sleep. Six times she woke me up with her rustling around, pawing through her damn suitcase, trips to the bathroom, water running, more trips to the bathroom, sitting up to read, belching and burping. I got two winks, no more, and she got none.

"How'd you sleep?" she asked in the morning as we headed west on I-40.

"Fine," I said. "You?"

"Fine."

We had breakfast at the Kingston rest stop. I spread out the map of Tennessee and studied it over my third cup of coffee, looking for the fastest way to Pikeville. The restaurant was empty except for one other table, a family of sorts. The old man saw my map and came over. "Are you lost?" he asked, hoping we were.

I didn't feel like talking to this old man, so I just said, "No." And I pointedly looked back at my map.

"Have you been to Gatlinburg? If not, you should go," this old man said. "You'll love it." While he was talking about how great Gatlinburg was and how when he went there someone he hadn't seen since high school recognized him, his middle-aged daughter came over and stood by his side, talking up the Blue Ridge Parkway. They had a way of alternating sentences, of looking at me, then at each other just as they were about to pass the baton.

"You're right up *in* the mountains . . ." she said. "You can see for miles. . . . You'll think you are in heaven. . . . You can feel the presence of God everywhere."

Next the old guy's wife came over with her address book, going through it page by page with big slobbery licks of her thumb, until she found the name of a cheap motel to stay at outside Gatlinburg. It was an Irish name.

Finally the granddaughter came over. She was a cross-eyed little thing about eight years old. She elbowed her way in between her mother and her grandmother and proceeded to jump up and down and ran her fingers over my spread-out map in itsy-bitsy spider fashion.

These people were literally surrounding us, all talking at once, giving us instructions, seeming to agree yet constantly gently correcting each other.

Eppie, God bless her, vomited a little tiny bit right on the yolk of her fried egg and they left.

"Look at that goddamn thing," I said when we passed the Tennessee River dam they had made such a big stink about years back. They were right not to want it. It looked inhuman. "What a monstrosity," I said. "What an outrage. A dam doesn't have to look like that goddamn thing. A dam can be a work of art." And in the process of explaining it to her, I missed the turn to the bridge.

"Goddammit," I said. I hate to backtrack so we kept going. "There's got to be another goddamn bridge." I said it every mile.

Eppie turned on the radio to drown out my cursing. Every station either had a Bible-thumping Baptist promising you you'd go to hell or a fast-talking furniture salesman selling you suites of all sorts, bedroom, living room, dining room, on the installment plan. Furniture for who? All we saw was tarpaper shacks with rusted-out trucks parked in front.

I went up to one of these shacks to ask where the next bridge was across the Tennessee River. The screen door was wide open. The television was on. No one was home or if they were home, they were hiding. *Recipe No. 387,* read the television screen. *One navel orange. One bunch cilantro.*

We were a stone's throw from Georgia by the time we got over. I was following the backroads toward Pikeville when we came to a little wooden State Park sign with yellow letters. *Fall Creek Falls,* it read, *2 mi.* "Clark," Eppie said. "I want to see that waterfall."

We turned at the entrance. Do you think I could find that goddamn waterfall? By the time we parked and found the trail and I got Eppie up there, I was ready to kill. She hardly made it. I had to carry her the last hundred yards. She put her feet in the pool at the base of the falls and watched it nonstop for an hour. Then I carried her back. And do you think I could find my way out of there?

When I finally saw a ranger rolling toward us in his Jeep, I parked the 4×4 in the middle of the road and walked up to give him a piece of my mind.

Well, it was a her. That threw me off. That smoke-glass driver's-side window went gliding down with its brand-new hum and there is a gal with bright red spiky hair and that kind of orange lipstick that makes a man want to bite a woman's lips to see if they are real or artificial. She's got her little wrist resting on the steering wheel and here, she's wearing a big new diamond engagement ring. Her whole fuckin' life's in front of her.

"What's up?" she said—in a goddamn New York accent. No way was I asking *her* directions.

"Your signs are very misleading," I said. "You'd be well advised to correct them. You've caused two people a lot of hardship today. And that's not a good advertisement for Tennessee if you catch my drift."

"Which signs are those?" she asked.

"Your signs to the falls. Beginning out on the route there." And of course I pointed in the wrong direction because the road into the parking lot winds like a bastard, this way and that way.

"There's no sign there."

"Well, wherever the signs are, they are wrong," I said. And I explained it. While I laid it out for her piece by piece, she was looking over my shoulder at the traffic piling up behind my truck. "Nobody else has complained," she said.

"You goddamn little bitch," I said, "My wife almost died getting to your fucking falls."

"Don't you curse at me, sir," she said and she whipped out the walkie-talkie. "I'll write you up in a second." She clicked her monitor on and said, "Zero two niner, this is forty-six." I let her have it. I said some things I shouldn't have. I knew it at the time, but I couldn't stop myself. "White male, late fifties," she said into the CB, "six feet four, two hundred and thirty pounds, sandy gray hair, glasses, driving a Dodge 4×4, dark green, female passenger. Pennsylvania license plate NZ442D."

There were four or five cars lined up behind us. The drivers were all frowning and scowling at me. One guy called me an asshole. Here he was dressed in Eddie Bauer from head to toe, driving a metallic gold Lexus version of a jeep. I walked over and opened his car door. "You got a problem, pal?" I said. At least I got the satisfaction of seeing that shit-in-the-pants look on his face before we both heard the siren and saw the flashing red light.

Jo-Jo's BBQ was right where that girl ranger's superior said it would be. He told me not to pay any mind to her. She's a New Yorker, he said. He said she's a good egg but she's a little sensitive about the guff she gets from men in this state. He offered me a chew from his little tin of Red Dog and pointed me in the right direction. He weighed three hundred pounds if he weighed an ounce. His name was Randy Bright. If he had not given me flawless directions, I would have passed right by Jo-Jo's. I would never have dreamed that this tiny little unpainted roadside lean-to had the best barbecued pork and Southern fried chicken in Tennessee.

"Two of those," I said to the gal, pointing to the sign over the door: *Southern Fried Chicken. Fried to your order. Please allow 45 minutes.*

"Now it does take the full forty-five minutes, sir," she said, all apologies.

"We were told to order it by Randy Bright," I said.

Her face turned all smiles and sunshine. "Do y'all know Randy? Ain't he fun?" she said.

This gal brought us our ice tea, then she took the slip of paper with our order on it and walked up the hill to a ranch house. Out came Jo-Jo himself, a happy, fat, red-faced man wearing a clean white T-shirt and madras bermuda shorts and carrying a cast iron skillet as big as an automobile tire.

"You watch," I said to Eppie. She looked a little vague. Her eyes were glazed over and she was bone tired. I realized later instead of getting mad like I did with the lady ranger and showing off like I was doing now with Jo-Jo, I probably should have just shut up and got Eppie to the faith healer. But I didn't see that then. It was still all about me and what I needed to prove.

Jo-Jo went to town. He cut up a whole chicken and fried it for us and while he fried he talked. "Bless you Yankees," he says to us. "I cannot get my own next-door neighbor to wait forty-five minutes for my chicken. Everybody has got the Kentucky Fried mentality. They want everything right now. Well, they don't know what they're missing."

"Did you learn this recipe from your mama?" I asked.

"No sir," he said. "They made me a cook in the Army. Then when I got out, I worked my way up through Restaurant Associates. My first big hotel restaurant was in Chattanooga. I ran that restaurant for nine years. I had a black woman there who was the best restaurant manager I'd ever had. She did the work of three people. And she never forgot anything. That woman was smart.

"One day I noticed she was kind of down. And this woman always had a smile on her face. So I said to her, what's wrong. She said she'd been down to the furniture store to buy some furniture on the installment plan and even though she'd had a steady job with me for nine years, they wouldn't sell her a stick of furniture.

"'I'll be a goddamn son of a bitch, I said. So I went down there with her and I co-signed the papers and she got the furniture and she never missed a payment.

"Now listen to this. A few years later when my sister was in the hospital with some problems and she needed a big operation, the doctors told me to have all my friends come to the hospital and give blood—because they had to have lots of blood on hand in case she needed a big transfusion. I made about five calls and I told my friends how important this was to me. Well a few days went by and the doctor called and said to me, Jo-Jo, we've got to do better than this. We've only got five pints of blood.

"Five pints of blood. I thought I had friends. So I was kind of down about that and here this black lady noticed this and she said to me, what's wrong. And I told her. And wouldn't you know, by that afternoon, a hundred black people were lined up at that hospital to give blood for my sister. And she needed it too. She needed a lot of blood. And do you know what? That Negro blood improved her. She was nasty before the operation and much better afterwards."

"What a story," I said to Eppie. She just stared straight ahead. I didn't know then how bad she was feeling.

"I had nigger friends all over Chattanooga," Jo-Jo said. "They'd come to the back door of the restaurant and I'd give them free food. I could never get them to come to the front door. Even though I invited them to. Many a night, I'd play cards with them. See that trophy?" Jo-Jo pointed to a Rook championship trophy on a little wall shelf over my head. I'd forgotten about Rook. "Many a night I'd play cards with them down on Nigger Street. They used to call it Nigger Street. Now they call it Martin Luther King Street. Well, there you are, folks. Taste that and tell me if you ever ate a better piece of fried chicken."

I ate straight through mine and Eppie's. I thanked him. I promised him we'd see him again. And then when I went to pay— he wouldn't let me. He said, "This is on the house. I enjoyed talking to you two so much, it wouldn't be right to ask you to pay."

I hugged that man. He was so fat, he was hard to hug—but I did my best. And when we got back in the car, I was so happy I thought I was drunk. "Wasn't that funny," I said to Eppie, "the way he said nigger so freely? Nigger this, nigger that. How long has it been since we could say nigger? Over twenty years, I believe."

"This is it," Eppie said. And I hooked a left into a little mud driveway next to a purple rural route mailbox. And out of this purple trailer comes the biggest, fattest old black woman either of us have ever seen.

"Hold on here," I said. "Did you know she was black?"

"Yes," she said.

"Hold on," I said. "Did you just make me drive you 1,200 miles to a black woman's house?"

"Clark," she said. "I just want to live."

I felt sick to my stomach. "I'm waiting here," I said. "This is as far as I go."

The black woman was stepping down off her stoop and waddling out to the truck. She was wearing a big old black-and-white polka-dot dress with a big clean white collar and three big black shiny buttons down the chest, the kind of dress I haven't seen on a woman since I was seven years old.

"Roll your goddamn window down," I said to Eppie after a few minutes because Eppie was staring at her lap while the black woman looked through the window at her. Eppie rolled it down.

"Are you Eppie?" she asked.

"Yes I am."

"Then you must be Clark."

I wouldn't answer.

"Well, I am Willie Mae," she said. "Won't you please come inside!"

Inside. The way she said the word hit me like a ray of light shining through the bars of a man serving a life sentence. I got out of the truck and opened Eppie's door for her like a gentleman. We went inside. Everything in the living room was purple. Somehow that made it easier.

"Would y'all like a cool drink?" Willie Mae said. She clasped her hands before her big chest.

Eppie said, "Yes, please."

Willie Mae brought us both a long, cool glass of ice tea with a purple crocheted sock ring around it so you can hold your cold drink without your damn fingers going numb. I took mine and put it on the purple rug.

"Look, miss," I said to Willie Mae. "I would not have driven all this way if I knew you was black—nothing against blacks."

Willie Mae smiled at me. Not a smile with the lips but a smile with the whole face. She smiled so long I reached down and drank some of her ice tea just to break the tension.

She bowed her great big head and clasped her hands delicately together in front of her big white collar and she closed her eyes. "Let us pray."

I don't pray. I never have prayed and I didn't intend to start. So while she and Eppie prayed, I sipped my drink and looked at the white undersides of Willie Mae's heels spilling out over the backs of her shoes as if with all the scrubbing and washing, the black color was starting to rub off her skin.

Her voice went up. Her voice went down. I don't know what all she said, but when she said, "A-men," Eppie was crying a little. "She needs you to comfort her when she cries," Willie Mae said to me. I don't much like anyone telling me what to do, let alone a woman. I'm a bastard of the first water who never did anything he was told to do except in Korea. And I wished I hadn't done it there. I wished I'd had the balls to say the hell with you and let them just court-martial me.

I looked at Eppie, sniffing and sighing, and something came over me. I did what Willie Mae said. I put my arms around her and she leaned into me and cried a little more. Not the big wailing stuff, because she didn't have enough life left in her for that. *Son-of-a-bitch,* I thought to myself, because it felt so good to have her all soft and sweet in my arms like that, *you could have been doing this when she cried for the last thirty years!*

"Where are your children?" Willie Mae asked me.

"Ask *her,*" I said as if it was Eppie's fault.

"I will," Willie Mae said. "But first I'm asking you."

"Deeana, she's in the foreign service in Cairo, Egypt. And Charles, he lives with Eppie."

"Do they know their mama is not well?" Willie Mae asked Eppie.

"No, ma'am," she said.

"Well, *why the hell not?*" Willie Mae said it with one of those great earthy gospely growls that makes you feel the presence of the truth, the whole truth and nothing but the truth. I was starting to like this woman.

"Charles, he's a basket case," Eppie said. "And Deeana, she has a job as a schoolteacher over there in the American school. They have finals about now."

"Thank the *Lord Above* for ex-husbands," Willie Mae said. I sat up straight. I wished to hell we'd have come here when we started having trouble. I would have comforted Eppie whenever she cried and she would have learned she was a damn pushover and a door-mat with these kids.

"Let's invite these children into the room with us," Willie Mae said. She sat back in her big purple chair, rested her arms on the armrests with her white palms facing up, and let her head fall back a little. Her eyelids fluttered and I could see the whites of her eyes. I got a chill in my spine.

"Come in, Charles," she said, just as if a real person had knocked on the front door. I could feel a little wispy curl of hate in my gut. I never liked my son once he turned five.

"Come in, Deeana," Willie Mae said. I couldn't feel Deeana come in, but Eppie could. Eppie started to twitch a little. Her daughter could lie straight to her face and Eppie never knew.

"Children," Willie Mae said with a little bit of a reprimand. "Your mama is dying."

A noise filled the room. It sounded like a wolf who'd been shot in the side and was running around in circles, dragging its back half by the guts. It took a moment for me to realize the noise was coming out of me.

"Children," Willie Mae said, taking Eppie's hands in hers. "God is calling your mama home. Can you let your mama go home to God?" More wailing. "She *needs* you to release her. Her body is *wracked* with disease." She put that gospely growl in for emphasis. "She is sick from her *throat* to her *knees*. And she needs to shed this little body that's tying her to this earth and *join* the Lord as a beau-tiful spirit. Are you with me children?"

The wailing stopped. Eppie's eyes were closed, her face as still and calm as if she were asleep. The two of them were holding all four hands. Eppie started to glow. I mean glow. I loved that woman. I loved her more than life itself.

Willie Mae asked the children, first one, then the other, to give their mama a special message filled with details that were new to me, things that made me realize they'd had a whole life together, Eppie and the kids, that I had never been a part of and didn't know anything about. And I forgave her for letting them take advantage of her. You love your kids to death and they need to push you to the limit and you think it's love to give in.

I must have fallen asleep. All I know is when I woke up, I was alone in the living room. I snooped around the trailer, wondering how that woman found everything in purple, purple toilet seat cover, purple toilet brush, purple soap, purple mini-blinds, purple bedroom slippers, a purple Bible.

I walked out back. Eppie was in the hammock with a little quilt over her and Willie Mae was sitting in a metal lawn chair at her side, rocking her gently to and fro.

I killed her. That's what it comes down to. I got Eppie the morphine she asked me to. And I gave her the overdose she asked me to. You wouldn't think a thing like that would bring a man and a woman closer, but it *made* my life, having her whisper personal things right into my ear when her voice didn't have any noise left. She told me it was the most beautiful experience in her entire life, having me pick her up and carry her up to the lovely flat stone lookout over the waterfall. "Because of that," she whispered into my ear, "my life is complete." And hearing her say that, I knew mine wasn't and never would be.

And then she couldn't even whisper. All she could do was answer questions by squeezing my hand twice for yes and once for no. My last question was, *Now?* Meaning the overdose. She squeezed twice.

I killed her there in Tennessee and I buried her there. And the kids flew in and they got into a big fight and wouldn't speak to each other and they blamed me for not letting them help decide the details of her treatment. I just smiled at them with my whole face like Willie Mae had smiled at me and I forgave the little shits for everything.

I tried to go home. I really did. I gassed up the truck, set the alarm for 4:30 A.M. and took off. I got as far as the Tennessee border, but I couldn't bear to leave the state. The name itself, Tennessee, had a hold on me. It was only 10 A.M., but here I was, looking for a motel where I could spend the night. I found one, the Shamrock.

Shamrock, Shamrock, it sounded familiar. As I sat in the little aluminum lawn chair in front of my room, number 39, looking at the blackbirds swirling through the sky with the door wide open behind me and the television on inside so I wouldn't feel too lonely, I remembered. This was the motel *outside* Gatlinburg the old woman in the rest stop told me to stay in. Life was becoming pure magic now. Imagine that, magic coming to an old bastard like me.

2003

Paul Prather

THE FAITHFUL

Paul Prather is the pastor of a rural church near Mount Sterling, Kentucky, and the son and nephew of country ministers. He formerly was a staff writer and now is a contributing columnist at the Lexington Herald-Leader, *where he has won several prizes from the Kentucky Press Association. He says he has photographed two abandoned churches, one covered with graffiti and another similar from the outside to the one described in this story. "The time-worn church buildings and my memories of the women in my family eventually joined up in my head and out came 'The Faithful.'" He is working on more stories about the spiritual lives of various people in this same Kentucky town.*

Lucille Johnson eases her Plymouth off the bypass onto Johnson Branch Road. In the passenger seat Betty holds a bowl of pea salad in her lap with both hands. Betty's purse is on the floorboard between her feet. She sits knock-kneed.

The turn takes them east. The sun strikes Lucille nearly blind, even though she's wearing sunglasses. Laser surgery has left her eyes generally improved but sensitive to light. She's humped over the steering wheel squinting. Johnson Branch Road is more difficult to negotiate than the four-lane bypass. It rises, falls and winds. No sooner have they started down it than a huge pickup comes flying at them around a curve, riding the middle of the road.

"Oh, Lord!" Betty cries, hitting a phantom brake pedal with her foot. She kicks over her purse.

Lucille wrenches the Plymouth to the right. The pickup's driver swerves to his side of the road. Lucille glimpses just enough of the truck's cab to see that the driver is wearing a white Sunday shirt and has his wife in the cab with him. Lucille's car wobbles as she wrestles the steering wheel. She keeps the Plymouth on the blacktop.

"This road makes me a nervous wreck," Betty says.

Every Sunday when they go to church they're taking their lives in their hands. Lucille dreads the trip, but believes it's worth the danger. In any case she won't be making it anymore. Today's the day they're closing Johnson Branch Baptist Church.

Right behind the truck follows a whole line of traffic headed toward the bypass: a couple of minivans, another pickup, three or four SUVs. Lucille tries not to clip mailboxes or fence posts. The people who live on the road now all go to town to church, if they bother to go at all. They mainly are city folks who have built houses in new subdivisions with names like Shady Acres or Oaklawn. They don't farm. During the week they teach school in Ephesus or drive clear to Georgetown, an hour-and-a-half away, to the assembly line at Toyota.

Lucille has made the opposite migration. She had to sell her forty-eight-acre farm and move to a seniors' complex in town because she couldn't find anybody but Mexicans willing to work the land, and she couldn't communicate with them. When she sold the place five years ago she got $94,400 for it after the Realtor's fees, and she's had to spend most of that on living expenses and medicine. Betty, who faced identical problems, occupies the apartment next door to her. On pleasant evenings they sit on their adjoining concrete porches in plastic chairs and talk about their children.

"Lord, honey, will you watch what you're doing?" Betty says.

Lucille has let the tire dip off the pavement onto the gravel shoulder. "Hush, Betty," she says. "I do well to be on the road at all."

She successfully dodges another line of vehicles. If her eyes weren't so aggravating and the traffic weren't so heavy she would love to study the scenery going by. When she was a girl, she and her family traveled from Johnson Branch to town and back every Saturday, in a mule-drawn jolt wagon. This road was hardly more than a rutted dirt path, and the five miles could take hours. But you got to see and hear things: cardinals singing and darting among the maple trees that lined the road, or the glint of sunlight off John-son Branch itself, or the lush grass of the green knobs behind the creek. Her family knew the names of the owners or tenants of each farm along the way and called to them as they passed. When they got to Ephesus, they would window shop at the dime store and go see a western at the Virginia Theater. Her daddy loved westerns. They would ride home exhausted and happy about dusk, in time to listen to the *Grand Ole Opry*. Her parents didn't buy a car or get electricity until after Lucille was married, but they did have that table-top, battery-powered radio.

They make it to the church in one piece. Lucille steers the Plym-outh up the gravel path and parks by the door of the fellowship hall, so she and Betty won't have to carry their dishes far. Lucille's contributions are lined across the car's backseat: a sliced ham, dressed eggs, mashed potatoes, a butterscotch pie, her purse with the spe-cial gifts in it.

She leaves Betty in the car, unlocks the hall, and flips on the lights inside, then passes into the musty sanctuary, where she un-locks the church's front door. When she returns to her Plymouth, Betty is half in and half out, still fumbling with the purse she kicked over. Lucille has to go around to the driver's side and help her get it. She takes Betty's pea salad into the fellowship hall. Betty is only seventy-nine, younger than Lucille, but has every ailment from congestive heart failure to gout, and already was slow as Christmas when she was young and healthy. By the time Lucille makes sev-eral trips to get her own dishes, the rest of the congregation has arrived bearing food. Counting Lucille and Betty there are six of them now, all women, the youngest sixty-seven and the oldest ninety-two.

"It's a wonder somebody's not killed on that road," says Sister Lib Thomasson, the oldest, as she hobbles through the door on her walker.

"That Engels woman was killed on it last year," says Atha Holtz-claw, Mrs. Thomasson's niece and driver. She's the youngest. She carries Sister Thomasson's brown casserole dish atop her own Tup-perware bowl and two baking pans covered in tin foil.

"That was three years ago," Lucille says. "Sister Thomasson, do you need help?"

"Honey, I need about every kind of help you can name. Just not any kind they can give me."

"Aunt Lib, why don't you go on into the sanctuary and sit down?" Atha says. All business, she's already arranging the cold dishes in the refrigerator.

Instead, Mrs. Thomasson stops and leans on her walker and looks around the low-ceilinged hall. Her husband, Brother Edwin Thomasson, was pastor of Johnson Branch Baptist for forty-three years. "My oh my. I hate to give this place up."

"Now Aunt Lib, don't get on a jag," Atha says. "You'll have us all bawling. Why don't you go on to the sanctuary?"

"Do you remember the time way up one winter when little Mar-vin Shawcross wanted to be baptized?" Sister Thomasson says.

"I think so," Lucille says. She hands Atha a macaroni salad.

"Well it was too cold to go to the creek. The water was froze so deep we couldn't break the ice. Edwin got this bright idea about baptizing Marvin here in the church, in a galvanized washtub."

"A washtub?" Betty says. She never remembers anything. She's sitting off to the side in a chair, one shoe off, rubbing her foot. "I never heard the like."

"Put your shoe on, Betty," Atha says. "You're in the Lord's house."

"I'm only in his dining room. The Lord knows this gout's kill-ing me."

"Anyway," Sister Thomasson says, "this was before we got in-door plumbing here, much less a baptistery, you know. Me and Edwin hauled the tub up from our house on the back of the truck. Then we liked to never have got any water out of the pump outside, for the handle was froze, too. But somehow we did. We carried the water in one bucketful at a time. Edwin put that big old tub of cold water right in front of the pulpit."

"Are you sure?" her niece Atha says. "I don't recall that either, Betty."

"Why Atha, you were right *there*. How can you not remember that? You were on the first row, for your mama was mad at you and she made you sit down front."

"She was always mad about something."

"Will you all let Sister Thomasson tell her story?" Lucille says.

"Well," Sister Thomasson says, "what Edwin didn't know was that Marvin was scared to death of water, even a little dab. So Marvin did sit down cross-legged in the tub, but when Edwin went to put him under—he said, you know, 'I baptize thee Marvin Shawcross, my brother, in the name of the Father and the Son and the Holy Ghost'—and just as he put his hand over Marvin's nose, well, Marvin starts thrashing like a scalded dog. Hit Edwin in the eye"—she raises upright from her walker and cackles—"and turned that tub over on the floor. Ruined the rug. And the water seeped down and buckled the floor. That spring we had to tear the boards out and re-lay the front of the sanctuary."

"I do kind of remember that," Atha says. "Whatever happened to Marvin Shawcross? He was an ugly boy. Had that wiry red hair."

"We never did get him baptized, love his heart," Sister Thomasson says.

"Didn't he get killed in Korea?" Betty says, working her shoe back on her foot.

"Missing in action," Lucille says. "They couldn't ever find him. His poor mother grieved herself to death."

"Now that I think of it, he asked me out one time before he went to the service," Atha says. "Mama wouldn't let me go. She always said, 'Never go out with a boy you wouldn't want to marry someday.' And when Marvin asked me out Mama said, 'I don't want no red-headed grandbabies.' She couldn't stand red hair."

The dining hall door swings open. "Praise the Lord!" the guest preacher announces in a voice way too loud and eager. "Here you are. I looked in the front door."

Lucille flinches. She's never met him. Generally she calls around the larger Baptist churches in Ephesus, or even way over at Georgetown College, and finds a retired pastor or a Bible professor who's willing to drive out to Johnson Branch for a few Sundays. For the past month they've had Brother Clifton Devine, who runs Living Word Bible College, a two-year school in Ephesus that holds classes in a former liquor warehouse. Lucille had hoped Brother Devine could conduct this last service. He's not Baptist, but he's a good preacher and a sensitive man. On Thursday he phoned to say his daughter was sick in Georgia, and he would have to send one of his pupils instead.

This boy is in his twenties. He weighs about two hundred and fifty pounds. His hair is slicked back. His navy suit looks cheap and shiny under the artificial lights. He's got a great big Bible tucked beneath his left arm.

"I'm Lucille Johnson."

The boy strides over and pumps her hand. He looks at her strangely and Lucille realizes she's still wearing her sunglasses. "Eye surgery," she says. His hand is soft as biscuit dough; Lucille's is hard from a lifetime of milking and hoeing.

"Brother Mitch Fowler, praise the Lord. I brought my wife, Linda." As the boy says this, a mousy little thing of about nineteen enters. She glances at the older women, forces a half smile, then ducks her head. Her flowered cotton skirt reaches to her ankles. Her brown hair hangs down her chest. She stays near the door, as if prepared to run.

Lucille takes off her glasses, blinks, then goes over to introduce herself. The girl's hand is as soft as the husband's, but thinner. She doesn't say hello.

By this time the preacher has made his way around the room and greeted the other women. "Where is everybody?" he announces.

"This *is* everybody," Betty tells him. She's got her other shoe off now.

The preacher's countenance falls.

Lucille leads the singing. Sally Barclay plays the old upright piano. Sally is as out of time as the piano is out of tune. She's the only one who still lives on Johnson Branch. She never married. Instead she took care of her parents until they passed away, then stayed on in their farmhouse. But she had to sell her land, and her house is surrounded now by the vinyl homes of a subdivision called Foggy Bottom.

They try three verses of "Standing on the Promises." On the front pew, facing Lucille, the young preacher booms out the song as if he's singing on national TV, on a Billy Graham crusade. His wife sits beside him but never looks up from her hymnal. Her lips scarcely move. Lucille recalls how Brother Edwin used to joke that while Christians ought to stand on God's promises, mostly they sit on His premises. The older women are scattered around the front half of the sanctuary, which was built to hold two hundred. Of the members, only Atha is dry-eyed.

They attempt two verses of "Bringing in the Sheaves" and two more of "Farther Along" before Lucille gives up. She asks Hazel Stamper, her second cousin on her mother's side, to take the offering. Hazel, a gangly woman gone stiff with age, used to be a secretary for the county extension office. As she totters up and down the aisles each of the members drops a few ones or a five into the plate. Hazel makes her way to the front again and extends the plate toward Brother Fowler and his wife but quickly withdraws it when they ignore her. All the while Sally pounds out what Lucille thinks is "Church in the Wildwood." During the war they had a piano player who got saved in a saloon in Ephesus. Brother Edwin walked in off the street and preached the gospel and led her out. Her name was Nancy. One Sunday during the offertory she forgot where she was and started playing "Brother, Can You Spare a Dime?" Nancy married a boy from Bethel and moved to Detroit in the late forties.

"You know," Lucille says to the flock when Sally has finished playing, "I wanted us to do something really nice today, it being the last Sunday. But there aren't enough of us left for much of a ceremony, and those of us who are here aren't able to celebrate."

The old women smile. Brother Fowler says, "Praise God." Betty frowns at the back of his head.

"I do have a little treat for us later. You'll have to wait for that. I've been going through the church records. I don't know if I remembered to tell everybody, but I moved them to my apartment so they don't get lost. This church started out in an old log house in 1831. A couple of years after it was founded a cholera epidemic swept through Kentucky. A third of the congregation died. Isn't that something? That must have been so awful. But the rest came back when the epidemic was over. They built this building in 1876. People have been worshiping here ever since. It's a sight to go over the rolls. Of course there's lots of Johnsons, who were Fred's people. And lots of my people, Cundiffs. There's Thomassons and Holtzclaws and all the rest, just generation after generation. All gone to be with the Lord. Or moved north. And our kids have all run off."

"Lord, Lucille," Atha says. "Just shoot us while you're at it." Atha's first husband left her for another woman. Her second husband, Den Holtzclaw, drank himself to death. She's been down on the world ever since.

"I'm sorry, Atha," Lucille says. "Sister Thomasson, I've been thinking an awful lot about Brother Edwin."

"Love his heart," Sister Thomasson says and dabs her eyes with an embroidered handkerchief.

"He was my pastor from the time I was just a teenaged girl until I was nearly sixty. He married Freddy and me. He buried Freddy. He baptized Freddy Junior and Horace. Brother Edwin used to say, 'Folks, I'm not the prettiest man in the county. I ain't the smartest. But if I can't do nothing else I can be faithful.'"

"That's what he said," Sister Thomasson agrees. "Edwin always said that."

"And so here we are, us old women. We've tried to be faithful like Brother Edwin, all these years. We've kept the doors open while the world went off and left us. But we can't keep them open anymore. The place needs too much work we can't do, and too much money we don't have. That Keath man bid five thousand dollars just to put on a roof. And there's cracks in the foundation to deal with. And—well, you know how much else there is. We can all hold our heads up before the Lord, though, I think, and say we did our best. I feel good about that."

"Amen," Sister Thomasson says. "That's a comfort, honey."

There's a lot more Lucille would like to say, but it's not a woman's place to preach and, besides, she doesn't want to lose her composure. So she nods at Brother Fowler and takes her seat on the end of the empty third row, where she has sat for sixty-five of her eighty-one years. Freddy's family, the Johnsons, always sat near the front. When she married she joined them. Her people sat halfway back on the left.

Brother Fowler stalks to the podium like he's about to whip somebody and spreads his Bible on the pulpit. Freddy's grandfather built the pulpit from an oak tree he'd cut on his farm, in the 1880s or '90s. It's worn and stained on the edges from a century of preachers gripping it. Lucille would love to keep the pulpit, but there's no place in her apartment for it and no one to move it there without hiring it done.

"This is an emotional day for all of us," Brother Fowler announces. "An emotional day. Fortunately we have a rock we can cling to in difficult times amen?"

Only Sister Thomasson answers, "Amen."

"Turn in your Bibles to John, chapter 3, verse 16."

Obediently the women find the passage. They know it by heart, which is fortunate, Lucille thinks, because they can no longer read the fine print for themselves. Young Brother Fowler intones it loudly, though, and deliberately, as if they've never heard the verse before and they're all a little dense: "For God . . . so . . . loved . . .

the world . . . that . . . He gave . . . His . . . only . . . begotten . . . Son . . ."

Afterward he lifts the Bible on his outspread palm. Its cover flops with each movement of his arm. He tears into a salvation message, shouting as if he's preaching on a noisy sidewalk in some heathen city like New Orleans. He strides back and forth across the narrow stage. He rakes loose the knot in his tie. His face reddens. He tells the ladies Jesus died on the cross in their place. They're sinners who have fallen short of God's grace. Unless they repent they're bound for eternal fires like so much kindling. Lucille thinks it's probably the only sermon he knows—and he probably heard *it* from somebody else. From where she's sitting she can see the profile of the preacher's wife. The girl stares straight ahead, looking bored stiff.

Atha arches an eyebrow at Lucille as if to say, "This is a fine fare-thee-well." Lucille shrugs. The pew makes her hips ache. The doctor wants to replace her left hip. At her age it's not worth the trouble, she thinks; she won't have to endure the pain all that much longer. Brother Fowler's agitated voice echoes around the room, intruding on her. He's getting more worked up, preaching himself happy, as Brother Edwin used to say.

Lucille remembers when Johnson Branch Baptist Church was the hub of the community, the site of pie suppers and gospel singings and cake walks and vacation Bible schools and two revivals a year, after spring planting and when the crops were laid by. In the fall of 1958 Brother Edwin invited in an evangelist from Knoxville, a Brother Sinclair, for a revival. Now that man could preach. They had seventy-some saved, and so many rededications the preachers lost count. The ushers had to put out folding chairs in the aisles. People sat on the floor and stood around the walls. Freddy Junior and Horace got saved in that revival.

Lucille tried to get Freddy Junior to fly back for today. He always loved church when he was young. He has retired early from the shipyard in California and he and Connie have moved to Arizona, where they play golf every day. He said he was too busy to come all the way to Kentucky for one service, but to tell everybody *hi*. He claims he belongs to a church in Flagstaff, but Lucille doubts he attends much; he never talks about the Lord on the phone. She didn't even ask Horace to come. He's in Boulder and hasn't been home since IBM transferred him out there in 1985. Horace sends her cards for Christmas, Mother's Day, and her birthday—or his new wife, Jeannie, does. The only other time Lucille hears from him is if she calls. He did fly her out there for the wedding. Colorado is pretty and Jeannie and her kids seemed sweeter than Horace's last wife and stepchildren. Still, Lucille was glad to get home.

When Brother Fowler has worn himself out, he calls Sally up to play an invitation. She gamely tries "Just as I Am," but the ladies don't walk down the aisle to grab Brother Fowler's arm and repent. They've been Christians since before his parents were born. Lucille kind of feels sorry for him. He's just a boy, really. He's got a lot yet to learn about the Lord and about himself. Most of it isn't going to be much fun for him.

In the fellowship hall they arrange the food on the counter and take the towels and plastic wrap off the dishes. In the old days there were so many people they had to eat their potluck dinners outside. They would place long boards across saw horses in rows and crowd the makeshift tables with bowls and pans. "Lord forgive us for the sin of gluttony we're about to commit," Brother Edwin would pray, grinning.

Still, even on this day there's too much food given the size of the group. None of the members is in the mood to eat, and anyway most of the ladies are on restricted diets. Lucille takes a dab of everything so as not to hurt anybody's feelings. The members congregate at one table. Brother Fowler and his wife sit at another. Lucille chooses a chair beside the Fowlers so the church won't appear unfriendly in their memories.

Brother Fowler's plate is heaped. "My, this is great," he says. "Praise God for good cooks." He empties his plate in nothing flat and returns to the counter to refill it.

"You're not eating much, honey," Lucille says to Mrs. Fowler.

"I don't like most of that stuff," the girl says.

Brother Fowler overhears. "She doesn't like anything but hamburgers and french fries."

"I do too."

"We had an evangelist who came through here," Lucille says. "One of the kids asked him how he realized God wanted him in the ministry. He said, 'Well, I woke up one morning craving fried chicken and feeling lazy—and I knew I had the call.'"

Brother Fowler and his wife don't even smile. "I don't get it," Brother Fowler says as he sits down and shoves a piece of ham into his mouth.

"Well, you know, people used to always take a preacher home with them for Sunday dinner. And nearly everybody fed him fried chicken. It got to be kind of a joke."

Brother Fowler tears a yeast roll in half. "But preachers aren't lazy. I would resent that, as a man of God, if somebody said I was lazy. The Lord's work is the most important work there is."

"I reckon you're right," Lucille says. She pushes around the food on her plate.

Before long Brother Fowler goes back to the counter for a third helping. His wife leans toward Lucille and whispers, "I never wanted to be married to a preacher."

The warm sun hangs overhead now instead of in Lucille's eyes. There's a breeze. Lucille walks among the tombstones that take up most of the churchyard. Walking helps her hips sometimes. Other times it makes them feel worse.

She drifts to a section where the stones are mossy and worn. There's one stone a bit newer than the others. It says, "Naomi Holtzclaw, Beloved Wife and Mother, 1858–1933." Old Mrs. Holtzclaw was Lucille's Sunday school teacher when Lucille was a girl. She sat in a wooden wheelchair that had a woven cane back. She used to tell Lucille and the other children stories about the Civil War, which Mrs. Holtzclaw had survived during her own childhood.

One tale was about some Yankee soldiers who came through Johnson Branch scavenging for food. Mrs. Holtzclaw's mother hid the family's hams in an ash barrel. The soldiers found the hams but didn't want them because they were ash-covered and moldy. Being from the north, they didn't know Kentucky hams always looked moldy, and the ashes were easy to rinse off. So the Holtzclaws had ham meat all winter. Mrs. Holtzclaw looked as ancient to Lucille as a crone from a storybook. Lucille is older now than Mrs. Holtzclaw was when she died. There's nobody on earth besides Lucille and the old women in the fellowship hall who would have any idea who she was.

Lucille continues down the cemetery's rows. She finds Brother Edwin's stone. Beside his inscription, Sister Thomasson's date of birth already is carved in, her death date left blank temporarily. Beneath all that sod Brother Edwin must be spinning in his coffin to think the church's last service was preached by the likes of young Brother Fowler. Brother Edwin was convinced that only Baptists would make it into heaven. Lucille doesn't believe that herself, but she feels bad on his behalf.

After he died, Lucille kept praying the Lord would send another pastor like him, a man who would take the church into his heart and give his life to it, but that didn't happen. In Brother Edwin's declining years the attendance already had started to wane. The pastors who followed him didn't stay long. They planned bigger futures for themselves than they were likely to find at Johnson Branch Baptist.

The women haven't been able to decide what to do with the church property. The sanctuary is in too bad a shape and too far from town for another congregation to be interested in it. They might be able to sell the property to a developer, but Atha's the only one who wants to and, besides, what would a developer do with all these graves? For now they're just going to shut the utilities off, lock the building and leave it. Lucille knows it won't take vandals long to realize it's been abandoned. Teenagers from the subdivisions will knock out its windows and then eventually venture inside to spray-paint their names and ugly words on the walls. They'll build bonfires on the floors and drink beer and hold séances and claim the church is haunted. They'll tip over gravestones. She's seen it happen to other churches that were as dear to their people as this one is to her.

Two rows over from Brother Edwin she reaches the Cundiff plot, where her grandparents lie near her mama and daddy, her brother Chester and her sister Marie, who was three when she died of the whooping cough. Lucille decides she needs to come back next spring, if she lives and keeps her health, and plant new flowers on their graves even if the vandals just trample them down. To her it's the principle of the thing: You do what you can, and what you should, even if the results are out of your hands.

And then she makes it to Freddy's stone. It has a polished granite facing and rough-hewn sides. "Johnson" is engraved near the top on the front and, lower, in a small square it says: Frederick William, June 16, 1917–August 8, 1981. Next to that: Lucille Cundiff, March 22, 1920, with a hyphen.

The door to the fellowship hall opens. Brother Fowler emerges, followed by his wife. His suit jacket is folded across his arm. His wife is carrying his huge Bible. The preacher spots Lucille and bounds toward her. "Mighty fine meal! You all are wonderful cooks praise the Lord!" His wife hangs back.

He walks up beside Lucille. "If you ladies don't need us anymore, I guess Linda and I had better be getting on back to town bless God."

"Well, thanks for coming."

But Brother Fowler lingers. "Did you know a lot of these people?"

"Most of them. Knew *of* all of them."

"Praise the Lord. There must be some great saints out here."

Lucille doesn't answer. The preacher shifts from one foot to another. "We're to mourn at the day of birth and rejoice at the day of death, amen."

Finally, Lucille realizes what he's after. "Oh," she says. "I left the church's checkbook in the glove box." She leads him back across the graveyard.

The cars are loaded, the counter wiped. The women sit in the fellowship hall facing one another around a table. No one wants to be the first to go. Betty is in her stocking feet. Sister Thomasson has one baggy arm propped on her walker. Sally has gathered a sheaf of music as a keepsake.

"Did you all think this day would really come?" Hazel Stamper says. "After a hundred and seventy years?"

Atha says, "Everything in this world is born to die. Churches pass just like dogs and squirrels and people. That's a fact."

"It may be a fact, but that doesn't keep it from being a shame, too."

Sally shuffles her sheet music. Sister Thomasson starts to cry. "Lordy, lordy," she says. "Poor Edwin. Love his heart."

"Aunt Lib, it's time for us to head out," Atha says sternly.

"Wait." Lucille bends toward the floor. Opening her purse, she takes out several white envelopes and drops them on the table. "I've been asking the Lord for the right time to do this."

Each of their names is written on one of the envelopes.

"Now what's this?" Atha says.

"This is a little gift."

"A gift? From who?"

"I don't know, exactly," Lucille admits, feeling her cheeks blush. "From the church. Or me. Or the good Lord."

Lucille explains that, when she sat down to balance the books, the church still had over $900 in its account. "I left enough in to pay the preacher today and to keep the grass mowed 'til fall," Lucille says. "But then I got to thinking that if I left it all in there it would just end up going to the bank, or some lawyer, or the state, or whoever gets it when a church closes. I don't even know where it goes, really. I didn't ask. The men listed on the papers as trustees are dead and gone."

"Honey, what did you do?" Sister Thomasson says.

"Well, I drew out six hundred dollars. And I brought each one of us a hundred dollars apiece as a going away present."

"That's not right," Sister Thomasson says. "Is it? I mean, is it legal?"

"I don't know. But I'm eighty-one, and I've been treasurer since Kelvin Brashears died in nineteen seventy. I've never taken a dime. If the law wants to come after me for this, let 'em come."

"I am on a fixed income," Betty says. Her eyes have lit up. Last month she had to do without her blood thinner.

"We've endured," Lucille says. "I don't think the Lord will mind." She pauses. "Think of it as a reward. Or a little down payment on glory."

"To the victors belong the spoils," Atha agrees. "Isn't that in the Bible?"

"No, honey," Sister Thomasson says.

"Well, it ought to be."

They stare at the envelopes.

"Oh, I don't see why not," Sister Thomasson says at last, and that decides it.

They tear open the envelopes and eagerly pull out crisp hundred-dollar bills. Betty lifts hers by the ends and pops it. That makes Hazel Stamper pop her bill, too.

Then, to the astonishment of them all, Sister Thomasson rolls her hundred-dollar bill into a stick like a cigarette. Holding it between her liver-spotted fingers, she acts like she's smoking it. "I always did think I'd make a good tycoon," she says between puffs.

The others giggle like foolish schoolgirls.

Trying to outdo Sister Thomasson, Betty folds her money in half, raises a gouty foot and pretends to use the edge of the bill to clean her toenails through her stocking.

"That's nasty!" says Sally Barclay. But Sally's laughing so hard her upper plate slips loose from her gums. She catches it with her thumb.

All the women shriek. They laugh until they're wiping their eyes and patting each other's backs. They're so caught up that, as Lucille holds her stomach, shaking, she thinks she must be the only one aware of the treacherous drive back to town they still must survive, with the traffic coming the opposite direction, trying to run them off the narrow road.

2004

Chris Offutt

SECOND HAND

Chris Offutt grew up in Haldeman, Kentucky, a tiny former mining community. A recipient of awards from the American Academy of Arts and Letters and the Lannan and Whiting foundations, he is the author of three collections of short stories, a novel, and two memoirs, The Same Rive Twice *and* No Heroes. *"The early versions of 'Second Hand' were based on my strained relationship with my eight-year-old son," says Offutt. "He was miserable in the Kentucky school system. . . . When I look at this story today, I realize it was not about Kentucky or my son." But it's certainly a story about communion between an adult and a child groping towards a tenuous relationship.*

My prize possession is a pair of ostrich-skin cowboy boots standing by the bed. I never keep my boots in the closet because a part of me suspects that this house is haunted. There is one room in particular, the family room, that I stay out of. Maybe it is haunted by a failed marriage that is now interfering with me and my boyfriend.

He is talking to someone on the phone in another room. His voice lowers slightly, and I'm not sure if he has shifted his body, or doesn't want me to overhear. He says, "I don't know, I just don't know. Lately, she's just so, you know."

I'm still half asleep and wonder if he is talking about me or his eight-year-old daughter. She's a lonely kid, a little withdrawn, and very smart. She doesn't call me "Mommy" which is understandable, but sometimes I wish she did.

An acorn hits the roof. Our house is at the end of a country lane, surrounded by white oaks—not a bad house, but still a rental. People don't take care of rentals the way they do their own house and I am no exception. Eventually someone will buy this house after

249

an advertisement says it's a fixer-upper. It's definitely not a starter home, nor a golden years home. It's a dump is what it is, and I decide to remain in bed the rest of the day and maybe my life. I'll tell my boyfriend it's cramps. I'll never own a house or be a real mother. I'll become a bed person.

Six months back, I moved here on a temporary basis for a secretarial job that went bad fast. I can't remember ever having a job that didn't go bad fast. I either get mad and quit or get mad and get fired. Most bosses think that having authority is a license to treat you poorly, and I won't let anyone do that to me.

Another acorn hits the roof. I used to like that tree until nuts covered the driveway, and last weekend I asked my boyfriend's daughter to dump them in a groundhog hole near the door. She did it for about ten minutes, then wanted to get paid.

"Paid," I said. "What about family chores?"

She held the bottom of her shirt high on her chest to make a pouch for the acorns. She didn't say anything but I knew what she was thinking—the same thing I was thinking—that filling a hole with acorns wasn't much of a family chore. Still it ticked me off because she didn't know the first thing about a mean boss or a bad job, or some guy brushing against your backside while you're leaning over the water fountain, or straining his neck to peek down your shirt when you bend forward. I wanted to tell her all this but I didn't. For one thing, she's in the third grade. For another, she already knows some things that aren't so hot. She's an only child to a single parent. Her mother is on parole in another state.

I am a new presence in this girl's life, one who made her fill a hole with nuts. I wondered if a real mother would do that. It occurred to me that she was probably wondering the same thing, and I told her to drop the acorns. She looked as close to happy as she'd been in months. Right then I knew things were not just going bad, they'd already got there.

Lying in bed bores me until I have no choice but to rise and dress. I can't even stick out staying in bed. I pull on the cowboy boots that were a gift from a man in Colorado with twins—one boot per kid is how I look at them. Payday just went by, and after the bills, I am sixty bucks to the good and there's a thousand things to do, chief among them taking that money to the beauty parlor and going for the makeover—haircut, manicure, mud wrap. Maybe buying my boyfriend a new belt buckle will make him feel better. On the other hand, maybe I shouldn't worry so much about making him feel better.

I fix coffee and the girl shuffles through the house, head down like a crippled dog. Her clothes fit loose. For a minute I consider moving on down the road until I find a new man's life to fit into. I've done it before. I don't need much of a push.

Every man I find seems like he needs more than one woman—one for money, one for sex, one to cook and clean and raise his kids, and one to make him feel better at all times. Each woman is supposed to wait at home while he stays out all night or serves jail time or goes fishing for a week. I'm good at picking the wrong man, or maybe they're good at picking me. One trick is to sit by the TV in a bar and they can't help but notice you. I know the right guy's out there, but then again, I thought my boyfriend was. He's a good man, just out of work, and his kid needs a mom. The problem is, I don't know if I'm fit for the job.

"Let's take a drive," I say to her.

"Where?"

"Anywhere. Just a drive. That's what living in the country means. Follow back roads and see where they lead."

"They don't lead anywhere."

"Maybe we'll find a road that leads to a new place."

"There's nothing new here. It's all just old."

"What I mean is a new place we haven't been to yet."

"I get car sick."

"On the school bus, you do. But we're not taking the bus today."

"I don't know."

"Tell your father."

She looks at me a long time, as if realizing I am truly serious, and that despite her overall mood, it might not be a bad idea to roam the land in my company. My boyfriend waves from the couch, an impatient kind of wave like someone warding off bugs at a picnic.

Outside, the day is full of autumn with a sky so blue and clear that it's not sky any more but water in a bowl. My old Chevy starts on the third try. The shocks are bad and the girl sits at the far edge of the bench seat. I ease down the road, hitting every pothole in sight. I tell the girl about hay stacks. I grew up in the country and it makes me feel good to let her know I have some knowledge that surprises her. I'm more than the newest woman to take up with her dad. I have worked on a farm. I own a car and can drive a tractor. I explain how hay is harvested in rounded rolls to shed water instead of the old-time square bales. Out West, I tell her, they still use square bales because it hardly ever rains and the sun is so clean you can see a bird a hundred miles away.

The girl looks out the window and says that she's car sick. She wants to go home and read a book in which magic works. She believes in magic and who am I to tell her she's wrong? People go to church, read the horoscope, and have lucky rocks. Sometimes I feel like I'm starving and everybody else has just finished a big meal and I'm still scratching holes in the dirt looking for a seed.

I park under a leafless willow beside a little dry creek bed that feeds into a bigger dry creek. I can't recall ever being alone with my own mother in a car. It must have happened, but it was either so long ago that I've forgotten, or nothing occurred that mattered. She never left the house until she left for good. I was seven years old.

I want to speak to the girl, but don't know how to pierce her misery, so I just shoot from the hip.

"Do you ever get scared of the family room?" I say.

"I'm scared of the whole house."

This surprises me. I don't know what to say because all I can think is how children are more sensitive than adults and if she's scared of the whole house, not only must it be haunted, but she is sure messed up.

"How come?" I say.

"Just am."

"What is it that scares you?"

"All of it."

"Like it's haunted or something?"

"Maybe," she says. "Do you think it is?"

"Of course not. There's no such things as ghosts."

"How do you know?"

I put the car in reverse and have to hold the brake and give it gas until it jerks into gear. We drive along the road. The transmission slips, and I remind myself not to get in a spot where I have to go backwards. Always forward is my motto.

The trees look like somebody dumped buckets of bright paint out of a helicopter and I start thinking how that would be a cool job, one you couldn't get fired from, then jerk the wheel hard to miss a dead raccoon. The girl makes a face. She is a city kid who likes bagels, video stores, and pizza delivery. There is no life outside this car for her and roadkill is living proof of this.

"What will make you happy?" I say.

She shrugs and shifts her body away, the same motion my boyfriend has used on me for two months.

"How about a bike?" I say.

"There's not any good places to ride."

"A mountain bike, then. It's perfect for the country. You know how to ride, right?"

She looks at me as if I've given her the worst insult possible, then rolls her eyes. She's only eight. I don't know how to talk to her. When her life doubles, she will drive a car. In thirty years she might be me—a woman trying to get by. The problem is, as I get older, the love gets harder to find. Sex used to be important but these days I just keep an eye out for somebody to team up with.

The girl turns her head to me.

"What," I say.

"What what?"

"What what what?"

"What what what what?"

A fragment of a smile flees across her face, and the rest of the drive goes smoothly. Town is town, full of people who went to town. I stop at a pawnshop, thinking that for sixty bucks, I can get a bike with three gears and tell her it's a mountain bike. The store smells like sweat and dust, which is really the smell of hope and loss. The small room is packed with guns, watches, video games, guitars, tools, stereo systems, fishing rods, cell phones, and radios. Cheap jewelry lies in a glass case with tape over the cracks. There is a row of leather jackets chained to each other through the sleeves, and if you wanted to steal one, you had to steal them all. This is a room of last resort, like a chapel before an execution. Everything in this place has been handled by people at the end of their rope, and that despair fills the air.

Against a wall are two big touring bicycles with ram's horn handles and tiny seats. Beside them is a little kid's bicycle with training wheels. In the corner stands a mountain bike with shock absorbers on the front tire, fifteen gears, and a water bottle. It has no bell, no streamers, and no fenders. It doesn't even have a kickstand. It looks like a bike that got stripped by a thief, and I wonder if the guy is going to try and sell me the rest in parts.

The girl goes right to that bike like a fly to sugar. Her entire posture is full of desire, a feeling I know well. My problem is I keep getting what I want— a new man, another job, a fresh start in a different place. As soon as I get it, I don't want it anymore. I stand in a room surrounded by all this stuff that people are supposed to have, and I have no desire for any of it. There's nothing in this store for me, nothing in any store. Six months ago I told myself that life with a new man would be different. It must be true, because this is the first time I've ever entered a pawnshop as a buyer. Usually I'm trying to raise money to leave town.

I ask if the girl can test ride the bicycle in the parking lot. He pushes the bike across the dark carpet. The girl follows and I watch through the plate glass window. She rides in a circle with a joyous look on her face.

"It's sold," I say. "How much?"

"Three hundred."

"New, sure. But what's the pawn price?"

"That is the pawn price. New is eight hundred."

"That's a lot of money."

"I can see it's been a while since you bought a new bike."

I don't say anything because it's been a while since I bought any-thing new. Somebody else's body has already filled all my clothes. Even my boyfriend was married before. I wish I had a career and the same man for a few years, but I'm stuck with this life. Every wrong decision I ever made has led me here, to this place at this moment—standing in a room full of things I don't want, facing a man alone.

"Let's talk turkey," I say. "You can see the jam I'm in. She wants that bike but three hundred's beyond reach. I don't have anywhere near that. I'm in a pickle and you can help. Let's work something out."

The pawnshop guy looks me up and down like I'm something pawnable that he doesn't really want, but might hold for a while. I know what's coming, too. He'll say something that hints at pay-ing the other way, and if I pick up on it, he'll be more direct. Men are predictable. The key is to head them off early. This place is guar-anteed to have two things hidden—a loaded pistol near the front, and a mattress in the back. I look at him and think about his body naked. I start taking off a cowboy boot. He is watching me care-fully. He's probably seen people pull everything out of their boots— a wad of cash, a switchblade, a gun. All that comes out of my boot is a foot.

I lower my eyes to look at him through the lashes. I wet my lips and speak low.

"Ostrich," I say. "The toughest leather of all. Seven rows of stitching on the uppers. Heels are in good shape. These are thou-sand dollar boots."

He takes the boot and I remove the other. It gets hung because that foot is a little bit bigger than the other, which has always been a problem. Once I bought a pair of pumps that were a half-size apart. They fit well, and I worry about the poor woman who bought the other two shoes. The pawnshop guy looks the boots over. He is a lucky man. People walk in his store every day and place valuable things in his hands.

Outside, the girl rides back and forth across the lot. She is smiling and when a girl smiles that way, her whole body is happy and she can't remember when it wasn't. The bike swerves. She jerks the handlebars for balance, and glances through the window, and I do the right thing and pretend as if I didn't notice.

"Straight up swap," I say. "The boots for the bike."

"You wearing a belt?"

"No."

"Got anything in the car?"

"Like what?"

"CD player. Pistol. Different people carry different things. Maybe a coat. I had a man show up with forty car batteries once."

I follow him outside. The pavement hurts my feet and I am careful to avoid walking on broken glass. He looks in the car windows, checking for something to sweeten the deal. The back seat holds a grocery bag and a math book. There is nothing else in the car. It suddenly looks old and ratty, exactly what you'd expect to see parked in a pawnshop lot. I wonder if people driving by think I'm the kind of woman they'd expect to see standing here. My feet are cold. None of this is what I had in mind today.

The girl rides near. She's the most free creature in the world—a kid on a bike—and I envy her. She's only walked this earth for eight years. I've been here for thirty-eight and don't even have shoes to show for it. At this moment, to keep her happy, I will trade the whole car for the bike. I glance at the pawnshop guy to see if he can somehow read my mind and hold out for the Chevy, but he is looking in the trunk. The slot for the spare tire is empty. There is a dirty blanket and a jack. The pawnshop guy lifts the jack from the trunk. It is newish. It is the most newish part of my life.

"Your daughter," he says, "is very pretty. Just like her mother."

"Thank you. But she's not my daughter."

"I know," he said. "I was trying to be nice."

"How did you know?"

"Most people don't bring kids in here."

"I didn't have a lot of choice."

"Let me finish," he says. "Parents don't want their kids to see them in a tough spot. An aunt or a step-mom doesn't mind that much. Myself, I think it's good for children to see that grownups have it hard sometimes."

"Do you have kids?"

"Yes, but I don't live with them. I'm a good dad though. And I make sure they see me vulnerable."

"You don't seem like the usual pawnshop guy."

"It's just a job."

"Then how about leaving me that jack?"

"Can't," he says. "A deal's a deal."

He walks away and I realize that he didn't come on to me and I'm grateful for that. This surprises me because in my younger days I never thought I'd feel this way. Maybe I'm maturing. That strikes me as funny, because if it's true then I'm a mature woman with bare feet and no jack. I like to travel light.

I wave the girl over.

"Help me put it in the trunk," I say.

She says nothing.

"It's yours," I say.

She doesn't speak, and I wonder if she understands. The trunk won't close all the way. Driving will make the lid bang against the bike and I don't have any rope. I look at the pawnshop, but there's no way I will ask that man for help. I search the weeds at the edge of the lot and find nothing to tie the trunk with. The girl knows something is not right, but doesn't want to ask. I don't know what to say to make her feel better. A real mother would, but I can't think of anything. I just look at her and nod.

She watches me unsnap my bra under my sweater. I wriggle the strap off one shoulder, hook it past my elbow, and over my hand. The other side comes off easy. I pull the bra from my sleeve. As nonchalantly as possible I tie it to the inside of the trunk, and knot it around the bike like a bungee cord. The bra is ruined, but that doesn't matter since it was used to begin with.

We drive out of the lot and the girl never shifts her eyes away from me. This is the most she's ever looked at me. Her attention makes me nervous.

"Nice bike," I say.

She shrugs.

"It's yours," I say.

She stares at the dark trees flashing past in the dusk. I suddenly remember endless trips to town with my father, looking out the window, counting telephone poles and mail boxes, seeing the same houses and the same railroad tracks, all the time wishing I lived somewhere else. The memory is shocking because it runs dead against how I see my childhood now, one I hoped to give the girl, that of gathering wildflowers for a supper table and listening all day to the singing of birds. Instead, I hated where I grew up and resented my folks for living there. I was mad at God for having the gall to stick me in a world where I had no friends, nothing to do, and nowhere to go. It was a dead place. I left early.

I park near the house and get out of the car. The blacktop is broken into chunks like brownies. I untie my bra and remove the bike and place it on the road. The girl straddles the seat and pushes off. The bike wobbles until she gains speed, then she stops. She has to get off the bike to turn it around. Instead of riding, she pushes it back toward me. Her face is serious and I wonder if something is wrong—a broken spoke or a loose wheel. Maybe I got gypped on the deal. Somebody might already be wearing my boots and I am ready to get mad—at the girl, at the pawnshop guy, at myself. I didn't start going to pawnshops until I was an adult, but her whole life is secondhand, even me.

She looks at me and says, "Thanks, Lucy."

"You're welcome," I say.

She pushes hair from her face with shaking hands. I want to

watch forever. It is the most beautiful sight I've ever seen, a child's hands trembling with delight. I can't remember my hands ever doing that. When mine shake, it is always with fear. She climbs on the bike and pedals away. I wonder if I'd have made the same trade for my own daughter.

2004

Jill McCorkle

INTERVENTION

Jill McCorkle says, "Usually my stories begin with a line of dialogue or the idea of a particular character and then take shape along the way. With this one, my idea was the ending; I imagined a person getting into a car with someone she knew should not be driving." The result is a story about, in the author's words, "a marriage bond that because of all it weathered is now indestructible." McCorkle, a native of Lumberton, North Carolina, is the author of eight books of fiction, five of which have been named New York Times *notables. She now lives near Boston.*

The intervention is not Marilyn's idea, but it might as well be. She is the one who has talked too much. And she has agreed to go along with it, nodding and murmuring an all right into the receiver while Sid dozes in front of the evening news. They love watching the news. Things are so horrible all over the world that it makes them feel lucky just to be alive. Sid is sixty-five. He is retired. He is disappearing before her very eyes.

"Okay, Mom?" She jumps with her daughter's voice, once again filled with the noise at the other end of the phone—a house full of children, a television blasting, whines about homework—all those noises you complain about for years only to wake one day and realize you would sell your soul to go back for another chance to do it right.

"Yes, yes," she says.

"Is he drinking right now?"

Marilyn has never heard the term "intervention" before her daughter, Sally, introduces it and showers her with a pile of literature. Sally's husband has a master's in social work and considers himself an expert on this topic, as well as many others. Most of Sally's sentences begin with "Rusty says," to the point that Sid long ago made up a little spoof about "Rusty says," turning it into a game like Simon Says. "Rusty says put your hands on your head," Sid said the first time, once the newly married couple was out of earshot. "Rusty says put your head up your ass." Marilyn howled with laughter, just as she always did and always has. Sid can always make her laugh. Usually she laughs longer and harder. A stranger would have assumed that she was the one slinging back the vodka. Twenty years earlier, and the stranger would have been right.

Sally and Rusty have now been married for a dozen years— three kids and two Volvos and several major vacations (that were so educational they couldn't have been any fun) behind them— and still, Marilyn and Sid cannot look each other in the eye while Rusty is talking without breaking into giggles like a couple of junior high school students. And Marilyn knows junior high behavior; she taught language arts for many years. She is not shocked when a boy wears the crotch of his pants down around his knees, and she knows that Sean Combs has gone from that perfectly normal name to Sean Puffy Combs to Puff Daddy to P. Diddy. She knows that the kids make a big circle at dances so that the ones in the center can do their grinding without getting in trouble, and she has learned that there are many perfectly good words that you cannot use in front of humans who are being powered by hormonal surges. She once asked her class: How will you ever get ahead? only to have them all— even the most pristine honor roll girls— collapse in hysterics. Just last year— her final one— she had learned never to ask if they had hooked up with so-and-so, learning quickly that this no longer meant locating a person but having sex. She could not hear the term now without laughing. She told Sid it reminded her of the time two dogs got stuck in the act just outside her classroom window. The children were out of control, especially when the assistant principal stepped out there armed with a garden hose, which didn't faze the lust-crazed dogs in the slightest. When the female—a scrawny shepherd mix—finally took off running, the male—who was quite a bit smaller—was stuck and forced to hop along behind her like a jackrabbit. "His thang is stuck," one of the girls yelled and broke out in a dance, prompting others to do the same.

"Sounds like me," Sid said that night when they were lying there in the dark. "I'll follow you anywhere."

Now, as Sid dozes, she goes and pulls out the envelope of information about "family intervention." She never should have told Sally that she had concerns, never should have mentioned that there were times when she watched Sid pull out of the driveway only to catch herself imagining that this could be the last time she ever saw him.

"Why do you think that?" Sally asked, suddenly attentive and leaning forward in her chair. Up until that minute, Marilyn had felt invisible while Sally rattled on and on about drapes and chairs and her book group and Rusty's accolades. "Was he visibly drunk? Why do you let him drive when he's that way?"

"He's never visibly drunk," Marilyn said then, knowing that she had made a terrible mistake. They were at the mall, one of those forced outings that Sally had read was important. Probably an article Rusty read first called something like "Spend time with your parents so you won't feel guilty when you slap them in a urine-smelling old-folks' home." Rusty's parents are already in such a place; they share a room and eat three meals on room trays while they watch television all day. Rusty says they're ecstatic. They have so much to tell that they are living for the next time Rusty and Sally and the kids come to visit.

"I pray to God I never have to rely on such," Sid said when she relayed this bit of conversation. She didn't tell him the other parts of the conversation at the mall, how even when she tried to turn the topic to shoes and how it seemed to her that either shoes had gotten smaller or girls had gotten bigger (nine was the average size

for most of her willowy eighth-grade girls), Sally bit into the subject like a pit bull.

"How much does he drink in a day?" Sally asked. "You must
know. I mean, *you* are the one who takes out the garbage and does
the shopping."

"He helps me."

"A fifth?"

"Sid loves to go to the Food Lion. They have a book section and
everything."

"Rusty has seen this coming for years." Sally leaned forward and
gripped Marilyn's arm. Sally's hands were perfectly manicured with
pale pink nails and a great big diamond. "He asked me if Dad had
a problem before we ever got married." She gripped tighter. "Do
you know that? That's a dozen years."

"I wonder if the Oriental folks have caused this change in the
shoe sizes?" Marilyn pulled away and glanced over at Lady's Foot
Locker as if to make a point. She knows that "Oriental" is not the
thing to say. She knows to say "Asian," and though Sally thinks that
she and Rusty are the ones who teach her all of these things, the
truth is that she learned it all from her students. She knew to say
Hispanic and then Latino, probably before Rusty did, because she
sometimes watches the MTV channel so that she's up on what is
happening in the world and thus in the lives of children at the junior high. Shocking things, yes, but also important. Sid has always
believed that it is better to be educated even if what is true makes
you uncomfortable or depressed. Truth is, she can understand why
some of these youngsters want to say motherfucker this and that
all the time. Where *are* their mommas, after all; and where are their
daddies? Rusty needs to watch MTV. He needs to watch that and
Survivor and all the other reality shows. He's got children, and unless he completely rubs off on them they will be normal enough to
want to know what's happening out there in the world.

"Asian," Sally whispered. "You really need to just throw out that
word Oriental unless you're talking about lamps and carpets. I
know what you're doing, too."

"What about queer? I hear that word is okay again."

"You have to deal with Dad's problem," Sally said.

"I hear that even the Homo sapiens use that word, but it might be the kind of thing that only one who is a member can use, kind of like—"

"Will you stop it?" Sally interrupted and banged her hand on the table.

"Like the 'n' word," Marilyn said. "The black children in my class used it, but it would have been terrible for somebody else to."

Sally didn't even enunciate African American the way she usually does. "This doesn't work anymore!" Sally's face reddened, her voice a harsh whisper. "So cut the Gracie Allen routine."

"I loved Gracie. So did Sid. What a woman." Marilyn rummaged her purse for a tissue or a stick of gum, anything so as not to have to look at Sally. Sally looks so much like Sid they could be in a genetics textbook: those pouty lips and hard blue eyes, prominent cheekbones and dark curly hair. Sid always told people his mother was a Cherokee and his father a Jew, that if he was a dog, like a cockapoo, he'd be a Cherojew, which Marilyn said sounded like TheraFlu, which they both like even when they don't have colds, so he went with Jewokee instead. Marilyn's ancestors were all Irish, so she and Sid called their children the Jewokirish. Sid said that the only thing that could save the world would be when everybody was so mixed up with this blood and that that nobody could pronounce the resulting tribe name. It would have to be a symbol— like the name of the artist formerly known as Prince, which was something she had just learned and had to explain to Sid. She doubts that Sally and Rusty even know who Prince is, or Nelly, for that matter. Nelly is the reason all the kids are wearing Band-Aids on their faces, which is great for those just learning to shave.

"Remember that whole routine Dad and I made up about ancestry?" Marilyn asked. She was able to look up now, Sally's hands squeezing her own, Rusty's hands on her shoulders. If she had had an ounce of energy left in her body, she would have run into Lord & Taylor's and gotten lost in the mirrored cosmetics section.

"The fact that you brought all this up is a cry for help whether you admit it or not," Sally said. "And we are here, Mother. We are here for you."

She wanted to ask why Mother—what happened to Mom and Mama and Mommy?—but she couldn't say a word.

There are some nights when Sid is dozing there that she feels frightened. She puts her hand on his chest to feel his heart. She puts her cheek close to his mouth to feel the breath. She did the same to Sally and Tom when they were children, especially with Tom, who came first. She was up and down all night long in those first weeks, making sure that he was breathing, still amazed that this perfect little creature belonged to them. Sometimes Sid would wake and do it for her, even though his work as a grocery distributor in those days caused him to get up at five A.M. The times he went to check, he would return to their tiny bedroom and lunge toward her with a perfect Dr. Frankenstein imitation: "He's alive!" followed by maniacal laughter. In those days she joined him for a drink just as the sun was setting. It was their favorite time of day, and they both always resisted the need to flip on a light and return to life. The ritual continued for years and does to this day. When the children were older they would make jokes about their parents, who were always "in the dark," and yet those pauses, the punctuation marks of a marriage, could tell their whole history spoken and unspoken.

The literature says that an intervention is the most loving and powerful thing a loved one can do. That some members might be apprehensive. Tom was apprehensive at first, but he always has been; Tom is the noncombative child. He's an orthopedist living in Denver. Skiing is great for his health and his business. And his love life. He met the new wife when she fractured her ankle. Her marriage was already fractured, his broken, much to the disappointment of Marilyn and Sid, who found the first wife to be the most loving and open-minded of the whole bunch. The new wife,

Sid says, is too young to have any opinions you give a damn about. In private they call her Snow Bunny.

Tom was apprehensive until the night he called after the hour she had told everyone was acceptable. "Don't call after nine unless it's an emergency," she had told them. "We like to watch our shows without interruption." But that night, while Sid dozed and the made-for-TV movie she had looked forward to ended up (as her students would say) sucking, she went to run a deep hot bath, and that's where she was, incapable of getting to the phone fast enough.

"Let the machine get it, honey," she called as she dashed with just a towel wrapped around her dripping body, but she wasn't fast enough. She could hear the slur in Sid's speech. He could not say slalom to save his soul, and instead of letting the moment pass, he kept trying and trying—What the shit is wrong with my tongue, Tom? Did I have a goddamn stroke? Slllllmmmm—sla, sla.

Marilyn ran and picked up the extension. "Honey, Daddy has taken some decongestants, bless his heart, full of a terrible cold. Go on back to sleep now, Sid, I've got it."

"I haven't got a goddamned cold. Your mother's a kook!" He laughed and waved to where she stood in the kitchen, a puddle of suds and water at her feet. "She's a good-looking naked kook. I see her bony ass right now."

"Hang up, Tommy," she said. "I'll call you right back from the other phone. Daddy is right in the middle of his program."

"Yeah, right," Tom said.

By the time she got Sid settled down, dried herself off, and put on her robe, Tom's line was busy, and she knew before even dialing Sally that hers would be busy, too. It was a full hour later, Sid fast asleep in the bed they had owned for thirty-five years, when she finally got through, and then it was to a more serious Tom than she had heard in years. Not since he left the first wife and signed off on the lives of her grandchildren in a way that prevented Marilyn from seeing them more than once a year if she was lucky. She could get mad at him for *that*. So could Sid.

"We're not talking about my life right now," he said. "I've given

Dad the benefit of the doubt for years, but Sally and Rusty are right."

"Rusty! You're the one who said he was full of it," she screamed. "And now you're on his side?"

"I'm on your side, Mom, your side."

She let her end fall silent and concentrated on Sid's breath. He's alive, only to be interrupted by a squeaky girly voice on Tom's end—Snow Bunny.

Sid likes to drive, and Marilyn has always felt secure with him there behind the wheel. Every family vacation, every weekend gathering. He was always voted the best driver of the bunch, even when a whole group had gathered down at the beach for a summer cookout where both men and women drank too much. Sid mostly drank beer in those days; he kept an old Pepsi-Cola cooler he once won throwing baseballs at tin cans at the county fair, iced down with Falstaff and Schlitz. They still have that cooler. It's out in the garage on the top shelf, long ago replaced with little red and white Playmates. Tom gave Sid his first Playmate, which has remained a family joke until this day. And Marilyn drank then. She liked the taste of beer but not the bloat. She loved to water ski, and they took turns behind a friend's powerboat. The men made jokes when the women dove in to cool off. They claimed that warm spots emerged wherever the women had been and that if they couldn't hold their beer any better than that, they should switch to girl drinks. And so they did. A little wine or a mai tai, vodka martinis. Sid had a book that told him how to make everything, and Marilyn enjoyed buying little colored toothpicks and umbrellas to dress things up when it was their turn to host. She loved rubbing her body with baby oil and iodine and letting the warmth of the sun and salty air soak in while the radio played and the other women talked. They all smoked cigarettes then. They all had little leather cases with fancy lighters tucked inside.

Whenever Marilyn sees the Pepsi cooler she is reminded of those days. Just married. No worries about skin cancer or lung cancer.

No one had varicose veins. No one talked about cholesterol. None of their friends were addicted to anything other than the sun and the desire to get up on one ski—to slalom. The summer she was pregnant with Tom (compliments of a few too many mai tais, Sid told the group), she sat on the dock and sipped her ginger ale. The motion of the boat made her queasy, as did anything that had to do with poultry. It ain't the size of the ship but the motion of the ocean, Sid was fond of saying in those days, and she laughed every time. Every time he said it, she complimented his liner and the power of his steam. They batted words like throttle and wake back and forth like a birdie until finally, at the end of the afternoon, she'd go over and whisper, "Ready to dock?"

Her love for Sid then was overwhelming. His hair was thick, and he tanned a deep smooth olive without any coaxing. He was everything she had ever wanted, and she told him this those summer days as they sat through the twilight time. She didn't tell him how sometimes she craved the vodka tonics she had missed. Even though many of her friends continued drinking and smoking through their pregnancies, she would allow herself only one glass of wine with dinner. When she bragged about this during Sally's first pregnancy, instead of being congratulated on her modest intake, Sally was horrified. "My God, Mother," she said. "Tom is lucky there's not something wrong with him!"

Tom set the date for the intervention. As hard as it was for Rusty to relinquish his power even for a minute, it made perfect sense, given that Tom had to take time off from his practice and fly all the way from Denver. The Snow Bunny was coming, too, even though she really didn't know Sid at all. Sometimes over the past five years, Marilyn had called up the first wife just to hear her voice or, even better, the voice of one or more of her grandchildren on the answering machine. Now there was a man's name included in the list of who wasn't home. She and Sid would hold the receiver between them, both with watering eyes, when they heard the voices they barely recognized. They didn't know about *69 until a few months ago when Margot, the oldest child, named for Sid's mother, called back. "Who is this?" she asked. She was growing up in Minnesota and now was further alienated by an accent Marilyn only knew from Betty White's character on *The Golden Girls.*

"Your grandmother, honey. Grandma Marilyn in South Carolina."

There was a long silence, and then the child began to speak rapidly, filling them in on all that was going on in her life. "Mom says you used to teach junior high," Margot said, and she and Sid both grinned, somehow having always trusted that their daughter-in-law would not have turned on them as Tom had led them to believe.

Then Susan got on the phone, and as soon as she did, Marilyn burst into tears. "Oh, Susie, forgive me," she said. "You know how much we love you and the kids."

"I know," she said. "And if Tom doesn't bring the kids to you, I will. I promise." Marilyn and Sid still believe her. They fantasize during the twilight hour that she will drive up one day and there they'll all be. Then, lo and behold, here will come Tom. "He'll see what a goddamned fool he's been," Sid says. "They'll hug and kiss and send Snow Bunny packing."

"And we'll all live happily ever after," Marilyn says.

"You can take that to the bank, baby," he says, and she hugs him close, whispers that he has to eat dinner before they can go anywhere.

"You know I'm a very good driver," she says, and he just shakes his head back and forth; he can list every ticket and fender-bender she has had in her life.

The intervention day is next week. Tom and Bunny plan to stay with Sally and Rusty an hour away so that Sid won't get suspicious. Already it is unbearable to her—this secret. There has only been one time in their whole marriage when she had a secret, and it was a disaster.

"What's wrong with you?" Sid keeps asking. "So quiet." His eyes have that somber look she catches once in a while; it's a look of hurt, a look of disillusionment. It is the look that nearly killed them thirty-odd years ago.

There have been many phone calls late at night. Rusty knows how to set up conference calls, and there they all are, Tom and Sally and Rusty, talking nonstop. If he resists, we do this. If he gets angry, we do that. All the while, Sid dozes. Sometimes the car is parked crooked in the drive, a way that he never would have parked even two years ago, and she goes out in her housecoat and bedroom slippers to straighten it up so the neighbors won't think anything is wrong. She has repositioned the mailbox many times, touched up paint on the car and the garage that Sid didn't even notice. Sometimes he is too tired to move or undress, and she spreads a blanket over him in the chair. Recently she found a stash of empty bottles in the bottom of his golf bag. Empty bottles in the Pepsi cooler, the trunk of his car.

"I suspect he lies to you about how much he has," Rusty says. "We are taught not to ask an alcoholic how much he drinks, but to phrase it in a way that accepts a lot of intake, such as 'How many fifths do you go through in a weekend?'"

"Sid doesn't lie to me."

"This is as much for you," Rusty says, and she can hear the impatience in his voice. "You are what we call an enabler."

She doesn't respond. She reaches and takes Sid's warm limp hand in her own.

"If you really love him," he pauses, gathering volume and force in his words, "you have to go through with this."

"It was really your idea, Mom," Sally says. "We all suspected as much, but you're the one who really blew the whistle." Marilyn remains quiet, a picture of herself like some kind of Nazi woman blowing a shrill whistle, dogs barking, flesh tearing. She can't answer; her head is swimming. "Admit it. He almost killed you when he went off the road. It's your side that would have smashed into the pole. You were lucky."

"I was driving," she says now, whispering so as not to wake him. "I almost killed him!"

"Nobody believed you, Marilyn," Rusty says, and she is reminded of the one and only student she has hated in her career, a smart-assed boy who spoke to her as if he were the adult and she were the child. Even though she knew better, knew that he was a little jerk, it had still bothered her.

"You're lucky Mr. Randolph was the officer on duty, Mom," Tom says. "He's not going to look the other way next time. He told me as much."

"And what about how you told me you have to hide his keys sometimes?" Sally asks. "What about that?"

"Where are the children?" Marilyn asks. "Are they hearing all of this?"

"No," Rusty says. "We won't tell this sort of thing until they're older and can learn from it."

"We didn't," she whispers and then ignores their questions. Didn't what? Didn't what?

"The literature says that there should be a professional involved," she says and, for a brief anxious moment, relishes their silence.

"Rusty is a professional," Sally says. "This is what he does for a living."

Sid lives for a living, she wants to say, but she lets it all go. They are coming, come hell or high water. She can't stop what she has put into motion, a rush of betrayal and shame pushing her back to a dark place she has not seen in years. Sid stirs and brings her hand up to his cheek.

Sid never told the children anything. He never brought up anything once it had passed, unlike Marilyn, who sometimes gets stuck in a groove, spinning and spinning, deeper and deeper. Whenever anything in life—the approach of spring, the smell of gin, pine sap thawing and coming back to life—prompts her memory, she cringes and feels the urge to crawl into a dark hole. She doesn't recognize that woman. That woman was sick. A sick, foolish woman, a woman who had no idea that the best of life was in her hand. It was late spring, and they went with a group to the lake. They hired babysitters round the clock so the men could fish and the women could sun and shop and nobody had to be concerned for all the needs of the youngsters. The days began with coffee and bloody marys and ended with sloppy kisses on the sleeping brows of their babies. Sid was worried then. He was bucking for promotions right and left, taking extra shifts. He wanted to run the whole delivery service in their part of the state and knew that he could do it if he ever got the chance to prove himself. Then he would have normal hours, good benefits.

Marilyn had never even noticed Paula Edwards's husband before that week. She spoke to him, yes; she thought it was Paula's good fortune to have married someone who had been so successful so young. ("Easy when it's a family business and handed to you," Sid said, the only negative thing she ever heard him say about the man.) But there he was, not terribly attractive but very attentive. Paula was pregnant with twins and forced to a lot of bed rest. Even now, the words of the situation, playing through Marilyn's mind, shock her.

"You needed attention," Sid said when it all exploded in her face. "I'm sorry I wasn't there."

"Who are you—Jesus Christ?" she screamed. "Don't you hate me? Paula hates me!"

"I'm not Paula. And I'm not Jesus." He went to the cabinet and mixed a big bourbon and water. He had never had a drink that early in the day. "I'm a man who is very upset."

"At me!"

"At both of us."

She wanted him to hate her right then. She wanted him to make her suffer, make her pay. She had wanted him even at the time it was Paula's husband meeting her in the weeks following in dark, out-of-the-way parking lots—rest areas out on the interstate, rundown motels no one with any self-esteem would venture into. And yet there she had been. She bought the new underwear the way women so often do, as if that thin bit of silk could prolong the masquerade. Then later, she had burned all the new garments in a huge puddle of gasoline, a flame so high the fire department came, only to find her stretched out on the grass of her front yard, sobbing. Her children, ages four and two, were there beside her, wide-eyed and frightened. "Mommy? Are you sick?" She felt those tiny hands pulling and pulling. "Mommy? Are you sad?" Paula's husband wanted sex. She could have been anyone those times he twisted his hands in her thick long hair, grown the way Sid liked it, and pulled her head down. He wanted her to scream out and tear at him. He liked it that way. Paula wasn't that kind of girl, but he knew that she was.

"But you're not," Sid told her in the many years to follow, the times when self-loathing overtook her body and reduced her to an anguished heap on the floor. "You're not that kind."

People knew. They had to know, but out of respect for Sid, they never said a word. Paula had twin girls, and they moved to California, and to this day, they send a Christmas card with a brag letter much like the one that Sally and Rusty have begun sending. Something like: We are brilliant, and we are rich. Our lives are perfect, don't you wish yours was as good? If Sid gets the mail, he tears it up and never says a word. He did the same with the letter that Paula wrote to him when she figured out what was going on. Marilyn never saw what the letter said. She only heard Sid sobbing from the other side of a closed door, the children vigilant as they waited for him to come out. When his days of silence ended and she tried to talk, he simply put a finger up to her lips, his eyes dark and shadowed in a way that frightened her. He mixed himself a drink and offered her one as they sat and listened with relief to the giggles of the children playing outside. Sid had bought a sandbox and put it over the burned spot right there in the front yard. He said that in the fall when it was cooler, he'd cover it with sod. He gave up on advancing to the top, and settled in instead with a budget and all the investments he could make to ensure college educations and decent retirement.

Her feelings each and every year when spring came had nothing to do with any lingering feelings she might have had about the affair—she had none. Rather, her feelings were about the disgust she felt for herself, and the more disgusted she felt, the more she needed some form of self-medication. For her, alcohol was the symptom of the greater problem, and she shudders with recall of all the nights Sid had to scoop her up from the floor and carry her to bed. The times she left pots burning on the stove, the time Tom as a five-year-old sopped towels where she lay sick on the bathroom floor. "Mommy is sick," he told Sid, who stripped and bathed her, cool sheets around her body, cool cloth to her head. It was the vision of her children standing there and staring at her, their eyes as somber and vacuous as Sid's had been that day he got Paula's letter, that woke her up.

"I'm through," she said. "I need help."

Sid backed her just as he always had. Rusty would have called him her enabler. He nursed her and loved her. He forgave her and forgave her. I'm a bad chemistry experiment, she told Sid. Without him she would not have survived.

On the day of intervention, the kids come in meaning business, but then can't help but lapse into discussion about their own families and how great they all are. Snow Bunny wants a baby, which makes Sid laugh, even though Marilyn can tell he suspects something is amiss. Rusty has been promoted. He is thinking about going back to school to get his degree in psychology. They gather in the living room, Sid in his chair, a coffee cup on the table beside him. She knows there is bourbon in his cup but would never say a word. She doesn't have to. Sally sweeps by, grabs the cup, and then is in the kitchen sniffing its content. Rusty gives the nod of a man in charge. Sid is staring at her, all the questions easily read: Why are they here? Did you know they were coming? Why did you keep this from me? And she has to look away. She never should have let this happen. She should have found a way to bring Sid around to his own decision, the way he had led her.

• • •

Now she wants to scream at the children that she did this to Sid. She wants to pull out the picture box and say: This is me back when I was fucking my friend's husband while you were asleep in your beds. And this is me when I drank myself sick so that I could forget what a horrible woman and wife and mother I was. Here is where I passed out on the floor with a pan of hot grease on the stove, and here is where I became so hysterical in the front yard that I almost burned the house down. I ruined the lawn your father worked so hard to grow. I ruined your father. I did this, and he never told you about how horrible I was. He protected me. He saved me.

"Well, Sid," Rusty begins, "we have come together to be with you because we're concerned about you."

"We love you, Daddy, and we're worried."

"Mom is worried," Tom says, and as Sid turns to her, Marilyn has to look down. "Your drinking has become a problem, and we've come to get help for you."

I'm the drunk, she wants to say. I was here first.

"You're worried, honey?" Sid asks. "Why haven't you told me?"

She looks up now, first at Sid and then at Sally and Tom. If you live long enough, your children learn to love you from afar, their lives are front and center and elsewhere. Your life is only what they can conjure from bits and pieces. They don't know how it all fits together. They don't know all the sacrifices that have been made.

"We're here as what is called an intervention," Rusty says.

"Marilyn?" He is gripping the arms of his chair. "You knew this?"

"No," she says. "No, I didn't. I have nothing to do with this."

"Marilyn." Rusty rises from his chair. Sally right beside him. It's like the room has split in two and she is given a clear choice—the choice she wishes she had made years ago, and then maybe none of this would have ever happened.

"We can take care of this on our own," she says. "We've taken care of far worse."

"Such as?" Tom asks. She has always wanted to ask him what he remembers from those horrible days. Does he remember finding her there on the floor? Does he remember her wishing to be dead?

"Water under the bridge," Sid says. "Water under the bridge." Sid stands, shoulders thrown back. He is still the tallest man in the room. He is the most powerful man. "You kids are great," he says. "You're great, and you're right." He goes into the kitchen and ceremoniously pours what's left of a fifth of bourbon down the sink. He breaks out another fifth still wrapped with a Christmas ribbon and pours it down the sink. "Your mother tends to overreact and exaggerate from time to time, but I do love her." He doesn't look at her, just keeps pouring. "She doesn't drink, so I won't drink."

"She has never had a problem," Sally says, and for a brief second Marilyn feels Tom's eyes on her.

"I used to," Marilyn says.

"Yeah, she'd sip a little wine on holidays. Made her feel sick, didn't it, honey?" Sid is opening and closing cabinets. He puts on the teakettle. "Mother likes tea in the late afternoon like the British. As a matter of fact," he continues, still not looking at her, "sometimes we pretend we are British."

She nods and watches him pour out some cheap Scotch he always offers to cheap friends. He keeps the good stuff way up high behind her mother's silver service. "And we've been writing our own little holiday letter, Mother and I, and we're going to tell every single thing that has gone on this past year like Sally and Rusty do. Like I'm going to tell that Mother has a spastic colon and often feels 'sqwitty,' as the British might say, and that I had an abscessed tooth that kept draining into my throat, leaving me no choice but to hock and spit throughout the day. But all that aside, kids, the real reason I can't formally go somewhere to dry out for you right now is, one, I have already booked a hotel over in Myrtle Beach for our anniversary, and, two, there is nothing about me to dry."

By the end of the night everyone is talking about "one more chance." Sid has easily turned the conversation to Rusty and where he plans to apply to school and to Snow Bunny and her hopes of having a "little Tommy" a year from now. They say things like that they are proud of Sid for his effort but not to be hard on himself if he can't do it on his own. He needs to realize he might have a problem. He needs to be able to say: I have a problem.

"So. Wonder what stirred all that up?" he asks as they watch the children finally drive away. She has yet to make eye contact with him. "I have to say I'm glad to see them leave." He turns now and waits for her to say something.

"I say adios, motherfuckers." She cocks her hands this way and that like the rappers do, which makes him laugh. She notices his hand shaking and reaches to hold it in her own. She waits, and then she offers to fix him a small drink to calm his nerves. "I don't have to have it, you know," he says.

"Oh, I know that," she says. "I also know you saved the good stuff.

She mixes a weak one and goes into the living room, where he has turned off all but the small electric candle on the piano.

"Here's to the last drink," he says as she sits down beside him. He breathes a deep sigh that fills the room. He doesn't ask again if she had anything to do with what happened. He never questions her a second time; he never has. And in the middle of the night when she reaches her hand over the cool sheets, she will find him there, and when spring comes and the sticky heat disgusts her with pangs of all the failures in her life, he will be there, and when it is time to get in the car and drive to Myrtle Beach or to see the kids, perhaps even to drive all the way to Minnesota to see their grandchildren, she will get in and close the door to the passenger side without a word. She will turn and look at the house that the two of them worked so hard to maintain, and she will note as she always does the perfect green grass of the front yard and how Sid fixed it so that there is not a trace of the mess she made. It is their house. It is their life. She will fasten her seat belt and not say a word.

2005

Gregory Sanders

GOOD WITCH, BAD WITCH

Born in Baytown, Texas, Gregory Sanders now lives in West Hollywood, California, where he works as a film editor. He says of this story, "It's a highly fictionalized account of my own relatives. Begun as a humorous anthropology of family rituals, the story took on a darker tone as it approached this question: How should we react when a person we love holds hateful ideas?" Sanders's short fiction has appeared in many periodicals, including River City, Snake Nation Review, *and* Chiron Review. *He is at work on a novel.*

In my family, the word "aunt" did not rhyme with either "ant" or "font." Instead it was pronounced "ain't," and while strictly speaking, "ain't" was just a pronunciational variant, it had become a word in its own right. And that is the way I still hear Aunt Aubria's name in my head—Ain't Aubria.

Every Christmas, it was Ain't Aubria who threw the party in Houston, and Grandmother Gertrude who supplied the wet blanket. Christmas morning would begin in Port City with Grandmother Gertrude's querulous plaint at the breakfast table. Didn't my father realize that she had been up all night wrapping presents? Couldn't he see that she still hadn't finished? And until all her presents were wrapped, we couldn't possibly leave for Houston.

Her son considered these objections unworthy of refutation, so every time she raised them, he just pounded his gavel and upheld his previous ruling. "We have to leave here by eight," he would tell her, "because Ain't Aubria expects us at nine." This kowtowing to Ain't Aubria always cut Grandmother Gertrude to the quick. Insensitive to personal insults, she was mortified by social slights. After all, my father was *her* son, not Ain't Aubria's. Her sense of

278

grievance made her all the more determined to drag her feet and if necessary dig in her heels. By the time my father had finally herded her out of the house, he would be worn out from flogging her like Balaam's ass. And always, always we would already be at least a half hour late.

Grandmother Gertrude would hobble along, refusing to be hurried, and although she had the doctors' diagnoses to prove that her arthritis and tendonitis and bursitis and osteoporosis and diverticulitis were real physical maladies, it was hard to believe that the severity of her suffering was not subject to a psychological rheostat. On Christmas morning, when the dial was always spun all the way over to maximum, she could barely maneuver her body onto the front seat, let alone the back. (That was why she always rode in the passenger's seat next to my father, while my mother, who usually sat there, was displaced to the backseat, where she straddled the hump, separating my brother and me.) My father would open the car door for Grandmother Gertrude and she would gingerly lower herself down until at last gravity overcame her and she plopped into place with an oomph. Then, one by one, she would lift her legs in as though they had been paralyzed by polio and were now weighed down with metal braces.

Before pulling out of the garage, my father would remind her to put on her seatbelt. Grandmother Gertrude would protest that it curtailed her freedom of movement, that she could not bear the thought of being strapped in because she might be trapped if the car caught fire. And besides, she could never figure out how the blessed thing worked. When it came to technological innovation, Grandmother Gertrude was *not* an early adapter. After she had made several halfhearted attempts that ended with the belt being retracted instead of fastened, my father would have to reach over and fasten it for her. From the way she squirmed in her seat and noised her discomfort, you might have thought he was catheterizing her.

Once we were underway, she would revisit the ruling that had gone against her that morning. There was no earthly reason why we all had to get up every Christmas at the crack of dawn. Ain't Aubria never had dinner on the table before one o'clock anyway. This was the gist of her brief. Now it would be my mother's turn to remind her that Ain't Aubria would not allow her own grandchildren to open any of their gifts until everyone had arrived so we could all have our Christmas tree together. Ain't Aubria saw us as one big extended family, not two separate nuclear ones. And it was just this hegemonic vision that Grandmother Gertrude had so set her face against. She would have much preferred to remain in Port City and have my mother fix us Christmas dinner. As long as we stayed on the family estate, she could at least lord it over her daughter-in-law. In Houston, Ain't Aubria held court, and Grandmother Gertrude was only a dowager empress by marriage. Ain't Aubria had money, and if you had money, things were very different, as Grandmother Gertrude never ceased to remind us. The implication was that if she'd had money herself, she too could have had a big house where everyone foregathered at every holiday. And if *that* were so, everyone would have loved her instead, and deferred to her wishes the way we now deferred to Ain't Aubria's.

Architecturally, Ain't Aubria's house was without distinction. What immediately grabbed your attention was the enormous oak tree smack in the middle of the front lawn, its trunk a good six feet in diameter, as great as Herne's oak in the last act of *Falstaff*. Since it was the only tree on the half-acre lot, its imposing canopy had spread without obstruction. By Christmastime each year, it had buried the grass in brown leaves.

Usually, one of the children would spot the car pulling into the long narrow driveway. Everyone inside would have come out to greet us before we were even out of the car, including Ain't Aubria in her apron (unless she had some sauce on the stove that had just reached critical mass). We would all embrace and say that we were all glad to see each other. Then each of us would individually avow that all the others looked great. While we frantically gibbered and chattered and groomed each other, the two-toed sloth that was Grandmother Gertrude glided stately through our midst. Stretching before her was an arduous trek through the garage and the kitchen, then down an endless corridor that led to the bathroom at the back of the house.

Once she was out of earshot, we would lower our voices like conspirators and someone, often Ain't Aubria's daughter, would ask, "Did Ain't Gertrude give you all a lot of trouble this morning?" This would let loose the floodgates of our disloyalty. Grandmother Gertrude being none of ours, we easily disowned her, and could hardly wait to stab her in the back. This gleeful treason relieved the stress we had always been under of biting our tongues at everything she said, and swallowing our fury every time she enforced some petty tyranny. Only my father declined to swear his fealty to our faction. But if he would not turn his coat outright, neither would he defend his mother. How could he? Instead he remained silent. By the time she returned from the bathroom, we were all in collusion against her.

If Grandmother Gertrude saw the little looks and smiles we exchanged behind her back (and sometimes not even behind her back, but almost to her face), she either refused to take notice, or noticed but failed to interpret these smiles and looks correctly. Like Falstaff, she was oblivious to what we merry wives really thought of her. Hermetically sealed inside her own self-regard, it would have been inconceivable to her (literally unimaginable) that she had become a figure of fun, that we were all sitting around waiting for her to say something self-congratulatory or Pharisaical so we could then repeat what she'd said out loud and laugh about it the next time she went to the bathroom.

Now would have been the time to crowd into the living room and have our tree. My father and Ain't Aubria's son-in-law, who handed out the presents, would read aloud from the tag, who it was for and who it was from. We would all wait until a gift had been found for each of us before we opened our gifts together. Admiration would be expressed and thanks shouted across the room. Then the process would have been repeated with another round of gifts. With so many gifts for so many different people, the gifts always spilled far out into the room as though poured from a horn of plenty. It would be several rounds at least before we reached the ones that were actually under the tree.

We were profligate of wrapping paper, tearing it off in great shards like barbarians sacking a city, but we were thrifty when it came to bows. "Don't throw your bows away," we children would be reminded. "Be sure to save your bows." Even as we were wadding up the discarded wrapping paper and stuffing it into garbage bags, we were sifting through the rubble like archaeologists in search of any bows we might have overlooked earlier. And we would make jokes about how we just exchanged the same bows among us every year.

From her chair in the corner, Grandmother Gertrude would observe us the way a director in an auditorium might observe a rehearsal on a stage. Always when you failed to appreciate the gift she had given you in quite the way she had hoped, she would interrupt your performance to italicize that gift's valuable significance for you.

"Those are *Russell Stovers* candies," she would tell you. "I bought them at *Neiman Marcus.*"

Thus enlightened you were expected to improve your line reading. "Oh, really? From Neiman Marcus? Well, I'm sure they'll be real delicious. Thank you so much."

Grandmother Gertrude was one of those people who truly believed it was more blessed to give than to receive. But in her case, you got the feeling this belief had little to do with a spiritual view of material things, and everything to do with putting others in her debt while incurring no corresponding debt of her own.

Could this be why she always received her own gifts so ungraciously? I remember the time Ain't Aubria gave her a bed jacket from Kaplan's Ben-Hur. Grandmother Gertrude held it up and cooed the same admiration as everyone else, "Oh, it's just lovely, Aubria, just beautiful." But then Cinderella's gown became Cinderella's rags as she dropped it back down into the box and added, "Unfortunately, I can't wear it, it's polyester."

Everyone knew that Grandmother Gertrude believed herself allergic to polyester, to rayon, to all synthetic fibers of any kind. Only cotton, silk, linen, and wool could touch her delicate skin. Otherwise, she would break out in hives. Furthermore, her allergies neither began nor ended with fabrics. Like the Gadarene demoniac, a legion of them bedeviled her. She was allergic to margarine. Her system simply could not tolerate anything but butter. And onions gave her intestinal cramps. Every year she would call upon Ain't Aubria to furnish a verbal guarantee that the cornbread dressing contained no onion. "Oh, honey, you know I wouldn't put onion in your dressing," Ain't Aubria would tell her. On the strength of this assurance, Grandmother Gertrude would then wolf down three servings, apparently with no ill effects even though the dressing actually did have onion in it. Quite a lot of onion, in fact. Hardly a secret, as my mother pointed out. "Why, you could see it with the nekkid eye."

In addition to turkey and dressing, there were mashed potatoes and candied yams, buttered carrots and Kentucky wonder beans, broccoli with cheese sauce and pearl onions, plus olives stuffed with pimento and celery sticks stuffed with pimento cheese, not to mention giblet gravy and cranberry sauce, and dinner rolls that reached the table warm from the oven in two shifts, the first when we sat down to eat, the second halfway through the meal.

Ain't Aubria, and Ain't Aubria alone, had cooked everything spread out before us, since she did not permit either her daughter or my mother to bring a covered dish of any kind, not even so much as a pie. "There's no need," Ain't Aubria insisted. She always had plenty of deserts on hand: pumpkin, pecan, and chocolate pies, plus heavenly salads, such as fruit cocktail with miniature marshmallows folded in whipped cream; also pineapple upside-down cake, and a wide array of cookies and candies.

Especially admired were her kiflins. These little cylinders of sweetened pie crust mixed with nuts and rolled in confectioner sugar could not be duplicated, even using the same recipe, by lesser cooks like my mother.

There was no beer, no wine, no aperitifs, and certainly no brandy or cigars. As good Southern Baptists, we washed our meal down with iced tea and our desserts down with hot coffee. On the whole, we benefited from this arrangement, the conviviality it may have curtailed being more than offset by the aggression it surely forestalled. From all the horror stories I have heard over the years about the alcohol-fueled family feuds that erupted at other people's holiday boards, I have come to see how lucky I am that caffeine was my own family's drug of choice. Passive aggression is so much more peaceful than aggressive aggression, especially if it is the men as well as the women who swallow their rage and suffer in silence. From the way my father, as well as the rest of the family, always placated Grandmother Gertrude, you might have thought she would be disposing of a great fortune upon her death.

She would not of course, but even so, we would all sit there in respectful silence, nobody interrupting, just eating our turkey while she rambled on, some interminable story until at last Ain't Aubria interrupted. "Would anyone like another roll? How about some more iced tea?"

Was there any wound iced tea could not salve, any wrong a hot roll fresh from the oven could not assuage, any grief that could not be comforted by an enormous slice of chocolate pie topped with a half-pint of heavy whipped cream? I always had chocolate pie, instead of pecan or pumpkin, for dessert. Always. When the main meal was over and the women were taking dessert orders, whoever was asking me, would not actually ask but say, "You don't have to tell me, I know what *you* want." Everyone would laugh because it had been a family joke, me and my chocolate pie, for as long as I could remember.

I must have been quite small when the joke got started, no more than three or four, and in those days, it was easier for Ain't Aubria to cater to my finicky tastes since I was her only grandchild. An honorary grandchild to be sure, but even after her real grandchildren came along, the two of us still shared our special memories of the time when Santy Claus came to her house only for me.

At Ain't Aubria's, I had my own room and my parents had theirs, just like at home. I remembered getting up early one morning when the light was still gray and the door to my parents' room still shut. But since the door to Ain't Aubria's room was open, I had wandered in and gotten into bed with her. The two of us lay there and talked for the longest time.

Then we got up and went into the kitchen, where Ain't Aubria made biscuits from scratch. She rolled the wet, tacky dough out and let me help by cutting out big circles with the mouth of an iced tea glass. Ain't Aubria had never judged me for wanting to help her make biscuits or play with the vacuum cleaner or even traipse around the house in a pair of her old high heels.

"If that's what he wants to do, I think that's all right," she would say.

I was also afraid of the dark. And she never judged me for this either. On the contrary, she always made sure there was a nightlight burning in my room, a little Christmas-tree bulb in a blue translucent hood that plugged directly into the wall socket. One night in particular, I can remember her putting me to bed in that dark bedroom, darker than my room at home on account of the dark green walls illuminated only by eerie blue light, and at first I had thought she would tuck me in, but instead she pulled back the sheet and lifted my foot in the air. I was lying on my back, looking up at her with my tiny foot suspended in front of her face and my big toe grasped between her thumb and forefinger as she proceeded to count my toes.

"This little nigger went to market," she said. "This little nigger stayed home, this little nigger had roast beef, this little nigger had none, and this little pickaninny went wee, wee, wee all the way home."

If Ain't Aubria had cut her finger with a kitchen knife and let fly a volley of oaths, I would have been shocked, but I would have been titillated as well, because deep down, I understood that however bad most bad words might be, they were still just words that could not hurt you. But "nigger" was more like a stick or a stone; that was why you never said it, not under any circumstances, because it really could hurt people, and for Ain't Aubria to say it, not just once, but again and again, upended the moral order. I was not only shocked, I was frightened, and with each repetition, I wanted to shout at her to stop, to *please* not say it again. She had already said it four times and was about to say it a fifth when confused, I asked: "What's a pickaninny?"

"*What's a pickaninny?*" It was as though I had asked her who Jesus was, or whether eggs came from cows.

"Why, a pickaninny's a little nigger child," she told me.

She seemed peeved that she had to explain the punch line to her own joke, but she soon recovered, being a good-natured woman, and having wee wee wee'd my pinky toe to her heart's content, she returned to my big toe and said, "Now you say it."

She had put me on the horns of a dilemma. Ain't Aubria was not allowing me to remain just an observer. She was insisting that I become a participant. I would have much preferred to let the cup pass from me, but she had left me no alternative. "This little nigger went to market," she prompted. And that was when I spoke out.

"You're not s'posed to say that," I told her.

"Say what?" Ain't Aubria seemed genuinely puzzled.

"You're s'posed to say 'Negro,'" I said. "Either 'Negro,' or 'colored.'"

It was as though I had, as a full-grown man, clenched my fist into a tight little ball and slammed it full force into her forehead. That was how shocked she looked, and how hurt. Because she had never judged me, she never dreamed I would ever judge her.

"You told her *what?*" my mother had said, horrified, when I told her the story. With Grandmother Gertrude always scheming against her, my mother needed Ain't Aubria as an ally.

"You should not have said *that* to her," said my mother.

But my father defended me, so she had to back down. "So what *did* you say?" my mother asked.

This was much the same question Ain't Aubria had asked, though with entirely different emphasis. "So what do *you* say?" she had said, her voice clipped, her face frozen. I could tell she was veiling her anger, and not just her anger, her humiliation. I told her that I always said "This little piggy" at home. So she said, "Why don't you just say that?" And I did.

This was in the 1950s. By the 1960s, "nigger" was no longer a socially permissible word, not even in Texas, not even when used by old people who insisted they were just too old to change. But long after others had made the change, Ain't Aubria still resisted. She never got as far as "African-American." She never got as far as "black." She never even got as far as "Negro." The best she could manage was "nigra." She would make some untoward remark about the nigras just as she was disappearing into the kitchen with somebody's empty iced tea glass, and her daughter and my mother would exchange knowing glances, then smile back down at their plates. "Nigra" had become Ain't Aubria's running gag, what chocolate pie was for me.

But why had she been so stubborn about it? Two little vowels and she would have been there. According to my mother, Ain't Aubria was keeping faith with her mother whose real name my mother could no longer remember, everyone had just called her Mammy. My mother did not seem to think this was strange, that a white woman should have been called Mammy, especially a white woman who was a racist.

Well, not a racist exactly. That was too strong a word, my mother insisted. Mammy was never mean to people, she was not hateful, she just had this idea that everyone should keep to their place.

I heard a lot of that in those days, the idea that African-Americans had a right to exist, so long as they knew their place. It made racism sound like a particularly virulent form of snobbery, which it was in a way, and Ain't Aubria's brand of it reminded me of Proust's remark about Charlus: that just because a man was a snob, it did not necessarily have to infect every aspect of his life. I would have liked to think that Ain't Aubria's racism could be compartmentalized, leaving the rest of her untainted, but I was far from sure this was possible. If she had admitted that it was wrong to say "nigger," and wrong to regard segregation as a moral imperative, then she would have been forced to admit that Mammy had been wrong. And this, above all, she could not do. Thus did racism pollute even the best thing about her, her unconditional loyalty to the people she loved, whether they were living or dead.

"Rex, honey, come sit here by me," she had said. (Ain't Aubria had always called everyone honey, and she pronounced my name to rhyme with "rakes.")

She had made this request the last time I saw her, the Christmas before she died, when I was in my late forties. The seating chart at the big table had never been set in stone. Each year, it was renegotiated. But since I was the only left-handed person in the family, I had always been seated at the end, far from Ain't Aubria. Now, if I sat at her left, I would be fencing elbows with the right-handed person to my left. But how could I gainsay her? She was ninety-three and her health was failing.

We all knew that even if Ain't Aubria lived until next Christmas, it was unlikely she would ever again fix us dinner. How had she done it this year? She had started long beforehand, for one thing. The cookies and candy and piecrusts had all been baked or rolled out weeks in advance and then frozen. She was very picky, so her daughter had taken her to the grocery store and pushed her around in the wheelchair so that she could select the celery, the broccoli, the onions, all the produce, herself.

Ain't Aubria was not wheelchair-bound in the sense that her legs were no longer functional. It was just that after two heart attacks she was so weakened, she could only walk a short distance on her own. With a little help from one of her grandsons, she had gotten into a dining room chair, then her daughter had rolled the empty wheelchair into the den and out of sight. It was obviously important to Ain't Aubria how we would all remember her, and she did not want us to remember her sitting in a wheelchair at the table.

"Come closer to me, Rakes honey," she said.

I scooted my chair close to her and she leaned in even closer as though about to show me how big her teeth were, when really, she was just trying to get a good look at my face. Her eyesight failed her at the end, but she was never completely blind. The TV was a blur of color. But she could still read her large-print Bible with a magnifying glass. And she could make eye contact with you if your face was no more than a couple feet away.

"Can you see my tree?" she said.

For a moment, I was not quite sure which tree she meant, the Christmas tree or the great live oak in her front yard, and I realized that when the Christmas tree was not there, you could sit in the living room and look out at the real tree, as perfectly framed by the picture window as the Christmas tree would be when seen from the other side. Since I was always here during the holidays and at no other time, the tree that had been merely decorative, like a flower in a vase, had obscured my consciousness of the tree in the ground that had been Ain't Aubria's proudest possession. This tree was her idea of luxury; it was what made this piece of land so valuable. When she was selling off the property Uncle Otis had left her, she could have sold this lot for a princely sum and then spent it on travel or furs or status-enhancing philanthropy. Instead, she had kept the tree for herself, and built her house in its shadow where she could sit in her living room and look out at it every day for the purely aesthetic pleasure it gave her. She could still see it now in her memory better than I could in real life, my view being obscured by the Christmas tree.

"Yes, I can see your tree," I told her.

"I've always loved that tree," she said.

Her far-off gaze suggested oracular trance, and it struck me that her devotion was more druidic than horticultural.

"This year I hired a nigra man to come rake up my leaves," she told me.

Did I visibly flinch, or did it just feel as though I had? Why did she have to show me this side of her in what might well be our last conversation? It was not as though it turned out to be a great story either. It was just a meandering incident. Her tree had grown so large, it seemed, that for this nigra man to rake up and bag all her leaves took more than one day. On the second day she had noticed that he seemed unhappy ("dragging his feet" was the phrase she used). She had asked what the problem was and he told her that his wife had gone into the hospital that morning. She told him not to worry about the leaves, that he should just go be with his wife, that he could come back and finish raking her leaves after Christmas. And, not only that, she had given him an extra twenty-five dollars.

That was it. That was all there was to the story. And now, she waited for a response. But what could I say? "When a man throws a coin to a beggar, he throbs with contempt"—these were the words that sprang to mind, but of course I did not quote de Sade to her. What I actually said was, "I'm sure he must have really appreciated your doing that."

Clearly, this was not the response she had hoped for. She nodded in disappointment and said, "Yes, I think he did," in a vague distracted way.

I had failed to connect. So I had tried again.

"Do you remember when I was a little boy and spent the night, and we'd get up the next morning and make biscuits?" I said.

Her face lit up. "Do you really remember that?" she said. "I thought you might have forgotten."

We had loved each other then, when I was three or four years old, not that we did not love each other now. But then, we had been Romeo and Juliet of the balcony scene. Now, we were Anthony and Cleopatra with Rome closing in on us, and, if this great tree of hers really was a Herne's oak, this would be the final fugue we sang beneath its naked limbs and danced upon its buried roots. Sitting this close to her, you could not miss the truth. She was so fragile, so frail, and death was so near. The last leaf hung by the merest thread; the slightest breeze would bring it down. It was more than poignant, it was tragic. The terror of death, the pity for her.

It was only after her death a few months later that I finally realized why she had been so eager to tell me that patronizing story about her yardman. She too had never forgotten the time I had rebuked her for counting my toes the way Mammy had always counted hers, and before she died, she had wanted this barrier of my disapproval to be broken down between us.

But how can sins be absolved, unless they are acknowledged as sins? Had she told me some story that illustrated how much she had changed over the years, I could have absolved her easily. But with this story about the yardman, she was saying that she and Mammy never really needed to change, that they had always empathized with and been generous to their nigras, that in their hearts, they were guiltless. But noblesse oblige is no substitute for justice, and I could not bring myself to pretend that it was, not even for her benefit, not even at the end of her life when she was leaving the world and it no longer mattered how she behaved in it. I do not see this as a particularly admirable stance on my part. When a final choice had to be made, it was real people Ain't Aubria was loyal to, whereas my ultimate loyalty was to abstract ideas. When I was absolutely certain that I was absolutely right, I could be very unforgiving. Judgmental even. Self-righteous. Just like Grandmother Gertrude.

2005

Stephanie Soileau

THE BOUCHERIE

"Several years ago, a livestock trailer did in fact tumble off the interstate into down-town Baton Rouge, and there was speculation that the missing members of the herd ended up in stewpots and freezers," says Stephanie Soileau about the impetus for her story. She goes on to say, "Fatima is based on several Sudanese refugee women I knew in Iowa City. One of those women was the daughter of a significant Muslim politi-cal leader who had spoken for peaceful coexistence among ethnicities and equality for women; he was ultimately hanged for sedition and apostasy." A graduate of the Iowa Writers' Workshop, Soileau lives in Chicago.

Of course it would be exaggerating to say that Slug had so es-tranged himself from the neighborhood that a phone call from him was as astonishing to Della as, say, a rainfall of fish, or blood, or manna, and as baffling in portent. Still, as Della stood, phone in hand, about to wake her husband, Alvin, who was sleep-ing through the six o'clock news in his recliner, she sensed with a sort of holy clearness of heart that what was happening on the tele-vision—two cows dropping down through the trees and onto somebody's picnic in the park—was tied, figuratively if not causally, to the call from Slug. "*Mais,* the cows done flew," she thought.

The anchorwoman for the Baton Rouge news announced that a livestock trailer carrying over a hundred head of cattle on their way to processing had plunged over the entrance ramp's railing at the Interstate 10 and Hwy 110 junction that morning. The driver had been speeding, possibly drunk, though definitely decapitated. More than a dozen cattle were crushed outright. Several others sur-vived the wreck only to climb over the edge of I-110 and drop to their deaths in the park below, while the remaining seventy-or-so, dazed and frightened, fled down the interstate or into the leafy shelter of the surrounding neighborhoods, followed by a band of cowboys called in for the impromptu roundup.

Fifty-three of the seventy cows had been recovered already, and all carcasses promptly removed from the roadway in time for the evening rush. Calls were still coming in, however: from kids who had a cow tied with cable to a signpost on their street; from riverboat gamblers who saw a small herd grazing on the levee downtown; from a state representative who stepped in a sizeable patty on the lawn of the Capitol. The search would continue into the night.

It was not the first time an eighteen-wheeler had gone over that railing, Della remembered. Back in the late '70s, absurd but true, some poor woman driving northbound on I-110 was killed when 40,000 pounds of frozen catfish dropped on her Volkswagen. Della thought then, as she did now, that it was certainly a shame to lose all that meat, with so many people starving in this world.

When Alvin finally snorted himself awake, he first tried to make sense of the man on horseback in a cowboy costume, waving a lasso at a red shorthorn under the statue of Huey Long—another advertising bid for Texas gamblers?—before he noticed his wife in the doorway, waving the phone and hissing, "*Ç'est* Slug! *Ç'est* Slug!" Alvin yanked the lever on his recliner, sending the footrest down with an echoing concussion that catapulted him up and out. "*Ç'est* Slug?" he said. The name dropped out of his mouth in the Cajun-French way, with a drawn out *uuhh.* "Let me talk to him."

Della held the telephone out, covering the mouthpiece with her palm. "Poor thing, you can't hardly understand what he says." She rushed to a notepad on the coffee table and scribbled Slug's name under the names of her four children and five grandchildren, all scattered to the ends of the earth. Next to Slug's she wrote: *Face. Visit, cook, clean?* Tomorrow, in a quiet moment, the list of names on the notepad would be passed to Pearl, then from Pearl to Estelle, from Estelle to Barbara, and on down the telephone prayer line.

Alvin squinted at her and leaned into the phone. *"Quoi?"* he said quietly. *"Ain?"* he said gently. *"Ain? . . . Ain? . . . Quoi t'as dit?"*

Della thought of how foolish Slug's wife Camille had been. A doctor had told Camille she needed to watch her cholesterol, so she cut all meat but chicken from their diet, and would not at all countenance an egg. They stopped visiting their neighbors, terrified of the gumbos and *etouffées* that threatened their blood at every house. At church each Sunday for two years, the neighborhood watched Camille grow thin and papery, painted with watercolor bruises, and when finally she died of pneumonia, no one wondered why. Many now attributed Slug's present condition to the two years he'd been deprived of meat's vital nourishment. Why else would the removal of a tiny melanoma turn into an infection that, having started at such a small place by Slug's ear, crept fast over his face like mold on bread? It was so simple. Why couldn't the doctors see?

"Ain?" Alvin said. *"Une vache?"*

Alvin wasn't much of a carpenter; measurements bored him, and he didn't have the tools or the fascination with things intricately wooden. While a gibbet did not have to be intricate, only sturdy and built to fit inside his fourteen-by-twenty-foot garage, Alvin could not even vouch for that. But Claude, down the block, could do amazing things with wood. He made reclining porch swings out of cypress, which never rotted. He whittled his own fishing lures. Many years ago Claude had helped Alvin right a fallen chicken coop in exchange for a dinner of the last pullet left alive.

Because Alvin could not build, he butchered, and he was not so sure, despite what his wife said, that the stink of guts and mess of feathers, or the old ways of village barter, were at all worse than the mad relay at the Winn Dixie on senior discount days: he and Della in separate lines, each with the limit—two nine-cent-a-pound turkeys—then the dash for the car, turkeys into the trunk, and right back for two more each at different registers before some faster senior citizen in one of those go-carts snatched them all up. These cheap and plentiful turkeys provoked his wife's instinct to hoard. In three deep-freezers, Della had turkeys for the next five years' holidays, and they were not to be traded, these hard-earned birds. At the same time, she fussed, she threatened: no more live chickens, no more rabbits, no more pigeons, doves, or squirrels in traps. She griped that she would never live to see the end of this meat.

Around the neighborhood though, Alvin's garage butchery was held in the highest esteem, so for Alvin's promise of a fresh brisket and sweetbreads, Claude traded woodworking consultation, even at this late hour. He took one look at Alvin's paper-towel blueprint and smeared on a few changes with a leaky pen. "That's how they do for deer," he explained. "But deers aren't near as heavy."

"Us, we used to do it from a tree," Alvin said.

Claude said, "Us too. We from the same place, you know. Or you forgot that?"

Claude traced over Alvin's lines until the paper towel split into a fuzzy stencil of an A-frame, and he deliberated aloud over weight limits and angles. Then he sketched his own design on the back of a receipt from his wallet. To the basic frame, he added a crossbar with two hooks. He attached the crossbar to a block and tackle that could be tied to a truck, in case the bare strength of all the neighborhood's aging men wasn't enough. He even drew the truck.

"You got him tied in your yard right now?" Claude said.

"Aw, no, man," said Alvin. "He went in those Indians' yard. Slug says we better come get him quick before that little lady gets scared and calls the cops."

"He's a peculiar fella, Slug."

"Aw, yeah, he is."

A moment of silent contemplation passed in observance of Slug's peculiarities. It had been a long, long time since anyone had seen Slug up close. It had been a long, long time since Slug had participated in the give and take.

The Indians were actually from Sudan, and had been living in the house next to Slug's for three years now. Through the mail carrier,

Della stayed informed about them and their funny ways. There was a mother named Fatima, a little girl, another littler girl, and the oldest, a boy. Their last name was Nasraddin. They sometimes got packages of meat, frozen over dry ice and labeled PERISHABLE, from HALAL MEATS WHOLESALE, through overnight mail. There had been no sign of a father, but they had twice received official-looking letters from Sudan. Wasn't Sudan, Della guessed, a part of India? She never thought to look it up.

When the Sudanese first moved in—the woman and the three children on their own—the neighborhood watched from windows and porches. After hauling each heavy piece of furniture from truck to house, the mother and son, both small and narrow, stood panting in the driveway while the little girls picked at acorns on the ground. The neighborhood watched them survey the remaining pieces for the next lightest, putting off the inevitable six-foot hideaway sofa, bulky and impossible as a bull. The bright flowered shawl wrapped around the woman's head was wet with sweat and kept sliding off. When Alvin and a few other men offered to help, the woman waved them away. She and her children climbed into the truck and surrounded the sofa. They pushed. "Not heavy," she said. The sofa shifted slightly toward the loading ramp. Her shawl slipped off again, but this time she untied it and draped it over her shoulders, like an athlete drapes a towel. The woman said, "Thank you." The men, so ox-like and unsmiling, might have seemed presumptuous, a little crude, even threatening perhaps, advancing uninvited onto her lawn, but still Alvin thought it was a shame she didn't have someone to help her get along in a strange place, tiny as she was, with three kids.

For months, the neighborhood watched as the woman came and went at odd hours in the familiar uniforms of food service and checkout counters, with her long hair pulled tight into a bun at the back of her neck. When they sometimes found her at the end of a line, bagging their turkeys and toilet paper or wrapping their hamburgers, the people of the neighborhood wanted to say something to her, if not *welcome,* then *hello,* maybe, or *what do you need;* but she would thank them and look away before they had decided; and then, they would doubt that it was her at all, but perhaps one of the many other dark people whose faces under fleeting scrutiny looked, quite frankly, alike.

The neighborhood watched when, a year later, the mother and son stood again on the lawn, this time with a garden hose and scrub-brushes, washing splattered eggs off their windows and bricks. Much to the neighborhood's surprise, Slug emerged from his hermitage next door to cut down the deer skin that was strung like a lynching from the low branches of the Nasraddin's oak tree. News of a bombing in a government building had goaded the restless college and high school boys, who for love of country and trouble patrolled these neighborhoods in their pickups, rattling windows with speakers bigger than their engines, and shouting: "U! S! A!" and "Arabs, go home!" Fatima's boy for days afterward lurked on the front porch with a baseball bat or lingered at the gate. He silently dared the white faces in every passing car, and when no one took his dare, he battered the knobby, exposed roots of the oak tree instead.

By the end of the second year, the neighborhood had accepted the Sudanese in that they had lost interest in the family altogether. From time to time, Della still sent a prayer around for the woman Fatima and her three children. She knew the name Fatima only as the holy site of Virginal apparitions somewhere off in Europe, Italy or France maybe. To Della, that a brown woman could be so named was another sign that all the world's people more or less worshiped the same god. When she called Claude's wife Pearl to deliver the prayer list, Della said, "They just like us, them Indians. They love Mary and Jesus, same as us." Pearl said, "I don't think they're the same."

Last year when Alvin slaughtered the last of his rabbits, Della put in a busy morning of head smashing and fur scraping, and sent him around the neighborhood, a gut-reeking summer Santa with a bag full of carcasses and orders to visit the Indians. Alvin knocked at Slug's door first, encouraged by the blue television light flashing on the curtains. He saw a shadow, movement across the room, and knocked again. He waited, knocked, prepared himself for the shock of Slug's disfigured face should the door finally open; but it did not open.

When he rang the bell at the Nasraddin house, all at once he heard many bare feet running on linoleum. A dense uneasiness pressed on the door from the inside, but here too the door stayed shut. Alvin thought maybe he could just leave a rabbit on the front steps, and as he was fishing in the bag for a nice big one, the chain clattered, the door opened. Fatima, swathed in a purple cloth that dragged the floor, said, "You are bleeding?"

There were spatters of blood on Alvin's coveralls and, though he'd washed his hands, red on his elbows. "No, ma'am. I'm Alvin Guilbeau. I brought you a rabbit."

Fatima shook her head. She smiled and waved him inside her house. The shy little girls, eyes wide and wet, peeked around her purple cloth.

"I raise rabbits. Me and my wife, we can't use them all, so I give them away."

Behind his mother, the boy, about thirteen by then, leaned against the wall dressed in tight yellow sweatpants and a red T-shirt. He had grown since Alvin first saw him out on the lawn shoving hopelessly at furniture. His shoulders were wide, his chest thick. He was almost as tall as any man. "Mama," he said, "he brought us a rabbit. *Arneb.*" His voice was still a boy's voice, but it had an oscillating croak. He grinned a wicked grin at Alvin, then said to his little sisters, "Do you want a bunny?"

Fatima said, "No, no," and shook her head so vigorously that long fuzzy hair exploded out of its bun. She blurted Arabic at her son. "No," she said to Alvin.

"It's cleaned and skinned. Fresh," Alvin said. Alvin reached into his bag again, yearning to prove they were pretty rabbits, but Fatima swung her purple cloth around and scurried to the kitchen. The two big-eyed girls were marooned; they drew closer together.

Over her shoulder, Fatima communicated something to the boy in what sounded to Alvin like angry coughs and gurgles.

"She says we cannot eat that meat. That's what she said." The boy's English bubbled and flowed, smoother and more proper than Alvin's.

"It's clean," Alvin said. "Y'all don't eat meat, maybe?"

"We eat meat." His eyes took in and then avoided the blood on Alvin's coveralls. "That's what she said to tell you."

Alvin was deciding whether or not he should be offended when Fatima returned, her purple cloth pinched into a sack in front of her. "Thank you," she said. She jutted her chin at Alvin's bag. "Open," she said. He did. She stood over it and let the cloth drop, dumping several pounds of candy over rabbit meat. "Thank you," she said.

"Thank you," Alvin said.

"Sorry. We cannot eat this meat," she said. "Stay for tea?"

"No, no, thank you," Alvin said, backing toward the door. "I got to go give these rabbits away."

"Come for tea."

"Thank you."

"Tell your wife," Fatima said, smiling, thanking, waving, closing the door.

Alvin stopped on the sidewalk and dug a caramel out of the bag. He unwrapped it thoughtfully, popped it into his mouth and continued down the block, wondering what in the world people eat if not meat.

All the way to Slug's, flashlights in hand, Alvin and Claude scoped a route to Alvin's garage that would avoid attention. They met no one on their two-block trek. One or the other of them knew almost every resident within a four-block radius, many of whom would be invited to share in this lucky blessing from the Lord, but it was the passers-through, like the students from the college, who might make trouble, or the policeman, a neighbor's grandson, who rolled down the block every now and then to check on the old folks.

Claude and Alvin turned the flashlights off near the Nasraddin house and paused at the chain-link gate to look and listen. Light from Fatima's windows overflowed the curtains and pooled in a narrow moat around the brick walls. Alvin clicked on his flashlight and made a quick sweep of the yard, but the beam only fell upon a droopy fig tree and a rusted barbecue pit.

The sound of an opening door sent Claude and Alvin ducking to the ground. "Y'all signaling planes out here?"

Alvin shined the beam on Slug's porch where Slug stood, one hand holding him up against a column and the other lingering self-consciously near his chin. Only one eye, the left, reflected back under one silvered, bristling eyebrow. Half of Slug's head, from brow down to chin and back over an ear, was taped up in brownish bandages, and Alvin thought of the cartoons he'd watched with his grandchildren: the sweating, pink pig who dabbed with a handkerchief and wiped his face right off, then thrashed around, grabbed blindly, a bewildered pink blank until the cartoonist leaned in with a giant pencil and gave the pig back to the world. "You looking good, Slug. You feel good?"

"Jesus," Claude said.

Slug pulled down one corner of his mouth to straighten it. "I feel alright. Can't do nothing 'bout it anyway." The words melted, dribbled down the steep slope of his mouth and drained out.

Slug's front room was tidy, tidier than Alvin expected considering how long the man had been hiding out with no company except his son, who drove two hours every other weekend from Alexandria to haul his father to specialists in New Orleans, another hour away. But the house did not feel clean. Dust coated the furniture, evidence of a life in stasis, like gangrene in an occluded limb. Slug's house had always been neat, thanks to his fastidious wife, but a fishing magazine might be left here, or an empty glass there. Alvin saw nothing to indicate that Slug did more than mope from room to room, or sit contemplatively, brooding or resentful in his armchair. The only thing not coated in dust was the TV remote control. There was a sour-and-bitter odor hanging around Slug, of clothes left too long in the washing machine then scorched in the dryer. Alvin noticed wetness on the bulge of bandages over his ear. He tried to focus on Slug's speckled blue eye, yolk-yellow all around like a crushed robin's egg. "You doing everything them doctors tell you to?"

"*Ça connaisse pas rien,* those fool doctors." Slug dared Alvin or Claude to say otherwise.

"Okay," Alvin said.

"Y'all want that cow or not? She's in those Indians' backyard," Slug slurred. "The boy didn't see her and he shut the gate."

On the way to the back door, Slug tied a lasso out of a rope that was waiting on the kitchen table. When Claude turned on his flashlight, Slug swatted at it, nearly knocked it out of his hand. "You gonna scare that little lady," he said.

The men crossed Slug's dark, tangled lawn with their flashlights off. Something wild and quick jetted back to its den in the hedgerow at the rear end of Slug's property, and in answer, from beyond Fatima's chain link fence, came a snort. Alvin felt the heavy presence of the animal all of a sudden. It was startling and near—all the more real for being unseen. He remembered: cows have horns, hooves, heads, tails, and they are so damned big. Ever so slowly, a very large and pale silhouette developed against the darkness like a photo negative. Grabbing up a wad of grass, Slug clucked and cooed, and the silhouette trudged closer. The big white head swung up and took the grass from Slug's open hand. He rubbed the wide space between her eyes, pinpointed one spot with his thumb, just right of center. The cow shook her head and puffed out a wet breath.

Each holding a handful of grass, the three men edged down the fence toward the gate, and the cow followed. The lights in the Nasraddin house were still on, and shadows moved against the curtains, the two little girls jumping on the sofa. Once the men were nearer the gate, Slug widened the lasso and slipped it around the cow's neck. Alvin lifted the gate latch, but the gate hung badly on its hinges and as Alvin dragged it open, it scraped against the driveway.

The cow stomped her feet. Slug bent his knees and held on to the end of the slack rope as the cow backed away. Alvin could only see the blank side of Slug's face, impassive as the moon. The rope tightened. "Grab it!" Claude yelled. The cow swung her head from side to side. Pulling against them, she let out a loud and awful *moo*.

The little girls in the house stopped jumping and poked their heads between the curtains. The men dropped the rope. The cow retreated to the backyard.

With her boy behind her, Fatima stepped out of her front door waving a baseball bat. "Who's that?" she said.

Alvin turned a flashlight on his own face. "It's Alvin Guilbeau." He presented himself to her in the light of the open door. "You got a surprise in your backyard."

She let the bat drop to her side and said something in her language to the boy, who then disappeared into the house. Tonight, instead of a long sheet, she wore a maroon fast-food uniform with yellow stripes on the sleeves. There was a turquoise shawl wrapped around her shoulders. Her feet were bare. In the air, Alvin smelled spices he couldn't name and remembered, for the first time in many years, the Indian markets he'd seen during the war, the cyclone of dark people in bright colors.

"*Chere*, you seen the news report tonight? You got one of them cows in your backyard," Alvin said. Fatima shook her head slightly. "A cow," Alvin said. He gestured at the backyard. There was, to Alvin, a shroud about the faces of people who spoke languages other than his. Even when silent, they wore a vagueness about the eyes; their body language spoke in impossible accents. "Cow," Alvin said again. "Cow. Cow." Fatima readjusted her shawl, and seemed to teeter between frustration and understanding.

Then Slug and Claude rounded the corner, tempting the animal with grass and leading it by the rope. All at once, the vagueness lifted from Fatima. With the baseball bat hanging like a billy club to one side of her hips, she swaggered down her front steps. The little girls watched from the window.

"I saw on the television!" she said.

"That's right."

"Khalid!"

The boy appeared again, his arms crossed over his chest, trying very hard to fill his doorway, to be the man of his doorway. "She wants you to have some tea." His voice had changed entirely. Alvin and Fatima both pointed at once, and the boy gasped.

"We should call the police?" Fatima walked boldly up to the animal and motioned for her boy to do the same. Alvin watched the mother and son as they patted the cow's haunches. While the boy whispered to the creature, Alvin wondered if the Nasraddins could be trusted.

"Come inside, use the phone," Fatima said.

"You don't want to call the cops," Claude said. He sounded, Alvin thought, absurdly menacing. The boy pushed between his mother and Claude, and his smooth, brown face radiated outrage as clearly as any man's. Fatima only looked from Claude to her son, and she made pensive birdish noises between her lips, unable to decode the language of a threat, or maybe just not threatened.

"I don't think we should call the police," Alvin said, "tonight."

Slug said, "Let's wait and see."

"What should we wait to see?" the boy said. He glared at Claude. "We will call the police."

"Khalid!" Fatima wrapped an arm around her boy's waist and drew him close to her. She spoke to him in their language, and Alvin saw a mother like any he had known, who could calm her son, and entreat, and explain, and who was confident in her own wisdom. "We will not call tonight," she said to the men.

"So she'll call tomorrow?" Claude said. "The cow can't stay here."

"It can stay in the yard. We can close the gate," Fatima said, "until tomorrow."

"No, ma'am," said Alvin. "We need to take it to my garage."

"Why take it? I don't mind."

Slug emerged from the shadows. He tugged at his mouth.

"Ma'am," he said, "Ma'am. We don't want to call the cops at all." He spoke very slowly, took care to make each word clear. "Miss Fatima, one cow is a lot of meat."

Khalid yelped. "You're going to eat this cow!"

"Y'all welcome to some of it," said Slug.

The boy bubbled over with Arabic. He flung his hands around, pressing closer and closer to his mother, and trailed off into English. "They're crazy!" he said to her. "They want to eat it!"

The woman said, "If you want to share, my son must kill her with a knife." Even her laughter rippled with foreignness; the men could not translate it. By way of explanation, she only said, "Khalid is a big boy," and laughed again. The boy seemed both astonished and very embarrassed. She patted his arm.

In the humans' confused silence, the cow tore at grass and swished her tail.

Fatima poked the bandage around Slug's ear, not so gently, with three fingers. "You need to change this."

"Maybe so, yeah."

"You are not listening to the doctor." Next, she addressed Alvin: "Will you come tomorrow for tea? Will you bring your wife?"

Before he meant to, Alvin said, "Yes, ma'am." Fatima turned back to her house. Khalid started to follow, but Fatima threw out the baseball bat to stop him. "Help them, Khalid," she said. She gave him the bat and went in to her little girls.

The boy walked along the animal's right shoulder and stroked her swaying neck. Her hooves thudded on the grass, clopped on the pavement as they passed through yards, across driveways, and behind houses. On the cow's left side, Slug and Claude each sulked in his own way, for his own reasons. Alvin walked ahead, leading the cow by the rope and listening for cars.

Claude said, "You got your daddy over there in India?"

The boy didn't answer.

"Ain't none of your business," Slug said.

In one backyard, the cow took control of the men. She dragged them over to a garden of mustard greens and devoured half of a row before haunch-swatting and rope-tugging finally coaxed her on. The boy dropped far behind. He took swings with the bat at dirt, trees, and telephone poles.

"I got to see India," Alvin said. "During the war. They let the cows roam the streets."

"I seen on TV," Claude said, "how they make the women walk behind the men."

"I don't know about that, but I seen the cows for myself." Alvin looked around for the boy. "I guess his momma's used to having cows all over the place."

"I'm telling you, they don't even let them show their faces, those women."

"We aren't from India," Khalid shouted from the darkness behind them. "We're from Sudan!"

By the time they came to Alvin's house, the boy had disappeared. They led the cow into the garage and tied her to one of the beams overhead. She lifted her tail and dumped a heap onto the concrete floor. With a shovel that he took down from the rafters where it balanced along with rakes and fishing poles, Alvin shoveled the crap into a paper bag so that he could use it later to fertilize the muscadine vines that crawled up a lattice at the back of the garage and covered the only windows.

"She's crazy," Claude said. "We ain't gonna let a boy kill that cow."

"Aw, she was pulling our leg. Don't get all worked up," Alvin said.

"You don't know what she's joking about or not. I wouldn't be surprised if she was dialing 911 right now."

"*Bouche ta gueule!* She won't call no cops!" Slug stood at the garage door, his one eye peeping through a crack for any sight of the boy. "You know that little lady," he whispered, "she went to school for law in her country."

"Is that right," said Alvin.

"And her husband. He was some kind of politician. They didn't like what he had to say over there. They shot him dead."

"Aw, no," Alvin said.

"So don't you ask that boy about his daddy no more."

Slug slipped out of the garage into the darkness and crept homeward like a possum, along walls and fences and hedges.

Della, in bed and asleep by eight o'clock, long before Alvin came in, and awake again at dawn long before Alvin awoke, had no idea, when she went out to the deep-freezers in her housedress and slippers for a package of *boudin* to boil for breakfast, that she would find a cow in her garage. When she saw it there, smelling like a circus and totally composed, she turned immediately back toward the house, and just as she opened her mouth to yell, Alvin rounded the corner, still in his pajamas. He started at her in French before she could argue. He told her about Slug and the Sudanese, and he made her see that it would be just like at Pepere's farm on autumn Saturdays when their children were still babies. God knew what He was doing, sending that trailer-truck flying in November instead of July. The flies had slacked off. The air was light and thin, perfect weather for slaughter. The neighbors would come and ask for this or that part, the brisket, the ribs, the sweetbreads, or the brains, and there would be no fights about it, only merry hacking and sawing and yanking at skin. She would stuff her red sausages. Pearl would make liver gravy. Inside, their house would be close, wet with the boiling of sausages and the heat of a crowd sweating from homemade wine. "Besides," he said, "if we don't slaughter it ourselves, they just going to haul it off, cut it up, and send it right back to us at three dollars a pound. That cow came to us. She's ours." He made it sound like a good idea.

By noon, thanks to Della and the Catholic sisters of the prayer line, word got around that God had delivered unto the neighborhood a fat, unblemished cow, and they planned, sure enough, to eat it. Although some of the ladies had concerns, they had to admit the price of beef had gone up, and their little bit of social security certainly did not allow for steak and brisket every night of the week, and furthermore, if so-and-so down the block was in for a piece of the cow, then they should be, too. Della passed along all her prayers for Slug, for her children and her grandchildren who never called or wrote or prayed for themselves, and for Fatima, her little ones, and that angry young man of hers. "And pray," she said finally. "Pray tonight we don't get caught."

It took little for Alvin to convince Della to visit Fatima with him in the very early afternoon. Della did her hair and powdered her face, Alvin tucked in his shirt. They found a jar of fig preserves in the back of a cabinet, dusted it off, and wondered if the Nasraddins would say they could not eat figs.

The boy answered the door, slouching in his jeans and sweatshirt. He said nothing, only stepped aside to let them in. The little girls played dominoes on the carpet. The littler one said, "Hi." She looked like she wanted to say more, but the bigger one shushed her and started to pick up the dominoes. The boy led them into a tiny green kitchen, where Fatima stood before the stove stirring milk in a saucepan.

"You are Mrs. Guilbeau?" Fatima smiled. Della and Alvin smiled back. "Sit down," Fatima said, and gestured to the kitchen table. Della and Alvin sat.

"Your house is very nice," Della said. She searched the walls and countertops for anything unique to a Sudanese woman's kitchen but saw only the usual things: clock, potholder, sugar bowl, flyswatter. Della wondered what strange foods had been cooked on that stove and stored in that refrigerator. She wondered especially what might be in the freezer.

"Do y'all like figs?"

"What is *figs*?"

Della held up the jar for Fatima to see.

"Yes," she said. "Thank you." She said something to the boy in her language, and he went to the pantry and took out some bread. Meanwhile, an itch grew in Della to talk about the cow, cows, any cow; it seemed frivolous to talk about anything else.

Alvin said, "We weren't sure if y'all could eat figs."

"Just meat sometimes we can't eat," the boy said.

"You can eat beef?" Della asked.

"Sometimes." The boy started to leave the kitchen, but his mother spoke again, and he sat down at the table across from Della and Alvin. Fatima set four cups and saucers on the counter. To Della's surprise, five ordinary little tea-flags dangled by strings from the lip of the saucepan from which Fatima poured.

Fatima served the tea then sat down next to her son.

She smiled at her guests and sipped from her cup. They smiled back and sipped from theirs. The boy kept adding sugar to his. He frowned and sighed.

"My father had cattle in Sudan," Fatima said.

"Is that right," said Alvin. "For milk?"

"Some for milk, some for eating. We always had food."

"You were blessed," Della said. "All those people starving." She did not know for sure if there were people starving in Sudan, but she thought it was a good guess. "When I was a little girl, we didn't have nothing for a long time. No cows. No chickens. Nothing. That was the Depression."

Alvin said, "No, ma'am, we didn't have much."

Della held the cup close to her mouth and blew at the surface of the tea, wrinkling the milk skin, which she then dabbed with a forefinger, lifted out of the cup, and deposited on her saucer. Fatima graciously handed her a napkin.

"We wish you and your children would join us tonight," Alvin said. "There's going to be plenty." He sounded to Della like the door-to-door peddlers of peculiar religions who would show up every spring to invite them to revivals.

Fatima looked to her son, who had not drunk his tea, but was staring down into it. "You see?" she said.

"I thought you were joking."

"Khalid does not know where meat comes from."

"I do!"

"He's a good boy," she said, "but he does not remember Sudan."

The boy pushed his chair away from the table and left. A moment later, a door slammed somewhere in the house.

As best she could, Fatima explained about meat, what Muslims could and could not eat, and also about something she called *ummah*. She kept using that word to describe the people among whom she now lived, and this word sounded more lovely, and because of its newness to their ears, more important than the words they might have used to describe themselves and their gentle loyalty to each other. Behind her halting English was a persuasive warmth and insistence, a tenor that made every word seem lawful and good. She had been a lawyer, Della could see, and what a shame, she thought, that in this great country such a gifted woman had to wrap hamburgers.

In the *World Book Encyclopedia,* copyright 1965, that they'd bought for the children, volume by volume per ten-dollar purchase from the grocery store, Alvin read that Sudan is the largest of all African countries. Its capital, a town called Khartoum, sits on the banks of the Nile like Baton Rouge sits on the Mississippi. There is a North and there is a South. The North has cities and deserts. The South has swamps and mosquitoes, and months of nothing but rain. These people are poor. Poor, poor. Some parts of the year, they starve, even though certain tribes hoard millions of cattle, sheep, goats, and camels for social prestige, and because there just aren't enough trucks to haul them anywhere.

The name "Sudan" comes from the Arabic expression *bilad as-Sudan,* Land of the Blacks, which seemed to Alvin to mean that the Sudanese are as likely to look like your run-of-the-mill African American down at the Wal-Mart as they are to look Indian, that is, from India Indian. They are Muslim. There are some Christians, in the South, who have been Christians longer than the French have been Christians, longer than the French have been French. How about that. There are some who believe in spirits—water spirits, tree spirits. The Muslims are moving in on them. When boys become men in Sudan, Alvin read, when they kill an enemy, their backs and arms and faces are cut in stripes of scars. A picture showed a young man in a white gown and turban with three dark hatch-marks across his cheeks. *Cicatrization,* it was called. *Ci-ca-tri-za-tion.*

Alvin's eyes gave out just before the section on the History of Ancient Nubia. He closed the encyclopedia, closed his eyes, and saw Fatima propped up by a walking stick and her little girls with distended naked bellies. Sand spun around them like sleet. Or maybe there was no sand. Maybe their bare feet were sinking into an island of mud and swamp grass. Mosquitoes and deerflies swirled around them like slow sand. They were part of a circle of many people: Arabs and Africans and some lean-looking and dusty white people. In the center of the circle, a black man, shriveled, desiccated—by sand or by mosquitoes—held Fatima's boy by the shoulders. The boy, Khalid, faced his mother and sisters. Alvin saw Khalid's wide back bisected by the skinny and dark line of the old black man. The man withdrew a straight-bladed knife from the toolbelt-thong that hung cockeyed on his hips. One smooth stroke across Khalid's shoulders, and blood swelled and overflowed. While the circle of men and women and children hooted and raised fists over heads, Khalid stood perfectly still. Alvin wished he could see the boy's face. He seemed so very young.

Alvin went to the garage and opened the long, flat, wooden case where he kept his butchering tackle. He surveyed the contents: fillet knife, boning knife, a cleaver as heavy as a hatchet, a carver, a simple and gently curved butcher knife. None of these would slice through a cow's thick neck, not neatly, not painlessly. The cut would have to be smooth, straight, decisive. The boy's hand would have to be steady. Not one of them could handle a thrashing cow.

Then he thought of the thirty-inch blade from his riding lawn-mower and spent the rest of the afternoon sharpening it, in the backyard so as not to upset the cow. Round and round, on one side and then the other, Alvin honed the blade against the whetstone. There could be no nicks or dull spots. He knew from cutting his own hands so many times that the dull knives hurt, while he never felt the nick of a sharp one at all. So he sharpened and sharpened, took a break for a glass of wine, and sharpened some more.

The boy came early in the afternoon. "Mama sent this," he said.

He had an armful of old newspapers and a nearly empty roll of butcher paper. Before sending him home, Alvin took him out to the garage. With the garage light on, they both looked smaller— the boy and the cow—big but not quite fully grown. Maybe they could handle her. Maybe the boy could handle her. He had thick arms, and she really seemed to be a placid cow.

The cow pissed, loud as a rainstorm on the concrete floor, and Khalid jumped back from her. "She almost splashed me," he said. Then he said, "Gross," and the word sounded silly and even more American dressed up in the boy's lilting accent. Alvin had heard his grandchildren say it hundreds of times, about *ponce,* and chicken livers, and the orange-yellow fat of crawfish tails, among other things. It was a silly word, in any case. "That's gross, yeah," Alvin said. "I'll hose it off tomorrow. Come here, boy."

He handed Khalid the lawnmower blade to make him understand. He said, "You think you can do that, what your mamma wants? You think you can, boy?"

Khalid balanced the blade on his flattened palms with his fingers stretched back, away from the edge. He looked incredulously at Alvin. "You know she was joking," the boy said. "They don't do this in Sudan."

At eight in the evening, the neighborhood began to gather in Della's kitchen where she sat steadfast on a stool by the stove, stirring hot praline goo with one hand and doling out wine with the other. Claude and Pearl came first, with a loaded shotgun and the A-frame gibbet, which the men quickly installed in the garage. When Alvin saw the shotgun, he motioned for Claude to follow him to the backyard. He pointed to the long, sharp blade lying across an old sycamore stump. Claude said, "For them Indians, you'd do that?"

"They're from Sudan," Alvin said. "She'll call the cops if we don't let the boy do it." This was a lie, of course, and Alvin hated to tell it, but he knew that no diplomatic somersaults in French or English, no Arabic invocation of community could justify such a strange decision to Claude. Claude picked up the blade and strummed it with his thumb. "Be careful," said Alvin. "It's sharp, sharp."

"It better be sharp," Claude said.

There was a small crowd gathered in the driveway when the neighborhood policeman pulled over to the curb and rolled down his window. "How y'all?" he called, and cracked good-natured jokes about drunken old Cajuns until his own grandmother came out of the house and pressed a bottle of homemade wine and a tin of pralines, still warm, into his hands. "Go bring that to your wife," she said, and then, "Y'all still looking for them cows?"

"They still can't find some of 'em," her grandson said.

"They done got ate, I bet you."

The policeman drove away and his grandmother came back to the group laughing from her rolling belly. "Us coonasses been stealing cows since the dawn of time," she said. "That's part of our culture, that." Most of them laughed, but some, Claude especially, speculated in French that Fatima had called that cop after all, that he was reconnoitering and most certainly would be back.

By nine o' clock, Alvin and Della's house was teeming, the table crowded with food. Many had brought the Saturday paper, which featured on the front page a photograph of yesterday's accident: a dead steer, roped by the neck, dangling from an overpass. They would use this page, they decided with glee, to wrap up their takings this evening.

From time to time, Alvin checked on the cow. She had been quiet all day, but now, with so much commotion, she huffed and stomped her feet. Alvin, who could not stand to see an animal suffer, cooed at her in French and patted her flaring nose. He had not given her anything to eat or drink—she would clean easier that way—and wondered how thirsty she was. When he held a mixing-bowl full of wine under her nose, she sniffed it, tested it with her tongue, then drank up every drop and flipped the bowl looking for more. Alvin gave her more.

• • •

At ten o'clock, the crowd, pressed elbow to elbow in the steamy kitchen, quieted down. The ominous booming from the students' passing cars shook the windows and pulsed like tribal drums in the chests of the old people. There had been no word from Slug or the Sudanese. Della called Slug's house but got no answer, and none of them could spell Nasraddin to find it in the phone book.

Had they been in their own homes, rather than here in Della's kitchen, those who lived across the street from the Nasraddins might have looked into Fatima's brightly lit living room and seen her winding bold cloths around her daughters, combing out and braiding their long hair, before she finally took up a roll of bandages and, with blunt efficiency—as though grooming her children, packing groceries, slaughtering cows and disinfecting old men's lesions were all the selfsame gesture—ministered to the ruined face of her neighbor as he sat on her couch and hid behind his hands to spare the little girls. The spies then might have pulled shut their drapes quickly, embarrassed when they saw Fatima glance out of her own window, searching the shadows for her son, who had not returned from Mr. Guilbeau's that afternoon.

And had the people all over this neighborhood been watching from their windows, as they were accustomed to do after nightfall, flipping on their porch lights and peering out at their street, hands cupped around eyes, they would have seen a figure moving in and out of the orange light of streetlamps and trespassing fearlessly into one yard after another. What a shock they'd have had when the face drew close to their windows, as close as they had ever imagined ominous faces in the night, and gazed at them; no, not at them— beyond them, into their homes, at their plain and barely valuable things. And the old couple who lived in the gray brick house on the corner—what would they have done, what would they have thought, when the expression on that face changed suddenly from curiosity to anger, when the young man at their window reared back the baseball bat he carried and swung it with a grown man's strength into the glass?

• • •

Under the light of a single bald light bulb dangling from a rafter, the neighborhood gathered into Alvin's garage and formed a circle around the cow. They watched Alvin offer her another bowlful of wine. They watched Claude cross to the center of the circle, shotgun in hand.

It had gotten around, what the brown woman wanted. Everyone knew and agreed to allow it. There was beef in this world before there were guns, they reasoned; people must have killed cows somehow. As the night grew later, though, they began to believe that they had been fooled, not through spitefulness on Fatima's part, but rather through their own provincial ignorance of foreign places and customs; they hadn't gotten her joke. They had been propelled by momentum into this circle and this ritual that was at once familiar and very strange, but now as they saw Claude aiming the shotgun after all, their momentum flagged. Claude set the shotgun aside. He said to Alvin, "Somebody will hear it. If that cop comes by . . . . What do you want to do?"

Alvin took the lawnmower blade from where it lay on top of a deep freezer. "If you hold her head up, I'll do it. She won't feel a thing." One of the men suggested his teenage son hold the gun aimed at the cow, just in case, and this seemed like a reasonable compromise.

Claude held her gently but firmly by the jaws. Turning the blade this way and that, switching it from hand to hand, Alvin walked around to one side of the cow and then the other. He draped one arm over the cow's neck and poised the blade under her throat, but he could find no leverage. He stood back and considered, as Claude hummed and massaged her broad buttery jowls. The teenager stood poised with the shotgun on his shoulder. They all prayed he would not shoot Claude by mistake.

"Hit her in the head with something," the teenager said. From the dark perimeter of the circle, his father said, "Hush boy."

"I can't watch, me," Della said. She cringed back with all her body.

Alvin stood further back. "Somebody look for that cop." Della rushed to the door and opened it just a crack. "Oh!" she squeaked. Hearts pounded and fluttered all around the circle. "Oh! Oh, *chere!* I didn't know you at first. Come in!"

When they saw Slug, most of them for the first time in several years, the people of the neighborhood were less surprised by the bandages and deformity of Slug's face than by the young man who came in right behind him, hanging onto Slug's sagging belt.

It was Slug who had gone looking and heard the shattering glass, who had found Khalid in a dark house picking up and examining all the small, un-incriminating remnants of desk drawers and bookshelves. Somewhere in the circle now, the boy realized, were the old couple whose check stubs and prayer lists he had handled, whose refrigerator he had opened and closed, who would immediately believe it was the work of those college boys, drunk on a Saturday night, when they later found their window broken and things upset. Khalid let go of Slug's belt and stood up straight, seeing no one and nothing but the cow and the blade cocked under her throat.

Fatima followed, with her two little girls, all three draped in bright fabrics. A silk veil covered Fatima's head and black hair. To the neighborhood, which had seen her only in uniforms—tired, bagging groceries—Fatima seemed in these foreign clothes strangely like the Virgin Mother.

Slug's one eye winked at all of them as he looked around the circle. When his eye landed on them, they wondered, each in turn, why they had not knocked louder at his door or longer, why no one had insisted on driving him to doctors, or cleaning his house, or helping him change his bandages.

Like an altar boy presenting the Bible, Alvin held the blade out to Khalid. "Take it," Slug said, and Khalid picked up the blade.

Alvin lunged for a mop bucket near the door, and positioned it on the ground under the cow's head. They all knew it would never contain the blood. Alvin took the shotgun from the teenager, who stepped back into the circle, pressed close to his father. Alvin aimed, just in case.

Claude cupped his hands around the cow's jaws again. He pulled her head up so the skin on her neck stretched flat, taut. Slug and the boy stood by her side, on the right. The boy was losing his color. He held the blade feebly. It trembled in his hands.

The neighborhood watched the boy move his lips, but no words came out. The mother said, "Khalid—*Bismillah ArRahman.*" The boy tried again. His face blanched.

Slug laid his hand over the boy's. He hugged the boy against his chest, pressed him tightly to stop his quaking. The cow snorted. She stepped back and nearly broke free of Claude's hold. They all heard the shuffle and click when Alvin set the shotgun.

Slug and the boy cocked the blade at the cow's neck. She pounded one hoof and took a deep breath that swelled her. As she started to moo, Slug and the boy leaned forward together. Slug said, "Y'all say a prayer."

The blade wrenched across the tight white line of throat, like a bow on a silent fiddle. Claude stroked her cheeks while blood gushed from her neck, saturated his jeans, and pooled in the bucket at his feet. The bucket filled and spilled over, and the pool spread fast, outward and outward to Slug and the boy who had fainted in his arms, to Alvin, to Della, to the woman Fatima and her wide-eyed girls, to the circle's perimeter, to the feet of the people who watched and remembered the country farms, the spoken French, the good of home-stuffed sausage. The blood spread out toward the garage doors, and under the doors, out to the driveway, into the street. Enough blood, they all thought, to flood the neighborhood.

APPENDIX

A list of the magazines currently consulted for *New Stories from the South: The Year's Best, 2005,* with addresses, subscription rates, and editors.

The Antioch Review
P.O. Box 148
Yellow Springs, OH 45387-0148
Quarterly, $35
Robert S. Fogarty

Apalachee Review
P.O. Box 10469
Tallahassee, FL 32302
Semiannually, $15
Laura Newton

Appalachian Heritage
CPO 2166
Berea, KY 40404
Quarterly, $18
George Brosi

Arkansas Review
P.O. Box 1890
Arkansas State University
State University, AR 72467
Triannually, $20
Tom Williams

Arts & Letters
Campus Box 89
Georgia College & State University
Milledgeville, GA 31061-0490
Semiannually, $15
Martin Lammon

Atlanta
1330 W. Peachtree St.

Suite 450
Atlanta, GA 30309
Monthly, $14.95
Rebecca Burns

The Atlantic Monthly
77 N. Washington St.
Boston, MA 02114
Monthly, $39.95
C. Michael Curtis

The Baffler
P.O. Box 378293
Chicago, IL 60637
Annually, $24
Solveig Nelson

Bayou
Department of English
University of New Orleans
Lakefront
New Orleans, LA 70148
Semiannually, $10

Bellevue Literary Review
Department of Medicine
New York University School of
    Medicine
550 1st Ave., OBV-612
New York, NY 10016
Semiannually, $12
Ronna Weinberg

Black Warrior Review
University of Alabama
P.O. Box 862936
Tuscaloosa, AL 35486-0027
Semiannually, $14
Fiction Editor

Boulevard
6614 Clayton Rd., PMB 325
Richmond Heights, MO 63117
Triannually, $15
Richard Burgin

The Carolina Quarterly
Greenlaw Hall CB# 3520
University of North Carolina
Chapel Hill, NC 27599-3520
Triannually, $12
Fiction Editor

The Chariton Review
Truman State University
Kirksville, MO 63501
Semiannually, $9
Jim Barnes

The Chattahoochee Review
Georgia Perimeter College
2101 Womack Rd.
Dunwoody, GA 30338-4497
Quarterly, $16
Lawrence Hetrick

Chicago Quarterly Review
517 Sherman Ave.
Evanston, IL 60202
Quarterly
S. Afzal Haider

Cimarron Review
205 Morrill Hall
Oklahoma State University
Stillwater, OK 74078-0135
Quarterly, $24
E. P. Walkiewicz

The Cincinnati Review
Department of English and
  Comparative Literature
University of Cincinnati
P.O. Box 210069
Cincinnati, OH 45221-0069
Semiannually, $12
Brock Clarke

Columbia
415 Dodge Hall
2960 Broadway
Columbia University
New York, NY 10027-6902
Semiannually, $15
Fiction Editor

Confrontation
English Department
C.W. Post of L.I.U.
Brookville, NY 11548
Semiannually, $10
Martin Tucker

Conjunctions
21 East 10th St.
New York, NY 10003
Semiannually, $18
Bradford Morrow

Crazyhorse
Department of English
College of Charleston
66 George St.
Charleston, SC 29424
Semiannually, $15
Bret Lott

Crucible
Barton College
P.O. Box 5000
Wilson, NC 27893-7000
Annually, $7
Terrence L. Grimes

Denver Quarterly
University of Denver
Denver, CO 80208
Quarterly, $20
Bin Ramke

The Distillery
Motlow State Comm. College
P.O. Box 8500
Lynchburg, TN 37352-8500
Semiannually, $15
Dawn Copeland

Epoch
251 Goldwin Smith Hall
Cornell University
Ithaca, NY 14853-3201
Triannually, $11
Michael Koch

Fiction
c/o English Department
City College of New York
New York, NY 10031
Quarterly, $38
Mark J. Mirsky

Five Points
Georgia State University
MSC 8R0318
33 Gilmer St. SE, Unit 8
Atlanta, GA 30303-3083
Triannually, $20
Megan Sexton

The Florida Review
Department of English
University of Central Florida
Orlando, FL 32816
Semiannually, $10
Pat Rushin

Gargoyle
P.O. Box 6216

Arlington, VA 22206-0216
Annually, $20
Richard Peabody

The Georgia Review
University of Georgia
Athens, GA 30602-9009
Quarterly, $24
T. R. Hummer

The Gettysburg Review
Gettysburg College
Gettysburg, PA 17325-1491
Quarterly, $24
Peter Stitt

Glimmer Train Stories
710 SW Madison St., #504
Portland, OR 97205
Quarterly, $32
Susan Burmeister-Brown
   and Linda B. Swanson-Davies

Granta
1755 Broadway
5th Floor
New York, NY 10019-3780
Quarterly, $37
Ian Jack

The Greensboro Review
English Department
134 McIver Bldg.
University of North Carolina
P.O. Box 26170
Greensboro, NC 27412
Semiannually, $10
Jim Clark

Harper's Magazine
666 Broadway, 11th Floor
New York, NY 10012
Monthly, $21
Ben Metcalf

Harpur Palate
English Department
Binghamton University
P.O. Box 6000
Binghamton, NY 13902
Semiannually, $16
Letitia Moffitt

Hobart
9251 Densmore Ave. N.
Seattle, WA 98103
Biannually, $7
Aaron Burch

The Idaho Review
Boise State University
Department of English
1910 University Dr.
Boise, ID 83725
Annually, $9.95
Mitch Wieland

Image
3307 Third Ave., W.
Center for Religious Humanism
Seattle, WA 98119
Quarterly, $36
Gregory Wolfe

Indiana Review
465 Ballantine Ave.
Indiana University
Bloomington, IN 47405
Semiannually, $12
Laura McCoid

The Iowa Review
308 EPB
University of Iowa
Iowa City, IA 52242-1492
Triannually, $20
David Hamilton

The Journal
Ohio State University

Department of English
164 W. 17th Ave.
Columbus, OH 43210
Semiannually, $12
Kathy Fagan and Michelle Herman

Kalliope
Florida Comm. College–
  Jacksonville
South Campus
11901 Beach Blvd.
Jacksonville, FL 32246
Triannually, $16
Mary Sue Koeppel

The Kenyon Review
Kenyon College
Gambier, OH 43022
Triannually, $25
David H. Lynn

Land-Grant College Review
P.O. Box 1164
New York, NY 10159
Semiannually, $18
David Koch, Josh Melrod

The Literary Review
Fairleigh Dickinson University
285 Madison Ave.
Madison, NJ 07940
Quarterly, $18
René Steinke

Long Story
18 Eaton St.
Lawrence, MA 01843
Annually, $6
R. P. Burnham

Louisiana Literature
SLU-10792
Southeastern Louisiana
  University
Hammond, LA 70402

Semiannually, $12
Jack Bedell

The Louisville Review
Spalding University
851 South 4th St.
Louisville, KY 40203
Semiannually, $14
Sena Jeter Naslund

Lynx Eye
c/o ScribbleFest Literary Group
542 Mitchell Dr.
Los Osos, CA 93402
Quarterly, $25
Pam McCully, Kathryn Morrison

Meridian
University of Virginia
P.O. Box 400145
Charlottesville, VA 22904-4145
Semiannually, $10
Jett McAlister

Mid-American Review
Department of English
Bowling Green State University
Bowling Green, OH 43403
Semiannually, $12
Michael Czyzniejewski

Mississippi Review
University of Southern
  Mississippi
Box 5144
Hattiesburg, MS 39406-5144
Semiannually, $15
Frederick Barthelme

The Missouri Review
1507 Hillcrest Hall
University of Missouri
Columbia, MO 65211
Triannually, $22
Speer Morgan

The Nebraska Review
Writers Workshop
Fine Arts Building 212
University of Nebraska at Omaha
Omaha, NE 68182-0324
Semiannually, $15
James Reed

New England Review
Middlebury College
Middlebury, VT 05753
Quarterly, $25
Stephen Donadio

New Letters
University of Missouri at
  Kansas City
5101 Rockhill Rd.
Kansas City, MO 64110
Quarterly, $17
Robert Stewart

New Millennium Writings
P.O. Box 2463
Knoxville, TN 37901
Annually, $12.95
Don Williams

New Orleans Review
P.O. Box 195
Loyola University
New Orleans, LA 70118
Semiannually, $12
Christopher Chambers, Editor

The New Yorker
4 Times Square
New York, NY 10036
Weekly, $44.95
Deborah Treisman, Fiction
  Editor

Nimrod International Journal
University of Tulsa
600 South College

Tulsa, OK 74104-3189
Semiannually, $17.50
Francine Ringold

The North American Review
University of Northern Iowa
1222 W. 27th St.
Cedar Falls, IA 50614-0516
Six times a year, $22
Grant Tracey

North Carolina Literary Review
English Department
2201 Bate Building
East Carolina University
Greenville, NC 27858-4353
Annually, $10
Margaret Bauer

Northwest Review
369 PLC
University of Oregon
Eugene, OR 97403
Triannually, $22
John Witte

Ontario Review
9 Honey Brook Dr.
Princeton, NJ 08540
Semiannually, $16
Raymond J. Smith

Open City
270 Lafayette St.
Suite 1412
New York, NY 10012
Triannually, $30
Thomas Beller

Other Voices
University of Illinois at Chicago
Department of English (M/C 162)
601 S. Morgan St.
Chicago, IL 60607-7120
Semiannually, $12
Lois Hauselman

The Oxford American
201 Donaghey Ave., Main 107
Conway, AR 72035
Quarterly, $29.95
Marc Smirnoff

The Paris Review
541 E. 72nd St.
New York, NY 10021
Quarterly, $40
Fiction Editor

Parting Gifts
March Street Press
3413 Wilshire Dr.
Greensboro, NC 27408
Semiannually, $12
Robert Bixby

Pembroke Magazine
UNC-P, Box 1510
Pembroke, NC 28372-1510
Annually, $8
Shelby Stephenson

PEN America
PEN American Center
568 Broadway, Suite 401
New York, NY 10012
Semiannually, $20
M. Mark

Pindeldeboz
23-55 38th St.
Astoria, NY 11105
Annually, $12
Whitney Pastoree

Ploughshares
Emerson College
120 Boylston St.
Boston, MA 02116-4624
Triannually, $24
Don Lee

PMS
Univ. of Alabama at Birmingham
Department of English
HB 217, 900 S. 13th St.
1530 3rd Ave., S.
Birmingham, AL 35294-1260
Annually, $7
Linda Frost

Post Road Magazine
853 Broadway, Suite 1516
Box 85
New York, NY 10003
Semiannually, $16
Rebecca Boyd

Potomac Review
51 Mannakee St.
Rockville, MD 20850
Semiannually, $18
Eli Flam

Prairie Schooner
201 Andrews Hall
University of Nebraska
Lincoln, NE 68588-0334
Quarterly, $26
Hilda Raz

Puerto del Sol
Box 30001, Department 3E
New Mexico State University
Las Cruces, NM 88003-9984
Semiannually, $10
Kevin McIlvoy

River City
Department of English
University of Memphis
Memphis, TN 38152-6176
Semiannually, $12
Mary Leader

River Styx
634 North Grand Blvd.

12th Floor
St. Louis, MO 63103
Triannually, $20
Richard Newman

Roanoke Review
221 College Lane
Salem, VA 24153
Annually, $8
Melanie Almeder

Rockhurst Review
Department of English
Rockhurst University
1100 Rockhurst Rd.
Kansas City, MO 64110
Annually, $5
Patricia Cleary Miller

Santa Monica Review
Santa Monica College
1900 Pico Blvd.
Santa Monica, CA 90405
Semiannually, $12
Andrew Tonkovich

The Sewanee Review
735 University Ave.
Sewanee, TN 37383-1000
Quarterly, $24
George Core

Shenandoah
Washington and Lee University
Mattingly House
Lexington, VA 24450
Quarterly, $22
R. T. Smith

So to Speak
George Mason University
4400 University Dr., MSN 2D6
Fairfax, VA 22030-4444
Semiannually, $12
Nancy Pearson

The South Carolina Review
Center for Electronic and Digital
  Publishing
Clemson University
Strode Tower, Box 340522
Clemson, SC 29634
Semiannually, $20
Wayne Chapman

South Dakota Review
Box III
University Exchange
University of South Dakota
Vermillion, SD 57069
Quarterly, $30
John R. Milton

Southern Exposure
P.O. Box 531
Durham, NC 27702
Quarterly, $24
Chris Kromm

Southern Humanities Review
9088 Haley Center
Auburn University
Auburn, AL 36849
Quarterly, $15
Dan R. Latimer and Virginia M.
  Kouidis

The Southern Review
43 Allen Hall
Louisiana State University
Baton Rouge, LA 70803-5005
Quarterly, $25
James Olney

Southwest Review
307 Fondren Library West
Box 750374
Southern Methodist University
Dallas, TX 75275
Quarterly, $24
Willard Spiegelman

Sou'wester
Department of English
Southern Illinois University at
  Edwardsville
Edwardsville, IL 62026-1438
Semiannually, $12
Allison Funk and Geoff Schmidt

StoryQuarterly
online submissions only:
www.storyquarterly.com
Annually, $10
M.M.M. Hayes

Swink
244 5th Ave., #2722
New York, NY 10001
Semiannually, $16
Leelaila Strogov

Tampa Review
University of Tampa
401 W. Kennedy Blvd.
Tampa, FL 33606-1490
Semiannually, $15
Richard Mathews

Texas Review
English Department Box 2146
Sam Houston State University
Huntsville, TX 77341-2146
Semiannually, $20
Paul Ruffin

The Threepenny Review
P.O. Box 9131
Berkeley, CA 94709
Quarterly, $25
Wendy Lesser

Timber Creek Review
8969 UNC-G Station
Greensboro, NC 27413
Quarterly, $16
John M. Freiermuth

Tin House
P.O. Box 10500
Portland, OR 97296-0500
Quarterly, $29.90
Rob Spillman

TriQuarterly
Northwestern University
629 Noyes St.
Evanston, IL 60208
Triannually, $24
Susan Firestone Hahn

The Virginia Quarterly Review
One West Range
P.O. Box 400223
Charlottesville, VA 22904-4223
Quarterly, $18
Ted Genoways

West Branch
Bucknell Hall
Bucknell University
Lewisburg, PA 17837
Semiannually, $7
Robert Love Taylor

Wind Magazine
P.O. Box 24548
Lexington, KY 40524
Triannually, $15
Chris Green

The Yalobusha Review
Department of English
University of Mississippi
P.O. Box 1848
University, MS 38677
Annually, $10
Joy Wilson

Yemassee
Department of English
University of South Carolina
Columbia, SC 29208
Semiannually, $15
Fiction Editor

Zoetrope: All-Story
The Sentinel Building
916 Kearny St.
San Francisco, CA 94133
Quarterly, $19.95
Tamara Straus

ZYZZYVA
P.O. Box 590069
San Francisco, CA 94159-0069
Triannually, varies
Howard Junker

NEW STORIES FROM THE SOUTH, 1986–2005

Previous volumes of *New Stories from the South* can be ordered through your local bookstore or by calling the Sales Department at Algonquin Books of Chapel Hill. Multiple copies for classroom adoptions are available at a special discount. For information, please call 919-967-0108.

THE YEAR'S BEST, 1986

Max Apple, BRIDGING

Madison Smartt Bell, TRIPTYCH 2

Mary Ward Brown, TONGUES OF FLAME

Suzanne Brown, COMMUNION

James Lee Burke, THE CONVICT

Ron Carlson, AIR

Doug Crowell, SAYS VELMA

Leon V. Driskell, MARTHA JEAN

Elizabeth Harris, THE WORLD RECORD HOLDER

Mary Hood, SOMETHING GOOD FOR GINNIE

David Huddle, SUMMER OF THE MAGIC SHOW

Gloria Norris, HOLDING ON

Kurt Rheinheimer, UMPIRE

W. A. Smith, DELIVERY

Wallace Whatley, SOMETHING TO LOSE

Luke Whisnant, WALLWORK

Sylvia Wilkinson, CHICKEN SIMON

The Year's Best, 1987

James Gordon Bennett, DEPENDENTS

Robert Boswell, EDWARD AND JILL

Rosanne Caggeshall, PETER THE ROCK

John William Corrington, HEROIC MEASURES/VITAL SIGNS

Vicki Covington, MAGNOLIA

Andre Dubus, DRESSED LIKE SUMMER LEAVES

Mary Hood, AFTER MOORE

Trudy Lewis, VINCRISTINE

Lewis Nordan, SUGAR, THE EUNUCHS, AND BIG G. B.

Peggy Payne, THE PURE IN HEART

Bob Shacochis, WHERE PELHAM FELL

Lee Smith, LIFE ON THE MOON

Marly Swick, HEART

Robert Love Taylor, LADY OF SPAIN

Luke Whisnant, ACROSS FROM THE MOTOHEADS

The Year's Best, 1988

Ellen Akins, GEORGE BAILEY FISHING

Rick Bass, THE WATCH

Richard Bausch, THE MAN WHO KNEW BELLE STAR

Larry Brown, FACING THE MUSIC

Pam Durban, BELONGING

John Rolfe Gardiner, GAME FARM

Jim Hall, GAS

THE YEAR'S BEST, 1989

The Year's Best, 1990

Tom Bailey, CROW MAN

Rick Bass, THE HISTORY OF RODNEY

Richard Bausch, LETTER TO THE LADY OF THE HOUSE

Larry Brown, SLEEP

Moira Crone, JUST OUTSIDE THE B.T.

Clyde Edgerton, CHANGING NAMES

Greg Johnson, THE BOARDER

Nanci Kincaid, SPITTIN' IMAGE OF A BAPTIST BOY

Reginald McKnight, THE KIND OF LIGHT THAT SHINES ON TEXAS

Lewis Nordan, THE CELLAR OF RUNT CONROY

Lance Olsen, FAMILY

Mark Richard, FEAST OF THE EARTH, RANSOM OF THE CLAY

Ron Robinson, WHERE WE LAND

Bob Shacochis, LES FEMMES CREOLES

Molly Best Tinsley, ZOE

Donna Trussell, FISHBONE

The Year's Best, 1991

Rick Bass, IN THE LOYAL MOUNTAINS

Thomas Phillips Brewer, BLACK CAT BONE

Larry Brown, BIG BAD LOVE

Robert Olen Butler, RELIC

Barbara Hudson, THE ARABESQUE

Elizabeth Hunnewell, A LIFE OR DEATH MATTER

Hilding Johnson, SOUTH OF KITTATINNY

THE YEAR'S BEST, 1992

THE YEAR'S BEST, 1995

THE YEAR'S BEST, 1996

THE YEAR'S BEST, 1997

The Year's Best, 1998

THE YEAR'S BEST, 1999

THE YEAR'S BEST, 2000

THE YEAR'S BEST, 2004

THE YEAR'S BEST, 2005